D1414153

Fever Dreams

Other Five Star Titles by Laura Leone:

Fallen from Grace

Fever Dreams

Laura Leone

Five Star • Waterville, Maine

This novel is a work of fiction. Names, characters, places and incidents are either the product of the author's imagination, or, if real, used fictitiously.

First Edition
First Printing: June 2004

Set in 11 pt. Plantin by Ramona Watson.

Printed in the United States on permanent paper.

Library of Congress Cataloging-in-Publication Data

Leone, Laura, 1962–
Fever dreams / by Laura Leone.—Five Star rev. ed.
p. cm.
ISBN 1-59414-087-1 (hc : alk. paper)
1. Children of the rich—Fiction. 2. Bodyguards—Fiction. 3. Jungles—Fiction. I. Title.
PS3568.E689F48 2004
813′.6—dc22 2003061271

This book is dedicated to my friend,
best-selling and award-winning author Mary Jo Putney,
with thanks for her unswerving support over the years.

ACKNOWLEDGEMENTS

Special thanks to Joyce Ferree, Laurie Grant, and Don Pape for answering my many questions about guns, bullets, and the physical damage they can do. Extra special thanks to Jerry Spradlin, who took me to a shooting range so I could learn what it's like to fire a gun, and who taught me most of what I know about physical combat. Any mistakes in the text are, of course, all my own.

AUTHOR'S NOTE:

This book is a revised and updated version of the 1997 edition of *Fever Dreams*. Since friends and readers who enjoyed the original version of the novel have asked me how and why I'm revising it for rerelease, here's the scoop.

Due to misfortunes which are typical of the publishing industry, *Fever Dreams* was almost impossible to find during its initial release in January 1997, and it went out of print even more quickly than most mid-list novels do. Since then, I've always wanted to see the book reissued, and, happily, my Five Star editor Russell Davis recently offered me such an opportunity.

However, when I opened the book and took a good look at it, I realized how young and inexperienced a writer I still was when I wrote it, and I decided I'd have to revise it thoroughly before I'd want to see it in print again.

For those (few) of you who discovered the book during its original release and enjoyed it then, rest assured that nothing substantive has changed. This version is simply a much better written (I not-so-humbly assert) version of the exact same story about the exact same characters. Far from changing the tone or heart of the story, I've merely cleaned up sloppy prose, clarified motivation, polished clumsy dialogue, added dialogue to bring more layers to characters and their relationships, and expanded some scenes which clearly needed it. Unless you read this version while simultaneously reading the former version (and, good grief, why would you do such a thing?), I doubt you'll even spot the changes. And that's as it should be, since the changes are meant to make the story more absorbing, not to call attention to themselves.

So here's the new and improved version. Enjoy!

—Laura Leone, January 2004

CHAPTER ONE

The heat in Montedora City was sticky and oppressive, even after sundown. The dimly lighted bar wasn't air-conditioned, and the ancient electric fans overhead, which groaned with each sluggish rotation, only managed to push the hot, damp air around the room, as if trying to ensure that everyone enjoyed an equal level of discomfort. Even the omnipresent flies seemed heat-stunned; they had taken to buzzing in a strange calypso rhythm, flying straight into the walls, and then falling to the floor, apparently unconscious.

Madeleine Barrington sipped glumly on her tepid rum and coke; the Andrews Sisters would never have sung so cheerily about the drink if they could have tasted this one. Madeleine wished desperately for a glass of mineral water with a slice of lemon, a cool, fragrant bath, and the comfort of a firm mattress and clean sheets. But all of that, she acknowledged with resignation, was several thousand miles away in her Manhattan apartment. And she was stuck in Montedora for another night.

A poor South American country, Montedora boasted only one real city, Montedora City, its chaotic capital. Not exactly a tourist mecca, the entire city had only two big hotels. The Hotel Tigre, which hadn't been decorated in nearly twenty years, was the safer of the two; it really wasn't all that bad if you didn't mind threadbare towels, peeling paint, squeaking ceiling fans, and sullen service.

Madeleine minded.

She took another sip of her drink and closed her eyes,

sternly fighting the wave of depression which threatened to engulf her. What a rotten day it had been. After spending ten hours in miserable discomfort at the airport, she had been informed that her flight, scheduled to take off this morning, had finally been cancelled. The news had been disappointing enough, after a whole day of unexplained delays, but then, when she tried to reclaim her luggage, she was informed that it had been lost. Perhaps loaded onto another flight by mistake, perhaps stolen. In any case, gone.

So here she was, stuck for another night in Montedora City, and she couldn't even change into a fresh set of clothes. She couldn't even buy some, since—due to the curfew—all the shops had already closed by the time she caught a taxi back into the city. Well, she supposed she could wash out her things in the bathroom sink in her room.

She sighed and decided that she had better finish her drink in the Bar Tigre and go across the courtyard to the reception desk, where she could get a room for the night. Perhaps the taxi-sized cockroach which had shared her room last night would still be there. It could keep her company. She grimaced and finished her drink. Then, although she was usually abstemious, she ordered another. She'd need a little fortification if she was going to face one of those sullen desk clerks again. Not to mention the slightly brown water in the bathroom.

"Make it a double, please," she said to the bartender.

"Ah, you like?" The chubby man smiled.

"Actually, I'm trying to get the mosquitoes drunk," she said.

He didn't get it.

It had not been a good week, and Madeleine regretted that another trip to Montedora would probably be necessary before her goal was accomplished. Her grandfather had bought a huge plantation in this country over fifty years ago and misnamed it El Paradiso. It hadn't been a bad investment at the time; the year-round growing climate and rich soil produced tomatoes, sugarcane and other crops for Barrington Food Products.

However, social, economic, and political conditions had changed considerably over the years. Montedora had become unstable, for one thing; President Juan de la Veracruz was the country's fourth ruler in a row to seize power through violence. Moreover, the plantation was only producing half of what it used to, due to bad local management. Madeleine had been urging her father, Thackeray Makepeace Barrington, to sell the plantation for several years. Not only did she worry about losing the property to nationalization, but she also believed that Barrington Enterprises should support the U.S. agricultural economy rather than operating a feudal estate in a foreign country.

Her father had finally listened to her. Having gotten him to agree, she had come here to Montedora to inspect the property and examine the local management before putting El Paradiso on the international market.

It had been a grueling, lonesome, and depressing week, and she wished that her flight home hadn't been cancelled. She also wished she could feel more optimistic about her chances of getting out of here tomorrow. The airport seemed more like a county fair on its last legs than an international flight center.

"Another, señorita?" the bartender asked, noticing she had finished her second drink.

She shouldn't. She hadn't eaten all day, and she was feeling a little light-headed now. And Madeleine never had three drinks in a row . . . But what else was she going to do with her evening? Go check into a shabby room and stare at its four walls? Reread the two books she had brought from home and already finished? Review the paperwork which made her despair of ever being able to sell El Paradiso?

"Yes, I'll have another," she said.

She felt her elegant dress of thin silk clinging to her back, and her brow was damp with moisture. She pulled out a monogrammed handkerchief and pressed it delicately to her overheated face. She was sweating. Amazing. She never sweated. It was one of the many things her sisters disliked about her.

Oh, she knew they loved her, but there were a lot of things about her they didn't like. In fact, she supposed the same thing could be said about almost everyone who knew her. The uneasy, slightly snide jokes about her magna cum laude degree from Princeton, her mastery of every area of the enormous family business, her fastidious personal appearance, and her general competence were legion. The more she proved herself, the less affection she seemed to inspire.

Sitting here alone in a strange, seedy bar at the ends of the earth, she had to admit that, despite a large family, a prominent social position, and a vast personal acquaintance, there was no one she could call long-distance right now simply to say she was feeling lonely and demoralized. She wasn't that close to anyone.

She was thirty-one years old, healthy, wealthy, and socially and professionally successful. And, as she downed another swallow of flat coke and cheap rum, she felt . . . empty.

What had gotten into her? It must be the heat. She should stop being so maudlin. Thank goodness there was no one around to see her in this condition—sweaty, cranky, and wallowing in self-pity. She never permitted people to see her this way. She never permitted herself to feel this way. Fortunately, the bartender didn't seem to care, and the three other patrons of Bar Tigre were all involved in a poker game in the corner.

Still, she was a disciplined woman who never gave in to despondency. There was a dirty, cracked mirror lining the wall behind the bar. She looked up at it, staring forcefully into her own eyes, and ordered herself to feel capable and confident, as usual.

That was when she saw him staring at her.

Feeling moody after his final day at the Presidential Palace, Ransom walked through the dark, muggy, dirty streets of Montedora City. He had dismissed his chauffeur-driven car twenty minutes ago, wanting to clear his head with an evening stroll. Besides, despite the danger which lurked in the city's streets after dark, Ransom figured Miguel's driving was more likely to kill him than any mugger.

What a hell of a job this had been. Ransom liked working for Marino Security International, and he had willingly accepted this assignment to recommend and implement new security measures for President Juan de la Veracruz. He'd done his duty here, but he wouldn't be sorry to say good-bye to this miserable, oppressed country and its squabbling, egocentric rulers.

The assignment was finally over. Today he had finished reviewing the new security measures, and his written report would be done soon. Veracruz had invited him to spend the night at the palace, but he had declined, preferring the quiet privacy of his shabby hotel room to the ostentatious glitter of the palace, where everyone seemed to scheme and plot even in their sleep.

Ah, well. Tomorrow morning, the President's private car would pick Ransom up and take him to a military airfield, where the President's private plane would fly him back to the States.

He could hardly wait. He wanted some time off. He wanted some decent company, after putting up with Veracruz and his cronies. He wanted to get a little pleasure out of life after being stuck in Montedora for nearly a month. He wanted to undress and relax, after wearing a tie at yet another formal dinner tonight; ever since leaving the Secret Service, he seldom wore a tie for anything but weddings and funerals. He wanted someone to soothe his guilty conscience about having worked so hard to help preserve the power, position, and lifestyle of a greedy dictator. Despite the moral ambivalence he felt about it, Ransom had done a good job here, and because of that, he wanted a reward.

He pushed open the door of the Bar Tigre and saw the answer to all of his wants and needs sitting right there at the bar.

She was so beautiful she was almost intimidating. But he'd never been easily intimidated, so he stalked forward, eyes fixed on her.

Her flaxen blonde hair was starting to wilt in the heat, its fine tendrils clinging to her neck and shoulders as she pressed a lace-edged handkerchief to her cheeks and forehead. Her wide eyes were a rich, deep blue, fringed by long, curling lashes. Her skin was as fair as a pearl, as smooth and perfect as alabaster, as firm and enticing as ripe young fruit. She wore an expensive-looking dress of thin, dark purple silk with a high neck and a belted waist. It left her shoulders bare, and the hem stopped just above her knees, revealing long, shapely legs. Her simple bracelet and matching earrings were gold, and her shoes had probably cost $200.

He wondered what a woman like her was doing in a place like this. Her fine, aristocratic bone structure and perfect posture confirmed his impression that she was a class act. What was she doing sitting alone in Bar Tigre? She obviously wasn't a prostitute. No woman from the embassy staff would venture out alone after curfew, Peace Corps workers didn't dress like that, and not many foreigners did business in Montedora City anymore. Most of them had pulled out after the last coup.

If she was a traveler, she sure didn't seem to be enjoying herself. He had seldom seen such a bleak expression. What was she thinking about?

Whatever it was, it made her look into the mirror with a flash of cold fire. God, she was gorgeous! Whoever she was, whatever she was doing here, he was half-willing to believe she had been sent by the angels, expressly for him, to be his comfort and his reward. Except, of course, that Ransom's just deserts were more likely to come from someplace other than heaven.

Their eyes met in the mirror. He smiled slowly. No, this woman hadn't been sent by angels. There was too much challenge in her gaze. She had been sent by someone who understood Ransom very well indeed. He never liked anything to be too easy.

Hot as hell, he loosened his tie, undid a couple of his buttons, and joined her at the bar.

Madeleine glanced askance at the man who had looked her up and down so boldly, then sat beside her at the bar without even asking.

"Hi, there," he said easily.

"Good evening." She held his gaze for a moment, letting

him know that she wasn't shy or flustered, but that she wasn't interested in talking to him. Then she accepted another rum and coke from the bartender.

"It's on me," the man said when the bartender asked her for payment.

She said, "No, thank you. I—"

"Then do you want to buy me one?" he asked.

She frowned. "But—"

"Thanks! Señor, the lady's buying my drink. Make it a beer."

She looked at the stranger with rising irritation. "Excuse me, but I'm—"

"You're American, aren't you?"

"Yes. But—"

"So am I."

"Yes, I can tell. However—"

"You staying at the Hotel Tigre?"

She glared at him. "Your technique is very clumsy."

"I know. I usually have to rely on charm and sex appeal."

To her surprise, she laughed. It must be the rum.

He grinned. An undeniably sexy grin. "That's better."

"Better than what?" Why was she talking to this man?

"Better than the expression you had on your face when I walked through that door. You looked like you were thinking of jumping off a bridge."

"No, I wasn't."

"You looked like you were moping about being all alone in this rotten city on such a miserable night."

"Well . . ." She paid for his beer, suddenly glad for the company. Talking to anyone, even this impertinent stranger, seemed better than being alone with her morbid thoughts.

He raised his glass. “Here’s to golden days and purple nights, both of which have been in short supply lately.”

“As you say.” She clinked her glass against his, wondering what his version of a purple night would be. Probably a waterbed motel and the sort of woman whom Mother would describe as “obvious.”

“Had any purple nights lately?” he asked, his green eyes sparkling at her.

“I don’t believe so.”

“Nice accent. You sound like a debutante.”

“Please, don’t say that.” Visions filled her head of the silly, overdressed girls she had never been able to understand or emulate.

“Ah, a working woman, huh?”

“Yes.”

“What do you do?”

“I don’t want to talk about it.”

He shrugged. “Okay. No shop talk. It’s been that kind of a day for me, too.”

“No shop talk,” she agreed, surprised at herself. She was never this blunt. Perhaps it was the heat. Or perhaps it was the man himself. It was funny how easily she had accepted his presence at her side, strange how comfortable she felt with him. She’d heard about such things, about people who told their most intimate secrets to a stranger, comforted by the anonymity, freed by the lack of a shared past and all the baggage it carried. That probably explained it.

God, it was hot! She had never known such debilitating heat. It played tricks on her mind and heightened her senses. She was aware of the stranger’s body heat, his musky scent, the subtle sound of his breathing.

He was a good-looking man, though not at all the sort of man she would ever date. About six feet tall, he was slim without being skinny, muscular and athletic-looking without being bulky. His thick hair was light brown, streaked with shades of gold. One rebellious lock hung over his forehead, and he occasionally brushed it out of his eyes as he enjoyed his beer at her side.

His brows and lashes were dark, framing bright green eyes which sparkled with interest and energy. His long, lean face revealed two heart-stopping dimples when he smiled, and his mouth was full and wide. A slightly crooked nose and a faint scar at his temple gave him a certain roughness and added to his rakish air.

His clothes were ordinary. Indeed, in a less generous mood, Madeleine would have called them cheap—khaki pants, an old leather belt, scuffed shoes, a factory-made shirt, and a tie that some woman had given him. He couldn't possibly have chosen that wine-colored background and paisley design for himself.

"A woman gave you that tie," she said without thinking.

His brows moved in surprise. "That's right. How did you know?"

"I'll bet it's your only tie, except for the black one you wear at weddings and funerals."

He smiled, studying her with interest. "Have you been peeking in my closet?"

"Men are so predictable."

"Really? Then tell me what my briefs look like."

"Oh, I'm not an expert on underwear."

"Just ties."

"It doesn't look like you. And it doesn't match your shirt. You wouldn't wear it if you owned a few more." She realized what she had just said. "Sorry. That was rude." She frowned. "I'm never rude."

"Never say never."

"No, I'm never rude." She blinked at him, feeling light-headed. "But I just was, wasn't I?"

"It's the heat," he assured her blandly.

She pushed her drink away. "I think I've had too much to drink."

He removed his tie and put it in his pocket. "I hate this thing, to tell the truth."

"Who was she?" None of her business. She shouldn't have asked, but she wanted to know.

"The woman who gave it to me?" He shrugged. "Just someone."

"She wanted you more than you wanted her," Madeleine surmised. Funny how freeing it was to say the things she always knew but usually didn't mention.

He peered into her glass. "Are you reading tea leaves or something?"

She shrugged. "It wasn't hard to guess."

He was the sort of man women wanted. Not her, of course. Madeleine had refined tastes, and this stranger was anything but refined. His shoulder muscles bulged against the cotton of his shirt. His pants were as tight as plastic wrap around his narrow hips and hard thighs. He had stalked toward that bar stool like a predatory cat. And his gaze, as he continued looking at her, was frankly sexual, yet full of enough humor and curiosity to make a woman feel singled out, special, and admired.

"Women love that sort of thing," she murmured. She took another sip of her rum, then remembered she had decided not to drink any more.

"What sort of thing?" he asked, propping his cheek on his fist.

He had nice hands. Long, strong, and neat. They were lightly tanned, like his face and arms. She noticed another scar on the heel of his hand.

"You're either a soldier of fortune or very clumsy," she said.

"Hmmm?"

She pointed to his scar. He clearly didn't understand what she meant. Emboldened by his comfortable response to whatever inappropriate thing she said, she reached over and traced the scar on his hand.

"Oh, that." His voice was husky.

"And this one." She reached up to his temple. He went very still, looking into her face as she traced the fine, white line that disappeared into his hair. "And your nose . . ." She ran her finger down its bridge. "It goes a little sideways." Her own voice sounded raspy to her. She wanted to run her fingertip across his full lower lip, too. But there was no scar there, so she pulled her hand away.

He moved a little closer. "Yeah. Broke my nose a couple of times."

"How?"

"Fighting."

"You must have quite a temper."

His smile made her catch her breath. "Nah. I'm a pussycat."

"You're flirting with me," she said in surprise.

"It's either you or those three guys in the corner, and I don't think they'd like my tie." His teasing gaze was perceptive. "You don't like flirting?"

"I'm . . . unaccustomed to it, shall we say."

"We can say whatever you like. But you must live in a guarded tower if you're not used to men flirting with you."

"A guarded tower?" She grew pensive and took another sip of her drink. "A guarded tower," she repeated.

"Are you married?" he asked quietly.

She blinked. "No." No guard needed. She was the tower.

"Oh. Okay."

"Why? Would you get up and leave if I said yes?"

"No. There's no harm in talking. But I wouldn't . . ."

"Wouldn't what?" What else did this flirtatious, impertinent stranger intend?

He shrugged and looked around the room. "If you'd said yes, I wouldn't ask you to dance."

"We can't dance. There's no dance floor."

He grinned again. "No dance floor? Damn. We sure don't want to break the rules in a fine, upscale establishment like the Bar Tigre, do we?" He slid off his stool and took her hand without asking. "Come on. There's an empty space, there's music, and there's a handsome guy like me. What more do you need?"

There was indeed music, though she hadn't noticed it until a moment ago. Blaring out from the dusty speaker of an ancient radio, which the bartender obligingly turned up, the rumba had a scratchy, tinny sound.

"How's your rumba?" the man asked, taking her in his arms.

"It needs work."

"Now's your chance."

He made her laugh, because he couldn't rumba any better than she could, but he sure knew how to enjoy trying. Anyhow, a man that graceful, that comfortable with his body, could fake it pretty well. She was giggling when the dance ended. Absurd.

"I never giggle," she said fastidiously, her hands still imprisoned by his.

"You should. It makes you look pretty."

He sounded so sincere that she flushed. She had been

complimented often by the most sophisticated of men, but it must be fifteen years since the last time she had felt shy and tongue-tied in the face of a man's honeyed words. "Oh."

The music changed. The new song was a slow, sensual Latin melody with a languid, suggestive beat. Madeleine nervously tried to pull away. The stranger held fast to her hands. She looked up, and their gazes locked. He tilted his head a little, and the suggestion of a smile played around his lips, making the corners of his eyes crinkle. He looked four, maybe five years older than she. His eyes narrowed and beckoned to her from behind their fringe of dark lashes, his expression a combination of laughter, challenge, and sexual foreplay.

"One more dance," he murmured.

"Um . . ."

"I dare you."

"Dare me?" She stepped into his arms.

He nodded. "I knew you wouldn't resist a challenge. Comfortable?"

She drew in a steadying breath but didn't respond. He'd pulled her much closer for this dance than he had for their rumba. She braced a hand against his hard shoulder, trying to keep her distance.

"Don't you sweat?" he asked.

"I am sweating."

The hand at her waist moved up and down her back in a slow, exploratory caress. She shivered and moved forward a little, seeking to escape its pressure. The movement brought her breasts into contact with his chest. He pressed her closer and drew his palm slowly across her shoulders, then back down to her waist.

"Barely sweating," he concluded. "And it's hot enough to suffocate tonight."

Her back burned where he'd touched her. Her waist vibrated under the light pressure of his hand. To her embarrassment, her nipples were growing hard where they pressed against his chest. She wondered if he could feel them.

Their eyes met. His had lost their teasing look and were growing heavy-lidded and sleepy. It made him look softer. It made her want to touch his cheek, stroke his hair, nuzzle him. She stiffened and tried to pull away.

He resisted. Not enough to force her to stay in his arms, just enough to give her time to realize that she didn't really want to pull away after all. He shifted the hand that held hers and laced his fingers with hers. She complied and let him draw her even closer, so that their hips pressed together as he slid one leg between her thighs.

He lowered his head. She felt his cheek against hers, hard and slightly rough with his five o'clock shadow. She felt him nuzzle her hair, inhaling its fragrance, and she quivered against him, closing her eyes.

"Relax," he murmured, sensing her tension. "Don't you ever let your spine sag?"

"Never."

"Never say never," he whispered. His hand slid up her back to gently knead the tight muscles between her shoulder blades.

She sighed and slid her arm around his neck, running her fingers through the soft hair at his nape. He was a feast of different textures: warm, smooth skin; slightly abrasive stubble; hard, bulging muscle beneath damp cotton; silky soft hair; soothing, stimulating hands.

She felt dizzy. Her head was spinning. Was she under the influence of the rum or the man? Both, she supposed.

His strong, clever fingers unlocked all the secrets she

carried between her shoulders. All the anger she never showed, all the fears she kept hidden, all the weariness she never gave in to; he freed it all and let it flow between them. She sighed and pillowed her head on his shoulder, wondering at his skill, his understanding. It was as if this perfect stranger knew things about her that no one in her life had even guessed.

Wanting to hold him with both arms, wanting both his hands to be free to touch her, she pulled her other hand out of his grasp and slid it around his shoulder. He responded by embracing her and letting his hands roam freely over her shoulders, back, and waist.

The intensity of his touch increased, his warm hands releasing other, more deeply buried instincts. She clung to him, feeling the depth of her loneliness, wondering how she could bear it if he stopped touching her. Her belly throbbed with desire, with a pulsing, insistent need to be even closer to him.

The song ended. The chirpy voice of the disc jockey intruded on this drowsy, magical feeling. Madeleine raised her head. The man in her arms stilled, then caressed her cheek lightly before tilting her chin so that their eyes met.

"Ask me up to your room," he whispered, his eyes glowing with lush, emerald highlights, his voice heavy with promise.

"I can't."

His expression didn't change. "I won't hurt you."

"I . . . believe you." Crazily enough, she did.

"I've got condoms." When she lowered her gaze in embarrassment, he pointed out, "Well, it makes a difference. I thought that might be why you—"

"No. I mean, I haven't got a room."

He gave a short puff of laughter. "Then come up to my room."

"Uh, I . . ." She bit her lip, confused and astonished. She was actually considering it! She, Madeleine Barrington, was considering accompanying this total stranger to his hotel room and going to bed with him.

She had only gone to bed with three men in her whole life, and she knew everything about them, their families, and even their trust funds before taking that step. She never slept with a man unless she was dating him seriously and exclusively.

"What are you thinking?" he asked.

"I'm . . ."

Her behavior tonight would shock everyone she'd ever known. She was always the model of propriety, good sense, and self-control.

"It's okay to be nervous," he said. "We're strangers, after all." He pressed his forehead against hers and closed his eyes. "But I don't feel like a stranger with you. And I want you as much as I want to go on breathing."

She trembled in response to the hot longing in his voice. He smelled sharp and tangy, and his breath was a little faster than before. Of its own volition, her hand moved to cup his cheek. He turned his head and pressed a kiss into her palm. His lips were hot and soft.

She started breathing like a swimmer, struggling for fast pants of heavy, humid air. The music started again. She ignored it, focusing on the man who held her in his arms.

Who would ever know? She was all alone here in the middle of nowhere. She could be someone else for a night in Montedora City, someone wild and irresponsible, someone free and driven only by desire.

There was no one here to see her do something sordid, unconventional, and wholly out of character. She was so tired of being perfect, so tired of being Madeleine

Barrington. And tonight, she was so lonely. She couldn't bear the thought of letting this man go.

No one would ever have to know. It would be her secret. Their secret. She made a silent pact with this nameless stranger. For this one night, they would be partners in her detour from the straight and narrow. And then tomorrow, it would be over. She'd get on a plane for New York and forget about him. He'd forget about her, too; he didn't even know who she was.

She could do whatever she wanted tonight, and then put it behind her.

"Where's your room?" she whispered.

CHAPTER TWO

Ransom wished he had someplace nicer to take her than his hot, shabby room in the Hotel Tigre. She was a woman who deserved satin sheets, marble floors, a sunken bathtub, a balcony with a view, and a bed that didn't creak with every movement. However, the Hotel Tigre was as good as it got in Montedora, which was undoubtedly why the country had no tourist trade.

Carrying her briefcase for her, he took her elegant, manicured hand and led her out of the bar, across the overgrown courtyard with its dry fountain, and into the hotel lobby. It was empty. There was no one behind the reception desk either, though Ransom could hear a television set blaring in the staff room.

"The elevator is this way," he said, leading her down a corridor.

"How long have you been staying here?"

"Too long." He had a feeling she had only asked to cover her nervousness. She hid it well, but he could tell she was a little scared. It was a safe bet that she didn't do this often. Neither did he. But something about the things she said to him, the way she looked, and the way he felt when he touched her had made this as natural and inevitable as the tide rushing home to the waiting sable sand.

They rode the elevator up to the sixth floor, then walked down the hallway to his room. He glanced at her when he unlocked the door, wondering if she was going to change her mind while there was still time. Their eyes met and she raised her chin abruptly, making him smile at the look of challenge on her face. Did she think he wanted to wrestle her? Well, maybe they would wrestle a little, depending on her tastes. He opened the door and showed her inside.

He didn't bother to turn on the light as he locked the door behind him. The room looked better in the shadows. Anyhow, there was more than enough light to see her by; a movie theatre across the street flashed its bright neon lights directly into Ransom's window. He watched her look around the room.

"I asked for the honeymoon suite, but it was already booked," he said, setting down her briefcase.

She dropped her purse onto the dresser. "It doesn't matter."

He watched the light play on her silver blonde hair, making it glow like moonbeams in the shifting shadows. "No, it doesn't," he murmured, feeling a slow burn start deep in his belly. He dropped his jacket on a chair and came toward her. She didn't back away or flinch or do any of the things that would have made him feel like a heel for bringing her here. His throat felt tight when he put his hands on her shoulders and lowered his head to kiss her.

Madeleine felt the firm, confident pressure of his warm, full lips against hers and tasted the slight saltiness of his mouth. The flashing lights coming through the window played on the golden streaks in his hair. His eyes gleamed with reflected light, though his features were veiled in shadow as he lifted his head and looked down at her. She sensed the tension building in him. His fingers gripped her shoulders a little harder.

She felt a soft puff of laughter stir her hair before he

said, "I just realized I don't even know your name. Mine's—"

"No," she said. "No names."

He hesitated a moment, a little surprised. "Why not?"

"Not now." She slid her palms against his chest, feeling his breathing quicken. "Later."

He swallowed and pulled her closer, so that their thighs and bellies pressed together. "You'll tell me later?"

"Yes," she lied. If he insisted in the morning, she'd make up some name. He must never know who she was. She could never live down something like this if he turned out to be the kind of man who bragged about his conquests.

His hands moved down her arms, kneading her flesh, burning her skin with their possessive touch, then slid around her waist. His eyes grew heavy-lidded and sleepy as he lowered his head. She braced herself for his kiss, knowing that there was no question of turning back now. She only hoped she could control her nervousness, which was threatening to take over her whole body. It was an effort to keep her hands from shaking as she ran them over his shoulders and into the soft hair at his nape.

Their mouths met, and this time he kissed her without restraint. His lips were hot and moist, and he rubbed them against hers with such intensity that her mind reeled and she sagged against him. He supported her weight in his arms, arching her backward as he braced her against his body. The room spun around her, and she found herself clinging bonelessly to him, surrendering her strength to him. She felt his mouth on her cheeks, her chin, her eyelids, her forehead. Gentle, inquisitive, and tickling at first, then bold, wet, and seductive. She heard a harsh, rasping sound and recognized it as her own breathing. His breath gusted against her skin. She didn't know if she was excited or afraid or both.

He nuzzled her neck and buried his face in her hair, inhaling its scent. "God, you smell good," he said hoarsely.

His touch was elemental. She had never before felt her self-control disintegrate after just a few kisses. She struggled against her senses, resisting the wild rush of heat that coursed through her. Her nerves practically vibrated as she struggled against the total abandon her body was demanding. This quivering disorientation wasn't what she had expected. This overpowering surge of adrenaline panicked her. Feeling like a terrified virgin, she whimpered, appalled to hear herself do so.

The sound seemed to please him. He murmured against her neck. She had only a moment to contemplate pulling away, running from the room, and escaping this folly. Then his mouth was on hers again, and she felt the intimate, satiny intrusion of his tongue at the same moment that his hands slid over her bottom and pulled her hips against his. The hard bulge he ground against the cleft of her thighs made her cry out, but the sound was trapped in her throat. So was the sound he made, while their tongues twined and dueled and his hips moved aggressively against hers. She felt a hot, painful rush of lust flow through her body and pool in her loins, as if he'd opened a floodgate inside her.

Her nerves dissolved into a seething mass of needs, and all the expectations based on previous experience vanished and fled. Instinct and passion took over, and all she thought or cared about was the man who was satisfying those needs, even as he created others within her, voracious ones that were new to her. She answered the insistent pressure of his hips and made room for him by parting her thighs and nestling him even closer to the core of her body. She answered his pleased groan by digging her fingers into his bottom and pulling him still closer, reveling in the freedom to demand him, tease him, entice him.

Their kisses were hot and deep, wet and shameless, breathless and rough. She felt his fingers searching her dress for a zipper, and she bit his neck impatiently because he was looking in the wrong place. Eschewing the subtlety and careful staging she had always expected and received, she stopped caressing him long enough to fumble in the well-concealed seam at her side and undo her zipper herself. He took her cue and started tearing off his own clothes, his eyes devouring her boldly as she unfastened the buttons at her neck and pulled her dress over her head. He flung off his shirt, then pushed down his trousers and briefs, kicking them away.

His body was beautiful. Long and leanly muscled, he was lightly tanned everywhere except his loins. His chest was covered with golden brown hair, but the hair between his legs was dark and thick. His erection commanded respect. Madeleine stopped breathing for a moment as she stared.

"A garter belt," he muttered, his gaze sweeping hungrily over her body. She still wore her lacy bra, brief panties, silk garter belt, and sheer stockings. He dropped to his knees and wrapped his arms around her, pressing his face into her belly. "I knew you would wear a garter belt."

She closed her eyes and threw her head back, sagging at the knees when he nibbled on her abdomen. He licked his way across her stomach, massaging the backs of her thighs at the same time. Impatient with her own clothing, she unfastened her bra, tossed it aside, then slid to her knees. Chest to chest, they kissed ravenously as he pressed her down into the threadbare rug on the floor. She felt him yank her panties down her legs, then she kicked them aside, all the while returning his soul-destroying kiss. His wiry chest hairs tickled her breasts. She scraped her nails across his nipples, then soothed them with her fingertips.

He slid a hand between her thighs, forcing them apart. She yielded, sighing as she felt the inquisitive caress of his fingers. He propped himself up on an elbow and watched her face as he delved inside her.

Their gazes locked in the dim, flashing light of the darkened room. She gasped as she felt his thumb move over the exquisitely sensitive nub he found while his fingers continued to probe. She stiffened against the shock waves his touch sent through her.

"Easy," he murmured. "Easy. Relax." His lips brushed hers.

She tried to speak, but the words caught in her throat when he lowered his head to her breast and licked an aching peak with long, lazy strokes. Her hands balled into fists at her sides. Her hips started moving in response to his coaxing hand, even as she tried to hold still. She felt raw, close to implosion. The rasp of his tongue made her tremble with feelings her body couldn't contain any longer.

She flung a hand over her eyes, licked her lips, and arched her back. This was torture, sheer agony. And she'd die if he stopped. His intimate caresses grew harder and faster, and she found herself moaning and moving against his hand without inhibition. When he drew her nipple into his mouth and sucked hard, she went up in flames. Heat rippled through her again and again, and she arched and writhed and sobbed in response, lost in the searing pleasure he offered her.

She was dazed and panting when she became aware of the hard floor beneath her back and the sluggish breeze created by the overhead fan. His hand rested on her stomach, and she felt his breath on her face. She opened her eyes and met his glittering gaze. His face was sheened with sweat, and his golden brown hair was tousled from the touch of her hands.

He smiled at her, sharing a secret, sharing her pleasure, and she smiled back without embarrassment. She never would have thought it possible to feel so comfortable with anyone, let alone a stranger.

They didn't speak. They didn't need to. She felt the steely hardness of his erection against her hip, felt the urgency of his need as his hand roved freely over her body. Their gazes remained locked for a moment before he whispered, "I'll get the condoms."

Her stomach clenched with renewed desire. "I want you between my legs. I want to feel you . . . plunging inside me," she whispered. She had never before said anything so frank to a man.

His mouth was hard against hers, his tongue restless and insistent. Without breaking their kiss, he pulled her off the floor and deposited her on the bed. She pulled off her stockings and garter belt while he disappeared into the bathroom. She didn't have time to think about anything before he was with her again, pressing her into the mattress with his weight, inflaming her with the hunger of his kiss. He put the condom on, and she spread her legs for him.

"Not too wide," he whispered against her mouth as he settled himself between her thighs. He ran one hand along her leg, making her bend her knee. "Just like . . ." He drew in a sharp breath as her fingers closed around his engorged penis. He swallowed and started breathing much faster. "Yes," he rasped.

His first thrust was gentle, and he paused for a moment

to let her adjust to him. Then, bracing his weight on trembling arms, he arched his back and filled her with his flesh, thrusting long, deep, and hard. He looked down at her as she tilted her hips and braced her hands on his muscular buttocks. There was an exultation in his expression that made her feel like a captive love slave. The fierceness in his gaze promised he wouldn't let her off lightly now that he had her beneath him.

"It'll be a rough ride," he said hoarsely.

"Yes," she whispered. "Yes, whatever you want. Do it."

"What's your name?" he demanded, thrusting hard.

"What?"

"Tell me your name." He plunged into her.

"No." Her hips rose to meet him.

"Your name." Harder.

"Oh!" Her hands slid up to the small of his back.

"Tell me," he urged, lowering his head to kiss her briefly.

"Not . . . ohhh . . . not now."

"I'll stop," he warned, withdrawing for another thrust.

"No, you won't," she said fiercely, locking her legs around his hips and heaving against him.

He groaned and struggled against her for a moment, then gave up and thrust into her again and again, his movements fast, rough, reckless. She wrapped her arms around his back and held him to her, unleashing her own wildness, sinking her teeth into his shoulder and digging her nails into his flesh.

Their sweat-slick bodies writhed together in the eternal mating dance, taking and giving without restraint, adversaries and partners in this primitive struggle to both conquer and surrender at once. They plunged headlong into the storm together, clinging to each other as the bed rattled, the headboard thudded against the hollow wall, and their moans of satisfaction echoed around the room.

Ransom lit a cigarette and inhaled deeply. He'd already smoked his limit for the day, but he could never resist a cigarette after some really good sex.

Not good. Great. Better than great.

He looked down at his sleeping companion. She was the best. But he knew enough about women to know it wasn't the sort of thing you said to them. Especially not on such short acquaintance.

No, women liked flowery adjectives and romantic superlatives; they didn't ever like to think they were being compared to others, nor did they like to be reminded of a man's previous experience. But then, he supposed the exact same thing could be said about men.

Still, after what he and this woman had just shared, he'd like to be honest about it. Hell, what had just happened between the two of them was about the most honest thing he'd ever experienced. Once she had shed her nervous tension . . . God! She had been fearless. And demanding and giving and shameless and hotter than hell. Who was she?

He'd have asked her again, but she'd fallen asleep almost immediately afterward, and he didn't have the heart to wake her. Yet. He would soon, and she'd need all her strength for what he had in mind.

Her hair was spread out across the pillow, gleaming like corn silk, like spun silver and gold in the pale flashing light of his room. Her skin looked as beautiful as it felt, and her back moved slightly with every soft breath. She slept on her stomach, her face turned toward him and her hand enfolded in his.

Careful not to disturb her, he brushed a few strands of

hair away from her face and studied her. She was a few years younger than he, but not many. Her features were so peaceful, pure, and perfect in repose, it was hard to believe she had sweated, panted, clenched her teeth, and begged for more only an hour ago. But she had, and so had he, and just the memory of it made him start growing hard again. When he'd spotted her in the Bar Tigre, even when he'd held her in his arms for the first time, he hadn't guessed it would be like this between them. How could he? His experience with women was not inconsiderable, but there had never been anyone like her. He hadn't known what was waiting for him. For them.

He wondered what had made an elegant woman like this overcome her nerves, her common sense, and her unmistakable reservations about tonight. What had made her accompany a total stranger to his room and open herself up to him like this? A crisis point in her life? A tragedy? Boredom or loneliness? Or had she sensed that something special would bind them together in this hot, shadowed bedroom?

He stroked her hair as she slept beside him. "Could it have been just anyone," he whispered, "or did it have to be me?"

He knew what he wanted her answer to be. He didn't want to think this woman who had taken him to the moon tonight would have come to this room with anyone but him. He stubbed out his cigarette, suddenly impatient for her to wake up. He wanted her company.

"Hey," he murmured, sliding down in the sheets so that they were face-to-face on her pillow. "Hey." He slid his hand across her back.

"Hmmm?" She blinked and then opened dreamy eyes fringed by thick lashes. Their gazes locked.

"So are you gonna tell me now?" he asked, noticing a hundred little things about her face, her hair, the way she woke up.

"Tell you what?" Her voice was deeper, more relaxed than it had been in the bar. She sounded content. Had he given her that?

"Your name." He slipped his hand under the sheet and caressed her bottom. The sound of her sigh rippled through him.

She smiled sleepily. "In the morning," she promised. "Rub my back again. When you did that in the bar, it was heaven."

"What we did in this bed was heaven."

"Yes. It was." She closed her eyes and practically purred when he began massaging between her shoulders. "Ohhh, that's wonderful."

"I don't get it. Why the mystery?"

She hesitated, then a tiny smile curved those lush lips, which were still swollen from his kisses. "It's your reward," she said, "if you're still here in the morning."

"It's my room," he pointed out dryly.

"I like the anonymity, all right? It's been a sordid fantasy of mine for years. Indulge me."

He couldn't help grinning at that. "All right. But tomorrow, I want to see your passport, your driver's license, and your credit cards." For some reason, that sent her into peals of laughter. He didn't get it, but he was glad he had made her laugh. She had looked unhappy when he'd first seen her.

"I like the way you sound when you laugh." He massaged the small of her back and whispered, "And I love the way you sound when you come."

He felt her stiffen. She closed her eyes. "Do you? Really?"

"Yeah, I do. Really."

She relaxed a little. "I . . ."

"What?" he prodded. Her shyness made him feel protective. He kissed her hair. "Tell me."

"I'm not usually so, uh, vocal."

He rubbed his cheek against her shoulder. "I'm glad you were tonight, then. With me."

"And I . . ." She licked her lips.

"Go on," he urged softly, stroking his hand up and down her back. He wanted her again, but this time he wanted it to be slow and sultry.

"I like the sounds you make, too," she said in a rush. "You sound wild and . . . and . . . like you really enjoy . . ."

"Enjoy? Now there's an understatement," he teased. "I was out of my mind. I wouldn't have noticed if a bulldozer had come through the wall."

"It's not usually like that," she said pensively.

"No," he agreed. "Not like that." It had been special.

She responded to the subtle pressure of his hand and rolled over onto her back. Her body was beautiful, and he couldn't help paying homage to it. He felt her soft sigh when he lowered his head to kiss her breasts. Her fingers twined in his hair as he moved farther down to kiss her stomach.

"What are you doing?" she whispered a few moments later, closing her thighs against him.

"What do you think?" he murmured, pushing her legs apart.

Their gazes locked, and he smiled. She looked more aroused than uncertain. She couldn't hold back any more than he could; this thing between them had more strength than either of them. "Do you really want to?" she asked doubtfully.

"Oh, honey, just try and stop me," he said, and planted his first, soft kiss between her thighs. She quivered, then sighed and gave in to the passion that flowed so naturally between them.

The brash light of day crept across Ransom's bed and peered into his face. He was a light sleeper, but bone-deep exhaustion and soul-deep satiation had sunk him into a deep, dreamless slumber. He ignored the sun on his face and the heat of the room, and lay there, enjoying the well-being that flowed through his body. He felt good. He couldn't remember ever feeling so good. He also felt like he'd never be able to walk again. She had worn him out, drained him dry, and pushed him to the edge of collapse.

But I won't hold it against her. Eyes closed, he smiled. The smile turned into a grin.

In the breathless, trembling afterglow of their second time, they'd realized how hot the room was. He'd gone over to the window to open it wider, though he doubted the humid night air of Montedora City would really help matters much. He started to say so, but he never managed to get more than the first few words out of his mouth. She had risen from the bed, still flushed and gleaming, her sun-colored hair tumbling around her shoulders, her expression glowing with promises. She had crossed the floor, kissed his mouth, his chest, his belly, his thighs . . .

Ransom sighed and felt his body tighten. Christ, he couldn't seriously be thinking about doing this again, could he?

Her mouth, her hands, her whispers, the look on her face . . .

He swallowed. Well . . . maybe just once more. And then they'd sleep some more. And then . . .

"I'll have to be hospitalized," he muttered, rolling toward her to see if she was up to being wished a very enthusiastic good morning.

She wasn't there.

He opened his eyes and looked. Yes, he was definitely alone in the tumbled, twisted sheets. A quick glance around the room didn't discover her. He started to call her name, then realized he didn't know it. Cursing, he got out of bed. She wasn't in the bathroom, either, and her purse, briefcase, shoes, and dress were gone.

He hadn't imagined her, though. Her stockings and garter belt still lay on the floor at the foot of the bed, half-hidden by a pillow they'd sent flying in the middle of the night. She must have given up looking for her stockings and slipped out of the room before he woke up. He glanced at his watch. Ten o'clock! Damn it! She could have left hours ago.

Accustomed to acting quickly, he washed his face, threw on his clothes, tossed his belongings into his suitcase, and called down to the front desk to ask if anyone had seen a woman of her description. Realizing that no one on the hotel's staff cared about his love life, he claimed that the woman had to be located because she had stolen his wallet. He didn't know if she'd forgive him for that story when she was found, but he was getting too angry to care.

What the hell did she intend, running off like that? Was he supposed to not mind getting laid and then deserted just because he was a guy? Or had she run out on him because she was nervous about waking up with him? Did she fear they'd have an awkward morning after, despite how great they'd been together all night long? Or had she managed to make him feel like a mushy, lovesick kid while she was only using him to get through a dull night in Montedora City?

"Using me . . . Shit!" Suddenly realizing he might have been telling the truth, he checked his wallet. To his relief, everything was there. Whatever her motive, at least it hadn't been petty theft. He would have felt like a real chump.

The scent of her skin and the smell of their passion lingered in the room. Wondering where she'd gone, he permitted himself the sappy luxury of picking up her pillow and burying his face in it. He'd never even learned her name.

The shrill ring of the bedside phone startled him. Adrenaline flooded his system. They'd found her! He dived across the bed and picked up the receiver. "Yes?"

"Señor Ransom. Your driver is asking for you. He has been waiting for nearly an hour."

Miguel and one of the President's cars. "Tell him to keep waiting," Ransom said tersely. "I'll be down in a few minutes to find out about this woman."

"But, señor, there is no woman—"

"Keep looking." He hung up and headed out the door.

Ransom knew how to question people, and he knew how to track down someone who didn't want to be found. But the woman had vanished into thin air. Even though she had told him she didn't have a hotel room, he nonetheless made the sullen desk clerk review his records and look for a woman staying alone in the Hotel Tigre last night. There were only a few, and none was the woman he sought. No one had seen her come into the hotel with him, and no one had seen her leave. He wasn't even sure when she had left; sometime after four o'clock in the morning, since that's when he had fallen asleep.

When he questioned the bartender in the Bar Tigre, the man remembered the woman well. But it was the first and only time he had ever seen her, and he knew nothing more. There was only one other hotel in Montedora City where a lone foreign woman was likely to stay. Ransom phoned it, to no avail.

He was at a dead end. Whoever she was, he wasn't going to find her. He supposed she had known all along that she would leave before he woke up; that's why she had insisted he wait until morning to learn her name.

It's your reward, if you're still here in the morning.

"Hope you enjoyed your little joke, lady," he grumbled, tossing aside an empty pack of cigarettes.

It might have been the most memorable night of his life, but he promised himself he'd forget all about it the moment he left this miserable city.

CHAPTER THREE

"I'm worried about you returning to Montedora," Graham Powell III told Madeleine. They were lunching together in a French restaurant on East 53rd Street in Manhattan. "It's an unstable, violent backwater. And you were just there three months ago. Surely you can send someone in your stead this time."

"I'm afraid I can't," she contradicted politely, seething with impatience. For a man who had proposed marriage two weeks ago but had not yet been accepted—Madeleine had promised to think about it—Graham was being too proprietary. "I've been there before, I know all the details, and I'm the one in charge of selling El Paradiso. This German company's offer is the first nibble we've had since putting the plantation on the market. I want to sell that place this year."

"I can understand that, darling, but don't you have local people in Montedora who can handle this for you?"

"No, I don't, Graham." She heard the snap in her voice, saw the surprise on his face, and felt contrite. He was only showing understandable concern. He professed to love her, and Montedora was an unpredictable and unsafe country. In truth, she didn't relish the thought of returning there, either; she had spent three months trying to forget what she had done there—without success.

"I'm sorry, Graham. I didn't mean to be short with you. I appreciate your concern, and I'd honestly rather not go back there. But the local business manager is inefficient and, I suspect, dishonest. I don't want him to be the one to deal with the Germans." It was important to do a good job, regardless of her personal feelings.

"Of course. I see," Graham said, too courteous to argue any more with her.

"Besides, I'll be in good hands. My father is as concerned as you are. He's hired a security specialist to accompany me."

Graham frowned. "A bodyguard?"

"Well, I suppose that's a better description of the man's duties with regard to this trip. Apparently he's quite familiar with Montedora and has important contacts there. He has served as a security consultant to the country's President."

"Veracruz? I believe you mean 'dictator.' "

"Yes, I do, but it's not a good idea to get in the habit of saying that. If I let the expression slip out while I'm in Montedora, I could theoretically be arrested." She said "theoretically" because no one arrested, harassed, or intimidated a Barrington. Particularly not this Barrington.

"Good God!" Graham exclaimed. "Arrested? Well, yes, I must say I agree with your father, and I am considerably relieved to know you'll be accompanied by someone who can protect you from any unpleasantness. If this fellow knows Veracruz, perhaps you'll even meet him—and surely the 'President' wouldn't arrest an acquaintance."

In fact, Veracruz did arrest his acquaintances—and even his friends—when it suited him. But Madeleine passed over Graham's naive comment and said, "My father says we've actually been invited to stay with the President while we're there. I haven't yet decided what I'd rather do." She didn't want to be the guest of a petty tyrant, no matter what his title. On the other hand, she couldn't face returning to the

Hotel Tigre. There were too many memories there, all of them shameful. Unfortunately, there weren't many other options in Montedora City, particularly in light of the growing violence there.

Madeleine didn't know what to do. She was usually so decisive and determined. But the anticipation of returning to Montedora, where she had made the biggest mistake of her life, was shredding her confidence. Indeed, she hadn't been herself ever since returning from that country three months ago. She hid it well and didn't think anyone had noticed, but she had become habitually impatient, ill-tempered, depressed, and distracted ever since her return. And she only seemed to be getting worse.

"So have you checked out this security man?" Graham asked.

"Hmmm? Oh, no. No, I let my father handle that. It was his idea."

"But you're leaving the day after tomorrow, darling. Don't you think you should at least interview him? Not that I'm questioning your father's judgment, but surely—"

"No, you're quite right." She wished he wouldn't call her "darling." It irritated her. "I've been too busy to think about it, and the man has very good references. Mr. Ransom is apparently a top-level employee of Marino Security International."

"Those are good credentials," Graham agreed. "Nevertheless, it—"

"I'm scheduled to meet him today, in my father's office." She had interrupted Graham twice in a row. What had happened to her manners? She glanced at her watch and said, "In fact, I'm meeting him in fifteen minutes, so I'd better get back to work."

Graham's face went very still, as it usually did when he

wanted to snap or argue like a less well-bred person. However, he merely nodded and signaled the waiter for the check. Madeleine wondered if he'd had second thoughts about marrying her during the two weeks since he had proposed. She certainly hadn't been pleasant company lately. She didn't even know why she was still thinking over his proposal. She should just let him down gently and get it over with. She didn't love him and never would.

She was only hanging on, she realized guiltily, because her loneliness had intensified so unbearably since her return from Montedora. If she would never love anyone, then why not marry Graham? He was a good man from a respectable family, he cared about her, and their children were likely to be healthy.

As it always did when she thought about Graham's proposal, Madeleine's mind returned to that mad night in Montedora City. The haunting memory of that night was like a fever dream brought on by the antimalarial drugs she had to take while in Montedora: crazed, intense, surreal. She couldn't believe she had done what she'd done.

She'd done it, though. The marks the stranger had left on her skin left no doubt about that. They had taken days to fade.

And she still remembered the timbre of his voice as clearly as if she'd just escaped from his room five minutes ago. She recalled the teasing, slightly crooked smile he gave when he was amused. She saw his glittering green gaze when she closed her eyes, felt the touch of his hands in her dreams . . .

Stop, she ordered herself. Stop thinking about him.

Meanwhile, though she couldn't forget sleeping with the stranger, she was uncomfortable trying to imagine sleeping with Graham. He was a handsome man, well-built and elegant, who kissed and embraced with experienced skill, but Madeleine couldn't picture being intimate with him. If she married Graham, she could never behave with him as she had with the stranger.

And that was just as well, she suddenly realized as she preceded Graham into the lobby of the Barrington Building on Fifth Avenue. She could never look Graham in the eye again if something like that happened between them. It was far too embarrassing. But fortunately, neither she nor Graham was the kind of person who would abandon all dignity and initiate the sordid sort of things that had happened in that hot, shabby room in the Hotel Tigre.

But I am that kind of person.

No, no, not at all.

Yes. I bit and scratched and begged. I wrapped my legs around him and forced him to keep making love to me when he pretended he might stop. And later, much later, I followed him to the window and covered him with kisses, and I dropped to my knees and took him in my mouth. And I loved it! I loved every moment of it. When he pushed me up against the wall, so rough and impatient, I loved it so much I screamed. I didn't care who might hear. And now I want him again. I want him day and night. If he were here right now, I'd devour him, I'd . . .

"Oh, my God," she groaned in horror. Hot shame flooded her veins, but the pooling heat in her loins intensified, mocking her efforts to banish the visions she had just conjured up.

"Darling, are you all right?" Graham asked.

"Hmmm? Oh. Yes. Fine, thank you," she croaked.

"You look flushed. Do you feel feverish?"

"No, no, I, uh . . . Perhaps my lunch was a little too heavy."

"But you barely touched it."

"Well . . . that's because it was heavy. I'd better go up to my father's office now, Graham. I don't want to keep Mr. Ransom waiting."

"I'm coming with you," Graham said.

"But—"

He took her elbow in a firm grip and escorted her onto the elevator that led to her father's private office at the top of the building. "Not only am I worried about your health at the moment, Madeleine, but I also want to meet the man who will be responsible for the safety of my fiancée."

"We're not engaged," she reminded him faintly.

"No, I know. Sorry. I meant to say, er . . ."

He kept talking, but she barely heard him. She concentrated on trying to banish the memory of the stranger's hands on her body, of the way his back had felt beneath her palms, of the soul-deep way he groaned when he climaxed, of the way he looked when he slept.

She didn't want to know such intimate things about him. She hadn't been able to bear the thought of facing him in the morning. What could she say to him? How could she look a total stranger in the eye after she'd sweated and clawed, begged and screamed with passion in his arms? And what if he talked about that?

She had initially worried about him learning her identity and exposing the fact that Madeleine Barrington had had a one-night stand in Montedora. But she had never suspected, upon entering his room, just how thorough and potentially humiliating his knowledge of her would become before morning.

Although slipping out of his room before dawn may have been cowardly, she had simply been incapable of facing him again.

★ ★ ★ ★ ★

Ransom paced around the well-appointed penthouse office with ill-concealed impatience. Thackeray Makepeace Barrington, an elegant, stiff-necked guy of about sixty, watched him with detached curiosity. Ransom didn't care. He hadn't wanted this job, and he wasn't going to pretend to be happy about it. He felt irritable today—which was how he had felt most days since waking up alone in a hotel room in Montedora City three months ago. And now his boss, Joseph Marino, was sending him back to that hellhole, with all of its memories.

Barrington glanced at his watch. "Madeleine is late. This is unlike her."

"I can't wait all day," Ransom warned.

"I don't see why not. We're paying for your time."

Ransom said rudely, "You don't own me just because you hired me."

"Yes, that's quite clear, Mr. Ransom. However, I don't think asking you to wait for your client to arrive is unreasonable."

Ransom was annoyed. Didn't this guy know when someone was trying to get himself fired? He looked directly into Barrington's steel-blue eyes. What he saw there made him hesitate. Oh, yes, Barrington knew what Ransom was doing; he just wasn't affected by it. If anything, he was somewhat curious about why a highly recommended specialist was behaving like such a jackass when he was about to be well-paid for an ordinary assignment. Ransom sighed. Barrington was obviously a lot smarter than Steve Keller—which was probably just as well, since Keller was the whole reason Ransom had to leave the country.

But Montedora? No way. He decided to lay his cards on the table.

"Look, Mr. Barrington, I don't think I'm the right man to baby-sit your daughter on her business trip."

"Why not?"

"You know I'm in trouble, don't you?"

"I know that there's a rock group, er . . ."

"Sex On The Beach."

"Yes." Barrington frowned with distaste before he continued, "And a member of that band—"

"The lead singer. Steve Keller."

"—is threatening to file a lawsuit against you and Marino Security. I understand you publicly insulted him, and when he hit you, you hit back."

"So, that doesn't make me the kind of man you want looking after your daughter, does it?"

"I sincerely doubt that Madeleine will instigate a fistfight, Mr. Ransom. Nor will she give you cause to insult her, as I suppose cause might have been given by someone who would name his band Sex On The Beach." Barrington paused before adding, "My old friend Joseph Marino has confided that he hopes Mr. Keller can be convinced to forget the whole matter, if you're out of the country for a while."

"Out of sight, out of mind," Ransom muttered, not really believing it. Steve Keller was a malicious, vindictive sonofabitch, and Ransom wasn't convinced that Joe Marino could calm him down. "Anyhow, the truth is, Mr. Barrington, that whole mess wasn't entirely Keller's fault. I've got a temper."

"Yes, I gathered that." Barrington's tone was dry. "However, I trust you, and I'm rarely wrong about these things. My father may have built this empire, Mr. Ransom, but I've held it together through three decades of political, economic and social crises. I'm a good judge of men, and I judge you to be capable, honest, and intelligent."

"Oh." Ransom sagged into a chair across from Barrington's position behind his desk. However grouchy he had become in recent months, he was capable, honest, and intelligent. "Well."

"Besides, I have no doubt that Madeleine can handle a man with a temper."

"Oh?" If she was as hard-nosed as Ransom, this would be a hell of a trip.

"Indeed. I've never known anyone she couldn't handle."

"She sounds like a sumo wrestler," Ransom said dryly.

"On the contrary. She's an intelligent, beautiful young woman." With a subdued expression of paternal pride, Barrington picked up a framed photograph which sat facing him. "My daughters. Caroline, Stephanie, and Madeleine. Taken last year."

Ransom looked at the picture. There was a hippy in her mid-twenties, a plump woman in her late twenties, and a cool, beautiful blonde—

It was her.

He remembered those golden-lashed, blue eyes looking at him, first with hesitancy, then with passion. He remembered the scent of that blonde hair, the taste of that fair skin, the feel of those elegant hands skimming over his back. Her mouth was painted with lipstick in the photograph, but he remembered it soft and sweet against his forehead, hungry and wet against his chest, warm and passionate against his lips, hot and shameless as she knelt before him in the dark.

"So you do have a name," he whispered.

"Excuse me?"

Ransom swallowed. "The . . . really blonde one," he forced out. "Madeleine?"

"Yes." Barrington was looking at him intently. "You've met before?"

"We, uh . . ." His mind went blank. He didn't know how to respond. After all, he had done things to Barrington's daughter that would make most fathers want to shoot a guy.

Jesus! The woman in his hotel room had been Madeleine Barrington? Of the Barrington empire? Food products, hotels, land, stocks, and wealth beyond his imagining. There was a Senator Barrington, and there were other relatives in the Justice and State Departments. Ransom knew all this because of the background material Joe had given him before sending him on this assignment.

He didn't understand. How could Madeleine Barrington have been that pensive, lonely woman in the Bar Tigre, who'd had no luggage, no change of clothes, and no hotel room?

No names, she had said.

Ransom set down the framed photograph with a thud, avoiding Barrington's gaze. Had she kept her identity a secret because she expected him to blackmail her after they'd had sex? Is that why she had disappeared? Is that what she really thought of him?

The anger he had felt at her for the past three months was nothing compared to the fury that flooded him now. Did she think that because she was a Barrington she could simply pick him up to play with, then drop him again without a thought?

"Mr. Ransom, I sense an air of disquiet about you."

"Do you really?" Ransom muttered.

"May I ask why?"

"It's private." This was between him and Madeleine.

"I see." Barrington glanced at the photo. "Are you going to quit this assignment?"

"Quit?" He finally met Barrington's gaze. "Absolutely not."

There was no way in hell he'd let her go back to Montedora without him. He scarcely even understood the resolution that flooded him.

And he'd show that self-centered society bitch a thing or two about integrity. He wouldn't let his personal feelings enter into it for one minute. He'd take her to Montedora and make sure that her hair didn't even get ruffled. Let her remember that the next time she thought she was too good to tell her name to a guy after she'd fucked him.

"Mr. Ransom, while I don't wish to intrude on your privacy, I would like your assurance—"

"Of course. I'm a professional. She'll be safe with me."

"May I have your word on that?" Barrington held out his hand.

"You've got it." Smarting over Madeleine's deception, he added brusquely, "And my word is worth something."

Barrington said, "I believe you, Mr. Ransom."

After they shook hands, Ransom took a seat and tried to pull his thoughts together.

Barrington's secretary buzzed him on the intercom. "Miss Barrington is here, sir. She is accompanied by Mr. Powell."

"Send them right in," Barrington responded, going to the door.

The doors to Barrington's office opened a moment later. Ransom heard Madeleine and her companion enter and greet her father, but he remained in his chair, with his back to the door. Now that she was there, in the same room with him, three months' worth of memories and fantasies flooded his mind, and he was tense. He'd wanted to see her again so much, but he hadn't been prepared for this.

"Sorry I'm late, sir," she said.

Her voice rippled through him, making his belly clench. He remembered her whispers, her moans, her sighs, even her screams.

"It's all right, Madeleine. How are you, Graham?"

Ransom remembered how deep and lazy her voice sounded after sex. How sweet it sounded when she felt shy or uncertain.

"Very well, thank you, sir. But I'm afraid Madeleine isn't feeling quite herself."

"Are you sick?" Barrington asked.

That got Ransom's full attention. Sick?

"No, of course not," she said.

"She had quite a dizzy spell in the lobby."

A dizzy spell?

"And a bit nauseated, too, weren't you?" Graham continued. "I think her lunch didn't agree with her."

Dizzy spells. Nausea. Oh, no. Could she be pregnant? He had been so careful about that, but . . .

"I'm fine. Really," she said. "I've come to meet Mr. Ransom, sir."

"Of course."

Recognizing his cue, and unable to wait another moment to get a look at her, Ransom stood up and turned around. "I'm Ransom."

She looked at him. She was more stunning than he had remembered. How could he have forgotten the way her eyes tilted up at the corners? How could he have forgotten how subtly sexual her curves were? His heart pounded with recognition.

Her eyes flew wide open, then filled with an expression of such horror he felt the floor tilt. She went white as a sheet, and her jaw dropped. She swayed dizzily and looked like she might be sick.

"Darling!" The man at her side—Graham—seized her shoulders and hauled her over to a chair. She stumbled along without any of the grace Ransom remembered so well.

Once she was seated, Graham knelt at her side. "Are you faint? Are you ill? What's wrong?"

"I, uh, I'm just . . . I . . ." She closed her eyes.

Graham started patting her hand. Ransom rolled his eyes, then said to Barrington, "Get her a glass of water."

"Right."

Ransom bent over Madeleine and starting unbuttoning the high, tight collar of her pale silk suit.

"What are you doing?" she snapped, shoving his hands away.

"You're sealed up like a Victorian virgin," he snapped back. "Now we can all stand back and watch you pass out, or we can help you. Take your pick, Miss Barrington."

She gasped at his use of her name.

Graham said, "I think that tone is entirely—"

"No, no, Graham," Madeleine interrupted. "Don't provoke him."

"Yeah, you never know what a guy like me might do if he's provoked," Ransom said, shoving Graham out of his way so he could unbutton the cuffs of Madeleine's sleeves. "Violence, vulgar language, vandalism." He added deliberately, "Blackmail."

"Please," Madeleine croaked.

"Here's some water, Madeleine," Barrington said, returning to her side.

"Thank you." Her voice was barely a whisper. She took a few sips, then vaguely tried to set down the cup. Ransom took it from her, then used his fingers to splash her rather liberally with water.

"What do you think you're doing?" Graham demanded.

"Cooling her off," Ransom answered.

"I don't think—"

"Who are you?" He had noticed the man calling her "darling."

"I'm Miss Barrington's fiancé, and I don't like your—"

"No kidding?" Ransom struggled to conceal the shaft of pain that had just pierced him with vicious accuracy. On top of everything else, she was engaged?

"Graham . . ." Madeleine protested weakly.

"Well, nearly her fiancé," the man amended.

"I see. Any chance she could be pregnant?"

Madeleine gasped. Barrington cleared his throat. Graham flushed and snapped, "Certainly not! What kind of question is that?"

"It's a reasonable one," Ransom said. "Dizzy spells, nausea . . ." He shrugged. "Or maybe she's got the flu. Or a weak constitution. Or she's emotionally unstable."

"That's enough!" Madeleine yanked her hand out of Graham's and sat bolt upright. She pointed at Ransom and said, "You are not a doctor or a psychologist, so I suggest you keep your questions and your speculations to yourself."

"Madeleine," Graham interjected gently, "I think you should see a doctor—"

"There's nothing wrong with me!"

"You're fainting—"

"I'm not fainting!"

"Dizzy and sick and going pale and then getting flushed," Graham continued. "And, well, you must admit, you're acting strangely."

Ransom saw that that gave her pause. In fact, Graham and her father were both staring at her as if she'd grown another head. Apparently Madeleine wasn't prone to scenes.

While Ransom watched, she struggled to get control of the situation. She took a deep breath, cleared her throat, and looked at the other two men.

"Yes," she agreed. "Yes, I'm acting strangely, and I apologize. My behavior today has been reprehensible. I'm sorry. It's just that I'm . . . very nervous about returning to Montedora." Now she looked directly at Ransom. "I found it a dreadful place and I have nothing but bad memories of the time I spent there."

His anger was hot and cold at once. "Is that a fact?"

"Yes. That's a fact."

"Then, Madeleine," Graham said, "won't you please reconsider and send someone else?"

"No need," said Ransom. "She'll be safe with me."

"I hope you'll forgive me if I say I'm not entirely convinced of that," Graham said.

Ransom glanced at him. "Now why should I forgive you for saying a thing like that?"

He saw Madeleine sputter with involuntary laughter, which she quickly turned into a cough—drawing more concern from Graham. After an awkward moment, she turned to her father. "I'm sorry, sir. I know you're determined to hire a bodyguard for me, but I really think I'd rather go alone."

"I respect your feelings, Madeleine," Barrington said, "but I would feel much better if Ransom went with you. I have every confidence in his ability to keep you safe. Trust me on this, Graham," he added, when the man tried to protest.

Just to press the point home, Ransom added, "It's a dangerous country for a woman alone, Miss Barrington. I'm surprised nothing unpleasant happened to you your first time there."

"Something did," she said bitterly.

"Darling!"

"Madeleine!"

"You never mentioned anything!" Graham cried.

"Oh, really?" Wanting to shake her, Ransom said, "Just how unpleasant was it, Miss Barrington?"

"Oh, never mind." She shook her head. "I survived, didn't I?"

"Madeleine, you should have said something. It's not like you to keep secrets," Graham said.

Ransom snorted, drawing a warning glare from Madeleine.

Her father spoke in a tone that allowed no argument. "I'm afraid this alters the situation, Madeleine. My fatherly request must now be changed to an executive order. Mr. Ransom will accompany you, or you won't go to Montedora."

"Don't go," Graham urged, looking at Ransom as if he were a rabid dog.

"I have to," she said wearily.

"I think my daughter knows her duty," Barrington said stiffly. "She has never backed down from a challenge or an obligation."

"Then this should be fun," Ransom said.

"Don't count on it," Madeleine warned him.

"The last time I was in Montedora, I learned not to count on anything, Miss Barrington."

Their eyes locked, and they both counted on trouble.

CHAPTER FOUR

Madeleine splashed cold water on her face again and again, but her overheated blood kept pounding ruthlessly through her temples, flushing her face and making her head ache.

He's here, he's here, dear God, he's here!

She had excused herself five minutes ago and escaped to the relative safety of the private bathroom next to her father's office, putting a locked door between her and that man. But it wasn't enough. Her stomach churned as she stared at her wet reflection in the mirror.

Ransom!

How could this have happened to her? How could she have known on that hot, sultry night in Montedora that he would one day walk straight into Barrington Enterprises and consult with her father?

"Montedora," she moaned, realizing the full ramifications of the situation. He was going back to Montedora with her! Her vision swam, and she thought she might be sick. She sat down abruptly.

She had wondered many times—in the privacy of her bedroom, in the maddening Friday afternoon traffic leaving Manhattan, in the shadowy depths of her dreams—what the stranger had been doing in Montedora. And while she was planning this second trip to Montedora, she had worried about running into him again, all the while telling herself that such an event was improbable.

There was a part of her that had wanted to see him again, the part that tormented her with erotic dreams and a lingering taste of the wild pleasure she'd known with him. But even that part of Madeleine Barrington, so sternly repressed and smoothly concealed, was cringing with horror at the moment.

She ran shaking hands through her hair and realized it needed to be tidied. She searched her purse for the silver comb her mother had given her years ago and started pulling it through her hair with jerky little strokes.

He looked the same. Slim and agile, and just powerful enough to be intimidating. He'd combed his hair for this meeting, but one sun-streaked lock was already flopping down over his brow. Those dark-lashed eyes were greener than she had remembered, and they glittered with anger just as guilelessly as they had burned with passion at its height and shone with tenderness in its aftermath.

Helpless tears welled up in Madeleine's eyes. She swallowed and took several deep, steadying breaths. Makeup, she thought vaguely. She had to fix her makeup.

He looked just as dangerous as he had that night in Montedora, too predatory for these tame surroundings. For an awful moment, she'd been afraid he would hit Graham.

Graham! Madeleine's eyes flew wide open and her stomach lurched again. Good God! She had to get Ransom away from Graham! And from her father, too! What could she possibly be thinking? Why was she hiding in here while that man was saying God only knew what to her father and her almost-fiancé? She must separate them! Ransom mustn't be left alone with anyone until she'd had time to figure out what to do about him.

Hastily fixing her makeup, she wondered if he'd tracked her down, or if he was as surprised as she by today's turn of events. What would he want now? Money? Influence? More sex? Madeleine gripped the edge of the marble basin and tried to calm her nerves. There was no sense in jumping to conclusions. She'd get him alone and find out. Right away.

She finished applying her lipstick, took another deep breath, opened the bathroom door, and faced her demon.

Ransom looked up as Madeleine reentered the room, though he didn't bother to rise for her entrance the way Graham and Barrington did. She looked perfect again, he noted cynically. And not just physically—there was a coolness in her eyes and a composure in her face that hadn't been there five minutes ago. He had to give her credit. The woman had guts. He watched with bitter amusement as she smoothly took over the proceedings, suggested that her father would like to get back to work, and convinced her boyfriend to leave.

"Yes, of course," the fiancé said, accepting the dismissal with good grace. What did a woman like Madeleine see in this wimp? Wealth and position equal to her own, Ransom supposed. "I'll pick you up tomorrow at seven o'clock, then?"

"Fine," Madeleine answered absently.

"See you tomorrow evening, sir," Graham said to Barrington, shaking his hand.

"Hmmm?"

"The dinner party, sir," Graham reminded him.

Barrington tore his gaze away from Madeleine and said, "Oh, yes, of course. Tomorrow evening, then."

"Mr. Ransom." Graham barely nodded in his direction before departing.

"Nice guy," Ransom said blandly as the door closed behind Graham. "Are you really gonna marry him?"

"That's none of your business," Madeleine snapped. A look of alarm washed across her features a moment later, and she turned quickly to her father. "We'll leave you now, sir. I'm sure you have things to attend to."

"Yes, of course . . ." Barrington stared at his daughter for a moment longer before turning to smile briefly at Ransom. "I've enjoyed meeting you, Mr. Ransom, and I'm relieved to know that Madeleine will be accompanied by a capable protector."

Recognizing the dismissal, Ransom nodded and stood up. He saw a glint of steel in Barrington's eyes as the man shook his hand and added, "And I know you'll keep your word."

"She'll be safe with me," Ransom reiterated gruffly, starting to wish he hadn't promised. Why the hell didn't he just quit this assignment?

Barrington nodded and, to Ransom's surprise, clapped him on the shoulder. Then he turned to his daughter. "We'll expect you and Graham around seven o'clock tomorrow."

"Yes, of course. Mr. Ransom?" Without waiting, she turned and led the way out of her father's office.

Ransom followed Madeleine out the door, through the reception area, and toward the private elevator. Ignoring him, she pressed a button to call for the elevator and stared at a fern while they waited. The double doors swished open a moment later, admitting them to a plushly decorated elevator nearly as big as Ransom's first apartment. The doors closed behind them. Madeleine turned her back on Ransom and pressed a button on the control panel.

"Alone at last," he said.

She flinched, as if she expected him to jump her. "Don't say that!"

"You ca—"

"Don't say anything," she ordered, regaining her composure.

He frowned. "For how long?"

"Until we're in my office."

Irritated, he decided to ruffle her feathers some more. "Got a couch in your office?"

She glared at him. "That isn't funny."

"Damned right, it isn't funny." He loosened the leash on his temper. "Who the hell do you think you are? Where do you—"

"You have some nerve saying that to me! By what right—"

"What right?" he practically shouted.

"To come here—"

"I was hired—"

"And ambush me!"

"Ambush you? How was I to know?" He was shouting now. "Listen, lady, you were the one who said no names!"

"And I had a good reason!" she shouted back.

"Did you re—"

"How dare—"

The elevators doors swished open, and they both stopped in mid-shout. Madeleine drew in a quick breath and paled when a dozen people near the elevator bank stopped talking and turned to stare at her and Ransom.

Ransom shoved his hands into his pockets and lowered his head, trying to get control of himself.

"Um, is everything all right, Miss Barrington?" someone finally asked.

"Yes," Madeleine said in a tight voice. "Quite all right. Just a slight disagreement."

A young man stepped forward. Good-looking, well-dressed. "Do you, uh . . . Is this person leaving now?"

Realizing the guy was prepared to bodily evict him on Madeleine's say-so, Ransom felt his sense of humor returning. Fortunately, Madeleine pulled herself together and assured the guy that she didn't need any assistance.

"Shall we step into my office, Mr. Ransom?"

"By all means, Maddie."

Her jaw flexed in a way that made him suspect she was grinding her teeth. Awkward silences and curious stares followed them along the corridor to Madeleine's office. He didn't need anyone to tell him that she was never seen shouting in public like that. The office was at the end of the corridor. A discreet plaque informed visitors that Madeleine was the company's vice president in charge of operations. Her office was as big as Ransom's current apartment, but a lot more luxurious. It wasn't opulent, though. Every inch of the room evinced wealth beyond his wildest ambitions, but it was nonetheless discreet and tasteful. That annoyed him.

Hoping to annoy her in return, he glanced deliberately at the couch, looked at her, and nodded toward it in unmistakable invitation. She responded with an expression of such cold fury that he was sure she'd have slapped him if he'd been standing within reach.

Having told her secretary to hold all her calls, Madeleine took a seat behind the walnut desk with brass inlays; she gestured for Ransom to sit down opposite her. He suspected she felt better with this ponderous piece of furniture between them.

Now that the moment of truth was at hand, they stared uncertainly at each other, not sure how to begin this discussion. The last time they'd seen each other, they'd been involved in the most intimate act possible between a man and a woman. Now that the shock was wearing off, the change in circumstances suddenly seemed incongruous.

He knew the feel and taste and heat of her body. She knew what he enjoyed in bed and where all of his scars were. She had seen him asleep and had slept beside him. Yet, until today, they hadn't even known each other's names.

"Nice place, Maddie," he said at last, needing to break the silence.

"Don't call me Maddie," she said.

"Why not?"

She blinked. "Because no one calls me Maddie."

"Got a better reason?"

"Because I don't like it."

"Tough."

"I'm employing you," she reminded him.

"Your father's employing me," he corrected.

"I'd rather you call me Miss Barrington."

He leaned forward and spoke very distinctly. "I don't give a damn what you'd rather. About anything."

She swallowed. "I take it from your comments in the elevator that you . . . had no idea who I was. I mean, who Madeleine Barrington was."

"I'm beginning to think no one has any idea who Madeleine Barrington is. Your father, your fiancé, and your employees sure don't seem to know."

Ransom saw Madeleine's cool features crumble slightly. Her lower lip trembled, and he suddenly felt like a heel. Christ, he didn't want to make her cry. Or did he? Did he want some proof that she, too, felt a lead weight sitting on her chest right now? This whole thing had just gotten even more confusing.

"Look," he said at last, his voice softening, "I just showed up for a routine assignment, okay? I had no idea until I saw that photograph in your father's office." He smiled weakly, imagining how she must have felt when she'd seen him there. "Hell of a coincidence, huh?"

She took a steadying breath. "Not really, I suppose. There must be a very limited number of people who have business in Montedora these days."

"Apart from the CIA, the DEA, drug smugglers, the Red Cross, the Catholic Church, and UN Military Observers, hardly anyone has business there anymore," Ransom said dryly. "Which could explain your father's concern for your safety. I take it you were alone there last time?"

"I can take care of myself." Her chin rose a notch, just the way it had outside the door of his room that night.

"Oh, really?" Perversely, he said, "Do you know how crazy it was to go alone to a hotel room with a total stranger in Montedora City?"

"I'm beginning to realize," she said stonily.

"Anything could have happened to you! And who would have been there to help you?"

"I regret my actions more than I can say."

"You mean you regret going to bed with me?" he shot back. "Or you regret sneaking out like a thief while I was asleep?"

"I didn't steal anything," she snapped.

"No, you didn't. After all, what could a poor slob like me have that a Barrington woman could possibly want? Besides a hard-on, I mean."

She gasped and shot to her feet. "That's enough!"

"It sure seemed like enough for you at the time!"

She fell back a step, as if he'd slapped her. "You're fired," she choked.

"You can't fire me."

"Yes, I can."

He shook his head. "My contract is with your father."

"Then why don't you quit?"

He should, but he knew he wasn't going to. And since he

didn't know why, he lied. "I'm just a poor working stiff, Miss Barrington. I need the money."

"I'll pay you anyhow. I'll pay you double your fee if you'll turn around and leave now."

He felt like she'd slapped him. She reached into her desk and pulled out a checkbook. He shot to his feet, rounded the desk, and grabbed her wrist. The force of his grip made her gaze fly up to his face in wary surprise.

"Put that away before I break your arm," he growled.

Madeleine slowly opened her fingers and let the checkbook drop to the floor. "Let go of me," she said, staring him down. "Let go right now."

Their eyes held for a moment. He had to hand it to her, she had guts, all right. She could have threatened him with the power of her family, the machinations of her lawyers, or the wrath of her company's security guards. But she simply stood there and dared him to disobey her. A reluctant smile tugged at one corner of his mouth. In that moment, he almost liked her.

"Sorry," he said, releasing her arm. "I didn't mean to rough you up."

"Didn't you?" Her look was accusing.

"No. I'm nice to women. You of all people should know that."

She lowered her eyes at that. Rubbing her wrist absently, she turned toward the window. "If I can't fire you and you won't quit . . ."

"Yes?"

"Then I suggest we establish some ground rules."

"Sure, Maddie."

He saw her shoulders stiffen, but she had evidently decided to pick her battles, because she let the name pass without comment.

"There will be no familiar contact between us."

"Familiar contact? Would you care to elucidate, Miss Barrington?"

She gave him an impatient glance. "No touching."

"And especially no more wild, mind-blowing, frantic sex, right?"

"Exactly." She turned to face him. "Do you think you can manage that, Mr. Ransom?"

"Let me elucidate this time." He hoped she would remember every word he was about to say for the rest of her cheating, lying, superior life. "You fucked me and forgot me. And contrary to the popular misconception, men don't like that any better than women do. On top of that, you thought you were too good to tell me your name, or even say good-bye."

"You don—"

"I lost my virginity nearly twenty years ago, Maddie, but until I met you, no woman ever tried to make me feel cheap."

"I nev—"

"And," he added, raising his voice to drown out hers, "it seems you were using me to cheat on your wimpy fiancé, too."

"He's not my fiancé!" She looked surprised and added quickly, "And he's not a wimp. How dare you!"

"Me! How dare you? You were planning your escape from the moment you entered my room, weren't you?"

She flushed. He hoped she was ashamed. "I . . . I didn't plan to leave without saying good-bye."

"Then why did you do it?" he challenged.

"Because . . ." She started breathing faster. "Because . . . Never mind. It doesn't matter now." She lowered her head and refused to meet his gaze again.

It mattered to him, but he'd jump off the roof of this building before he'd admit it to her. "So let me clear up one point for you. When I found out who you were today, I promised myself I'd cut off my right arm before I'd ever touch you again. Got it, Miss Barrington?"

"Yes, I think you've made your position quite clear." He couldn't see her expression, but her voice was cool and distant. He realized with some surprise that he'd been counting on another shouting match. He had fantasized more than once about telling the mysterious blonde woman from Montedora exactly what he thought of her. And now that he'd finally done it, he felt deflated rather than satisfied. "Ah, hell." He turned and headed for the door, unable to bear her stoic demeanor for another minute.

She looked up. "Wait! Where are you going?"

"Straight to hell."

"What?"

"Home. My office. I don't know."

"We still have a few more things to discuss."

He studied her fragile but determinedly composed expression. "More ground rules?"

"Precisely."

He sighed, pulled a packet of cigarettes out of his pocket, and said, "Let's get it over with." He lit up without asking her permission.

She folded her hands. "When speaking to me, you will not indicate having a more personal knowledge of me than any ordinary employee."

"Well, now, just how personal is their knowledge, Maddie? That guy by the elevator seemed—"

"That is uncalled-for and just the sort of comment I expect you to refrain from making."

Her voice was so even that it grated on his nerves. He

felt pretty ridiculous for trying to annoy her again. They might as well do this as quickly as possible. "What else?" He took a long drag on his cigarette.

"You will not refer to that night in Montedora City again, under any circumstances, or in any way. Not when speaking to me, and particularly not when speaking to other people."

That figured. Upon realizing who she was, he had guessed she was terrified he would talk. Well, some guys did, but he'd never been one of them. She had no way of knowing that, of course, and he wasn't in the mood to soothe her fears.

"You don't seem to have a real close familiarity with the First Amendment, Maddie."

"That hardly applies—"

"Oh, I think it does. You have every right to tell me never to touch you again, and as I've already explained, I'm quite happy to cooperate. But nobody tells me what to say or not say. Ever. I say whatever I please, whenever I please, and to whoever I want to say it to. I thought you already knew that about me, but maybe you need reminding."

Her gaze was frosty. "Then let me explain, Mr. Ransom, that I am a woman of considerable reputation and credibility, and you will only succeed in making yourself look ridiculous if you start bandying about stories which, quite frankly, no one will believe."

"You don't think anyone will believe me?" He blew out a wreath of smoke. "Not even when I mention the birthmark on your butt? The one that's shaped like a sickle moon."

Her eyes sparkled with that sharp flash of cold fire which had first attracted him to her. After a moment of tense silence she decided to ignore his threat and closed the subject by saying, "If you're through reminiscing, perhaps we should discuss the details of our trip."

He nodded curtly. "Veracruz has invited—"

"Yes, I know. Please inform him that I accept his gracious invitation. I never want to see the Hotel Tigre again."

Ransom nodded again, then reached inside his jacket, pulled out an envelope, and laid it on her desk. "This is from our office. It's got our flight schedule in it, a list of recommended drugs and medical supplies for you, some safety guidelines, and an emergency number you can call anytime, in case something happens to me."

"Something . . . happens?" she repeated.

"In case I get shot, killed, captured, that kind of thing. Call this number, and they'll help you get to a safe place and wait for my replacement."

"What?" She blinked.

"Standard procedure. Unless, of course," he added dryly, "you wind up shooting me yourself."

Madeleine cleared her throat. "Why are you doing this?" she asked. "Just to get even with me?"

He scowled at her. "Protecting people is my job. And no casual roll in the hay with some nameless blonde is going to stop me from doing my job."

It was a brutal answer, but she had asked for it. "I see. Well, then, since neither you nor my father will relent on this, I suggest we at least try to be courteous to one another."

"Courtesy isn't my strong suit." Feeling restless, he said, "Are we done now?"

"Yes."

"I'll come by your apartment for you the day after tomorrow. Eight in the morning. Don't keep me waiting."

"I'll be ready." Her tone could have frosted glass.

"Right."

He remained where he was for a moment, just looking at her, taking in the silk suit, the pearl earrings, the skillfully applied makeup, the smooth waves of her hair, and the closed, arrogant expression on her face. He had a sudden, vivid image of her lying beneath him, naked and sweaty, flushed with pleasure, her hair spread around her in a wild tangle, her arms and legs enfolding him as she begged him not to stop. His body tightened and his mind clouded. He wanted to see her like that again. He wanted to see her abandon herself to pleasure and to passion. To him. He wanted it more than he wanted his next breath, which he drew in shakily before turning around and leaving her office without another word.

CHAPTER FIVE

"You look tired," Graham said with concern as he opened the passenger door of his Mercedes so Madeleine could get out of the car. The autumn wind was brisk, and she pulled the lapels of her coat around her neck as she stepped into the night air.

"Oh, I stayed up late last night. So many things have to be finished before I leave." And half of them were still undone, because she hadn't been able to concentrate. She'd been a distracted bundle of nerves ever since Ransom had seared her with a blatantly sexual gaze, then spun around and left her office without saying good-bye.

"You work too hard." Graham took her elbow and led her down the stone walk toward the front door of Chateau Camille, the Barrington family home on Long Island.

"I like hard work," Madeleine murmured, wondering if she would exchange these sort of banalities with Graham for the next fifty years if she married him.

Chateau Camille had once belonged to a mistress of the great nineteenth-century French writer, Alexandre Dumas. Madeleine's grandfather had bought the chateau during a tour of Europe some sixty years ago. He'd then had it transported stone by stone to the North Shore of Long Island, where it was rebuilt and renovated. The hand-hewn stones, the red tile roof, and the romantic turrets created a fairytale effect in this ten-acre setting of formal gardens and winding paths.

The house was lit up and welcoming tonight. All three of

the Barrington daughters were coming to dinner. Rosa, one of the domestic staff, admitted Madeleine and Graham to the grand foyer, whose eighteenth-century oak paneling was of museum quality. Rosa took their coats and showed them into the green sitting room, the least formal room on the main floor of the house, apart from the kitchen.

Madeleine wasn't surprised that she was the first to arrive. Her habit of punctuality had never rubbed off on her sisters. She embraced her mother, accepted a glass of club soda from her father—she'd been avoiding alcohol ever since that night in Montedora—and caught up on some family news. The news, of course, all came from her mother; Madeleine's father was a workaholic who paid little attention to anything but his vast business empire.

Most of Eleanor Barrington's family news, however, was about herself. Madeleine was concerned to learn that her youngest sister, Caroline, had been arrested (again) during a protest staged against Randall Cosmetics. However, any attempt to elicit information about Caroline's welfare only sparked more comments about Eleanor's own reaction to the incident.

"How could she have done it?" Eleanor cried. "Her own brother-in-law is a Randall!"

"Well, she's never pretended to like Richard," Madeleine said.

"I can't imagine what the girl was thinking of, Madeleine! You must talk to her. I'm so embarrassed! Everyone on the North Shore knows about it. I'm surprised you haven't heard before now."

"When did it happen?"

"Last week. And your father and I were supposed to attend a fund-raising dinner at the Metropolitan Museum of Art that night, too. Well, there was just no point in going, not when I wouldn't be able to enjoy myself at all."

"Caroline wasn't hurt, though?" Madeleine prodded.

"No, of course not. I was prostrate for two days, but she was out covering a story the very next morning for that radical, hippy, Communist, downtown magazine she writes for."

"I see." Madeleine caught Graham's eye as he tried to repress an amused smile. Caroline Barrington's radical politics and social activism had long been the bane of her parents.

"And now she's late for dinner," Eleanor added fretfully. "She never calls, either, even though she knows I sit here worrying that she's been murdered in that dreadful slum apartment of hers, or arrested again, or kidnapped by one of those political dissident groups she's always interviewing. What am I going to do with that girl?"

Deciding it was time to change the subject, Madeleine asked about her other sister. "And how's Stephanie? I haven't talked to her in almost three weeks."

"She did call. The children's soccer practice—or something—dragged on too long, so they'll be a little late. And Richard had to cancel."

"Ah." Madeleine sipped her drink, doubting that anyone would miss her sister's husband. She had never liked him, and now she suspected that he was cheating on Stephanie. It was none of Madeleine's business, but it didn't endear him to her. Besides, there was something about his manner toward Stephanie that always set Madeleine's teeth on edge.

She listened with half an ear as her mother continued to talk. Beyond saying, "How are you, dear?" her mother never asked Madeleine about herself. And Madeleine always responded that she was fine, busy at work (or, in previous years, at school), and looking forward to this or that event. For over twenty years, that had been the sum total of her relationship with her mother, and her mother clearly resented anyone who distracted her with more complicated behavior—the way both of Madeleine's sisters did. Rebellious Caroline with her radical affiliations, protests, sit-ins, and outrageous behavior. Sad Stephanie, with her uncertain health, extreme weight fluctuations, and psychotherapists. Madeleine shook her head and wondered how one couple had produced three such different daughters.

Still trying to distract herself from the growing panic she felt over going back to Montedora with Ransom tomorrow, Madeleine studied Graham as her mother continued to chatter. He was standing by the fireplace, talking with her father. He glanced at Madeleine from time to time. When their eyes met, she tried to bring some warmth into her expression. He was a good man, an attractive man, and he wanted to marry her. She suddenly wanted to feel something besides a mild fondness for him. She wanted to love and trust and need him. She wanted to want his passion.

"Ah, they're here," Thackeray Barrington said with a pleased smile, interrupting Madeleine's thoughts. His love for his daughters sometimes softened him, but his devotion to his grandchildren turned this driven, focused man into mush.

Jeff and Hazel Randall raced pell-mell into the room, followed slowly by their mother. The children flung themselves upon the aged golden retriever sleeping near the fireplace, then flung themselves at their grandfather. They ignored Graham, hugged Madeleine, and greeted their grandmother with an excited recitation of their day. Then they returned to the blinking dog and lavished their affection upon him. His tail thumped, and he presented an ear for scratching.

Madeleine willfully controlled her expression as she embraced her sister. Stephanie looked emaciated. Having regained the weight she had lost after bearing two children in a row, she had been dieting again this past year. But she had taken it too far. Madeleine had thought Stephanie a little too thin when she'd last seen her about six weeks ago. Now her sister looked gaunt, hollow-cheeked, withered, and unwell. Madeleine had never seen her so thin, not even during that terrible phase in Stephanie's adolescence.

As Stephanie moved on to greet their mother, Eleanor caught Madeleine's eye. Madeleine read the message there and realized she would be expected to talk to Stephanie. She nodded and resigned herself to the inevitable.

Caroline arrived a few minutes later, flushed, disheveled, and as unconsciously pretty as ever. Her faded jeans hugged her trim hips and long legs, her embroidered shirt was wrinkled, and she probably hadn't brushed her long, tangled hair since that morning. But that just-got-out-of-bed look suited her healthy, vibrant looks and uninhibited personality.

Eleanor went to the kitchen to check on the cook's progress. Upon learning that dinner was ready and waiting, she led the family into the formal dining room, and dinner was served.

An excellent hostess, Eleanor Barrington kept the conversation going throughout dinner, avoiding many unpleasant topics—including Caroline's recent arrest—with a skill born of long practice. Madeleine had to admire her mother's ability, even as some alien impulse inside of her longed to silence the ceaseless social chatter. Her father was absorbed in his two grandchildren, Stephanie was as quiet and self-effacing as usual, and Caroline seemed as determined as ever to start a huge row with her parents. Madeleine herself was distracted and quiet. Trying to banish her thoughts and fears about Ransom was using up all of her mental energy. So it fell to poor Graham to help Eleanor keep the chatter going, course after course.

Madeleine noticed that Stephanie scarcely touched her food. A bit of salad with no dressing, a few steamed vegetables, a single bite of chicken. On the other hand, Madeleine was doing little better, pushing food around her plate with a distinct lack of appetite.

Would Ransom really talk? Would he humiliate her, or was he bluffing? If he didn't want money or anything else from her, then why hadn't he spoken frankly in front of her father and Graham? Maybe, she thought with desperate hope, he was just angry and trying to shake her up. Maybe he had no more intention of telling other people about that bawdy night than she did.

But how would she spend the next week or so with that man, when every time she looked into his eyes she remembered that night and saw that he did, too? And he enjoyed reminding her! Oh, yes, whether or not he ever spoke to anyone else about it, he intended to keep taunting her with it, reminding her of how much she had wanted him, of how she had hungered for him and everything they did together, of how shameless and eager she had been. And he liked reminding her in the crudest language possible, too, knowing that it bothered her.

You fucked me and forgot me.

How she had tried to forget! But she couldn't.

What could a poor slob like me have that a Barrington woman could want? Besides a hard-on, I mean.

Stop it.

It sure seemed like enough for you at the time.

Well, it wasn't enough. She still wanted—

"That's enough!" Hazel cried.

Madeleine's gaze flew to her niece's face. The girl was telling her grandfather, most emphatically, not to put any more peas on her plate.

"Aren't you hungry, dear?" Madeleine's mother asked her a moment later.

"Hmmm?" Madeleine looked down at her plate and saw that she had smeared her soufflé into a pulpy mess. "Oh, uh, not really. Nervous, you know."

"Well, I'm sure I don't know why your father insists on sending his own daughter back to that dreadful place," Eleanor said with some asperity.

"He didn't insist, Mother."

"Madeleine knows her responsibilities and takes them seriously," Thackeray interjected. "And there's no one I'd trust in her place."

"And Mother tells me you're going to stay with Veracruz?" Caroline asked. When Madeleine nodded, she shook her head. "I can't believe it! I mean, I can't believe you, Madeleine! How could you accept hospitality from that thieving, murdering, fornicating dictator?"

"Don't say 'fornicating' at the table, dear," said Eleanor.

"Do you have any idea how many political prisoners Veracruz and his buddy Escalante have locked up? Do you know how many people are arrested without charge under their regime?"

"Caroline, dear—" Eleanor began.

"Arrested, beaten, tortured and—if they're not executed—locked up in some dank, rat-infested cell and forgotten about! Veracruz has leveled crippling taxes on everyone but his wealthy friends, and he has stolen from his own treasury. He has let Escalante and his secret police violate every—"

"I'm going to Montedora to sell the plantation, Caroline," Madeleine said. "The plantation you have always been ashamed of the family for owning. You've told me a dozen times this year how glad you are that I'm selling it."

"I didn't know you'd have to hold hands with Veracruz to do it!"

"With the escalation of crime in Montedora, particularly since last month's riots, I am fortunate to be offered the President's protection," Madeleine said. Involved in arguing with her sister, she momentarily forgot her mother's presence and blurted out, "Are you aware that rebel bands killed a journalist in the countryside two weeks ago, or that an agricultural consultant was robbed and murdered only a block from the Hotel Conquistador four days ago?"

"Oh, dear Lord!" Eleanor cried, clutching the delicate pearls she wore. "Madeleine!"

Realizing her mistake, Madeleine said quickly, "Veracruz has just completed major security improvements at the Presidential Palace. It's the safest place in the country right now."

"I'm going to be ill," Eleanor threatened.

"And the security improvements were all advised," Madeleine added for her mother's benefit, "by Mr. Ransom, the man who will accompany me."

Eleanor glared at her husband. "Well, you certainly left out a few things when you told me Madeleine was going back to Montedora for a business trip."

"I didn't want to worry you."

"Really, Mother, Mr. Ransom is very capable. There's nothing to wor—"

"I think I need to lie down," Eleanor said faintly.

"Yes, of course. Shall I help you up to your room?"

"Thank you, dear."

Madeleine escorted her mother up to the master bedroom suite her parents had shared for so many years, then called down to the kitchen and asked for some chamomile tea to be brought up. She got her mother calmed down and settled comfortably, then went back downstairs to join the rest of the family. They had adjourned to the library for coffee. Madeleine poured herself a cup and sat with her sisters while her father, Graham, and the grandchildren disappeared into an adjoining room to indulge in noisy games.

"How's Mother? Still having the vapors?" Caroline asked.

"Sleeping by now, I hope," Madeleine replied.

"Don't look at me like that," Caroline said. "It's not my fault. You're the one who's going to Montedora."

Madeleine studied her sister for a moment and then said, "Were you really arrested last week at Randall Cosmetics headquarters?"

"She handcuffed herself to the lobby doors," Stephanie said. "Richard told me about it."

Her lips trembled uncertainly for a moment. Then all three women started laughing. Their hilarity was partially a release from the tension which always pervaded family gatherings, but the image of Richard confronting his wild-eyed sister-in-law as she handcuffed herself to his company's glass doors made Madeleine laugh until her eyes watered.

"It's not funny!" Caroline insisted, laughing as hard as her sisters. "Oh, stop it!"

"Four years of college and a master's degree, all so you could go around chaining yourself to buildings," Madeleine choked out.

"Poor Richard!" Stephanie wheezed. "He was apoplectic about it for days!"

Pulling herself together, Madeleine asked on a sigh, "What on earth made you do it?"

"It was a protest against animal testing. I don't believe that it's complex or many-sided or controversial, Madeleine. It's just wrong." She glanced at Stephanie and added, "And Richard is a fool not to put a stop to it."

"You know Richard doesn't talk to me about business," Stephanie said.

"You gave Mother the vapors that day, too," Madeleine said to Caroline. "Are you trying to give her a heart attack?"

"She just needs a life," Caroline said with a shrug. "And she needs to let me get on with mine."

"Tonight wasn't Caroline's fault," Stephanie said.

"Thank you! You see?" Caroline looked triumphantly at Madeleine. "I'm not the one about to get shot by Montedoran rebels."

"It wasn't Madeleine's fault either," Stephanie insisted. "That little fit at the table was just Mother's way of ensuring that everyone's attention remained focused on her."

Caroline shrugged. Madeleine nodded and stared at her coffee. There was a long silence before Caroline said, "Will you really be safe down there?"

"Yes."

"Graham doesn't seem very convinced that this man—Ransom?—knows what he's doing. He told me the guy was a smart-ass."

"Surely Graham didn't say that?"

"No, he said something like 'impertinent to the point of belligerence.' "

"Ah. Well, yes, Mr. Ransom is a little abrasive, and he and Graham didn't hit it off. But Dad has every confidence in him."

"Do you?"

Madeleine blinked in surprise as she considered the question. She had been so busy worrying about her secret connection with Ransom that she hadn't even considered the very real issue of her personal safety until now.

"Yes," she said at last. "I do. He's not . . . I mean, I don't like the man, but he strikes me as extremely capable." That much, at least, was true. Whatever her personal problems with Ransom, he had seemed to her—from the very first moment—to be dangerous, able-bodied, and quick-witted. If anyone could protect her, it would be him.

To her relief, the conversation shifted away from her bodyguard. Caroline talked about her job, and Stephanie talked about the children. Madeleine finally brought up the subject of Stephanie's weight, only to be put off by the other woman.

"Come on, Madeleine, you know the saying: You can never be too rich or too thin," Stephanie said.

"Bullshit," Caroline said.

Madeleine asked Stephanie, "You're not still dieting, are you?"

Stephanie patted her stomach. "I still have some flabby parts I'm trying to get rid of."

"Stephanie, every woman's got some extra flesh on her. It's supposed to be there."

"Look, I take my vitamins. I know what I'm doing."

"Are you sure? You look very tired. In fact, I think you look too thin," Madeleine said gently.

Mingled hurt and anger flared in Stephanie's eyes. Her mouth tightened in her gaunt face as she said, "Thanks so much for sharing your opinion, Madeleine."

"I just meant—"

"You said exactly what you meant."

"I'm only trying to—"

"To do what? Help? Because I don't have your perfect understanding of what my weight should be?"

"I didn't mean that," Madeleine said. "But Mother's worried about you, and so am I."

"How thoughtful," Stephanie said sullenly. "Ever the perfect sister. Perfect daughter, perfect career woman. It must get awfully boring being so perfect!"

Madeleine blinked, taken aback. "Stephanie, I—"

"Just lay off, Madeleine! Do I hand out free advice on your life?"

"I'm sorry, I didn't—"

"Didn't you?"

"No, of course—"

"Leave it, Madeleine," Caroline advised. "The truth is, Steph, you look like death warmed over."

Madeleine glared at her. "Really, Caroline, that's—"

"And you," Caroline continued, turning to Madeleine, "should stop being so damn perfect. I agree with Stephanie on that. Would it kill you to act like a mere mortal for a change?"

Madeleine's mind was flooded with images from a shabby hotel room in Montedora City. She swallowed and wondered what to say to her sisters. She had always tried to be dependable and understanding. She had always wanted to be a role model for them. She had tried to shield them from all the pressures that inevitably made Stephanie crack and Caroline explode. And somehow, all her good intentions only made them resent her.

The taut silence of the room was broken a moment later by the entrance of the children, who tore through the doorway at top speed, shrieking wildly. Madeleine's father and Graham joined the group a moment later, and the atmosphere lightened as everyone's conversation focused on children and toys and games.

Needing something to do, Madeleine rose from her chair and walked to the far end of the room to pour herself another cup of coffee. Her father joined her there.

"I trust everything is in order for tomorrow?"

"Yes, Dad."

"No problems?"

She avoided his probing gaze. "No."

"And Mr. Ransom. He meets with your approval?"

"I thought the point was that he meets with your approval," she said, stirring her coffee.

"He does, but . . ." He seemed hesitant. "I had the impression that you might have met before."

Madeleine's belly clenched. "Did he say that?"

"No." He waited a moment, then added, "And neither, apparently, will you."

"He's abrasive, but his credentials are good," she said, still avoiding both his question and his gaze.

"I've never seen you take such an apparent dislike to someone so quickly."

"Haven't you?" she murmured.

"He's a good man, Madeleine."

Sheer surprise made her meet his gaze. "You like him."

"Yes. His behavior was rather rude today, but I like him." He shrugged. "Call it instinct. He's a man who can be trusted and counted on."

She considered her father's words. "And that's why . . ."

He nodded. "I wouldn't force unwanted company on you, Madeleine, but I am more concerned than I have admitted to you."

"Or to Mother?"

"Yes." He added a shallow spoonful of sugar to his coffee. "Ransom says he can protect you, and I believe him."

Her father's concern affected Madeleine. He had always been the first to push her toward new challenges. If he was worried about her safety, then she should be, too.

"I will follow his instructions to the letter, Dad," she said at last, privately wondering how safe she was from Ransom himself. Well, he had said he never intended to touch her again, didn't he? The thought did nothing to improve her mood.

"I think I'd better get going," she said, wanting to escape before the evening slid even farther downhill. "It's getting late and we've still got to drive back to the city."

"Yes, of course. I'll ask Rosa to bring your coats."

Madeleine's farewell with Stephanie was awkward, but Caroline was always able to forget an argument as quickly as she started one.

"Will you be back in time for Dad's birthday party?" Caroline asked Madeleine.

"Yes, of course. I'll be back well before that." Seeing Graham's inquisitive expression as he helped her into her coat, Madeleine explained, "It'll be my father's sixtieth birthday. The family's throwing a big bash here."

Thackeray added, "You're invited, of course, Graham."

"I'll look forward to it, sir."

Madeleine was quiet on the drive back to the city. Luckily traffic was light, and the journey went quickly. Her mind was awhirl with concerns, not the least of which was what she should do about Graham. How could she continue to think about his marriage proposal? Surely a woman knew when she wanted to marry a man, didn't she?

Madeleine looked across at his handsome profile. No answer revealed itself to her, and she was swept by a wave of loneliness. She wished she could tell Graham about Ransom. About her shame and embarrassment. About her fear of the man and the unpredictable emotions he aroused in her.

She leaned her head against the cold glass of the passenger window, wishing someone could hold her and make it all go away: the sudden, hurtful argument with her sisters; the heaviness she always felt after seeing her mother; her worries about going to Montedora; the weight of the responsibilities she bore; her whirling confusion over Ransom. She wished someone could cuddle and comfort her, and rock her to sleep.

She shifted her legs and remembered vividly how Ransom had done all of that, and more. He had taken a lonely, leaden night and turned it into magic. He had stripped her of all regrets and weariness. He had ravished her worries and cares and chased them into the darkness. He had taken her outside of herself.

If he weren't such an overbearing, foul-mouthed louse, she might even thank him for it someday. She might even ask him to do it again.

Madeleine's eyes flew wide open and she sat bolt upright. No! That was wrong. She would never, ever ask him to do it again. What could she be thinking?

She looked at Graham again as he steered the Mercedes down East 73rd Street. He was the man who wanted to marry her. Why couldn't he take away the demons tonight?

Graham brought the car to a stop outside Madeleine's building. He met her gaze. "Are you all right?"

Yes, why not Graham? They had never slept together. She had said she wasn't ready, and he hadn't pushed her. Yes, why not tonight? She had a feeling she was as ready as she'd ever be, and she needed . . . someone. Why shouldn't that someone be the man she might well marry?

"Why don't . . ." Madeleine's voice was dry and brittle,

fading before she could complete the sentence.

"Yes?"

"Would you like to stay with me tonight, Graham?"

Ransom rolled away from the woman beside him and lit up a cigarette. Sex had been a mistake. He'd known that even before they were done undressing. He shouldn't have done it, shouldn't have called her. But he'd desperately needed something. Someone.

"What's wrong?" Gwen lay on her side and studied his troubled frown. "Is it Montedora?"

He shrugged.

"I thought maybe it was," she said, "since you've been . . ."

"What?" he said tersely.

Stop it. Don't take it out on Gwen.

He liked Gwen, and his bad mood wasn't her fault.

Gwen was a divorced corporate executive who worked long hours, traveled often, and—in her own words—didn't need a man hanging around and driving her crazy. They had met on a plane a year ago and had been occasional lovers since then. There had never been more than that between them, and it had suited them both. Ransom didn't know if the relationship had been exclusive on her side, though her busy schedule made him suppose that it had. And except for that single night with Madeleine, he hadn't slept with anybody else. He was a one-woman-at-a-time kind of guy. And that was what was wrong tonight. The woman on his mind wasn't the one whose bed he was in.

"Well, you haven't been yourself since you came back from Montedora." Gwen sat up, pulling the sheet up to cover herself. "Did something happen to you down there?"

He shrugged again, uncomfortably aware that he was being churlish. "Sort of."

She hesitated. "Want to talk about it?"

He shook his head. "Nah. It's not your problem."

She stared at him for a moment, then shrugged. "Have it your way."

"I'm sorry, Gwen, I—"

"It's okay."

He gestured vaguely toward the twisted sheets. "No, I meant, I'm sorry about . . ."

She smiled. "Nothing to apologize for, Ransom. The sex was good. The sex is always good. That's why I let you disrupt my schedule from time to time."

He smiled wryly. "I suspect you're going easy on my fragile male ego tonight."

She shook her head. "No. I'll admit, it's been better. But even when you're obviously thinking about something else," she paused and raised her brows significantly before continuing, "you still know your way around a woman's body."

He drew on his cigarette. There was a companionable silence for a few moments before he said, "I should go."

She didn't try to keep him. Ransom drew on his jeans and slipped into his shirt while she watched. He pulled on his shoes and socks, picked up his jacket, and turned to say something to her.

"See you around, Gwen," seemed to be as eloquent as he could get tonight.

"See you around, Ransom."

He usually kissed her good-bye. He didn't tonight. She usually walked him to the front door. She didn't tonight.

He stopped in the bedroom doorway, turned around, and tried to think of how to tell her what he really needed to tell her.

"You won't be calling again, will you?" she said quietly.

"I . . ." He shook his head. "No, I won't, Gwen. It's nothing to do with you. I think I'm going crazy."

Her eyes watered a little. She looked away for a moment, then looked back, covering the moment with a bright, artificial smile. "Well, then I guess I won't be calling you either. So thanks for the good times and . . . take care, Ransom."

"You, too, Gwen," he said softly.

He drew on his battered, brown leather jacket as he left Gwen's apartment building and stepped out into the brisk night air. October. He loved October. Hell of a time to be going down to Montedora, where there would be heavy rains.

He pulled another cigarette out of his pocket and cupped his hands around it as he lit up, aware that he had smoked twice his usual number of cigarettes since seeing Madeleine Barrington yesterday.

The thought of her sent his blood rushing through his body in hot wonder and confusion. The memory of that night was like a fever dream, more real than reality. The colors, scents, sounds, and textures of that night were sharper and more vivid than any other sexual experience of his life, and they had stayed with him all this time, as sharp and stirring as if he'd held her in his arms only five minutes ago.

He thought briefly of the woman he had been holding in his arms just a few minutes ago, then shook his head. Damn Madeleine Barrington! Sex with Gwen had failed to satisfy the hungry beast stirring inside him ever since that night in Montedora, but seeing her from time to time had been more agreeable than contemplating pursuit of other women. He wasn't interested. He knew who he wanted, had known all along. He'd just never known where to find her.

Well, now he knew. Now he was going to be stuck with her day and night until this business in Montedora was over. And he had sworn not to touch her.

Christ, why did he always have to do things the hard way?

CHAPTER SIX

Sex had been a mistake. Madeleine had known that even before they were done undressing. She shouldn't have done it, shouldn't have invited Graham to spend the night. Now, as she faced him over her first cup of morning coffee, she castigated herself for not considering a few alternative options last night.

Why hadn't she cleaned her oven? Why hadn't she rented a few movies—some maudlin weepies, or maybe even a serial killer story? Why hadn't she gone online and shopped for some adult novelty items—a wriggling latex phallus, or perhaps something with fringe on it?

Madeleine gurgled with startled laughter, then choked on her coffee.

"Are you all right?" Graham asked.

She rubbed her forehead and muttered, "I think I'm going mad."

"Don't blame yourself, darling. It's my f—"

"No, it's not. Please, let's not have this discussion again."

"Of course. I didn't mean to—"

"What time is it?"

"Almost seven o'clock."

"He'll be here any minute," she said with dread.

Her suitcase waited by the door. She was dressed in a pale suit. She'd needed more makeup than usual this morning; the dark circles under her eyes had made her flinch when she'd first looked into the mirror.

"I'll miss you," Graham said, taking her hand.

Madeleine nodded, smiled faintly, and tried to think of a way to convince him to leave now. This very moment. But she hesitated, afraid of hurting him even more.

Graham was a considerate, if somewhat restrained, lover. He was attentive and experienced, and he had so wanted to give her pleasure last night.

"But, darling, why?" he had protested when she had finally suggested they try to get some sleep. "I know you haven't . . . Just let me—"

"No, please!" She had flinched away from his hands, hurting him even more than her unresponsiveness had already hurt him. "Not tonight, Graham. It's not your fault. Really. You must know it's not. I just can't relax. Please, I feel terrible about this, b—"

"I'm the one who should feel terrible," he protested. "And I do. I want to give you—"

"I should never have chosen tonight to ask you to stay." Then, wanting to soothe the hurt she had caused, she lied, "I'm just glad you're here with me tonight. Really, Graham. It means a lot to me that you're here."

Well, after that, the poor fellow had had no choice but to stay all night. Pouring herself another cup of coffee, Madeleine reflected that he must be puzzled and disappointed. Eager for forgetfulness, seeking safe harbor, she had thrown herself into his arms and kissed him with passionate longing. But by the time he had carried her into the bedroom, she knew beyond the shadow of a doubt that whatever she longed for, she would not find it with him. Her change of mood had destroyed the evening, and she couldn't even explain it to him, not without making things worse than they already were. She felt so ashamed.

And, oh, how she hated Ransom! In this moment, she

hated him more than she had ever hated anyone. She had found herself floundering with Graham, unhappily missing what she had never needed before meeting Ransom. In the absence of that heady, untamed passion she'd experienced in Montedora, she just felt sad, self-conscious, and eager to get the whole thing over with last night.

Poor Graham, she thought. Despairing of ever regaining her equilibrium, she looked at her watch again and felt her stomach heave. Eight o'clock. Ransom would be here soon.

Poor Madeleine, she thought. She grimaced with self-disgust and swallowed another scalding mouthful of coffee.

She jumped when the intercom phone rang in the entrance hallway. Ransom was right on time.

"I'll get it," Graham said with unexpected alacrity.

Madeleine said, "Tell him I'll be right down," and fled to the bathroom with inelegant haste.

When she returned, ready to leave, Graham informed her, "He's coming up."

"Here?"

"Yes."

"Why?"

"I asked him to."

"I don't want him in my home!"

Graham blinked.

She realized that had sounded a little hysterical, so she amended, "There's no reason for him to come up here."

Once again off-balance, Graham said, "I'm afraid it's too late. He'll be here any second."

She didn't need to ask why he had asked Ransom to come up. He was clearly intent upon staking his claim to her, just in case Ransom had any doubts. When he admitted Ransom to the apartment a moment later, Madeleine saw Ransom's eyes swiftly take it all in: Graham's presence in her apartment at this early hour; the tie and jacket which lay draped across a chair; the two cups of coffee on the table by the window.

Ransom responded to Graham's courteous greeting with a curt nod and impassive expression. He looked at Madeleine and said, "Ready?"

"Yes."

"Go ahead, darling," Graham said. "I'll lock up for you."

Madeleine looked at him helplessly. He didn't have a key for the dead bolt on her door, but she didn't want to embarrass him by saying so now. "I'd rather you came down with us," she said at last.

This seemed to please him, and he agreed. The elevator ride to the ground floor would have taken place in stony silence if he hadn't done all the talking.

"You'll call me when you get there, won't you? And let me know the moment you know the date of your return. I hope you won't have to be away for long, darling. And you're sure you'll be back before your father's birthday party?"

He was still chatting as they crossed the lobby and left the building. "You'll take good care of her, won't you, Mr. Ransom? I wouldn't like anything unpleasant—anything at all—to happen to her."

Ransom nodded, handed Madeleine's suitcase to the driver of the limousine parked in front of the building, and opened the car door for Madeleine. He glanced briefly at Graham, then met Madeleine's eyes with a sardonic expression. "Say good-bye."

She glared at him. "Would you mind giving us a moment alone?"

"On the streets of Manhattan?" he responded dryly.

"Get in the car and wait for me," she snapped.

"As you command, milady." He went round to the other side of the car and got in. She could have sworn he was smirking.

"Maybe I'll get lucky, and rebels will shoot him," she muttered.

"One can only hope," Graham said, taking her in his arms.

It was for his dignity that she had insisted on having a moment alone with him. Now she wanted to get it over with quickly. Best not to even mention last night. Taking command, she said, "I'll be back before you've had time to miss me. Don't worry."

"I miss you already," he breathed. His kiss was not inappropriate for a lover's public farewell, but it was more than she was comfortable with, knowing that Ransom might be watching.

"Good-bye," she murmured, sliding away from him.

"You'll call when you arrive?" he urged.

"I promise." The driver held the car door open for her, discreetly looking elsewhere.

She stepped into the car, her relief at leaving Graham behind overwhelmed by her apprehension at being in such close quarters with Ransom. He glanced up briefly from the newspaper he was reading as he lounged in the spacious backseat of the car.

Determined to stay in control of the situation, Madeleine sat back in the cushioned seat and placed her purse and briefcase between them. Once she was settled in, Ransom leaned forward and tapped on the glass separating them from the driver, indicating they were ready to go. The limousine pulled out into the street. Madeleine turned to wave to Graham. The car rounded the corner a moment later.

She wished she could love Graham. She wished he could have made her forget all about this dangerous man whose presence was like an electrical charge. She sighed and put Graham out of her mind with finality.

"So," Ransom said, turning a page of his paper, "I take it Graham got some last night?"

She was instantly furious. "Mind your own business."

"It certainly improved his mood more than yours," he observed. "Is he always this talkative after he gets laid?"

"Are you always this inquisitive about other people's love lives?" she shot back.

"Ah, so it's love, is it?" Ransom shrugged and continued perusing his paper. "Yeah, I guess it must be. You told him your name, after all."

Inexplicably compelled to sink to Ransom's level, she said, "Are you always this nasty when you don't get laid?"

He looked up from his paper. There was a wicked gleam in his eyes. "Ah, but I did get laid last night. Would you like me to tell you about it, Miss Barrington?"

Her stomach took another plunge. She felt her jaw drop. She swallowed and looked away. "No. No, I wouldn't." A horrible afterthought made her ask, "Did you tell her about me?"

"Somehow," he drawled, "the subject never came up."

"Oh." She felt a little light-headed as the limousine swung around another corner.

"I don't think she'd have been interested, anyhow."

"No." Her breathing was shallow. Her chest hurt, as if she'd been hit there. She looked out the window, willing him to be silent, willing him to look away from her.

After a few tense moments, she heard his newspaper crinkle. She risked a brief glance in his direction and saw that his face was now hidden behind it. She stared out the window again, stunned and confused.

Of course he slept with other women. Had she ever thought otherwise? Why had his comment come as such a surprise? Was he supposed to have turned celibate after Montedora?

Madeleine closed her eyes and tried to steady herself. Why did she feel as if he had just given away something that was rightfully hers? She opened her eyes and discovered her vision had grown misty. She blinked hard and clenched her jaw. This was absurd! And undignified—not that she had much pretense to dignity where Ransom was concerned. She must get a grip on herself. And she mustn't let him know she felt hurt. How he would ridicule her if he knew!

She had gotten off to a bad start, swapping insults with him like that. He could get under her skin faster than anyone she'd ever met, but it was time to start dealing with him the way she would deal with any other impertinent employee who tried to get the better of her. No one got the better of Madeleine Barrington, she reminded herself.

Firm in her resolve, and entrenched in her hatred of Mr. Ransom, she picked up the *Wall Street Journal* and started reading. But she didn't understand a single word of it today.

Ransom didn't stop hiding behind his newspaper until they pulled up outside their departure terminal at JFK Airport. He didn't absorb a word of the damned paper, but keeping it between him and Madeleine at least kept him from grabbing her and shaking her until her head flew off. The temptation to do so had been unbearable ever since she had dismissed him with a withering glance and begun calmly reading the *Journal.*

He wasn't sure whose idea it had been to make him go

up to her apartment, but there was no mistaking the purpose behind the request. The boyfriend wanted Ransom to know whose woman Madeleine was, and she wanted Ransom to know she wasn't pining for one wild night in Montedora City. It had taken a lot of self-control not to throw the boyfriend down the elevator shaft. It took even more self-control now not to draw the curtain across the glass separating them from the driver, pull Madeleine down into the cushioned seat, and do whatever it took to make her forget her boyfriend's very name.

No names, she had said.

No, why should she tell her name to some one-night stand in a crummy hotel room in another hemisphere? It wasn't as if some working stiff with a bad tie actually mattered. Not to her. He'd protected enough rich people to know that some of them were real shits. He was just annoyed at himself for getting taken in by Madeleine Barrington. He was just mad at her for treating him like a peasant. That explained the claw that had dug into his guts when he'd walked into her apartment this morning.

He tried not to think about those two in bed together. He tried so hard his head hurt. But the images flashed mercilessly through his mind as his eyes stared at the newspaper. Was it good between Madeleine and her society boyfriend? Was it frantic and noisy and juicy, tender and slow and sultry, easy and sweet and wild? Was it just the way he remembered it? Nah, probably not. Graham didn't seem like the kind of guy to really cut loose, even in bed. On the other hand, Ransom reflected uncomfortably, Madeleine didn't seem that way either, not at first glance. But when the time came, she had abandoned all her moorings and thrown herself into the storm.

Ransom gloomily redoubled his efforts not to think

about those two together. In bed. Fucking their brains out.

Stop it! What does the sports page say?

He had known she was no cloistered virgin, no green schoolgirl. Had he expected her to turn celibate after Montedora, for God's sake? It wasn't as if she was giving away something that rightfully belonged to him, after all. On the contrary, she was engaged to that supercilious jerk. Or nearly engaged. So Ransom really wasn't in a position to snarl at her for letting that guy into her bed.

The hell with the sports page! Where are the funnies?

That sigh she had given after waving good-bye to her boyfriend had cut through Ransom like a knife through hot butter. Was she really so crazy about that jerk?

He was going to stop thinking about it.

He needed to keep his mind on business. Letting himself get distracted over this woman would be dumb. Guys wound up getting shot—or worse—when they let a woman cloud their minds. He'd seen it happen to others and had always thought it was crazy. Sex had its proper time and place, and it was best left there. Gwen had understood that; it's what he had liked best about her. Wasn't it about time he started acting and thinking like a professional?

Yes, it was. For his own self-respect, if nothing else. He wouldn't let his temper—or this high-handed, sneaky society chick—get the best of him.

The driver pulled the limousine to a stop outside their departure terminal, unloaded their luggage, and drove away. Madeleine maintained her resolve to behave appropriately all the way from the car to the VIP check-in desk, about 100 yards away.

"Aisle, please," Madeleine said to the check-in clerk, presenting her with her passport.

"No, I need the aisle seat," Ransom said, handing over his passport.

Since they were clearly together, the clerk looked at them expectantly, waiting for them to settle the matter.

"I prefer the aisle," Madeleine said, her tone discouraging any argument.

"Company policy," Ransom replied. "I take the aisle seat."

"I'm the client," Madeleine said. "You can sit by the window if that's my preference."

"Would you like me to hold your coat and run your bath, too, milady?"

"Why can't you just accommodate me like a gentleman?"

"Why can't you just cooperate like a sensible client?"

"Because I'm going to have to get up a few times during the flight, and I don't relish the thought of having to squeeze past you every time I do."

"I sit by the aisle so that anyone trying to reach you has to go through me."

"I'm not worried about being attacked in the airplane," she said in exasperation, "I'm only worried about what happens after we get to Montedora."

Having run out of steam, they glared at each other.

The clerk said, "Uh, if I may make a suggestion . . ."

Ransom took a deep breath and forced himself to speak politely. "Miss Barrington will take an aisle seat. I would also like an aisle seat." He glanced at Madeleine and added, "In a separate row, please."

Madeleine muttered, "Or perhaps you could just strap him to the wing of the plane?"

The clerk twittered. They both glared at her.

Ransom lit up a cigarette, blatantly ignoring the sign

telling him not to. "I was down to four cigarettes a day when I met you," he told Madeleine.

"On Tuesday?"

"In Montedora."

"Oh."

"On Tuesday I was down to eight a day." He regarded the cigarette in his hand and added, "This is already my eighth today."

"Maybe you should take up knitting."

"Maybe I should have turned down this assignment."

"It's not too late to turn back."

He took his boarding pass from the desk clerk. "Oh, yes, it is, Maddie." His voice was surprisingly soft.

Their gazes locked. For the first time, Madeleine wondered if she had hurt him. It was an absurd thought, since she had never met anyone who seemed so invulnerable. And certainly his attitude about that night—and sex in general—seemed too cavalier for her to suppose he harbored any special feelings about what had happened between them. Everything he'd said these past couple of days indicated that his pride was wounded. Nothing more.

Nevertheless, for the first time, she wondered how she would have felt had the situation been reversed. What if she had awoken to find him gone with no explanation?

When passion was spent, he had been sweet to her, so very sweet . . .

"Uh, Mr. Ransom," the clerk said, drawing Ransom's gaze away from Madeleine's, "according to the notation on my screen, I believe you have some weapons to check?"

"Yeah." He turned to Madeleine, his expression impersonal now. "This will take a while. Why don't you go ahead? I'll catch up with you in the VIP lounge."

Relieved to have a little time to regroup, Madeleine agreed and left him on his own.

Ransom's tension eased a little as he watched Madeleine walk away. He turned his attention to the clerk, who was phoning one of her superiors to come inspect Ransom's weapons. She handed him a card to fill out which would go inside his checked luggage, along with his two unloaded, declared guns. As a member of the private sector, he wasn't allowed to carry a gun in the cabin of a public airplane.

His resolve to stop baiting and battling Madeleine hadn't lasted a moment beyond her first imperious order. Her regal manner and arrogant assumption that she needn't even listen to him pushed his buttons. And something about her coolness incited him to keep sparking the temper she kept trying to pretend she didn't have.

His papers and permits were all in order, and he knew the routine well, so the checking and approval of his firearms went smoothly. After passing through security and then through passport control, he found Madeleine reading a copy of *The Economist* and sipping a glass of juice. He ordered black coffee and sat down with her. One thing he had gotten used to as a Secret Service agent and still appreciated as a Marino Security executive was first-class travel all the way. It might seem natural to a Barrington, but Ransom had grown up without luxury, and he never took it for granted.

"Veracruz will have a car and driver waiting for us at the airport," he told Madeleine when she put down her magazine, apparently finished with it.

She looked at him with cool speculation. "Do you know him well?"

He shrugged. "I've spent time with him. I know a lot about him."

"You don't like him," she said perceptively, despite the careful neutrality of his tone.

"I don't like you either, but it doesn't stop me from doing my job," he said.

"So you've said." She refused to be ruffled. "So you're Marino's expert on Montedora?"

He shook his head. "No, I'm an expert on Veracruz's personal safety and the security of the Presidential Palace. Marino's expert on Montedora is an analyst who advises foreign investors about economic and political conditions there. He's the guy who briefed me before my assignment down there."

"I see. So your usual job description is . . ."

"Security advisor." He finished his coffee, vaguely suspicious of her polite interest in him. "I analyze, recommend, and implement security measures for individuals, companies, and organizations."

She frowned. "So you're not an expert on Montedora, and I gather you don't usually act as a bodyguard?"

"Not anymore. But I used to be in the Secret Service." He'd guarded some pretty important bodies in those days—as well as the American political system.

She nodded, still frowning. "So why did Marino send you to us when my father decided I needed a bodyguard in Montedora?"

He should have figured that she'd be bright enough to wonder about that sooner or later. He'd known from the first that she was a thinker, and he'd already guessed that she wasn't the operations director of Barrington Enterprises just because of her birth.

He considered lying to her, but he was no liar. He considered telling her to mind her own business, but he kind of thought his professional standing was her business, for as long as she put her safety in his hands. So he shrugged and told her.

"Joe—Marino, I mean—thought it would be a good idea if I left the country for a while."

She blinked. "Would you care to explain that to me?"

He wasn't proud of this. On the contrary. He'd really screwed up. He thought he should have been fired. But, without false modesty, he knew he was valuable to the company. Besides, Marino, who pretended to be such a tough guy, was a pushover who was too fond of Ransom to fire him.

"Marino thought my absence might help to diffuse a certain legal situation."

"What legal situation?"

He shifted and reached for a cigarette, ignoring another no-smoking sign. "I, uh . . ."

"Yes?"

He was ashamed to tell her. It was crazy. He'd lately been nastier to her than he'd ever been to a woman before, and now he was afraid of her bad opinion. Embarrassed by this stupidity, he said bluntly, "I slugged a client."

The surprise on her face made her look more like herself, and less like Madeleine Barrington, the cool, unruffled goddess of the upper classes. "You hit a client?"

He nodded and inhaled smoke. "It was a pretty big mistake."

"I know you've got a dreadful temper, but really." She stared at him. "How could you have done something so stupid?"

He grinned wryly, preferring her candor to her courtesy any day. "Funny. That's exactly what Joe said."

"Who did you hit?"

"Steve Keller." When she looked blank, he added,

"The lead singer of Sex On The Beach."

"The rock group?"

"Yeah."

"The skinny, long-haired man who wears tight bodysuits open down to . . ." She indicated a point slightly past her navel. "You hit him?"

He nodded.

"Did you hurt him?"

"Not really. Not seriously. Just his pride. But that can hurt a lot, you know."

"Yes. I know." She lowered her eyes. "What made you do it?"

"Good question. I haven't got a good answer. And I'd need a really good answer to keep Keller's lawyers from using me to clean up the floor of a courtroom."

"But what happened?"

He flicked ashes off the end of his cigarette and met her eyes. He noticed with surprise that they were a little bloodshot. She must have stayed up pretty late with the boyfriend. The thought of her with that wimp suddenly brought back the way he'd felt the day he'd slugged Keller. Close to implosion.

"You don't look as perfect as usual today," he commented.

"If you're trying to change the subject, that was a pathetic attempt," she shot back. "What were you doing working for Sex On The Beach?"

He couldn't help smiling at her sparks. "Keller had bought this huge estate out in California. House, pool, recording studio, the works. Celebrities have all kinds of people following them, threatening them, harassing them. So Keller wanted complete security for the whole estate, with back-up measures in case something went wrong."

Ransom shrugged. “It was a routine assignment. I didn’t think it would take long or be difficult.”

“I take it you were wrong?”

“I hadn’t counted on Keller. A high-strung, abusive slob who provoked everyone around him with impunity—thanks to his money and fame.”

“Come now, Mr. Ransom. I happen to know that no one provokes you with impunity.”

Their eyes met, full of acknowledgement. Yeah, sometimes he almost liked her. “Well, that was the problem. But I’m the one at fault in this. I was the professional; he was just some hopped-up guitar player with too much money and too little sense.” He drew on his cigarette, remembering. “And I was feeling pretty short-fused.” He’d been feeling that way ever since Montedora, but he wasn’t going to tell her that.

“Go on.”

“Keller had a girlfriend living with him. And . . . he pumped himself up by humiliating her in public. He liked to shout at her, belittle her. I’m pretty sure he hit her when they were alone, but I never . . .” He shrugged again, less easily this time. “And one day he made her cry in front of me and a dozen other people, and I blew my stack.”

“Well, that’s under—”

“No, I don’t mean I criticized him or suggested he cool off. I mean I lost it. And then he lost it. He hit me. And I . . .” Ransom sighed. “I hit him back.”

“If he hit you first,” she said, “surely—”

“My position’s pretty bad, Maddie. I was in his home. I intervened in a domestic squabble without authority. I insulted him first.”

“But he hit first.”

“But he’s a skinny guitar player, and I’m a trained

fighter. His punch barely made me blink. Mine knocked him across the room and made him bleed like a pig."

"Oh." She nodded slowly. "I see your point."

"His personal assistant had his lawyer on the phone before I even left the house."

"So he's going to sue?"

"That's what his lawyers and Joe's lawyers have been discussing. And Joe got pissed off when I refused to apologize to Keller."

"Why wouldn't you apologize?"

"Because I'm not a bit sorry I hit him. I'm just sorry my company is in trouble for it."

"So why don't you—"

"I just don't . . ." He shifted uncomfortably as he tried to picture himself telling that abusive bastard that he was sorry. "I don't think I can."

She studied him for a long moment. "I see."

"I mean, what was I gonna do? Just watch that girl cry while he kept shouting at her, saying things to her that a man should never say to a woman even in private, let alone in public? And it's not in my nature to get hit without hitting back. If he wasn't willing to fight, he shouldn't have taken the first swing." He ground out his cigarette. "So I told Joe I couldn't apologize. And that's when your father called him, looking for someone to keep you safe in Montedora."

"Out of sight, out of mind? Or did Mr. Marino hope that a week in Montedora would make you come to your senses?"

Ransom grinned wryly. "I think he figured I'd be willing to walk on my knees through broken glass after a second trip to Montedora."

"You hate the place that much?"

"I was . . . notoriously bad-tempered after I came back from Montedora three months ago." He watched her cheeks suffuse with color.

"Oh."

"Joe figured something down there just didn't agree with me."

She didn't look away, and he could tell that she wanted to. She spoke at last, so softly he could scarcely hear her: "I'm sorry."

He studied the embarrassed, regretful expression on her face and, strangely enough, he believed her. He just didn't know what to make of it. "Then—"

The intercom overhead announced that their flight was beginning to board. Madeleine slid out of her seat, picked up her belongings, and murmured, "We'd better go."

He watched her turn and walk away, and he wondered what he had started to say to her.

CHAPTER SEVEN

Madeleine was assaulted by a wave of hot, humid air the moment she emerged from the half-empty airplane in Montedora. Beneath the blistering sun, she crossed the cracked pavement to the airport building along with the rest of the passengers, most of whom appeared to be Montedorans. Ransom caught up with her as she reached immigration.

"Su pasaporte, por favor."

Ransom took Madeleine's passport and handed it, along with his own, to the stout, stern-faced immigration official.

"Viaje de negocios o de vacaciones?" Business trip or vacation?

"Negocios," Ransom replied.

An ordinary, well-dressed, and law-abiding person, Madeleine had been questioned for ten minutes at immigration the last time she had come to Montedora. Her minimal Spanish had, of course, made the process rather slow. Most of that ten minutes, however, had been taken up by armed men flipping through her passport, asking her exactly the same questions she'd already been asked, and then staring at her as if she might suddenly break down and admit to being a terrorist on the run. She was prepared to endure the same treatment again, but Ransom surprised her by pulling out several documents and saying, with uncharacteristic arrogance, "We're guests of President Veracruz, who assured me personally that we would be treated with respect."

The stern-faced official blinked in surprise, took the papers, and showed them to a bystander who was apparently his superior. That man, in turn, showed them to someone else.

"What are those papers?" Madeleine asked Ransom.

"A letter of introduction from Veracruz, a personal commendation from Veracruz, and special permits for my guns, signed by—"

"Veracruz."

"Uh-huh."

Thirty seconds later, Ransom and Madeleine were offered a personal escort into the main building, to the baggage claim area, and through customs. Whereas Madeleine's harmless toiletries bag had been subjected to a thorough search the last time she'd passed through Montedoran customs, Ransom's guns were now regarded as casually as if they'd been old shoes. It sure paid to have friends in high places.

"Señor, can you show me into a private room for a moment?" Ransom asked their escort, after clearing customs.

"Of course."

"And somewhere where I could freshen up?" Madeleine added.

Ransom ran his gaze over her. "Why? After four thousand miles, you haven't even wrinkled your skirt yet." He sounded annoyed.

"I have to go to the bathroom. Is that all right with you?"

Their chubby escort grinned and said, "Lovers' quarrel," in heavily accented English.

Madeleine gave him a look that quelled his grin. "You couldn't be more wrong."

As she turned away, she heard Ransom murmur, "Oh, yes, he could."

Her face flushed as she realized that, in the most technical sense of the word, they were lovers. Or had been. Once.

When someone showed her into the filthy, odorous bathroom, she rinsed her handkerchief in cold water and pressed it to the back of her neck. The heat, the tension, the embarrassment; she felt a headache coming on.

Ransom was waiting for her when she emerged from the bathroom. Their driver had found him and was already loading their luggage into the car outside. The airport, which hadn't improved any since her last visit, was crowded today; the vast piles of luggage suggested that people were leaving for a long time, perhaps forever. The metallic whine of the overhead speakers jarred Madeleine's nerves. A short, fat lady nearly knocked her over. A child started wailing. Someone stepped on Madeleine's foot. The man who had done it looked her up and down, nudged the man next to him, nodded at Madeleine, and said something. His tone was suggestive. His friend's snicker sounded obscene. She didn't like the way either of them grinned at her, and her frosty expression let them know it.

Ransom took her elbow, brushed past the two men, and kept hold of her as he guided her through the jostling throng. Something about his touch was reassuring, at a moment when she hadn't known she'd needed reassurance. Maybe he knew how much even a self-assured woman hated leers, snickers, and muttered obscenities. She maintained her dignity, but she was suddenly glad he was there.

A white limousine awaited them just outside the building. Ransom introduced Madeleine to the uniformed chauffeur.

"Miguel Arroyo. Madeleine Barrington. Miss Barrington is to be handled with care, Miguel."

The handsome young man grinned at her and took his

hat off, bowing slightly. He had a wonderful smile, full of zest and energy. She found herself smiling back.

"Ah, Ransom is worried about my driving," Miguel told Madeleine. "But I have improved very much."

"Glad to hear it," Ransom said dryly. "All the same, we'll both sit in back. With seat belts on."

Replacing his cap, Miguel opened the door for Madeleine. "Ransom taught me everything I know."

"Don't try to blame your driving on me."

"No, I mean the evasive maneuvers, the antiterrorist tactics, and the defensive procedures."

"Ah, I see," Madeleine said, getting into the car.

Ransom slipped in next to her. "Hopefully, we'll never have to find out if I was a good enough teacher."

"Ah, but you are very good!" Miguel assured him, leaning down to duck his head into the car. "You are—"

"Let's get going, Miguel." After Miguel closed the door on them, Ransom said, "He's a nice kid, but he talks a lot."

"I like him."

"I can tell." His voice was dry. "But we'd be here all day if someone didn't give him a shove."

"I see why you needed a private room back there," Madeleine commented. Ransom's lightweight sports coat had swung open when he climbed into the car, revealing the gun holstered at his side. The slender leather cases attached to his belt presumably held loaded magazines for the gun. He had chosen to arm himself before leaving the airport. She frowned. "Do you expect trouble between here and the Presidential Palace?"

"It's my job to expect trouble from now until I drop you off at your apartment in New York." The look he slanted her was slightly teasing. "If something happened during the drive, and I had left my guns in my suitcase in the trunk of this car, and you got hurt or killed as a result . . ." He sighed and shook his head. "It would be so embarrassing. Looks bad on a guy's record, you know."

"I can imagine." She glanced again at his gun. "You said 'guns'?"

He straightened one knee and pulled his khaki trouser leg up a few inches. As he did, she noticed a nondescript ring on his right hand. She'd never seen it before. It almost looked like a wedding ring. Then she looked down and saw a small, beautifully engraved revolver strapped to his ankle. "My backup gun."

"Oh." She gestured to the bigger gun at his side. "That one isn't very well-hidden."

"Doesn't need to be for this assignment." Seeing her blank look, he explained, "Some assignments call for discretion. The bodyguard is supposed to look like an assistant or colleague or companion. Nonthreatening. Or maybe he's just not supposed to call attention to himself."

"But this is different?"

He looked her over. "Well, we're calling attention to ourselves just by being here. A blonde, blue-eyed foreign woman and a man who's just as obviously foreign. Even without your tailored clothes and a good car, it would be assumed that we're wealthy. All foreigners are automatically considered wealthy here. So, since we aren't in a politically sensitive position, it makes sense to display the fact that you're well-protected and that it would be stupid for anyone to mess with you."

"An ounce of prevention?"

"Right. It does a pretty good job of discouraging muggers, rapists, and burglars."

"What about rebels and terrorists?"

"Hard to tell. Any time someone has a cause, they're not

as likely to be thinking of their own survival."

She thought about that. The breakdown of law and order in Montedora meant trouble could come from many sources. "How dangerous do you think it is for me to be here?"

"I think it's more dangerous than you think it is, which is why . . ." He stopped speaking and looked oddly surprised.

"What?" she asked, puzzled.

"Oh . . . Uh, why I think your father did the right thing, insisting you take me with you." He seemed distracted and avoided her gaze.

"I see."

After a few moments of silence, he leaned forward, slid open the glass partition, and asked Miguel, "Where are you going? This isn't the way to—"

"Must detour, Ransom."

"Why?"

"The direct route is closed."

Ransom frowned. "Why?"

"Explosion."

"What?"

"The LPM."

"What's that?" Madeleine asked.

"In Spanish, it stands for the Popular Liberation of Montedora," Ransom explained.

"I've never heard of it," she said.

"It's a much smaller rebel group than the Doristas."

"But getting bigger," Miguel grumbled.

"They blew something up?" Ransom asked.

"They were storing explosives in the back of a shop along the road. The shop exploded two days ago."

"How do you know it was LPM?" Ransom asked.

"The Seguridores questioned the owner of the shop. He

admitted that the LPM were planning to set a trap for El Presidente along that road."

Madeleine knew that the Seguridores were General Escalante's secret police, the most ruthless and powerful military entity in the country. She tried not to think about what the questioning had entailed.

"LPM—those bastards!" Miguel shuddered. "I drive on that road almost every day! Explosions!"

Madeleine nearly shuddered, too. How many people were hurt in the explosion? How many would have been hurt had the LPM carried out their plan to blow up the President's car as it drove by?

"I wonder why this wasn't in the news," she said aloud.

"El Presidente wants to make it quiet."

"Keep it quiet," Ransom corrected absently.

"Yes. He doesn't want to encourage the LPM with publicity."

"Still, the international press—" Madeleine began.

"They can't keep track of everything," Ransom said. "Especially not if the Seguridores won't release any information and everybody in the neighborhood is too scared to talk."

"Yes, people are frightened," Miguel confirmed. "Me, too. Someone aiming at President Veracruz could miss and hit—"

"Red light!" Ransom said.

The limo screeched to a halt when they were halfway across the intersection. They blocked traffic for a few moments before Miguel, following Ransom's instructions, drove the car forward and continued on his way, accompanied by the blare of horns. Once clear of the intersection, Miguel tried to apologize, but Ransom forestalled him.

"I should have known better than to distract you."

Ransom sounded resigned. "Keep your eyes on the road!" he ordered when Miguel turned to argue with him.

Ransom closed the glass partition and sat back. "He took out someone's front porch last time I was here."

"Why is he a presidential chauffeur then?"

Ransom shrugged. "He doesn't drive any differently than most Montedorans. Anyhow, he speaks four languages and . . . I'm pretty sure he's sleeping with the First Lady of Montedora. He's her driver, you see, more than Veracruz's."

"Ah." Madeleine watched Ransom open the small refrigerator built into the car. She accepted a bottle of chilled mineral water from him. "Four languages, did you say?"

He nodded. "Self-taught, for the most part. Miguel may be a lousy driver, but he's a bright, capable kid."

"Young man," she corrected. Miguel looked about the same age as her sister Caroline. "And very charming."

"Too young for you," he shot back.

"That wasn't—"

"Uh-huh."

She realized with surprise that he was teasing her, so she let it pass. "And in America or England or Canada, or a dozen other countries, he could have a bright future."

"But not many people in Montedora have bright futures," Ransom concluded.

"Why doesn't he emigrate?"

"You say that like it's as easy as moving from uptown to downtown in Manhattan."

"You mean Miguel has no money for emigration?"

"That's right. He supports his mother and two sisters. And this is his home." He shrugged. "Would you find it that easy to turn your back on your homeland?"

"I might, if it was Montedora," she said. "And judging

by the crowds at the airport, plenty of people do it."

He asked curiously, "And considering the situation here, why does anyone want to buy your plantation?"

"It's good land and I'm selling it cheap. Some people are gamblers. These buyers—these potential buyers—may be willing to bet that they can make it profitable enough to offset the time and effort they'll have to invest to increase its productivity."

"Not to mention the risk of losing it in another revolution."

"Do you think there's going to be another revolution here?"

"I think it's a strong possibility. People are dangerous when they've got nothing left to lose."

"Nothing but their lives."

"There are more civilians than soldiers in Montedora."

"But how many guns do the civilians have?"

"Probably more than anyone realizes." Not finding anything he liked, he closed the refrigerator and lit up a cigarette. "And if there is a revolution, whoever owns that plantation will probably lose it."

"For all I know, these buyers wouldn't mind losing it."

"A tax write-off?"

"Possibly. It's not uncommon." She shrugged. "My job is just to sell it."

"What'll you do if the Germans don't buy?"

"I'll find another buyer." She added, "I hope."

"When will they be here?"

"Four days. I've got meetings all day tomorrow here in the city. We leave for the farm the next day. I've scheduled the following day to make sure everything's in order there. And the Germans are supposed to arrive the day after." When the car came to a halt in the middle of the road, she asked, "Why are we stopping?"

Ransom opened his window, peered ahead, and said, "Bus accident." After a moment he added, "Get comfortable, we may be here a while."

After that thirty-minute delay, they resumed their journey. Ransom gazed out the window as the big car cruised down a rutted main road in a poor neighborhood.

Thirty people stood in line outside a bank. Forbidden revolutionary slogans were painted along a stone wall lining the street. Barefoot little boys ran up to the cars stuck in the heavy traffic, trying to sell flowers, newspapers, windshield washes, and bottles of Coca-Cola. Ransom knew that anyone buying the latter would be expected to drink it then and there, and to give the bottle back to the vendor before driving off. Bottles were too valuable to give up. The juvenile vendor would use the same bottle again and again, and he certainly wouldn't wash it between sales. As evening fell, prostitutes would join the boys, walking up and down the street in search of business, hustling the cars as well as the pedestrians. Most of them wouldn't even be old enough to be considered women, but grinding poverty had already stolen their childhoods.

"The usual route to the palace is, uh, much more showy than this," Ransom said to Madeleine. "Embassies, an old cemetery, that seven-million-dollar church the last President had built in honor of his mother. Of course, it's never been finished."

"My sister criticized me for coming here," she said pensively.

"Well, I wouldn't want my sister coming here either—"

"No, she meant I shouldn't accept hospitality from Veracruz. She said he . . ." She shrugged. "Well, you know."

"Yeah. But at least you'll be safe."

"That's what I said."

"And since you didn't want to go back to—"

"No," she said quickly. "I didn't."

After a long moment, he said, "You weren't registered there. I checked. The next morning." Though he saw her jaw clench, he wouldn't let it drop. "What were you doing there, with no room and no luggage?"

She smoothed her skirt and avoided his eyes. Her voice was cool as she said, "I'd spent all day at the airport waiting for my flight to leave. After it was finally cancelled, I learned that my luggage had been put on another plane." She frowned and added as an afterthought, "I never did get it back." She cleared her throat and continued, "So I had a drink. Several drinks, actually. I was just about to go across to the hotel lobby and get my old room, or another room . . ."

"When we met," he concluded, watching her. The sunlight gleamed on her pale hair. She was too disciplined to fiddle with the hem of her skirt or display her tension in some other ordinary way, but he felt it winding around her like a rope. "Well, that explains why no one could answer my questions the next morning. No one knew you were still in the country."

She didn't respond.

"Still," he mused, "I'd have thought they'd remember a woman like you, even without a name." When she looked at him inquisitively, he explained, "I described you to the morning desk clerk. Either he hadn't seen you before or he just didn't want to get involved."

"Oh."

She looked away again, staring out of the window. He wanted to ask her the important question: Why had she left like that? But the answer was probably not something he wanted to hear. Why should she have hung around, she'd ask? So they could exchange phone numbers over breakfast? Yeah, right.

He glared at her. She was still looking the other way.

He knew now why he had come back to Montedora with her, why he hadn't quit or let her fire him. It had nothing to do with Steve Keller or Joe Marino or his job or even promises made to her father. He'd made his decision the moment he'd seen her picture in her father's office, the moment he found out who she was. He just hadn't understood it until a moment ago, when he'd nearly blurted it out without thinking. He had come here with her because—however stupid or masochistic of him it was—he wasn't willing to entrust her safety to anyone else. If she had to come back to Montedora, then he had to come to make sure that nothing happened to her. It was that simple.

He wasn't at all happy about it. What the hell had she done, anyhow, to deserve such doglike devotion from him?

He glared at her again, annoyed with her for pretending she didn't need his protection. Did she think those frosty glances of hers would protect her down here?

The way those two guys had looked at her in the airport . . . leering, smirking, muttering and snickering. He had wanted to tear them apart, but he'd had to settle for getting her out of there fast. He didn't want her to endure looks like that. He wanted to fight for her, shield her, keep her safe.

Ransom leaned his head back against the cushioned seat. Christ, maybe what he really needed was a good long vacation when this was all over.

After another twenty minutes in traffic, they came to a military checkpoint along the road. Recognizing Miguel and one of Veracruz's own limousines, the soldiers waved them through.

There were two more security checkpoints when they reached the gates of the Presidential Palace. These were manned by the President's personal Guards. At the first gate, Ransom and Madeleine were instructed to get out of the car, which was then thoroughly searched, despite belonging to Veracruz.

When one of the Guards began going through their suitcases, Madeleine murmured, "Apparently being a guest of the President doesn't mean you get special treatment here."

"My orders." Ransom glanced at her. "When I first came here, a known Dorista could have stuck a pink bow on a bomb and carried it right into the President's bedroom without too much trouble."

Five minutes later, a stout female Guard arrived, took Madeleine to the far side of the car, and searched her. After this distasteful procedure was over, Madeleine found Ransom being relieved of his guns.

"I take it you don't think you'll need those inside the gates?" she asked.

"I'd rather have them with me," he admitted, "but it's nice to know they've stopped letting armed civilians enter the palace."

"Also your orders?"

He nodded. "Now no one except the President and the Guards carries a weapon beyond the gates. Not even the Seguridores."

"So I'm safe as long as none of the Guards decides to shoot me."

"Something like that."

Once cleared, they got back into the car. Miguel drove them through the first gate, which shut behind them. The second gate, up ahead, was still closed, effectively trapping them. A Guard at the second gate questioned them, verified something on his walkie-talkie, then permitted them to pass through.

A dozen more Guards were posted at the front entrance of the Presidential Palace. It was an enormous white mansion with marble steps and pillars, a red tiled roof, a sweeping driveway, and extensive gardens. It had been built more than fifty years ago by the ruler of what had then been a peaceful agricultural country.

As impressive as the palace was, it was reputedly humble compared to the country estate 100 miles to the south which one of Veracruz's recent predecessors had built, and where Veracruz spent his weekends and holidays.

Madeleine glanced curiously at Ransom as he helped her out of the car. "You preferred staying at the Hotel Tigre to staying here?"

"Too many wild parties," Ransom said briefly. "I need my beauty sleep."

That was clearly all he intended to say on that subject. Madeleine wondered what really bothered him about staying at the palace, since it seemed much more comfortable (and now much safer) than the city's hotels.

A pleasant–looking, middle-aged man came down the steps to greet them, introduced himself as Veracruz's personal secretary, and offered to show them to their rooms. Miguel would bring their luggage up in a few minutes.

They were given rooms on the second floor, where a long balcony overlooked the elaborate fountains and gardens behind the palace. Ransom gave Madeleine's room a brief search, then showed her the motion sensors installed at the door to her room and at the French doors leading onto the balcony.

"Punch in the security code before you go to sleep. Just remember to punch in the disarm code before you go through the door or out onto the balcony, though, or you'll set off an alarm that'll alert over a hundred Guards," he told her. "And there are video cameras trained on all the exteriors, so don't go out onto the balcony half-naked unless you want to give a thrill to some bored Guards monitoring the system."

"I'll try to remember that," she said.

He disappeared into his room when their luggage arrived, but returned a moment later. "We've been invited to dinner this evening. The President would like to know if you can spare my services between now and then."

Madeleine nodded. "I'm just going to stay in here and make some phone calls. I've got to talk to my local bankers and lawyers, confirm our meetings. Check in with my secretary in New York. That kind of thing."

"In that case . . . Veracruz has left a message asking me to do a follow-up review of the security here. It'll take me the rest of the afternoon." He handed her a small electronic device and showed her how to use it. "If you need me for anything, page me with this. I'll come right away."

She nodded again. He checked his watch and said, "I'll meet you back here around seven o'clock, local time."

He left. There was a discreet knock at the door only moments later, far too gentle to be Ransom. Madeleine opened the door and found a smiling maid awaiting her pleasure. Madeleine's Spanish was minimal, but she understood the woman's offer to unpack for her. She politely refused. She had never liked anyone touching her personal things, and she'd already watched the Guards investigate every single item inside her suitcase today.

She'd grown up in a wealthy home, but the security system at the Presidential Palace was like nothing she had ever encountered before. Although she doubted even a microbe could get past Ransom's security measures, let alone a person, she found the elaborate precautions depressing. Imagine living like this. Imagine being hated by so many people that you needed to live like this.

Madeleine sat down and made a few phone calls via the palace operator. She'd left her cell phone in the U.S., since it didn't work in Montedora; she'd discovered on her last trip here that local cell phone service was too unreliable for her needs. Having confirmed her appointments for tomorrow, she unpacked and showered. While drying her hair, she remembered that she had promised to phone Graham upon arriving. She might as well get it over with. Checking her watch, which was still on New York time, she picked up the phone, spoke to the operator, and gave her the number for Graham's private line at work.

He expressed pleasure at hearing from her, but she realized after a moment that he had someone in his office, so she kept the call brief. When he said he hoped they could talk again soon, she hedged rather than commit herself to that. After ending the conversation, she stared at the phone for a moment, finally reaching a clear decision.

She couldn't marry him. She didn't love him, and she couldn't envision spending the rest of her life with him. Being single was preferable to having a loveless marriage, or a marriage in which she constantly hurt a loving husband by not loving him back. The decision was so obvious to her now, so self-evident, she couldn't understand why she'd ever needed to think it over. She was fond of Graham, and her main regret was that she had, through her own blundering, confused him and led him on. And now she would have to hurt him.

She was appalled by her behavior. She'd like to blame Ransom for it—indeed, she would love to blame him for it—but, in truth, he hadn't forced her to use Graham, stall him, snap at him, lie to him, go to bed with him, or, having done so, to make such a fiasco of last night. Madeleine had to take full responsibility for all of that, and more.

She nodded as she faced herself in the mirror and styled her hair. If there was one thing Madeleine Barrington was used to, it was accepting responsibility. She didn't like to make mistakes, and she seldom made them, but she now admitted the mistakes she had made with Graham and acknowledged her failings.

She didn't like having failings. Not one little bit.

Then, as with every problem in her life except one—the one currently reviewing President Veracruz's security measures—she developed a plan to resolve matters.

The best thing for Graham—and herself—would be to let him off the hook as soon as possible. She was already planning what she would say to him, comments which would make her position clear without hurting him unnecessarily. Tactful, appropriate comments. The sort of comments that only seemed to desert her when she dealt with Ransom.

However, talking to Graham would have to wait until she returned to New York. A phone call was no way to tell a man you wouldn't marry him. She would tell him in person. He deserved at least that much consideration from her.

CHAPTER EIGHT

The sharp knock on her door came promptly at seven o'clock. Ransom was evidently a punctual person. Madeleine supposed it was the only trait they had in common. Dressed for dinner and ready to go, she opened the door.

"Hi, are you . . ." His voice trailed off as his gaze swept over her. Madeleine's mouth went dry at the look that blazed through those green eyes. She wore a black, knee-length sheath with a white, satin, off-the-shoulders neckline: simple, elegant, classic. She had considered her appearance appropriate for a formal dinner, but something in Ransom's expression suggested that he found it appropriate for things best done in private. Her cheeks felt warm. Her heartbeat thundered in her ears. He had looked at her that way once before, and she remembered exactly what he had done next.

"I'm ready." Her voice was faint.

He took a steadying breath. "Nice dress."

She looked him over and gave an involuntary start. "You're still wearing that tie," she blurted. He frowned. She clenched her teeth. She'd forgotten to watch her comments around him. Again.

"It's still my only tie, except for the black one I—"

"Yes, yes, I remember." She heard the arrogant dismissal in her voice. She knew how it must sound to him, but she couldn't face any more reminders of that night. Not now.

"Shall we?" His voice was bland.

She nodded, stepped into the hallway, and closed her door behind her. He silently led her to the central wing of the mansion, then downstairs, through a vast, elaborately decorated corridor, and out onto a covered patio where drinks were being served. Veracruz wasn't present, but there were a dozen other people already there.

Sipping from the glass Ransom handed her, Madeleine noted, "French champagne."

"Foreign aid buys the good things in life." He kept his voice low.

"Like security?"

"That, too."

"And it doesn't bother you?"

"If you're asking, does my professional help imply approval of my client, the answer is no. I keep people safe and alive, that's all. And it's not a bad day's work." He lit up a cigarette and continued, "The month before the President contacted Marino Security and hired me, someone nearly killed his two daughters while they were playing in the gardens."

"I didn't—"

"I think those girls deserve to grow up no matter who their father is, and no matter what kind of enemies he's made." He met her eyes. "That's the kind of thing I think about when I do a job like the one I did here."

At that moment, Madeleine liked him very much. Just the way she'd liked him when he explained why he couldn't apologize to rock star Steve Keller. She valued integrity. She valued the quiet nobility that he kept concealed behind cynical comments and an irreverent attitude. And she knew that these softening emotions she felt for him were dangerous, because they made her lower her guard. And she didn't think he was noble enough to resist the urge to prick her again.

"El Presidente!" someone cried.

Every Guard in sight saluted. Madeleine turned and saw His Excellency President Juan de la Veracruz coming toward her, surrounded by an entourage of nearly a dozen people. He was tall, overweight, and appeared to be in his late forties. His curly black hair revealed a few gray hairs, as did his mustache. He wore a white military uniform with gold braid and fringe on it. Assorted colorful ribbons decorated his chest.

"Ransom! My friend! So sorry I could not greet you when you arrived!" Veracruz pumped Ransom's hand.

"That's quite all right, sir. I'm pleased to see you now."

Madeleine blinked at Ransom. She'd never heard him sound so neutral and blandly polite. It was so unlike him, she guessed that he really disliked Veracruz.

Veracruz turned to her. "And this beautiful young lady must be Miss . . ."

"Barrington," she supplied, not surprised he'd forgotten. There must be twenty sycophants at tonight's cocktail party, all gathering round to meet the man. And this was probably a typical evening here, she supposed. "How do you do, Mr. President?"

Veracruz kissed her hand, bowing over it. Then he held on to it for a long time as he welcomed her to Montedora, expressed his pleasure at being able to offer her his hospitality, and asked if she found her room comfortable.

Ransom's eyes narrowed as he watched Veracruz stroke and squeeze Madeleine's hand. Perhaps trying to help, Ransom spoke to Veracruz, drawing his attention away from Madeleine. She used the moment to pull her hand out of the President's.

"So the security pleased you today, eh?" Veracruz asked, accepting a glass of champagne from his secretary.

"A little fine-tuning was needed. I took care of it," Ransom said. "I'll send you a written report after I return to New York."

"You! Ha-ha, you haven't changed!" Veracruz clapped him on the cheek, then lightly plucked the lapel of his sports coat. "You see this?" Veracruz said to Madeleine. "I was insulted by this, at first, but this is merely Ransom. For his own funeral, he will not dress well!"

"Indeed," Madeleine said, noticing how courteous and closed Ransom's expression was while Veracruz teased him.

Veracruz introduced them to his wife, some of his staff, and a few of the other people present, then went off to greet someone else, leaving the two of them alone again.

Ransom ground out his cigarette, then looked up when Madeleine asked, "Why don't you ever wear a suit?"

His face was typically expressive again, now that Veracruz was elsewhere. "All those years in the Secret Service." In response to her expectant look, he continued, "We almost always had to wear them. I never liked wearing a suit much anyhow, but then one day on the campaign trail, guarding a candidate, I sweated all morning in a wool suit that felt like body armor, while everyone in the crowd wore shorts and T-shirts. By the time we left New Orleans at noon, the thing was drenched. So that afternoon, I got off the plane in Chicago. They were having a sudden cold spell, with wind like you wouldn't believe. I nearly froze to death in that same damned suit."

"Sounds unpleasant."

"I swore that when I left the Service someday, I'd build a bonfire with all my suits and never wear another one. Stupid way to dress."

"And did you?"

He grinned. "Nah, I gave them to the Salvation

Army. And I kept one. The one I wear to—"

"Weddings and funerals."

"But nowhere else."

"All the same, Mr. Ransom, a new tie wouldn't hurt."

His eyes gleamed with amusement as she gave his tie a distasteful glance. "You don't have to say 'mister.' "

"I . . . don't know your first name," she admitted, feeling another wave of embarrassment. He'd taught her new sexual positions, and she didn't even know his first name.

"Nobody knows my first name. Just call me Ransom."

"Nobody?" she repeated.

"Well, my family know it, obviously. Hardly anyone else, though."

"How is that possible?" She frowned. "Isn't it on your driver's license, your bank statements, your passport?"

"Just my initials."

"Why the mystery?"

"This, from the woman who said, 'No names.' "

He was teasing, not bitter or angry right now, but she still felt her stomach drop. She passed over his mention of that night and asked, "Why is your name such a secret?"

"Because I don't like it."

"That's all?"

"Uh-huh."

"You don't like it?"

"That's right."

"But lots of people don't like their names."

"They didn't get stuck with mine."

"Which is?"

"Ah-ah." He grinned again. "I'm not that easily caught, Maddie."

She smiled and shook her head. "But you have to admit,

your surname is pretty ironic for someone whose expertise is in protecting people."

His eyes gleamed. "It's occasionally caused a little confusion. Someone calls and says, 'I demand Ransom,' and chaos ensues until someone figures out they don't mean, you know, ransom."

She laughed, surprised to realize she was enjoying herself. This was the last place she would have expected to find her spirits bubbling like French champagne. The last man she would have expected to find flirting with her again, and the last one she should be flirting with in return. But no one knew better than Madeleine how hard Ransom was to resist when he chose to exercise his charm.

"More champagne?" he asked.

"No, thanks. I never drink more than one."

"Never say never."

She took the risk and said, "I got into big trouble the last time I drank more than one."

It was the first time she had voluntarily referred to that night. Their eyes met. His expression softened. His voice dropped as he asked, "And was it really so awful?"

Her heart started pounding again. He'd looked like this before. Upon waking her up to make love again, his head resting near hers on the pillow, his eyes tender, his voice husky. She remembered his gentleness and suddenly ached for it, exhausted from being at odds with him.

"No." Her voice was weak, betraying her. "It wasn't . . . awful."

Whatever he saw in her eyes, he obviously decided that this wasn't the moment—or the place—to demand more from her. He distanced himself again with a wry smile. "Not awful? Wow. How can I control my ego after a compliment like that? It wasn't awful."

She smiled, relieved that he had chosen not to push—at least for now. "I never noticed you controlling your ego before. Why start now?"

"You know how to direct your barbs, Miss Barrington. Been practicing long?"

"It's a hereditary trait."

"I don't believe you. Your father seemed like a pushover."

"My father?"

"Well, 'pushover' may be an exaggeration."

"Delusion, I'd say."

"But I kinda liked him."

"That's funny. He liked you, too."

"Really?"

"Uh-huh."

"How do you know?"

He'd caught her. "Well . . ."

"You talked about me, didn't you?"

She brazened it out. "Naturally."

"What did you say?"

Her lips twitched, which surprised her. "I denied everything, of course."

He laughed. "And then?"

"And then he said he thought you were a good man who could be trusted, despite your atrocious manners. Or words to that effect."

"Yeah, he's all right, your old man," Ransom said magnanimously.

"I'm sure he'll be thrilled when I relay your compliment to him."

"He expects a lot from you, though, doesn't he?"

"Don't all fathers?"

"All fathers don't expect their daughters to be dutiful

enough to risk their safety in pursuit of business, or to learn to run multimillion-dollar empires."

"He should expect it of me."

"Why?"

"Because I can do it."

"Don't you think there's a limit to what he should expect of you?"

"Why? Because I'm a woman?" Before he could respond, she chided, "Don't be sexist, Ransom. You're too intelligent for that."

"Now that probably is the first compliment you've paid me."

"It just slipped out. I'll be more careful in future."

He grinned and was about to respond when dinner was announced. He gave both their champagne glasses to one of the obsequious waiters, then took her elbow. "The dining room is—"

"Ah, Miss Barrington! Ransom!" Veracruz pounced on them as they passed by. "Please, Carlos, not now! We will discuss this later!" he said to the thin military man talking with him.

Madeleine felt Ransom go tense beside her. She looked at him in surprise. His expression changed subtly as he gazed at the man with Veracruz. Anger flared briefly in his eyes. The hand on her elbow tightened, pulling her against him. His body radiated danger, readiness.

Distracted by this change in Ransom, when he had been so relaxed and charming only a moment ago, Madeleine barely heard Veracruz telling the thin man that he had guests to entertain. A moment later, Veracruz took Madeleine's free hand, tucked it into the crook of his arm, and insisted she and Ransom sit with him at dinner.

She felt Ransom's reluctance to release her, but he only

shook his head subtly when she looked at him. Covering her confusion, she responded to Veracruz's inane comments as he led her into a vast and lavishly furnished dining room. Veracruz sat at the head of the long table, seating Madeleine to his right and directing Ransom to sit to his left. The thin man took a seat next to Madeleine. The wooden set of Ransom's features told her that he wasn't pleased about the seating arrangements.

"Ah, forgive me, Madeleine. I may call you Madeleine, may I not?" Veracruz smiled at her. "Allow me to introduce you to your dinner companion. Miss Madeleine Barrington, General Carlos Escalante."

Madeleine called on years of self-discipline to keep her expression pleasant as she acknowledged the introduction. She began to understand Ransom's reaction: Escalante was the head of the Seguridores, the powerful security force so frequently denounced by Montedoran exiles, the U.S. State Department, and the international press. Who knew how many deaths Escalante had ordered?

Madeleine was suddenly glad, in a selfish way, that Ransom had implemented such thorough security measures here at the palace. She didn't doubt that every rebel in the country would like to have a clear shot at this table right now. Seated between the two most powerful—and hated—men in Montedora, Madeleine's back felt vulnerable. She lost her appetite for dinner even as the first course was placed before her.

Still, this might be her only opportunity to speak to Veracruz, and she mustn't waste it. Summoning her willpower, she resolutely applied herself to business. Upon accepting the President's invitation to stay at the palace, Madeleine had realized that Veracruz's influence could help her in dealing with the multitude of complex and contradictory regulations, not to mention petty officials, which could impede the smooth sale of El Paradiso to the German buyers. She hoped, before dinner was over, to get the President to give her the right to invoke his name in her business dealings down here; perhaps he could even be convinced to promise his support if she should need it. Madeleine liked to be prepared for every eventuality whenever possible.

As dinner progressed through soup, salad, and entrees, Ransom found his wariness turning into amusement. Madeleine was smooth, all right, smoother than twenty-year-old bourbon or satin sheets. The woman sure knew how to work a table. She hadn't even blinked upon being introduced to Escalante, though she must know his reputation. Nor did she rise to the bait as he questioned her about American foreign policy in Montedora, American economic imperialism, or "the insolent lies" of the American press. Ransom had been tempted to come to her rescue at first, but seeing how smoothly she set Escalante down, time after time, he wound up just sitting back and watching with considerable enjoyment. Oh, yes, the woman had class.

She worked her magic on Veracruz with equal skill. By the end of dinner, without knowing quite why he'd done it, the President had offered her the right to freely invoke his name in order to facilitate her business dealings here in Montedora. The poor slob had even promised to come to her aid, if necessary. Ransom was starting to think that Madeleine, if discovered by the government, could someday turn out to be the USA's most effective secret weapon.

They were lingering over coffee when Veracruz turned amorous and Escalante ran out of patience.

"But surely," Veracruz murmured, grasping one of Madeleine's hands before she had time to pull it out of reach, "you can arrange to stay in Montedora a little longer? I would so like to show you my country estate. It is so much more modern than this . . . mausoleum." He waved at their surroundings.

"Sadly, sir, I can't stay," Madeleine said. "I'm afraid I'm expected home as soon as my business here is concluded."

"We shall see." Veracruz caressed her hand. "And how is it that a beautiful, charming woman like yourself is not married? Is there no one who is man enough for you?"

"She's engaged," Ransom said, even though Graham didn't exactly strike him as "man enough."

"I don't believe El Presidente was asking you," Escalante said.

"Engaged? Really?" Veracruz asked Madeleine.

Madeleine promptly said, "Yes, and he's a very jealous man, sir." She tried to remove her hand from Veracruz's. She didn't succeed.

"We Montedoranos are jealous of our women, too," he told Madeleine, slurring his words a little. "But we are also men who see what we want—and take it!" His accompanying gesture was dramatic.

Madeleine blinked innocently at him. Ransom was torn between irritation and amusement. Escalante frowned and cleared his throat; he had clearly had enough of socializing.

"Your Excellency, though I regret to be the one to say it, the hour of the curfew approaches. Some of your guests should be warned," he said.

Gazing into Madeleine's eyes, Veracruz grunted in acknowledgement.

"And you and I still have important matters to discuss, Your Excellency," Escalante added.

When Veracruz didn't respond, Ransom could have

sworn that Escalante started grinding his teeth. Ransom smiled at him and said, "I don't think El Presidente wishes to discuss any more business tonight."

Glancing toward the far end of the table, where Señora Veracruz was watching her husband and Madeleine with venomous interest, Escalante said, "You seem to have made yet another enemy tonight, Mr. Ransom. How very foolish of you." Rising from his chair with the grace of a serpent, Escalante announced the approach of the curfew hour and suggested that the guests prepare to depart. Then, with eyes as cold as a snake's, he said good night to Ransom, Madeleine, and Veracruz.

When the party broke up, Ransom tore Madeleine away from Veracruz and sent her up to her room, telling her he'd follow her up shortly. True to his word, he knocked on her door fifteen minutes later.

"You overdid it," he said without preamble, brushing past her to enter her room. "Veracruz is in love."

"Just a little drunk, I think."

He sighed. "Well, don't worry about a late-night visit. I just finished explaining to him that, as your bodyguard, I have insisted that you activate the motion sensors at both entrances to your bedroom."

"I could have taken care of an unexpected visit, but I'd rather not need to. So, thank you."

He believed she could have taken care of it, but that didn't mitigate his irritation. "Uh-huh."

As if sensing his mood, she ventured, "I suppose this isn't the sort of danger you expected to have to protect me from."

"Oh, I expected it. Especially when you turned on the charm at dinner." He added cynically, "I've felt the force of it myself, remember."

"No, you haven't," she snapped. "I never tried to manipulate you."

"Didn't you?"

"No! If I had been clearheaded enough to manipulate you, do you think I'd have—" She stopped, practically falling over her own words.

"What?" he said. When she didn't answer, he stepped forward, tension flooding him. "What? Gone to bed with me?"

"Yes," she hissed.

They gaped at each other in surprised silence. After an awkward moment, too proud to look away, she added, "Tonight was . . . business. That's all."

"Do you always do business like that?"

"Like what?" She was angry again. "All I did was listen to his silly stories, ask him questions about himself, and let his ego reign. I didn't flirt with him. I didn't lead him on."

"But you let him . . ." He stopped, not quite sure what she had done that made him angry now. Because, in truth, she had discouraged the President from touching her, and she had turned down his advances and invitations.

"Yes! I let him think what he wanted to think," she said. "So what? I didn't put those thoughts in his head. They were his own." She slumped down on the edge of the bed. "All his own."

He stared. She was upset, no doubt about it. It was unlike her to slump. She usually held herself as straight as a queen. She looked vulnerable and soft now. So soft.

"You don't know," she said wearily. "What man would know?"

"Know what?" he prodded.

"Know what it's like to be condescended to, disregarded, and overlooked because of your gender. Know what it's like to suffer sexual advances no matter how clearly you've stated that you don't want them. Know what it's like to give in to the temptation to trade on a man's libido, in order to get the job done, because it won't get done any other way." She ran a hand across her face, lowered her head, and rubbed her neck. "You'd have to be a woman to know."

He sat down on the bed, too. She had surprised him. He had never expected her, of all women, to confess to frustrations like this. Not Madeleine, who used her influence with such regal confidence, who bore her responsibilities with such determined focus. Not Maddie, who could scorch a man with the cold fire of her gaze.

He remembered meeting her for the first time. The look she had given him had made it clear she didn't welcome his company, his advances. He hadn't cared. He'd seen her and wanted her, and he'd be damned if he'd leave her alone just because she wanted him to. She'd tried to tell him she didn't want to share a drink with him, and he'd bulldozed right over her objections. And however willing she had been in his bed, he had been the one who talked her into sharing it.

For the first time, he began to realize that their mutual history was not as one-sided as he had always thought. He placed a hand on her neck, squeezed it gently, and said, "I'm sorry, Maddie."

She turned her head and looked at him with surprise. He studied her face. It was the face she didn't like to show anyone: distressed, weary, vulnerable. And, to his amazement, a little messy. He smiled. She had smudged her eye makeup when she'd run a hand across her face.

Seeing his expression, she frowned. "What?"

"You're smudged." He stilled her hand as she scrubbed at her cheek. "Leave it there. I like it."

"You have very odd taste, Ransom."

"Especially when it comes to women."

She laughed ruefully. "Touché. I was right, you pricked me, after all."

"What?"

"Never mind. Look, how about a ceasefire until morning?"

"Okay. About tomorrow—what time do you want to leave?"

"Eight o'clock?"

"Fine by me."

"Good."

"Okay."

"Okay."

They ran out of words then, but the silence was speaking. Her scent. His heat. Her soft sigh. His tension.

Their eyes met. The gentle whir of the overhead fan, the soft give of the mattress beneath them, and the shadows of a tropical night reminded them both—with sudden, crashing intensity—of the night they had wreaked havoc on each other's lives.

Ransom drew in a sharp breath, suddenly there again, except that he had been so long without her. So very long . . .

God, to touch her again. To hold her and kiss her and bury himself in her. To hear her sighs, her murmurs, the deep moans of her satisfaction. To feel her caresses, her skin against his skin, her hand in his, her cheek against his shoulder, her legs entwined with his . . .

It would be worth his job, his career, his self-respect. Right now, it seemed worth the next billion years in purgatory. Hungry for her, for her warmth, for the sweetness of her kiss, he found himself leaning toward her, his lips parting in anticipation, his heart pounding as the rich blue of her eyes darkened with sudden passion and her breath caught shakily.

"No!"

Her cry was shrill and quavering as she slid off the bed, staggered away, and tripped on something. Filled with predatory heat, he shot to his feet, ready to go after her.

The tears clouding her eyes stopped him. Cold.

He couldn't even breathe. "Maddie?" His voice sounded strangled.

She swallowed. Looked away. Looked back. "Go. Please, go."

"I—"

"Go!"

No command in her voice now. No icy authority. Just panic. And fear.

Of him?

"Please. Go," she begged.

Feeling as if she'd just gutted him, he turned and went.

CHAPTER NINE

Ransom realized the moment he saw Madeleine the next morning that she was going to be her most standoffish today. Her silk dress and little matching jacket were pale blue, so pale that she looked like she was encased in polar ice. Her facial expression was so cool it could have frozen water. She couldn't have been more distant if she'd been on the moon. And her unfailing, unruffled courtesy got on his nerves within twenty minutes. God, the woman could be aggravating when she put her mind to it!

He got the message, all right. Hands off. It couldn't have been any clearer if she had written it across her forehead in fire engine–red lipstick—not that he supposed Madeleine would be caught dead owning such a vulgar color.

He'd spent half the night worrying about her. Had he upset her with that burst of desire? Was she afraid of being unfaithful to Graham? Afraid of incurring Ransom's contempt if they slept together again?

He'd spent the other half of the night castigating himself. He knew now that she'd been tired, depressed, and probably a little drunk the night he'd met her. Defenses down. Judgment impaired. In need of company and comfort. In need of things she normally didn't acknowledge, he figured, and vulnerable to emotions she normally kept locked away.

Okay, so she shouldn't have skipped out on him like that. But hadn't he overreacted, at least a little? He winced with shame when he thought of the things he'd said to her in her office a couple of days ago. He'd never spoken to a woman like that before, whatever the provocation. Hell, who could blame her for being afraid to sleep with him again after that? Who knew what insults she was afraid he would let fly the morning after? Sex needed a little trust, and why should she ever trust him again?

Well, that kind of thinking made sense at four o'clock in the morning. But now, sitting in an elegant conference room in a Montedoran bank, grouchy from a sleepless night and buzzed from too many cups of coffee, Ransom glared at Madeleine's back and called himself a softheaded chump. He'd been willing to trust her again last night, hadn't he?

"No," Madeleine said calmly to one of the three bankers meeting with her in this high-ceilinged, air-conditioned, paneled room. "That's not what I've calculated, based on the interest rates you quoted me."

Ransom saw the three men exchange a glance. One of them left the room while the other two smiled at Madeleine. The oldest banker leaned forward and suggested they go over it again. Ransom almost sneered at him. After what Madeleine had said last night, it was pretty easy to see now that these men had looked at her pretty blonde hair and her sexy legs and her long-lashed eyes and thought they could hoodwink her and get some extra profit on this deal, if the plantation sold. She'd eat them for lunch if they weren't careful.

No, not Madeleine, he realized. She was too subtle for that. She had her own methods, equally effective, and the younger banker was starting to sweat in the cool room. Ransom grinned wolfishly at him.

"Yes," Madeleine said. "Let's go over it again."

Okay, okay, Ransom was honest enough to admit that having a sudden and unexpected erection last night probably impaired his judgment as much as a few drinks had impaired Madeleine's on the night they'd met. And maybe trust wasn't precisely what he'd been feeling when he reached for her last night. Still, she hadn't been immune to him. He knew how she looked when she was aroused, and he'd seen the signs just a split second before she'd panicked.

"My lawyers will confirm that," Madeleine said. She glanced at her watch. "In fact, we'd better wrap this up soon, gentlemen."

Ransom stifled a yawn. They'd been here for three hours. They were due to meet Madeleine's lawyers for lunch around noon. Then, ignoring the traditional siesta (much to Ransom's regret), Madeleine and her lawyers would work through the afternoon and well into the evening. Ransom would continue to watch over Madeleine, and everyone else would continue glancing nervously at him. It promised to be an excruciatingly dull day.

He'd been right yesterday. He should keep his mind on business. He'd lost his head over this woman again, and look at the results: He was sleepy, a little slow, and dull-witted today. If anything went wrong, he'd be lucky not to get his fool head blown off.

And it was all Madeleine's fault, he fumed with more fury than fairness. Damn her. Why couldn't she just be like any other client?

Facts and figures blurred before Madeleine's eyes by the time they wrapped things up at her lawyers' offices. It had been a tedious day, the only comic relief being the wary looks everyone kept casting at her casually dressed bodyguard.

Well, he did look pretty ferocious today, she acknowledged. One might almost think he had been born with that scowl on his face. Madeleine knew better than to tell him to snap out of it. Ransom's mood would improve when Ransom decided he wanted it to improve, and not before. Besides, it was easier to deal with him this way. When he felt charming or kind or philosophical, it was too hard to keep her distance. She recognized the truth of this and realized that she must be more careful from now on.

My God, last night she had been moments away from tumbling into bed with him again! His touch, his soft apology, his tenderness, the sudden blaze of desire in his eyes . . . She'd wanted him enough to trade a year of her life for another night in his arms.

And then all the remembered shame and embarrassment and fear of exposure had flooded her, and she'd practically crawled across the room to get away from him. As contemptuous as he had been of her in New York, how could she even consider abandoning herself like that again? Would he wait until she begged, until she was nearly weeping with pleasure, and then comment that even a Barrington woman wanted a guy with a hard-on? Madeleine shuddered. Would she start worrying all over again that he would talk about what happened between them? Would he tell another woman, as he'd told her, that he "got laid" last night? And what about other women? Who was the woman he'd slept with on his last night in New York? Another one-night stand, or a regular girlfriend? Good God—did he have a wife? Madeleine realized she really knew nothing about Ransom.

She exchanged farewells with her Montedoran lawyers and turned to leave their offices. Ignoring the other men, Ransom rose with predatory grace to precede her, his jacket flashing open to reveal his gun; it had been returned to him upon leaving the palace this morning. Madeleine eyed the plain ring he wore as he opened a door and escorted her out onto the street. It could be a wedding ring, she supposed, but that didn't mean it was. For one thing, wedding rings were usually worn on the left hand, and this ring was on his right hand. Besides, why would—

"Damn it," Ransom said, startling her.

"What?"

He looked at her with some exasperation. "Notice anything?"

She frowned at the sarcasm in his voice. Then she realized the problem. "Miguel's not here with the car yet."

Ransom glanced at his watch. "He's late." He scowled again. "He mentioned something about taking Señora Veracruz on a 'shopping trip.' "

His tone made it clear that he didn't believe for a moment that Miguel and the First Lady of Montedora were actually shopping this evening. Remembering what he had said about Miguel's probable involvement with the woman, she asked, "Will he be long?"

"Could be," he said morosely.

It was dark, humid, and still hot. The noisy street was crowded with cars and people. Multicolored electric signs blazed in the night.

"Let's get something to drink across the street," Madeleine suggested, pointing to a fashionable café. "We can keep an eye out for him from there."

Ransom nodded and took her elbow, guiding her across the street. Traffic in Montedora City was a free-for-all, and pedestrians were fair game. She had to dash to the sidewalk when a noisy motorbike bearing two people roared right past her heels, nearly knocking her down.

When they entered the café, Ransom asked for a table by the window. Madeleine noticed other women looking at him as they were shown to their table. Sensual, smiling women. Women who hadn't spent all day closed up in meetings, going over facts, figures, and indecipherable real estate laws. Women who didn't spend their lives and their energy trying to prove their capability in a man's world. As Madeleine walked past the fashionable elite of Montedora City, she recognized that the elaborate dresses and hairstyles of the women indicated that they had their own way of getting what they wanted. After a day like this, their age-old methods seemed enviably easy.

"Buck up," Ransom said, startling her. "You knocked their socks off today. I was watching."

She laughed ruefully, set down her briefcase, and took her place by the window. "How did you know I was—"

"Brooding? I've seen you brood before. You brood like a silent film star."

"Oh. Well. As long as I'm not obvious."

"You were tough today. I was . . ." He changed whatever he had intended to say and concluded, "I was impressed."

She sighed. "Thank you, Ransom. I just hope it pays off."

"Hungry?" When she shook her head, he asked, "What do you want to drink?"

"A vodka tonic, if they've got good vodka here."

"I have a feeling they do," said Ransom, looking around at the clientele.

The café, like the law offices, was located in the small, central area that hosted the city's rare display of wealth. The Hotel Tigre wasn't far from here.

"What's wrong?" Madeleine asked, noticing Ransom frowning at something outside the window.

"A motorbike just went past."

"And?"

"It's the same one that nearly knocked us down five minutes ago."

She didn't understand. "So?"

"So I wonder why it's circling the block."

"Maybe they're lost."

"Maybe."

She wasn't interested in that. She was interested in getting something to drink. She gave her order to a waiter, then nudged Ransom, who was still looking out the window.

"Cerveza," he said absently.

The waiter nodded and left them. Ransom ignored Madeleine while she waited for the drinks to come, only once muttering "third pass" as he watched the motorbike speed past the window. She wondered how he could tell it was the same bike, or why it fascinated him so much. However, having spent all day talking, she was content with the silence. She glanced around the room and noticed a couple of young women watching Ransom. Maybe they hoped his lack of interest in her was a sign that he'd be interested in meeting them.

He was a man women liked to look at, she knew, having done her own fair share of looking at him. She studied his profile as he gazed out the window. How familiar that profile was becoming—the slightly crooked nose, the full lips and strong jaw, the lock of golden brown hair which fell over his forehead, the faint scar at his temple, a fine white line running into his hair . . . She would miss looking at that profile after they left Montedora.

Since the thought was not conducive to her peace of mind, she forced herself to focus on something else. Anything else. She looked around the café. To her surprise, she saw one of last night's dinner guests enter the front door.

"Who's that?"

"Who?" Ransom asked, following her gaze.

"Wasn't he at dinner last night?"

Ransom blinked. "Yeah. That's Martinez, Veracruz's Chief of Staff."

"And is that, er, lady at his side Mrs. Martinez?"

"I'd say that's his new mistress. I guess the old one didn't last very long."

"You knew her?" Madeleine asked.

"I saw her. Martinez isn't discreet."

"Not many men are."

"Sexism, Maddie? I thought you were too intelligent for that," he chided.

She smiled. "Do you th—"

"Not discreet," he said suddenly, vaulting out of his chair.

She flinched in surprise. "What—"

"Shit!" He hauled her out of her chair without ceremony and pulled her away from the window.

"What are you—" she began, confused and alarmed.

"Let's get out of here! But first let's warn that horny idiot that—"

"Ransom!" She lost a shoe in her haste to keep up with him as he dragged her through the café.

"Señor Martinez!" Ransom barreled straight into the man, hauling Madeleine behind him. "Get out of here! Two assassins are about to make another pass by this place. This time, they'll be signaled that you've arrived. Go!"

He spoke with such authority that the bewildered man barely protested when Ransom shoved him through the double doors leading into the kitchen and shouted something at the bemused cooks. Ransom turned around and shouted something at the patrons. Madeleine didn't entirely understand, but she caught the gist of it. Something about assassins coming here right now, everyone leave.

After more than a decade of civil unrest and violence, the Montedorans reacted quickly to Ransom's announcement. Madeleine thought she'd be trampled in the shrieking stampede for the door. Ransom turned and dragged her into the kitchen, still shouting in a mixture of English and Spanish.

Madeleine was as bewildered as she was frightened. The shrieking and chaos around her seemed surreal as the staff escaped from the kitchen by way of a back door. One fat old man, apparently the head chef, didn't want to leave. He glared at Ransom and argued with him in rapid Spanish, pointing at something he was cooking. The situation was so absurd that Madeleine wanted to laugh. Then Ransom pulled his gun out of its holster and pointed it right at the man. Madeleine gasped. The chef's eyes bulged. He followed Ransom's instructions and finally left his creation behind, but he complained all the way to the back door.

"Jesus, I hate perfectionists!" Ransom growled, following the man and pulling Madeleine so fast she was stumbling to keep up.

"I'm a perfectionist," she muttered, losing her remaining shoe as they fled for the door.

"I know. It's one of the things I find most aggravating about you." They emerged from the building and found themselves in a back alley.

"Ransom, I don't understand. What are you—"

Her question was cut off by an explosion that shook the ground beneath her stocking feet and seemed to split her skull wide open. Ransom flung her to the ground and threw himself on top of her. They waited, but nothing more happened.

When Ransom rolled off of her, Madeleine demanded, "What was that?"

"A bomb," he said, helping her rise. "They must have thrown it through the window, where we were sitting."

"Oh, my God!" she gasped, horrified. "We'd have all been . . . been killed." She started shaking.

"Listen to me." His voice was firm and urgent. "I want you to—"

"Mr. Ransom!" someone cried.

Ransom turned and saw Martinez and his wailing mistress emerge from a huge pile of rubbish in the alley. "Stay there!"

The couple obediently burrowed back into their hiding place.

"Ransom!" Madeleine grabbed his shoulder as he turned to go. "What are—"

"You stay here, too. Behind those barrels."

"But—"

"Do it!" He shoved her behind two large barrels, then ran through the alley and turned into the street. Madeleine didn't even think. She just followed him. They'd already nearly been killed once tonight. She wasn't going to let him risk his life a second time. She stumbled into the dark side street on shaking legs and saw him running toward the street corner. She ran after him.

The motorbike came around the corner and sped down the street toward them, the riders anonymous in their helmets. Madeleine saw Ransom stop and bring his gun up to fire. Still running, she saw the bikers ride into a pool of light cast by the only streetlamp. One of the riders raised his gun and pointed it at Ransom.

"No!" she screamed.

Ransom glanced over his shoulder and saw her.

The next thing she knew, she was lying facedown on the street, with Ransom's knee planted in her back and his gun firing directly over her head. Hot metal bullet casings kept flying out of his gun and hitting her. Her cheek scraped against rough pavement. Ransom's weight pressed relentlessly on her vital organs. She couldn't breathe. There was a roaring sound that rivaled the explosions directly overhead. The roaring faded, and then the explosions stopped. Her ears rang, but she could still hear the hysterical crowd in the distance and Ransom's harsh breathing directly above her. He was cursing.

He mercifully removed his knee from her back, but the hands that hauled her to her feet were not gentle.

"Goddamn you, Maddie! You could have been killed!" He shook her hard, his fingers bruising her arms, and shouted, "Are you out of your mind? You could have been killed, damn you!"

Breathless, dizzy, frightened, furious, and in pain, she hauled off and hit him. As hard as she could. A solid, open-handed smack right across his face. In a tone she had never before used, she cried, "So could you, you idiot! How dare you risk your life like that! How dare you scare me like that! How could you . . . Don't you . . . I . . ."

Her voice broke. Her heartbeat thundered through her ears. Blood raced through her shaking limbs. The imprint of her palm stood out whitely on his flushed cheek. She felt a tear trickle down her face.

They stared at each other in shocked silence for a moment. Then, without knowing quite how it had happened, she was in his arms, kissing him back as ruthlessly as he kissed her. His lips ground against hers, hurting her, and she pressed harder against him, wanting more, wanting to know he was really, truly alive and well and whole.

He broke off the kiss and buried his face in the hollow of her neck, hugging her with rib-bruising ferocity. She pressed her face against the warm, damp skin of his throat and dug her fingers into his back.

He said, "If you ever do anything like that again, I'll shoot you myself, do you hear?"

"Then you'll just have to shoot," she said fiercely, still angry at him. "Did you think their bullets would just bounce off you?"

"Do you have any idea of the odds against his hitting me while he was riding a bike, for God's sake?" He sounded exasperated with her. "Especially on a street full of garbage and potholes? And in the dark, no less? He couldn't h—"

"I don't care about your goddamn odds," she snapped. "You could have been killed!"

He pulled away and started shaking her again. "Damn it, Maddie, I nearly had a heart attack when I saw you running toward me. Why didn't you stay where I put you?"

She wanted to hit him again, but she restrained herself. "Why didn't you stay with me?"

"Because I wanted to bring them in. Whoever they are, they just tried to kill dozens of people."

"The café!" she blurted. "People might be hurt!"

She pushed past him. His hand clamped down on her arm.

"I'll go first," he said. "I am supposed to be protecting you."

"Oh, who cares about that now?"

"I care!"

"Pull yourself together, Ransom! This is serious!"

He laughed. He actually laughed. "Okay, okay. We'll go together."

By the time they reached the scene of the explosion, two local traffic police had already called for backup assistance and started pushing back the gaping crowd. A fire truck arrived then, but whatever part of the café hadn't been destroyed in the explosion was already consumed by fire. Madeleine watched the blaze soberly, realizing how close they had all come to dying.

Using the skills he told her he'd learned in the Secret Service, Ransom tended a young couple who had been wounded while passing by the café at the moment of the explosion. Miraculously, they seemed to be the only severe casualties, and they would survive if they got competent medical care. Luckily, Ransom murmured to her, they looked wealthy enough to get it.

Madeleine assisted him, following his instructions as she helped him deal with the two victims, one of whom was in considerable pain. She did her best to soothe the woman, whose hand she held while waiting for the ambulance. Madeleine had lost her head for a few moments back there, but she was focused and in control now. Ransom wryly admitted he was learning to appreciate both sides of her.

In the aftermath of the explosion, Madeleine was seeing some of the crucial differences between a wealthy country and a poor one. Public services here were poorly equipped, sparsely staffed, and inefficient. Thank God no more than two people had been seriously hurt, and that the café stood apart from the buildings on either side of it. And thank God for Ransom, too. Without him, they'd all have been dead. But, as he labored over the injured couple, he had no time to claim the mantle of a hero.

The situation remained chaotic even after the wounded couple was finally taken away by the ambulance. Some people with minor injuries had removed themselves from the scene, but most of the witnesses remained to answer questions from soldiers, police, and journalists. A huge crowd had also gathered to watch the proceedings. Having apparently sent his mistress home, a smelly and smeared Señor Martinez found Ransom in the crowd just as a black limousine pulled into the center of the scene. The spectators watched with fascination as General Escalante himself emerged from the dark car, accompanied by three Seguridores.

"Ah. Mr. Ransom," Escalante said, upon being shown the individual who could best explain what had happened here this evening. The general's tone dripped with dislike.

"Hi, General. And here I was afraid we wouldn't have another chance to get together."

Seeing Escalante's cold expression, Madeleine was tempted to elbow Ransom sharply in the ribs. It was stupid to bait the man. But she understood Ransom's behavior. In the aftermath of terror and near-death, the hormones kicking into her bloodstream made her feel heady and reckless.

Martinez broke the tension by crying, "This man saved my life! He saved me!" He seized Ransom's hand and kissed it.

Madeleine laughed out loud at the expression on Ransom's face. Everyone looked disapprovingly at her. Ransom's glance suggested he'd get even with her later.

Having already told the story to the police twice, Ransom was clearly in no mood to repeat himself for Escalante's benefit, so he kept it brief and ended by saying, "When I saw Señor Martinez enter the café, it just clicked, and I knew those guys on the bike were planning a hit."

"And you claim you had no inside information?" Escalante's tone implied a wealth of dark suspicions.

"Claim?" Ransom repeated. "Are you suggesting I'm in contact with rebels or terrorists?"

"You've evidently made yourself a hero today," Escalante

said. "Yet I find it very surprising that you leapt to such an extraordinary conclusion, based on so little evidence, and even more surprising that you proved to be correct."

"It's only surprising if you're a badly trained, overdecorated, under-qualified fool with delusions of grandeur," Ransom replied. "For example."

Escalante's expression grew coldly furious. "Your insolence does not improve your situation," he warned in a rigidly controlled voice.

"And your incompetence does not improve yours," Ransom shot back.

Madeleine winced and decided it was time to take charge. "Mr. Ransom is overwrought, General, and I beg you to excuse him."

Ransom glared at her. "Don't you—"

"I might have been killed, you see, and he takes his responsibility for me very seriously," she continued, giving Ransom a warning glare of her own. "Indeed, it is undoubtedly his alert mentality when on duty, combined with his many years of service to the President of the United States of America, which enabled him to instinctively suspect danger."

"Of course!" Martinez agreed jovially. He eyed Escalante and added, "We would all be dead if not for Mr. Ransom. *Por favor,* Carlos . . ."

"I'm sure President Veracruz will be pleased to learn that his faith in Mr. Ransom has not been misplaced," Madeleine added.

"And yet you let the terrorists escape you," Escalante mused, clearly trying to goad Ransom again.

"He did no such thing," Madeleine replied, stepping on Ransom's foot. She wished she were wearing football cleats instead of torn stockings. "I myself saw him risk his life in an attempt to prevent their escape, General." She briefly described the scene, omitting any mention of her emotional state.

"And where is this gun?" Escalante asked.

Ransom produced the Glock semiautomatic from his holster, already reloaded.

Escalante examined it. "I will have to confiscate this as evidence."

"No way," Ransom said. "I need it to protect Miss Barrington."

"Your needs are not paramount here."

"But the authority of President Veracruz is always paramount in Montedora, isn't it?" Ransom reached into his back pocket and produced a document. "Signed by El Presidente himself."

Escalante took the letter and read it. He then handed it back to Ransom with narrowed eyes and compressed lips. "Cleverly worded, Mr. Ransom. My compliments."

"Can we go now?"

"No. I may have more questions for you after examining the scene. You will be required to wait here for a little longer. You, too," he added to Martinez.

"But surely we can find a place for the lady to sit down," Martinez said.

Escalante's gaze swept Madeleine. His expression indicated that she looked like a bag lady. With a curt nod, he suggested they wait in his car. That wouldn't have been Madeleine's first choice, but the stone-faced Seguridore who turned and opened the limousine door for her looked quite capable of forcing her to get into the empty car if she balked.

"Handy," Ransom commented after the Seguridore closed the door on the three of them, shutting them inside.

He sat across from her in the spacious passenger area, while Martinez sat to her right. "He can keep us away from journalists this way, too."

"Why does he dislike you so much?" Madeleine asked, examining her ruined stockings.

Ransom seemed to notice her appearance for the first time. "Jesus! Are you all right?" He reached down and pulled her feet up into his lap. "You're cut and all beat up."

"Were you horrible to him last time you were in Montedora?"

"Where the hell are your shoes?"

"Did you try to seduce his daughter or something?"

"And your knees are all scraped," he remarked, massaging her calves. Studying the rest of her, he added, "And you're filthy. You look awful."

"Or did you insult his wife?"

"How did you get in this condition?"

His head bobbing back and forth, Martinez finally held up a hand and declared, "Enough of this! Do you always speak this way to each other?"

"Usually," Ransom admitted, examining Madeleine's feet. "You should soak these as soon as we get back."

"Then why have you not yet killed each other?" Martinez asked in wonder.

"My shoes fell off when you dragged me through the building. And I got those other abrasions when you threw me down on the street," Madeleine said.

"Escalante didn't like Veracruz calling in outside help," Ransom explained, stroking her feet soothingly. "He was hostile to me from the beginning, but things got really bad after I recommended that Veracruz not let anyone, including the Seguridores, carry a gun at the Presidential Palace. And that included Escalante."

"Ah, yes!" Martinez said. "I remember now. Didn't he have you arrested?"

"You were arrested? You never mentioned that. Ouch!"

"Sorry. When Escalante realized that Veracruz intended to follow all my instructions, he tried to convince me to change my recommendation. When threats and bribes didn't work, he tried a little old-fashioned coercion. Had me roughed up and thrown in prison."

"How could he do that?"

"Escalante can do almost anything he wants. Luckily, Veracruz found out about it and got me out after a day. They both decided to treat the incident like a practical joke."

"Oh, Ransom! You should never have come back here!"

"I had my reasons," he said laconically. "Does Escalante keep any booze in here?"

"Good idea. I could use a drink, too," Martinez said, investigating the small liquor cabinet.

"No, for her feet," Ransom said, taking a bottle away from Martinez. "We should disinfect these cuts."

"With French cognac?" Martinez sounded appalled.

"You can have some when I'm done," Ransom told him. "Give me your handkerchief."

"But . . . but it's a Ralph Lauren!" Martinez clasped a protective hand over his front pocket.

"Never mind," Madeleine said. "I've got one here." She opened the small, flat purse she wore slung across her body. Her money and personal documents were inside . . . The realization hit her at that instant: "My briefcase!"

"What?"

"Oh, no." She cradled her head in her hands. "My briefcase. I left it in the café."

"What was in there?" Ransom asked, taking her handkerchief.

"Copies of everything we worked on today. All my notes."

"Anything else?"

She thought it over. "Nothing irreplaceable, I guess." She sighed. "I'll call the lawyers and the bankers in the morning. At least I didn't lose anything until after meeting with them."

"Take off your stockings," Ransom ordered.

"What?"

He gestured with the handkerchief and the cognac he held. "Take off your stockings. And you, Martinez—close your eyes."

"This is hardly the time—" Madeleine began.

"Who the hell knows what kind of stuff is on those streets? Do you have any idea how well germs thrive in this climate?"

"With respect, Miss Barrington," Martinez said gently, "Mr. Ransom is right. A hot, damp climate like this breeds bacteria very quickly. You don't want to leave those cuts unattended."

"Oh, all right," Madeleine said, still brooding over the loss of her briefcase. "Well, at least I've got my passport and money."

"And your life," Martinez added. "To think those assassins were after me! Me!"

Ransom poured a generous amount of cognac on to Madeleine's handkerchief, then handed the rest of the bottle to Martinez. "Here," he said with a touch of sympathy. "Have a drink. And close your eyes."

Martinez accepted the bottle gratefully, closed his eyes, and took a long swallow of Escalante's cognac.

Madeleine reached under the hem of her dress, unhooked her garters, and rolled down her stockings. Ransom peeled them off her feet and dropped them on the floor.

"This'll sting," he warned.

"Go ahead."

He smiled at her tone. "Yes, milady."

He was right. It stung. She bit her lip as he applied the alcohol to the cuts and scrapes on her feet, knees, and elbows. When he was done, he offered her a swig of the cognac. She accepted, then passed the bottle to him. He swallowed a mouthful, then handed it back to Martinez, who drank some more.

"I tell you, I never thought things would deteriorate so," Martinez said, handing the bottle to Madeleine.

"Oh?"

"I think I shall resign my office and leave the country."

"Really?" Madeleine asked. "Are things as bad as that?"

He nodded. "The whole country is in turmoil. And now Veracruz is planning something dangerous."

"What?" Ransom asked, passing the cognac bottle back to him.

Martinez looked around nervously. After a pregnant pause, he whispered, "He intends to remove Escalante from power."

"Are you sure?" Madeleine asked, declining when Martinez offered her the bottle again.

"Of course I am sure! Do you think I am a fool?"

Madeleine refrained from answering that.

"Have another drink," Ransom suggested to Martinez. "How do you know this?"

"Know what?"

"That Veracruz plans to have Escalante de-clawed," Ransom clarified patiently.

"Oh, my mistress told me."

"How did she know?"

"Veracruz told her."

Madeleine frowned. "Why?"

Martinez shrugged. "Men are careless in the throes of passion. He let it slip out one afternoon, when they were in bed together."

"Oh." Madeleine wondered if the woman slept with Escalante, too. Then she asked curiously, "Veracruz talks politics in bed?"

"Not every man is as smooth as I am," Ransom told her. "So Escalante is on his way out?"

"Only if the plan of Veracruz is successful." Martinez took another swallow, then leaned forward and whispered, "But Escalante has ears everywhere."

"Still, it would be a smart move for Veracruz," Ransom mused. "Escalante has too much power, and his Seguridores are too dangerous."

"Yes," agreed Martinez. "They are dangerous to everyone."

"Can Veracruz do it?" Madeleine asked Ransom.

He shrugged. "It depends on the plan. And on who helps him."

"My health is very delicate," Martinez moaned. "This is very bad for me."

"Who do you think was behind tonight's assassination attempt?" Ransom asked him.

Martinez swallowed more cognac and wiped his mouth with a dirty sleeve. "Who knows? The Doristas? Or perhaps the LPM. They intended to blow up Veracruz in his car, you know."

"Yes, I know. Have you received any recent threats?"

"No. Oh, it is very hard to stay alive when one has so many enemies," Martinez said mournfully.

"Yes, I'm sure."

"I want to resign. I want to leave the country."

"Uh-huh."

"I want to go to Wyoming."

"Wyoming?" Madeleine repeated in surprise.

"They have real cowboys there. And everyone says it is a very quiet place."

"He's drunk," Ransom said.

"But sincere," Madeleine added.

"And how are you?" Ransom asked, his tone changing.

She met his eyes. "I'm fine. Just a little sore." She stretched and admitted, "My back hurts."

"I'm not going to apologize."

"I know." She glanced at his cheek, where the mark left by her palm had faded. "But I'm sorry I hit you. I've never hit anyone in my life."

He smiled wryly. "I seem to bring out your temper."

"I never used to have one," she muttered.

"Of course you did. You just didn't want anyone to know it."

That struck too close to home, so she changed the subject. "Thank you for saving my life. We'd all be dead now if—"

"You're lucky you're not dead." He brushed aside her thanks and admiration. "Next time I tell you to—"

"But how could I just—"

Another lively argument was prevented by the sudden opening of the car door. A Seguridore told them in gruff Spanish that they could go now. Eager to do so, they left behind Madeleine's ruined stockings and an empty bottle of cognac as souvenirs for Escalante, and slid out into the humid night air. The crowd had grown even bigger, and several cameramen were present. Martinez was recognized, and several journalists descended upon him.

"Let's find Miguel," Ransom suggested, steering Madeleine in the opposite direction. "He must be somewhere around here."

Sure enough, he was. They found him a few minutes later, searching frantically for them, very apologetic about having been late, and relieved to see them alive and well.

"Let's just get out of here, Miguel," Ransom suggested.

"Where's the car?" Madeleine asked.

"Over there. I was late because of the First Lady," Miguel explained, leading the way to where he had left the limo. "She wanted to go shopping one more time before she would let me leave this evening."

CHAPTER TEN

Madeleine awoke after a restless and largely sleepless night to discover that things could indeed always get worse. She was groggy, stiff, sore, and very cranky. She phoned the lawyers and bankers, explaining she would need updated copies of everything they had done yesterday. They promised to see to it immediately, but when she and Ransom arrived at their offices, she found that nothing whatsoever had been done since her phone call. So she didn't get back to the Presidential Palace until lunchtime.

Another surprise awaited them there. President Veracruz, moved beyond words by Ransom's reported heroism, hosted an impromptu luncheon in his honor, affectionately chastising Ransom for not having informed him himself of last night's events. Escalante attended the luncheon, remaining stone-faced throughout the ordeal, but if looks could have killed . . . Madeleine repressed a shudder. The effort of being courteous throughout this affair made Madeleine's head hurt, although Ransom's grim expression of forbearance when Veracruz kissed him on both cheeks was almost amusing enough to make the event worthwhile.

They had returned to the palace around ten o'clock last night and quietly retreated to their rooms. Madeleine phoned her father to explain the evening's events to him, forestalling his concern in case he should learn from other sources of her involvement in the affair. He was impressed with Ransom's performance, and she had to agree that her father had chosen her bodyguard wisely.

She then soaked her abused body in a hot bath, but she was unable to sleep afterwards. The realization that she had nearly died kept her wide-awake, as did her muddled analysis of her own behavior. The evening's events overwhelmed her, and she wanted to seek out Ransom, though she was a little fuzzy about what exactly she wanted from him. Not sex. Not tonight. Exhausted and sore and contemplating her own mortality, she didn't feel remotely passionate. But she wanted his company, his comfort, his offhanded common sense, and his ironic humor. She just wanted to be with him. And that realization kept her tossing restlessly for most of the night.

One look at Ransom today, however, left her in no doubt that he had slept like a baby last night, damn him. And his relaxed good humor irritated her as the day wore on.

When the formal luncheon was over, Madeleine hoped they could leave for the plantation at last. They were already six hours behind schedule. Then Veracruz informed her that only a presidential car was good enough to drive a hero like Ransom into the rugged Montedoran countryside. Consequently, the President's secretary had cancelled Madeleine's reservation for a rental car and was sending Miguel and a limousine to the plantation with her.

Madeleine ground her teeth and tried to talk her way out of it while Ransom watched, obviously amused by her efforts. She insisted that she didn't want to take advantage of the President, to inconvenience his employees, or to inconvenience Señora Veracruz by monopolizing her driver. The President's enigmatic response to this last sally made Madeleine suspect that he knew what the First Lady and her driver were doing on those shopping trips and intended to put a stop to it.

Madeleine made a few more attempts to elude

Veracruz's unwanted generosity, including pointing out that she had reserved a rugged vehicle from the rental agency for practical reasons; a limousine was not suited to Montedora's rural roads and might even be damaged.

When the President's obstinacy began to turn into annoyance, Madeleine gave up and thanked him for his generosity. They still couldn't leave, however. Upon receiving his instructions about the journey, Miguel had gone to see his family, and he still wasn't back. By the time he showed up, Madeleine felt ready to hop up and down with agitation, though she doubted that anyone but Ransom realized this. And he, damn him, continued to find it amusing. She said a courteous good-bye to her hosts, then waited with barely concealed impatience for Ransom to finish taking his leave of them.

"I am very excited, señorita," Miguel said as he finished putting her luggage in the trunk of the car. "I have only been out of Montedora City once before." He opened the car door for her.

"Then this will be an adventure for you." She tried to smile at him, remembering her discussion with Ransom. A young man of Miguel's charm and intelligence had so few opportunities here.

They pulled away from the imposing white palace and rolled down the sweeping driveway. Ransom collected his guns at the front gate, and Miguel steered the car down the Western Highway, heading into the vast Calentura Valley which lay between Montedora's two major mountain chains. Whatever lay ahead, Madeleine was relieved to leave behind the Presidential Palace and its scheming inhabitants. She fully understood by now why Ransom didn't like staying there.

"Veracruz is right, you know," Ransom commented,

lighting up a cigarette. "We'll never make the plantation by nightfall."

"Can you at least open a window if you're going to smoke that thing?" she snapped.

"And there are no Holiday Inns here," he continued mildly, rolling down his window.

"I'm aware of that. I have been here before." Her bad manners and lack of self-control actually seemed to please him, she noted grumpily. Men.

"Then I assume you have a plan?"

"Of course I have a plan. I always have a plan."

"That's what I thought."

"Doragua, a town of reasonable size, lies about two-thirds of the way to the plantation. Since the roads are unsafe after dark—"

"And not so safe by day," Ransom remarked.

"—we will stop there for the night. There is an inn there, the only inn for forty miles in any direction."

"I'll tell Miguel."

"I already told him while the First Lady of Montedora was draping herself around your body in poignant farewell."

"She likes me."

His complacent tone made her want to bite his head off. Her stomach burned from the once-a-week antimalarial pill she had taken before lunch. Her head hurt; so did the scrapes and cuts on her legs and feet.

Veracruz had had the car fully provisioned for their journey: food, beverages, magazines, pillows, and toilet paper (even if they saw a toilet between here and Doragua, it was unlikely to have toilet paper which, like everything else, had become prohibitively expensive due to Montedora's 212 percent inflation). Ransom picked up one of the pillows, put it on his lap, and patted it invitingly.

Madeleine gave him the frostiest look of inquiry she could muster. It made him grin.

"Come on," he said. "Lie down and take a nap. You're tired and cranky. If you get any meaner, I'll have to tie you to the roof of the car."

To her surprise, she laughed. "I'm sorry."

He put a hand on her neck and massaged gently. It felt too heavenly to resist, so she closed her eyes, letting him knead her taut muscles.

"You're as tight as a drum," he said. "Relax a little."

"No, I . . ." She felt blood flow into her cramped shoulders and sighed. "I should review my paperwork and . . . and . . ."

"Come on. Lie down." He brushed her hair away from her face and added, "I promise I'll behave."

She glanced at him. "Behave?"

"Uh-huh."

The warm expression in those changeable green eyes was at odds with his words, but she nonetheless believed him. Her pride and her sense of propriety urged her to refuse his offer, but the gentle pressure of his hand was too enticing to resist, and she let him guide her head to the pillow on his lap.

"Kick off your shoes," he urged, shifting to settle her more comfortably.

She did as he suggested, then drew her feet up onto the seat, comfortably curling up as he stroked her hair.

"Better?" he asked softly.

"Better," she murmured, feeling safe and contented. He was right. She needed sleep. She needed . . . She sighed again and closed her eyes, enjoying his soothing touch.

The flat fields around the capital city gradually gave way to the foothills of the mountains where, long ago, the

Spanish conquistadores had found rich veins of gold. They had enslaved the indigenous people of the region and set up vast labor camps of men, women, and children to work their gold mines, build and tend their villas, and haul their plunder through thick, perilous jungles on the long journey to the coast. For over a century, their galleons had carried the wealth of the New World home to Spain, the overloaded ships so slow and unwieldy that they were easy prey for the pirates of the Caribbean. There were other dangers on the long voyage, too; before reaching the Atlantic, well over a thousand treasure-laden ships floundered and sank in the violent hurricanes and treacherous reefs of the Florida Straits. But the rape of the Americas continued unabated.

When the mountain gold for which Montedora was named finally ran out, the country turned to agriculture. All the forests from Montedora City eastward were cut down for timber, and vast plantations took their place. The mountains to the west remained wild, untamed, and underpopulated to this very day. El Paradiso was in the Calentura Valley, the agricultural lowland lying between Montedora's two major mountain chains. Las Verdes—the Green Mountains—south of the plantation had been a haven for bandits ever since the days of the conquistadores. To the north were Las Lunas, the Mountains of the Moon, the stronghold of the Dorista rebels. Ransom looked down at his sleeping companion and was appalled to think that she had made this journey alone only three months ago.

The lack of direct access to the sea had kept the country isolated. Unskilled labor and corrupt leaders had kept it poor, as had its long history of warfare. Fifteen years ago, Montedora had gone to war with one of its neighbors over the disputed results of an international soccer game; the conflict had bankrupted the already impoverished society. One had to see the poverty here to understand how severe it was. The average income in the USA was at least fifty times the average income in Montedora, where two percent of the people held ninety-seven percent of the wealth. It wasn't surprising that a bright, ambitious kid like Miguel, born to a poor Montedoran family, drove a car for a living, slept with a middle-aged woman for extra tips and presents, and had only been outside of Montedora City once in his life; no, the surprising thing was that he had managed to get even this far in life. Ransom wondered if he'd ever have the chance to get any farther.

A military coup a decade ago had initially given Montedorans hope for a better future. They were promised schools, medical services, and jobs, as well as elections for the first time in nearly thirty years. However, rival military factions were soon vying for power and sabotaging each other's efforts to effect change. The new government was overthrown two years later by a violently oppressive right-wing regime. Then, three years ago, that junta was overthrown by the then immensely popular Veracruz and his supporters (the most forceful of whom had been the immensely unpopular General Escalante).

Although Veracruz's administration was less oppressive than his predecessor's, Escalante—using his new private security army, the Seguridores—had instigated a reign of terror which Veracruz seemed unable to control. Meanwhile, the corruption and excesses of the government continued unabated, and the population grew ever more discontent and restless. Another revolution seemed imminent, a popular one this time, led and backed by the long-suffering people of Montedora. The only people who had nothing left to lose, Ransom thought again, as the President's limo passed through a small, ramshackle village.

Though Veracruz was a greedy fool with no interest in the plight of his people, he was no worse than any of his predecessors of the past forty years. Indeed, Ransom acknowledged sadly, Veracruz was probably the best of the lot, mostly because his own popularity meant a great deal to him. He was more and more distressed by his growing unpopularity; the assassination attempts of the past year seemed to hurt his pride even more than they frightened him. And he certainly knew that the murderous intrigues of Escalante—and the Seguridores, who were loyal solely to Escalante himself—were a major factor in the Montedoran people's growing hatred of Veracruz.

Yes, Ransom thought, Martinez was probably telling the truth. In order to salvage the love of the masses, Veracruz would get rid of Escalante, the man who had put him in power. Clever, ruthless, uncharismatic, and widely disliked, Escalante had undoubtedly known, three years ago, that the country would never accept him as a ruler, no matter how much he wanted the job for himself. So he had chosen Veracruz, a popular public figure with a certain shallow charm and a gift for pleasing the crowd, to be his puppet. Escalante had counted on always being able to manipulate Veracruz. It seemed, however, that his confidence had been misplaced. Veracruz resented how his own position was endangered by Escalante's bloodthirsty excesses.

Ransom himself had been the instrument of Veracruz's first major defiance of Escalante's wishes. Ransom could still remember the fury with which Escalante had received the news that he and the Seguridores, like everyone else, would be disarmed at the palace gates from now on. For Ransom, it had been a commonsense measure. With no influence over how the Seguridores were chosen and trained, he considered them an unknown quantity who should not be trusted with weapons in a secure area. But Escalante had taken it personally. Very personally. Ransom believed that, if he could have gotten away with it, Escalante would have had him killed then. But an American passport and a close association with Veracruz had kept Ransom relatively safe, the arrest and brief imprisonment being Escalante's only revenge. And that had been bad enough.

"Ah, well, that's why I make the big bucks," Ransom muttered, stroking the blonde head resting against his stomach.

He silently wished Veracruz luck. Getting rid of Escalante would be like trying to pull the fangs out of an angry rattlesnake.

Turning his thoughts in a more pleasant direction, he studied Madeleine's sleeping face. She hadn't bothered to use makeup to conceal the circles under her eyes today. He wondered what had ruined her sleep last night.

He'd been so exhausted that nothing on earth could have kept him awake, and he'd awoken this morning feeling rested and buoyant. There was something very satisfying, after all, about knowing you had saved people's lives. He'd experienced it once before, during his days in the Service: the certain, indisputable knowledge that, except for him, someone would have died violently. And once the danger was over, there was no feeling to beat it. Whatever he did tomorrow, or next year, or thirty years from now, he had already done something that guaranteed his life wasn't wasted. Despite his failings and sins, he believed that when his number came up, he could look his Maker in the eye and say that for at least one moment, he had mattered, he had made a difference. And he felt damn good about that.

He supposed last night's tumultuous events were what

had kept Madeleine awake. She had been such a trouper. Except for impulsively leaving her hiding place and following him into the street, she had kept her head and done everything right. He still didn't think she understood how much she had endangered them both with that reckless act. Focused and clearheaded as he took aim against the terrorists, he had experienced a moment of overwhelming panic when he saw her running toward him. Fear for her had flooded him, paralyzing him for a precious, dangerous second—a second in which he could have lost her forever. He still felt chilled to the bone when he thought of it. She had surprised him, true, but he shouldn't have lost control like that in such a dangerous situation, not even for a second. It wasn't like him.

He'd been so angry with her afterwards that he'd left bruises on her arms where he'd grabbed her. He could see them now. He touched them with regret. Still, when the smoke cleared, he was gratified by the emotions which had prompted her crazy behavior, just as he was gratified by the way she returned his ruthless, life-affirming kiss. Whether she liked it or not, Madeleine cared about him. He'd have felt smug—if he didn't feel so vulnerable.

Jesus, why had she left him like that at the Hotel Tigre? Would she do it again, knowing him as she did now? Hell, why didn't he just ask her?

Because he'd feel like a fool, that's why. She had a fiancé to fill her nights in New York. She had tried to discourage Ransom's advances even in her softer moments down here. She had told him how much she loathed being the recipient of uninvited sexual advances. What more did he need to convince him that, even if she had started to care about him a bit, she didn't want to get involved with him?

He knew what he needed, all right. He needed to believe

the unguarded expression he sometimes saw in her eyes, before she covered it, wasn't desire. He needed to believe she wasn't becoming a little fond of him. He needed to believe she only shed her mask of perfection with him because she didn't care what he thought, rather than because she trusted him in some strange way, rather than because she, too, felt something special and unfamiliar happening between them. He needed to believe he didn't instinctively know her in a way he'd never known anyone else.

And he didn't believe any of that.

Damned if he knew what he did believe, though.

He liked her like this, though—even her bad temper didn't bother him much when she was being herself instead of playing lady of the manor. Why the hell other people were evidently satisfied with only knowing that one side of her baffled him, but he'd be damned if he'd let her pretend with him. And he was glad that she seemed ready to stop trying. It even made him able to find amusement in those moments when she fell back on old habits—eyeing him like a queen confronting an ill-mannered peasant, or coolly dismissing the First Lady of Montedora.

Yeah, despite all the water under the bridge, he was finding that he really liked his strong-willed, quick-thinking, occasionally imperious heiress a lot more than he had expected to.

The intercom system buzzed. Madeleine twitched and woke up. She sat up and looked around groggily. He leaned forward and opened the glass partition.

"Where are we?" she mumbled, blinking as her eyes adjusted to the dim light. It was nearly nightfall.

"Yes, Miguel?" Ransom added, "Don't look at me, keep your eyes on the road."

"We should be at Doragua in perhaps thirty minutes."

"Thanks." The going had been slow, since rains and flooding had rutted the dirt road. Miguel had driven with care to keep from breaking an axle, and Madeleine had slept soundly through the gentle rocking of the past few hours.

"A half-hour from Doragua?" Madeleine murmured. "We're not making bad time."

Unfortunately, Madeleine had spoken too soon. The road got increasingly worse, and the encroaching darkness made it harder to navigate. Then it started raining hard, making the muddy surface slippery and unstable. Water pooled in the ruts, creating quagmires in this, one of the nation's major rural roads. They had to get out four times on the way to Doragua to dig the car out of bogs or push it back onto the road, and the trip wound up taking almost two hours longer than Miguel had predicted. Never one to shirk her duty, Madeleine had been willing to help with the dirty work, but the men insisted that she drive while they pushed. Consequently, Ransom and Miguel were covered with mud by the time they reached Doragua.

The innkeeper at the Pensión Doragua laughed good-naturedly when the rain-soaked blonde woman and her two filthy companions finally turned up that night. That was the only way to deal with trouble and inconvenience, the little man assured Madeleine, you must laugh at it; otherwise you would cry all the time. She supposed that was how Montedorans survived.

Besides reserving three of the inn's six rooms, Madeleine had also had the foresight to book dinner at the Pensión Doragua, knowing that food might otherwise be unavailable. She had learned on her last trip to Montedora that most rural cafés and pensiónes didn't keep extra fresh food on hand in case of unexpected customers. They were far too poor to risk buying anything they couldn't be guaranteed of selling before it spoiled.

Instead of complimenting her on her foresight, Ransom grumbled something like, "I should have guessed," before trudging off to the pensión's only bathroom for a much-needed shower. The innkeeper's wife, Señora Gutiérrez, spoke to Madeleine then, offering to wash all their dirty clothes—by hand, of course, since washing machines were a luxury of the wealthy. She swore on the Cross that there would be enough morning sunshine to dry them tomorrow.

Having accepted the woman's offer without bothering to haggle over the fee, Madeleine informed Miguel of the arrangement, then went to tap on the bathroom door. "Ransom?"

"Yeah?" He opened the door and turned back to what he was doing—shaving.

He was stripped to the waist, his back smooth and naked before her as he faced the little mirror above the ancient sink. His muscled shoulders gleamed beneath the electric light humming over his dark golden head. Madeleine swallowed and forgot what she wanted to say.

He swiped the razor down his face a few times, then noticed her intent gaze. "I always shave at night. Don't like holding a razor against my throat first thing in the morning," he said, as if he supposed that was why she was staring at him.

"Oh."

It seemed an intimate thing, watching a man shave. Watching this man shave. And looking at his strong, straight back, his lightly furred chest, his stomach muscles . . . He'd been fully dressed every time she'd seen him since the Hotel Tigre.

She nearly stopped breathing as she thought of that night. It suddenly seemed like it had happened only moments ago. Like it could happen again. Like it should happen again. He'd welcome it, wouldn't he? It was what he wanted, wasn't it, despite his anger about her furtive departure? She could cross the space between them right now, wrap her arms around him, and rest her cheek against his shoulder. He would know, he would understand. He would respond. All the magic, all the warmth, all the heat she had known with him would blossom between them again.

And afterwards?

Oh, hell. Afterwards. Yes, there had to be an afterwards, didn't there?

"Did you come here just to watch me shave, milady?" Ransom asked dryly, keeping his eyes on his reflection as he shaved under his chin.

"Oh, um . . . No. Actually. No. If you'll give me your dirty clothes, Señora Gutiérrez will wash them."

He looked down at his mud-caked trousers. "I think it might be kinder just to bury them."

"She claims she can make them look brand-new. At least, that's what I think she said. My Spanish is very weak."

He shrugged. "What the hell, it's my favorite shirt. Why not see if she can work miracles?" He scooped the shirt off the floor, where he had dropped it earlier, and handed it to Madeleine. She held it gingerly away from her.

He had removed the gun and holster from his ankle before digging the car out of the mud for the first time two hours ago. She saw it now, along with his big gun, resting on a little table beside the mirror. As she stood watching, he unbuckled his belt and unzipped his trousers. The sound of that zipper heated her cheeks with a rush of searing memories.

He hesitated and caught her gaze again. "You've already seen all there is to see, but maybe you'd rather, uh . . ." He nodded toward the hallway.

"What?" She blinked at him, then realized what he meant. "Oh! Yes! Of course! Excuse me." She backed into the hallway and pulled the door shut behind her.

Already seen all there was to see?

She had done a lot more than see it, as he well knew. As she waited for him to finish undressing, she knew that he remembered it all as well as she did.

The door opened a moment later. He had wrapped a towel around his hips. She suspected it was more for her benefit than his; she doubted he had become modest since their first meeting. She looked down at the towel before she could stop herself. Its presence didn't stop her from remembering his body in every detail. When their eyes met again, she knew he knew it. She grabbed the trousers he handed her, abruptly turned, and fled down the hallway, belatedly realizing that she was clutching his filthy pants to her chest. She didn't remember until she was downstairs that she had also meant to tell him dinner would be ready in thirty minutes.

The storm killed the electrical power, and Señor Gutiérrez didn't think they'd get it back before morning. The señora posted kerosene lanterns around the inn and upon the few simple dining tables outside on the covered veranda. The heavy rain gradually settled into a gentle downpour, drumming lightly on the roof and freshening the night air.

Washed and wearing dry clothes, Madeleine, Miguel, and Ransom enjoyed a simple dinner in the now-cool evening air. When Señor Gutiérrez joined them after their meal and started asking about the car and where they had come from, Miguel readily admitted to working for Veracruz. He boasted of Ransom's exploits, too, until Ransom cut him short with unusual curtness. Neither Miguel nor the old man were daunted by this, and Miguel spent the next hour regaling the señor and his family with amusing stories about working for the inhabitants of the palace.

Madeleine had no trouble guessing the reason for Ransom's curtness. Three men had stopped for dinner at the pensión just as he came downstairs after his shower, and she could tell that something about them worried him. Despite not having called ahead, the men were angry that the wealthy foreigners and their driver were getting a hearty meal while they had to settle for beans and rice. Ransom had come to the aid of a flustered Señora Gutiérrez, putting the men in their place with a few clipped words.

However, Madeleine was sure that their rudeness wasn't the reason Ransom had told her not to leave his sight until the men had gone, and why he looked at them every few minutes with an expression that should have frozen their livers. She also noticed that he made sure they saw the gun holstered at his side. Surely those men would have to be suicidal to cause any trouble here tonight.

Fortunately, the men left soon after finishing their meal. When Madeleine felt ready for bed, Ransom took her to her room, checked the windows, then gave her his pager and told her to keep her door locked.

"Do you think those men will come back?"

"Not really," he said, pausing in the doorway. "But I don't want to take any chances."

"Do you think they're bandits?"

He shrugged. "Maybe. Or kidnappers. Or drug runners."

"What makes you th—"

"They were armed, and—"

"They were? I didn't see—"

"I did."

"Oh."

"And . . ." He shrugged again. "Call it instinct."

She nodded pensively. She had learned to believe in his instincts.

He hesitated. "Will you be all right?"

"Yes."

"Okay."

She spoke again as he turned to go. "Ransom?"

"Yeah?"

Their eyes met. There were a dozen things she ought to say to him. After a long moment, she settled on, "I'm glad you're here."

He looked surprised for a moment. Then he grinned. "So am I, God help me." He was laughing softly when he closed the door.

She stared at the door, wanting to open it and call Ransom back to her side. Then she heard the sharp rap of his knuckles on the wooden surface.

"Lock it!" he ordered.

She did.

Ransom did a patrol of the surrounding property after putting Madeleine to bed. Everything seemed quiet. Damp from the rain, he went back inside. In such a hot climate, there was no question of closing the hotel's windows, not even with tonight's rainfall. Nevertheless, Ransom double-checked the entire first floor of the pensión after Señor Gutiérrez finished locking up for the night. When he was done, he found Miguel waiting for him in the empty bar with two glasses of whiskey.

"Would you like a nightgown?" Miguel offered.

"Nightcap," Ransom corrected dryly. "Sure. Thanks."

They sat down to drink. Ransom lit up a cigarette, pleased that he hadn't smoked so many today. The rain pattered lightly outside the window, and the fan spun lazily overhead. The place looked soft and serene in the lantern light.

"You are different since you came back to Montedora," Miguel said, with the honesty born of strong liquor shared after dark in a strange place.

"Different how?"

"You never used to be afraid."

That surprised him. He raised both eyebrows and fixed Miguel with one of his meaner stares. "Afraid?" Ransom could make his voice as chilly as Madeleine's when he chose.

Miguel shook his head. "Not like that, amigo. I mean for her."

Ransom felt his stomach drop. He tightened his hand around his glass of whiskey and studied it, avoiding Miguel's eyes.

What could he say? It was bad enough that it was true, even worse that he'd let it show. Yes, he was afraid for her. Whether it was the hot panic he'd felt when she'd exposed herself to the escaping bombers last night, or the cold fear he'd known tonight when he'd found those three hard-eyed men arriving here for dinner, he was being tormented by unaccustomed feelings. And he feared, too, that his emotions would endanger Madeleine, because the first requirement of any good bodyguard was a clear, cool head.

"She's a very special woman," Miguel said. "I congratulate you."

"There's nothing to congratulate me for," Ransom snapped.

"Ahhhh . . ." Miguel grinned. "So that's why she got three rooms."

"It's a purely professional relationship, kid." Ransom took a belt of the whiskey and let it burn its way down his throat. It was strong stuff, and a little bitter.

"You know better than that," Miguel chided. "And so does she. I can see it when you look at each other."

"Oh, you can, can you?" Wow, what a gift for repartee I'm demonstrating, he thought sourly.

"And she trusts you."

He remembered the way she had fled from his touch two nights ago. Trusted him? "I don't think she does. Not that way." He sighed and added more honestly, "I think I made sure she wouldn't."

"How?"

"You're too young for this story." He finished his drink.

"Me? I'm the man who keeps the First Lady smiling," Miguel said with sudden bitterness. "A woman my mother's age."

"Sorry, I didn't mean—"

"I know." Miguel shook his head, then looked at Ransom with resolve. "I didn't want to speak of either woman, actually."

"Oh?"

"No. I meant only to say that I like you very much, Ransom. I am glad you came to Montedora."

"Well . . . thanks." Feeling self-conscious, Ransom stubbed out his cigarette and said, "I like you, too."

"I know. You have been good to me. And never condescending."

"You're too bright and too capable for me to condescend—"

"Many do, and you must know it," Miguel interrupted brusquely. "The wealthy of Montedora. The pitying foreigners I drive around for the President." He frowned. "It is the pity that I have hated most of all."

"Yeah," Ransom said slowly, wondering at Miguel's mood. "Pity cripples a man more than adversity."

"And hopelessness, too."

"Hopelessness most of all." He felt a little light-headed. That was damn strong whiskey.

"Yes. You would understand this. That's why I wanted to tell you."

"Tell me what?"

Miguel blinked and seemed to come awake suddenly. He smiled. "That I have always admired you, and that I like the lady." He stood up a little unsteadily. Ransom wondered if the kid had had too much to drink tonight. Or maybe it was the rain that was making Miguel so melancholy.

"Off to bed?" he asked, feeling rather tired himself all of a sudden.

Miguel nodded. "Yes. To bed."

"G'night."

"Good night, Ransom."

Frowning slightly, Ransom watched the young man go upstairs. Something wasn't right. Something was . . . Oh, hell. He was too tired to worry about Miguel's problems tonight. He had enough of his own.

He awoke at dawn, stiff and uncomfortable and disoriented. His eyelids felt as if they'd been glued shut. What had woken him?

He finally figured it out. There was a soft, repetitive,

abrasive sound. Somewhere nearby. Swish-swish, swish-swish. It took him back to his early childhood, to the mother he'd lost long ago, sweeping the kitchen after supper while he and his brother sat doing their homework at the kitchen table. Swish-swish, swish-swish. A comforting, homey sound, full of vague but good memories.

What was that sound doing in his room at dawn?

He forced one eye open. He saw a flat wooden surface. Ah, so that's what the hard thing under his cheek was. Wood.

Where the hell was his pillow? In fact, where the hell was his bed?

He blinked his other eye open and picked up his head. He immediately felt sick.

Oh, shit. He didn't want to be sick. He swallowed and held still, waiting for the feeling to subside.

By the time it did, he'd realized he wasn't in his room. He was sitting on a hard wooden chair in the bar, his head and arms resting on the table.

How the hell had he managed to fall asleep in this position?

His tongue felt furry, and his mouth tasted foul. His head hurt. The nausea was fading, but not disappearing. Surely he hadn't gotten stinking drunk last night? Not only was that unlike him, but surely he wouldn't have done anything so stupid while guarding Madeleine?

He thought back. The effort made his head hurt.

No, he'd only had one drink last night—that modest shot of whiskey. He remembered that the whiskey had been strong and slightly bitter, but still . . .

Oh, shit, he thought again, as things started coming together. He stood up slowly, and the way the room whirled confirmed his suspicions.

He'd been drugged.

"Buenas días, señor."

Ransom looked over his shoulder and found the source of the sound which had awoken him. A girl, about twelve years old, was sweeping the barroom floor. She smiled hesitantly at him. He tried to smile back, but she apparently didn't find the effort reassuring.

"Donde está el señor?" He asked for Gutiérrez in a gravelly voice, his mind working slowly. Who had drugged the whiskey? And why?

The girl replied that Gutiérrez was outside. Did the señor require something?

He didn't even hear her.

Why? Why else, you idiot? He was halfway up the stairs before he'd completed the thought. A wealthy woman, sleeping alone up there . . . Oh, God, please, please, please let her be safe.

He flung himself against her door. It was locked.

"Maddie!" He kicked in the door and barreled into the room.

She screamed and leapt out of bed.

Safe! Safe, she was safe.

"Maddie!" He scooped her up in his arms while she was still flailing in the tangled bedsheets that twined around her legs.

"What? What! What?" she cried breathlessly, squirming in his arms, trying to see what was in her room or beyond her door that had caused him to terrify her like this.

"Jesus, oh, Jesus, oh, thank you, God," he murmured incoherently, hugging her with bruising force.

"What? What? Ransom, what's going on?" she demanded, shoving at him.

He ran his hands over her possessively, still needing to assure himself that she was safe. "I thought . . . I thought . . . Oh, hell, I don't know what I thought, but—"

"You don't know? You don't know?"

"Well, no, but—"

"What's going on?"

"I'm not sure."

"Is something wrong?"

"Um. I'm not sure." He was starting to feel very stupid.

"You're not sure?" She looked like she wanted to hit him again. "Have you gone mad? You scared me half to death!"

Realizing that he wasn't behaving very sensibly, he mumbled, "I'm sorry."

"Sorry? You're sorry?" She seemed at a loss for words. Her pretty nightgown molded to her body as she slumped down on the bed and repeated, "You're sorry." She rubbed her side and said, "I think some of my ribs cracked when your gun rammed into them."

He glanced down, so accustomed to the feel of his holstered Glock that he'd forgotten he was wearing it. Yes, he must have hurt her. Shit. He had to pull himself together. He ran a hand through his tangled hair and tried to think. "Look, it's been a hell of a night, and—"

"I nearly had a heart attack!" She pressed a hand to her chest and threatened, "In fact, I may still have one!"

"Not now," he ordered absently, drawing a withering glare from her. "I've got to figure out . . ." It hit him like a ton of bricks. "Miguel."

He turned and ran from the room. Madeleine followed him. She caught up with him when he stopped to pound on Miguel's door, two rooms away.

"What's going on?" she demanded.

"Somebody drugged me last night," he said. Then he shouted through the door, "Miguel? Are you in there?"

"What?" Her eyes were wide with surprise.

"I thought it might be a kidnapping attempt."

"Oh! That's why you burst—"

"Stand back." He shoved her aside and kicked the door in. She followed him inside the room.

It was empty. The bed hadn't been slept in. There was no sign of Miguel or his battered valise. But there was a note on the bed. Ransom picked it up and read it in silence.

"What does it say? Where is Miguel?" Madeleine asked.

Ransom sagged onto the bed and handed the note to her. "He's gone. For good. And he's stolen the car."

CHAPTER ELEVEN

Ransom gave up the effort of being brave. He stumbled down the hall to the bathroom, where he fell to his knees in front of the toilet and was thoroughly sick. Through his misery, he could hear Madeleine at the door, calming the other inhabitants of the pensión, who had all been rudely roused from their beds by the racket.

After a painful and degrading interval, Ransom finally lifted his head. A cold, damp washcloth appeared out of nowhere and wiped his face. When it was pulled away, he saw Madeleine crouching next to him, concern warming her lovely features.

"What do you think he gave you?" she asked, brushing his hair off his forehead.

He sagged against the wall and watched as she rose to rinse out the washcloth. "Sleeping pills or tranquilizers. Stolen from Señora Veracruz, probably."

She flushed the toilet and commented, "It must have been a heavy dose."

"He probably didn't mean to make me sick." Ransom closed his eyes as she bathed his face and neck again.

"Why did he do it?" she wondered.

"To make sure I wouldn't wake up," he said irritably.

"No, I mean, why did he steal the car?"

"Oh. I guess he finally saw his chance," he mumbled.

"What chance? This isn't—"

"I should have guessed. His mood was so strange last night, I should have—"

"Stop it. You can't predict everything people are going to do, Ransom," she chided.

"Still . . ."

"Cut yourself some slack."

"Look who's talking." He eyed her with weary amusement, then said more seriously, "I think he decided this was his chance to get out of Montedora with some money. He's probably worked out a plan to get the car across the nearest border and sell it. Then he'll use the money to start a new life. Maybe in Canada or the U.S."

"And desert his family? I thought he wouldn't leave without them."

"That's why he's waited until now." When Madeleine pressed her hand to his forehead, he grumbled, "I'm hot."

"But not feverish. You feel normal."

"If Miguel were willing to leave without his family, he'd have gone long ago. He needed to get his hands on enough money for all of them, and that car is worth a lot. I'm sure he's arranged to meet his family somewhere. That must be what took him so long yesterday, while we were waiting to leave. When he realized he'd be taking the car so far away from Veracruz and Escalante, with only the two of us as passengers, he knew his opportunity had finally come. He had to make a lot of fast plans with his family."

"But . . . I thought he liked you." She rinsed the washcloth again.

He took it from her. "He did. He told me so last night." Ransom pressed the washcloth against the back of his neck. "Hell, I don't condone stealing, but . . . how much longer could he have lasted here? He said only a few days ago that he was afraid the next time someone aimed at Veracruz, they'd miss and hit him instead. I'll bet that LPM plot to blow up Veracruz's car made Miguel realize his time was running out."

"And even if he stayed alive, sooner or later the First Lady would want a new toy boy, or Veracruz would punish him for sleeping with her."

"And he probably had to sleep with her to keep the job in the first place—the best job he could get here."

"I liked him," she said sadly.

"So did I." He took her hand and squeezed it.

"He must have felt caught between the sword and the wall, to do this."

"He liked you, too, you know. He told me so."

"Last night?"

"Uh-huh. I can see now that he was trying to apologize for what he was about to do." He sighed. "Shit, if he just would have asked me for help. But he never did, not once . . ."

This time, she squeezed his hand. "He wanted your respect more than your help. I could see that."

"He said something about pity," Ransom murmured. "And about how hopelessness was the only thing worse than pity."

Her eyes were soft as she gazed at him. She summoned a faint smile. "Look, Miguel's bright and resourceful, and he can charm the birds out of the trees. I have a feeling that, as risky as this is, things are going to work out for him."

"I hope so."

Wincing at the stiffness brought about by sleeping in a barroom chair, Ransom rose slowly to his feet. Still muzzy-headed, he decided he'd better take a cold, bracing shower before they discussed what to do next.

"I'd ask you to join me," he quipped weakly, turning on the water, "but I have a feeling this will be an emasculating experience."

Her expression was a mixture of sympathy and laughter as she left the bathroom.

Madeleine was waiting for Ransom with a large pot of strong coffee when he came downstairs. He looked pale, hollow-eyed, and unhappy, but clearheaded. She knew that he felt he had failed Miguel, and that nothing she said would convince him otherwise, just as she understood why Miguel would never have accepted his help. They were too much alike. Only now that he was gone did Madeleine realize how much Miguel reminded her of her intriguing bodyguard, whose irreverent charm and innate sex appeal concealed a serious and responsible nature. His quick, adaptable mind never stopped working and was capable of an unsettling mixture of directness and complexity. The man had shrewd instincts, as well as a startling sensitivity that he seldom chose to reveal. And his pride—oh, his pride was merciless with him.

She knew that Miguel would never expect to be forgiven for what he had done to Ransom—not only the theft and the drugging, but also the betrayal—and she knew that Ransom had already forgiven him. In another reality, these two men could have been as close as brothers. But a bitter, hopeless poverty had shaped Miguel, just as ambition and opportunity had shaped Ransom, and so they were worlds apart.

She silently wished Miguel good luck as she poured Ransom a cup of black coffee and suggested he sit down.

"If I understand Señor Gutiérrez correctly, we won't have an easy time renting or even buying a car in Doragua," she announced without preamble.

Ransom thought it over. "Since the road from here to your plantation is bound to be as bad as what we encountered last night . . . Christ, can Miguel even make it to the border by himself?"

"He'll find a way. You would." He blinked at her, and she prodded, "You were saying?"

"Oh. Yeah." He fumbled in his pockets for a cigarette. "We'll have to call Veracruz. We'll have to tell him what's happened."

"I know." She could tell he wanted to give Miguel time to get away. "I'm sure Miguel planned on that, Ransom."

"Yeah. He would have." He frowned, took a long drag of his cigarette, then continued, "I say we tell Veracruz that we want the car you originally reserved from that rental agency. We need something reliable that can handle the road, especially if there's more rain. Veracruz can pay a driver to bring it out to us. I'll convince him that it's the least he can do."

"All right." She realized it meant they'd be stuck here for a day, but it was their best option. Besides wanting a better quality car than they were likely to find among the local farmers, they'd need something they could take back to the capital when they returned there in a few days.

"I'll go make the call," Ransom said without enthusiasm.

She put a hand on his arm. "You look awful. Why don't you go lie down for a couple of hours? I'll make the call."

He hesitated. "My Spanish is better."

"But my manners are better." Seeing that he wanted to give in, she urged, "Señor Gutiérrez can help me get through to the palace, and the operator there speaks English. All right?"

"All right," he agreed, still looking rather green around the gills. He turned and went upstairs without his usual predatory grace.

Madeleine watched him with concern, rather astonished

at the protective instincts coursing through her. It was ridiculous, really. She'd never met anyone less in need of protection than Ransom. Besides, she doubted he'd welcome it from her. Apart from their personal differences, it would insult his pride to be protected by a client.

The way it had insulted his pride to be abandoned by a nameless blonde after a one-night stand in Montedora City. How sordid it all was, she thought miserably. After a beginning like that, could two people ever . . . ever . . . What? she wondered in frustration. Flustered by the direction of her thoughts, she went in search of Señor Gutiérrez.

Eager to help his distinguished guests, despite the noisy scene they had staged at dawn, the señor was impressed to learn that Madeleine wanted him to help her phone the Presidential Palace. Although telephone connections had been restored after the storm, they weren't exactly reliable. Madeleine was cut off twice before she finally got a call through to the operator at the palace. The President was not available; he was at a meeting with Escalante at Seguridore headquarters. So Madeleine spoke to his secretary. The mild-mannered man she had met upon first arriving at the palace now took her message, expressed horrified astonishment at Miguel's desertion, and promised to inform the President of these events.

"We're at the Pensión Doragua," Madeleine shouted into the receiver. "In Doragua."

"Doragua? Yes, I know it. The army has troops stationed there."

Madeleine thanked the secretary for his help, hung up, and paid Señor Gutiérrez for the call. Then, feeling at loose ends, she offered to accompany Señora Gutiérrez on her morning shopping trip. Carrying a basket and two rough-woven sacks, they walked down the muddy street to a central square whose crumpled grandeur and fading beauty gave her a glimpse of Montedora's past.

Having seen nothing but rain, mud, and jungle last night, Madeleine now saw the soldiers that the President's secretary had mentioned. Some patrolled the town, some sat in the local café, and a cluster of them guarded the district governor's mansion. Though not as hated as the Seguridores, Madeleine knew they were not well-liked. Except for the officers, most of the soldiers came from poor families and had chosen the army as the only alternative to unemployment. Most of them were only interested in staying alive and collecting their pay, but some of them used their uniforms as an excuse to bully civilians, and there was no one to stop them.

Noticing how much attention her appearance attracted, Madeleine realized that Ransom would be annoyed with her when he learned she had gone out without him. A couple of soldiers stopped her and questioned her, demanding to see her passport. She pulled it out of the little purse she kept draped across her body and handed it over. They spent a long time looking at it. Señora Gutiérrez scowled at them, and several other villagers watched from a safe distance.

Madeleine didn't get worried until the soldiers demanded to see her money.

"Por que?" she asked coolly.

She didn't understand the answer completely. Something about wanting to make sure she had enough money to support herself and wouldn't try to seek work here. The pressure of the señora's hand on her arm warned her to be careful. Using her most queenly manner, Madeleine said, in halting Spanish, that she was a personal friend of El Presidente himself, and she didn't like all these questions. Nor did she think he would be pleased when she told him about it.

Seeing the soldiers start to look a little doubtful, Señora Gutiérrez spoke up. Madeleine lost the thread of the conversation after that, as several people spoke rapidly and all at once, but it seemed the soldiers were weighing their desire for some hard currency against the señora's repeated assurance that Madeleine really was a friend of the President's.

Finally, the soldiers backed down and let Madeleine and Señora Gutiérrez continue on their way. Her heart pounding with relief, Madeleine squeezed the señora's hand as they proceeded into the marketplace. Once they were safely lost in the crowd, the señora muttered angry comments about the soldiers and their greed.

Some of the villagers pressed Madeleine's hand, commented on her pretty hair, or smiled and tried to chat with her. One old man gave her a flower and patted her cheek, though she didn't understand a single word that came out of his toothless mouth. The friendliness of ordinary people reminded her that the greedy politicians and swaggering soldiers were not Montedora. The common people whose courage was expressed in endurance, who still had kind words for a stranger, and who suffered in ways she would never experience—they were Montedora. And that realization gave Madeleine a sneaking, surprising fondness for this scarred, sultry land.

Going from stall to stall, inspecting all the produce, and bargaining for a good price took a long time. Then the señora had to go to the bank. Madeleine waited for her outside, guarding their purchases. Despite the shade, the heat made her feel thirsty and light-headed. By the time they returned to the pensión, more than two hours after leaving it, she felt wilted.

Ransom was heading out the front door when they got

back. He stopped in his tracks and scowled at her. "I was just coming to find you! Where the hell have you been?"

"Shopping," she said, plodding past him with her sacks of produce. "You could offer to take one of these."

"Shopping?" he repeated, ignoring the heavy sack she tried to thrust at him. "Shopping?"

"Yes. You know—exchanging money for goods."

"You're not supposed to go anywhere without me," he snapped.

"You're feeling better, I see."

"Are you listening to me, Maddie?" His tone irritated her.

"Yes, I'm listening."

"Don't go wandering off without me again. I mean it."

"Fine," she snapped. It felt good to snap at someone; she hadn't realized how much tension was coiled in her belly from that encounter with the soldiers. For good measure, she snapped at him again. "Fine."

Señora Gutiérrez giggled at the expression on Ransom's face and said something about men and their silly demands. She tried to take the sacks from Madeleine, but Madeleine insisted on carrying them back to the kitchen for the old woman. When she came back out into the bar, Ransom had apparently decided to abandon the fight they'd been about to have.

"I'm hungry," he said instead. "What's for lunch?"

"It looked like twenty pounds of onions and carrots to me."

"I can hardly wait," he said. "Did you talk to Veracruz?"

"To his secretary." She recounted their brief conversation.

"Good. I think I'll call the palace again, though. Just to make sure someone has arranged the replacement car by now."

Madeleine went upstairs to shower off the sweat and dirt from her morning of shopping. When she came back downstairs, she found Ransom wandering restlessly around the veranda.

"There's no answer at the palace," he said, staring out at the jungle which began only a hundred yards away from the back of the pensión.

"No answer?" She frowned. "That's odd."

"It's weird. Even for Montedora, it's weird."

"Maybe the phone lines are down," she suggested.

He shook his head. "I asked the city operator. She said they're working. No one's answering."

"But they've got people on duty twenty-four hours a day. It's the Presidential Palace, the head of the national government," she said in bemusement. "How can—"

"I don't like it."

"What do you—"

"Let's turn on the radio."

He turned abruptly and went back inside. Madeleine followed him. He went behind the bar and turned on the ancient radio, tuning into one of Montedora's news stations—all of which were government-controlled. Madeleine couldn't follow the announcer's rapid, muffled Spanish and asked what was being said.

Ransom shook his head. "Nothing, really. It's just an agricultural report. Something about more foreign subsidies being made available in the Calentura Valley."

"They don't need subsidies there," Madeleine said with a disgusted sigh. "They're all big plantations, like mine. It's the small farmers who need—"

"Uh-huh."

Realizing he wasn't listening, and that her comments weren't relevant to the current situation, she stopped talking and sat down at the bar. After a few minutes, Ransom went upstairs and got a small twelve-band radio from his suitcase. He tuned into an English-language international broadcast and told Madeleine to listen to it.

An hour later, Señora Gutiérrez announced their lunch was ready on the veranda. Ransom asked her to bring it inside so he could stay by the pensión's radio and telephone. Curious about this request, Señor Gutiérrez came into the barroom and asked what was going on. After exchanging a few words with Ransom, he, too, sat down at the bar to eat his lunch.

Seeing that Ransom wasn't eating, Madeleine reminded him that, after the morning's unpleasant events, he should get some solid food into his stomach. He agreed absently and ate about half his meal before trying to phone the palace again. No answer.

The Montedorans were living under their fourth nonelected government in a row, and everyone knew it was only a matter of time before the elusive guerilla army of the Doristas mounted an offensive against Veracruz's regime. Neither the radio news nor the phone calls Ransom made to Montedora City suggested that the capital was under attack. Yet the palace had suddenly stopped answering the telephone.

Wondering if anyone else knew about this strange phenomenon, Señor Gutiérrez decided to stroll into the main square, where his friends would be gathering for coffee. Madeleine continued listening to world news, watching Ransom's quiet concentration with foreboding.

The señor returned an hour later, agitated and speaking so fast that Madeleine couldn't understand him. The expression on Ransom's face confirmed that it was alarming news.

"What?" she demanded.

"The army just cleared the streets and sent everyone home," he said. He asked Señor Gutiérrez to clarify something, then continued, "There's a curfew in effect until noon tomorrow."

"What?"

Señor Gutiérrez went to the kitchen to tell the news to his wife, daughters, and daughter-in-law. His married son and two grandchildren came inside, as did the other two guests of the pensión. Within minutes, a dozen people were gathering around the radio, which still rumbled with dull news about road construction and the First Lady's charity work.

"I don't understand," Madeleine whispered to Ransom.

"Neither do I," he murmured. "But something's happening."

"How—"

"Shhh, this is it." He turned up the radio. The room fell silent as the regular news broadcast was interrupted, everyone listening intently.

Unable to follow the announcement, Madeleine waited until Ransom turned to explain it to her. His expression was stark. "The entire country is under the same curfew as Doragua."

Her heart thudded. "Has the palace been attacked?"

"I don't know. Only the curfew was announced. No explanation."

"But that must mean—"

"Look, it might just mean that Veracruz has had an appendicitis attack. Or maybe there's been another assassination attempt. With two rebel forces and such an unstable government, they'd never announce any weakness or illness of his, but they'd be scared enough to shut down the country for a day or two."

She swallowed and nodded, realizing he was right. Things here were very different from what she was used to. There could be a dozen explanations. She mustn't jump to conclusions.

"Let's keep our heads, okay?" His voice was firm, calming.

"I will," she vowed.

He kissed her on the forehead.

The warmth of his lips on her skin, his hand on her arm, his soft breath stirring her hair . . . It comforted her even more than his sensible words. Surprised to feel her eyes mist, she ducked her head so he wouldn't see it and worry.

"Maddie?"

"I'm fine."

Whether or not he believed her, he squeezed her arm gently, then went back to his seat near the radio to listen for more information.

Señor Gutiérrez broke out a bottle of whiskey and started passing it around. Ransom lit up a cigarette. Madeleine took a chair by the window, avoiding the curious eyes of the children.

She was scared, she admitted to herself. They were in the middle of nowhere, in a country where they had no rights whatsoever. She didn't know what was happening at the Presidential Palace, or what effect it would have on her. For the first time, she truly understood the fear lurking in the faces of so many Montedorans. She understood their helplessness now, and she hated sharing it.

She must pull herself together. She couldn't help herself, or Ransom, or anyone else, if she let this lurking fear affect her judgment and her actions. She had told him she'd keep her head; she mustn't let him down. For now, that motivated her even more than not wanting to let herself down. She didn't think about why.

Madeleine saw them first, since she was still sitting by the window when they arrived an hour later. Four armed soldiers, all on foot. As they came up to the pensión and entered the front door, she wondered if they intended to occupy the building.

Clearly frightened, but summoning his courage, Señor Gutiérrez greeted them, identified himself as the proprietor, and asked what they wanted.

The officer in charge said something to one of his men, who nodded. Madeleine recognized the man as one of the soldiers who had questioned her in the street that morning. He pointed straight at her. The officer looked at her for a moment, then gave an order.

To Madeleine's horror, two soldiers seized her and started to haul her toward the door. Stunned beyond rational thought, her feet dragged as she babbled, "Wait! What are you doing? Wait! I'm not—"

Ransom had already moved to block their path, talking rapidly in Spanish which had suddenly grown a lot worse. The fourth soldier swung the butt of a rifle at him. He ducked and kept talking.

The officer put up a hand to forestall another attack on Ransom. Then he said, "I am Captain Morena. I speak English, señor."

"Surely there has been a mistake," Ransom said. "This lady is an American citizen. She has broken no laws."

"There is no mistake." Captain Morena's fat face was impassive, his tone cold and inflexible.

"What is the charge?" Ransom demanded.

"That is a classified matter."

"You cannot arrest this woman without—"

"Who are you to tell me what I can and cannot do?" The captain's tone became belligerent.

Seeing he had made a mistake, Ransom changed tactics. "You're quite right, Captain. My concern for the woman made me forget myself. You see, her father entrusted her to my care, and—"

"Why do you carry a gun?" Morena asked sharply, noticing the holster at Ransom's side. Two of the soldiers suddenly raised their rifles and pointed them straight at Ransom.

"Oh, please don't hurt him," Madeleine choked, still being restrained by one soldier. "Please."

"By whose authority do you carry this weapon?" Morena demanded, ignoring Madeleine.

"President Veracruz himself," Ransom said calmly. "I have papers signed by the President, here in my pocket. Would you like to see them?" He stood very still.

The captain gave a clipped order to one of his men. The man fumbled for Ransom's papers, then took away the Glock. He gave the papers to Morena, then unloaded the Glock; he handed the gun and Ransom's extra magazines to another soldier. Morena read the documents in question while the soldier continued searching Ransom with enough roughness to scare Madeleine even more. Ransom's face remained impassive as his pocket money and passport were taken away from him. The Smith & Wesson Bodyguard strapped to his ankle excited considerable comment. Madeleine had noticed before what a unique-looking weapon it was, beautifully engraved. Two of the soldiers apparently wanted it for themselves, and they started bickering. A barked order from their captain silenced them. Forgetting about the papers he was examining, Morena took the Bodyguard away from his subordinates, examined it with obvious pleasure, and then stuck it inside his waistband. He stared slyly at Ransom for a moment, fondling his new trophy with possessive fingers. If any of this worried Ransom, he wasn't letting it show.

Ransom's gaze focused on the documents in Morena's other hand. In a calm voice, he said, "As you can see, I am a special friend of El Presidente's, and I have his blessing to carry arms to protect Miss Barrington. Of course, if there are fines to be paid, we will gladly pay them . . ."

Money, Madeleine realized. Of course! The soldiers had wanted money earlier, and she had refused. But Ransom was getting control of the situation. Everything would be all right, she assured herself. Ransom knew what he was doing.

"A friend of Veracruz," Morena mused.

"That's right," Ransom said.

"You know him well?"

"Quite well. We dined with him only yesterday."

Morena grinned. "Only yesterday?" he repeated.

Ransom said nothing, watching the captain.

"You dined with him." Morena started laughing.

Something was wrong. Madeleine's stomach churned with renewed fear. Something was wrong.

Morena barked an order at his men. Two of them seized Ransom. The third kept hold of Madeleine. She heard the pounding of her own heart, a mad drumming in her ears. She was more frightened than she'd ever been in her life.

"A friend of Veracruz," Morena repeated, grinning hugely. He stepped forward and, without warning, brought his knee up with terrible force into Ransom's groin.

Madeleine screamed. Ransom collapsed, sagging between the two men who held him. Laughing, Morena slugged Ransom twice in the face and once in the stomach while his grinning subordinates watched. The children started crying. The Gutiérrez women turned away while their men watched in silent horror.

Morena took Ransom's chin in his hand and tilted his head up until their eyes met. Ransom glared at the captain with glittering green eyes.

"Still feel important?" Morena sneered.

Blood gushed out of Ransom's nose. "You're making a big mistake," he growled.

"It is you who are mistaken."

"Veracruz will—"

"You don't know, do you? It won't be publicly announced until tomorrow, when all is secure."

"What?" Ransom said warily.

Morena patted his cheek. "For the good of the people, for the good of Montedora, President Veracruz has relinquished his power to a more worthy man."

"A more . . . Oh, my God!" Madeleine blurted.

Morena grinned again. "At ten o'clock this morning, General Escalante took control of the government. And Veracruz's friends are now the enemies of Montedora."

"Shit," Ransom said.

Morena hit him again.

Ransom tried to fight back, and someone drove the butt of a rifle into his gut. Two soldiers dragged him outside and threw him down into the muddy road, where they began kicking him.

Madeleine was still screaming when he lost consciousness.

CHAPTER TWELVE

Everything hurt. His head, his face, his ribs, his belly, his arms, his groin. His groin . . . He vaguely remembered them throwing him down in the mud, then kicking the shit out of him. Mercifully, he remembered nothing after that. Nothing except Madeleine's screams.

Maddie!

Fear flooded him. He tried to sit up.

The exquisite pain and sudden dizziness forced a groan from him, and he fell back. God, it hurt.

"Stay still. Don't try to move just yet."

Her voice. Her beautiful voice. Her gentle hands on his skin, pressing his shoulders into the mattress as he stirred restlessly.

"Maddie?" he croaked.

He tried to open his eyes, but his body ignored his brain's commands.

"I'm here. I'm right here," she said.

Through the foul odors which surrounded them, he could smell her clean, womanly scent. He felt her hair brush his face as she leaned over him. With every ounce of strength he had, he raised his arm, found her head, and pulled her toward him. She resisted only for a moment, surprise tensing her muscles, then she relaxed. He rubbed his face against her neck, then buried it in the soft hollow between her breasts, where her blouse fell away as she bent over him. The lacy edge of her bra tickled his cheek.

He inhaled deeply and nuzzled her, wanting to

burrow into her. Soft, warm, fragrant, strong.

Madeleine.

The hand supporting his head gently rubbed the soreness at the nape of his neck. After a long, contented moment, she lowered his head back onto the mattress. And everything went black again.

Voices woke him. He couldn't understand what they were saying at first. He lay still, learning whatever he could without revealing that he was awake.

The woman's voice he finally identified as Madeleine's. Her Spanish wasn't good, but she got the point across. She wanted food, bandages, medicine, clean water, clean clothes, and a doctor, and she wanted them now. The gruff response was negative. She changed tactics, appealing to the guard's sense of decency. He apparently didn't have one. She didn't give up, though. She offered him a bribe. What did he want, she asked, money? She'd get money for him. How about her earrings? They were valuable.

The man told her what he wanted. Ransom doubted that Madeleine understood the vernacular, but the guard's tone made his meaning unmistakable.

There was a long pause. Worried, Ransom flexed and tensed, testing his muscles. God, he was sore!

"All right," Madeleine said in English, her voice weary. Then she switched to Spanish. "Bring me everything I have asked for, and then I'll—"

"Are you nuts?" Ignoring the protests of his body, Ransom shot off the bed, crossed their cell in three strides, grabbed Madeleine, and roughly shoved her behind him. "Over my dead body!"

"Ransom!" She gaped at him.

He turned to the guard, who had stepped back from the

heavy door, which was still ajar. The guard pointed the business end of a Colt .45 straight at Ransom's belly. Fixing the man with his meanest stare, Ransom told him in a garbled mixture of graphic Spanish and English what he would do to him if he ever laid a single finger on the woman.

"Ransom, don't antagonize him," Madeleine said. "You need—"

"*Entiendes,* you ugly sonofabitch?" Ransom growled.

Angry and shaken, the guard ordered him to step back. Testing him, Ransom stepped forward. Far enough to see what lay outside their cell: a small anteroom with a desk, the doors to three other cells, and a heavy door leading to the rest of the world. Getting out of this cell was possible. He could do it right now. But what lay beyond that door? He couldn't move until he knew.

"Please don't make him shoot you." Madeleine's voice was taut. "My first-aid abilities are very limited, especially under the circumstances."

The outside door opened. The guard looked away. Ransom didn't jump him, but he was tempted, so tempted. However, there was no point in escaping from this cell block if they'd be mowed down by guns the second they got out. So when another guard entered the anteroom, saw Ransom, and pointed his rifle at him, Ransom raised his hands, backed into his cell, and let them close and lock the door.

"Are you insane?" Madeleine snapped the moment they were alone.

He whirled on her, furious and scared. "Me? Have you lost your mind, offering to fuck one of the guards?"

"I'd have—"

"What—figured out some way to get out of it?" he snarled.

"I'd have thought of something."

"Don't be a fool, Maddie. Half a dozen of them could throw you on your back and gang-rape you until you passed out, and then keep on raping you, and you'd have no choice in the matter. And I couldn't stop them, because I'd be dead by then."

She gasped at that, but didn't back down. "Damn you! I was trying to help you—"

"You're not helping me by putting more bright ideas into their heads! Now that drooling bastard out there figures that I'm the only thing preventing you from giving him the blow job of his life." He took her by the shoulders, repressing the urge to shake her. He wanted her to listen. She had to understand how vulnerable she was. "Whatever fantasies he may have entertained about you, you just made them all seem possible, even if you never intended to keep your word."

"I'd have kept my word if I had to," she said stonily. "I don't know anything about medicine, Ransom. You've scarcely moved for two hours. For all I knew, you were dying! I'd have done anything to get what you needed! I had to . . . You might . . . I . . ."

Her voice broke. Tears welled up in her eyes and flowed down her cheeks.

"Oh, hell," he muttered, his heart aching at the sight.

"I couldn't bear . . ."

"Shhh, it's all right."

All the fight drained out of Ransom. He wrapped his arms around her and held her. Pride stiffened her spine for a moment, but then she gave in, buried her face against his bare shoulder, and wept openly. He rubbed her back and pressed gentle kisses into her hair, silently urging her to let it all out.

She was always so brave, so smooth, so focused, he hadn't even stopped to consider how frightened she must be, and how alone she had been since he'd been beaten unconscious back at the pensión. Her acceptance of the guard's proposition should have told him she had run out of ideas and was at the end of her rope.

"Maddie, Maddie . . ." he murmured against her hair. "I'm sorry, honey."

"Oh, God, the blood, all that blood . . ."

"Mostly from my nose," he guessed ruefully.

"And they just kept kicking you!" She pulled away, gulping back her sobs. Her nose was red. Tears streaked through the dust on her face. He tried not to grin at her appearance. "Are you badly hurt? Is anything broken?"

He took a deep, experimental breath and winced. "Definitely bruised. They didn't manage to break anything, though, for all their showing off. Amateurs."

"Amateurs?" She hiccupped.

He gave up and grinned. She scowled at him.

"Yeah, amateurs," he said, easing himself back down onto the little cot in the corner of their small, oppressive cell. "A good fighter can bust half your ribs with about a tenth of the effort those two guys put forth. They mostly got me in the legs and shoulders and . . ." He winced again and concluded, "And butt."

"And your head," she added shakily.

"What a hell of a day it's been," he grumbled.

"Quite." She sat down next to him, picked up a piece of torn cloth, and blew her nose.

"That's my shirt!" he said in surprise. He frowned. "Or what's left of it."

"They wouldn't give me any bandages, and I was trying to stop the bleeding." She looked him over. "There's a cut on your forehead, too, that bled all over your face."

"Oh."

"I don't think this shirt would have ever been the same, anyhow," she said.

"No, probably not," he conceded. She must have used her teeth to tear it into strips. "Everything happened so fast when I woke up and heard you talking to that guard, I didn't even wonder why I was half-naked."

He looked around. The cell was about the size of a small bedroom. The narrow cot and single chair indicated that it was intended for one occupant only. Madeleine must have convinced the guards to let her stay with him and tend his injuries. He hoped they wouldn't move her to her own cell now. He couldn't protect her if they were separated; even together, it would be touch and go.

A seatless toilet squatted at one end of the room, right next to a filthy sink. The toilet was probably the source of the odor he'd been noticing. He glanced at Madeleine and hoped she'd be able to set aside her modesty for practical considerations. He certainly could, and he said so.

"Oh. Now?" she asked.

"Uh-huh. Nature calls. Excuse me, milady."

He walked to the toilet and unzipped his muddy trousers. He glanced over his shoulder and saw that her back was discreetly turned. When he was done, he sat next to her on the cot again.

"Where are we?" he asked.

"Oh! Local army headquarters, at the south end of the village."

"What's the layout of this place in relation to where we are now?"

"I was so scared I probably missed a lot," she admitted.

She hadn't missed much, he concluded, after she spent

five minutes answering his questions. They were in the heart of a walled, wired military compound. The odds were against their escaping. Fear filled him, clouding his wits, because what he had said to her was true: she was in danger from these men. He had to get her out of here. But how? He had to pull himself together and think.

"It's all my fault," she blurted suddenly, surprising him.

"Why do you say that?"

"You were right. I should never have gone into town without you." She told him about her encounter with the soldiers. "If I hadn't attracted attention to myself, if I hadn't told them I was a friend of the President's, then none of this would have happened. They'd have never even known about us, if I had stayed inside the pensión. And you . . ." She added in a heartbroken tone, "You wouldn't be in this condition."

"Water under the bridge, Maddie," he said dismissively. "We wouldn't even be in Doragua if that terrorist attack in the city hadn't delayed the start of our trip. We wouldn't still be here if Miguel hadn't stolen the car. It doesn't do any good to—"

"If only I'd given them my money. Oh, why didn't I just give them my money?"

He took her hand. "Because most people raised in a democracy naturally object to military and government officials bullying them and stealing from them."

"But what would you have done?" she asked. "Would you have made a spectacle of yourself the way I did?"

"I doubt you made—"

"I did," she said morosely. "I was such a fool."

"Stop it," he ordered. "Pull yourself together. This isn't helping either of us." In fact, it was tearing his heart out. He couldn't stand to see her condemning herself like this, blaming herself for their imprisonment and his injuries.

"But I . . ." She swallowed and nodded. "Sorry. You're right. This isn't helping anyone."

He admired her resolve, knowing that she didn't summon it easily right now. "Hindsight is a waste. As far as anyone knew, you were doing the smartest, safest thing when you used Veracruz's name as a shield," he pointed out. "How the hell were you to know he would fall from power by lunchtime?"

"The meeting with Escalante!" she said suddenly.

"What?"

"When I called the palace this morning, Veracruz was at Seguridore headquarters for a meeting with—"

"Escalante set a trap for him," Ransom realized. "Away from the palace."

"Because you had made the palace too secure for Escalante to attack Veracruz there." After a pause, she asked, "Do you think he knew Veracruz was planning to get rid of him?"

"Hell, considering that even we knew, it seems likely that he found out. But I'd say he's been planning this for a while, and learning of Veracruz's plan probably only made him move sooner, that's all."

"What makes you think he's been planning this?"

"Captain Morena," he replied. "The army is supposed to be loyal to the President, not Escalante. Yet this army captain knows Escalante has seized power and knows that it won't be announced until tomorrow. And one of Morena's first moves was to act on a report by one of his men and arrest us—friends of Veracruz. Escalante has obviously been secretly securing support from army officers, probably with bribes and promises of promotion and power."

"That makes sense," she said slowly. "What do you

think Morena intends to do with us, though?"

"I don't know." He thought it over. "These cells are small and poorly guarded, and there are only four of them."

"So?"

"So I think this is just a temporary holding area, not a permanent prison." He gingerly rubbed the lump on his head. "Since Morena arrested us in the hope of garnering favor with Escalante, I'd say his next move is to notify Escalante that . . . Oh, shit." He met her eyes, and despite the fear he saw there, he had to be honest with her. "He'll notify Escalante that we're in custody. And Escalante hates me with a passion, Maddie."

"I know." Her voice was thin.

He shot to his feet. "We've got to get out of here."

"But we're Americans," she said. "Surely even Escalante wouldn't dare—"

"He can have a Seguridore blow us away with a Chinese-made AK-47 and claim that bandits got us after the President's chauffeur abandoned us in the hills." Ransom put the chair in front of the cell's single window, a little barred opening set high up in the wall. "He can get away with it, Maddie. We've got to get out of here."

"Can we?"

He climbed up on the chair, reached for the bars, and pulled himself up with the strength of his arms. One brief look was enough to assure him that it was useless.

"Not that way," he said. "Even if we could do something about the bars, it's a thirty-foot drop right into the central courtyard. Full of soldiers."

"What about—" She fell silent as they heard someone unlocking their cell door.

Ransom pushed Madeleine down onto the wooden chair and stood in front of her. A new guard—big, with a brutal face—opened the door, then stepped back. They heard Morena call him Alvarez. Then Morena entered the room, followed by two Seguridores. Ransom met their hard stares as the captain told the men that these were the prisoners and described with relish how they had resisted arrest.

One of the Seguridores was very young, and so handsome as to be almost pretty. He told Morena in clipped tones that the prisoners were to be ready for transportation to Seguridore headquarters first thing tomorrow morning, and that they expected the utmost discretion from the captain and his men. Moreover, they expected the prisoners to be in acceptable condition; Escalante wanted them for himself. The captain guaranteed it. He was practically kowtowing as the two men left the cell. Their voices could be heard briefly in the anteroom, giving similar, somewhat more explicit warnings to the two on-duty guards.

Then Morena turned and grinned at Ransom. "They were sent from their post in Santa Clara to escort you to Montedora City, and they tell me His Excellency President Escalante is pleased about the identity of my prisoners." He looked Ransom over for a moment, then remarked, "A private escort to Seguridore headquarters. Tell me, what did you do?"

"I made it hard for Escalante to kill Veracruz."

"Ahhhh." Morena wagged his finger at Ransom. "Choosing the winning side makes all the difference."

Ransom glanced down at the captain's ankle. "Ah. You took the ankle holster, too, I see. After I was unconscious, no doubt. How's the fit?"

"A little tight," Morena admitted. "You are too skinny."

"What a pity. And the gun?"

"The gun is more beautiful than a woman." Morena nodded. "I thank you for it."

"Oh, think nothing of it," Ransom said dryly.

Looking a little impatient, Madeleine asked, "Is Veracruz dead?"

"No, of course not," Morena answered reprovingly. "Think how that would look, señorita."

"Of course," she muttered.

"Veracruz gave Escalante a special escort into the Presidential Palace this morning, and then voluntarily confined himself to his private quarters with Señora Veracruz."

"Voluntarily," Madeleine repeated.

"Yes," Morena said, "after publicly recognizing his failure to lead the people of Montedora toward peace and prosperity."

"Then he ordered the Presidential Guards to turn in their arms and go home," Ransom said, "and he dismissed his cabinet."

Morena blinked. "That has not been announced yet. How did you know?"

"Just an educated guess."

"I see." Morena eyed him warily for a moment, apparently losing his sense of humor. "You will leave at first light. Do not cause me trouble, or I will deal harshly with you."

"As opposed to the restraint you have so far shown?" Ransom said.

"Vaya con Dios," Morena replied cheerfully, then turned and left. The guard—Alvarez—closed the door behind him.

"Gosh, we're gonna miss his wit around here." Ransom met Madeleine's gaze and instantly abandoned his levity.

"What do we do now?" She kept her voice even.

He appreciated her determination to stay calm; he could guess what it cost her. He put his hand on her neck and gave it a brief, comforting squeeze. "Now we plan our escape."

"Should we wait until morning and try to make a break for it when the Seguridores take us outside the compound?"

He shook his head. "I don't think so. They might, uh, disable us before they remove us from here. The Seguridores are elite forces, better paid, better equipped, and undoubtedly better trained than the army. They'll be harder to escape or eliminate."

Madeleine shivered at his reference to eliminating other men, but he needed to think like a professional, and he needed her help if they were going to escape. Still, there was no reason to frighten her with details of how the Seguridores might "disable" them.

"Anyhow," Ransom continued, "just because we've only seen two Seguridores, that doesn't mean there won't be more tomorrow."

"So we'll try to escape tonight?" She looked tense.

He nodded. "Sometime after midnight. In the empty hours. Men are less alert then." He gazed pensively at the ceiling, wishing he had a cigarette. "We'll need a plan."

To Madeleine's surprise, Alvarez brought them dinner a couple of hours later. With so many hungry people in Montedora, she didn't understand why the army bothered feeding two prisoners who were destined to disappear forever tomorrow; people taken to Seguridore headquarters were never seen again. Despite her churning stomach, the stuffy heat, her revulsion over the way Alvarez leered at her, and the unpleasant odors in their cell, she followed Ransom's orders and ate a little of the food—beans and rice—since they had no idea when they'd have an opportunity to eat again.

After their bowls were taken away, Ransom suggested she lie down on the narrow cot and try to get some sleep. If their plan was successful, they'd be on the run by morning and would need all their strength.

That "if" kept her wide awake, though.

They had argued heatedly before settling on a plan. Ransom's original scheme would have put him in danger while she hid in their cell. Her passionate declaration that she'd rather die than be stuck here alone after he got himself killed was the argument that finally overcame his stubborn refusal to let her help him.

If they disarmed their two guards and made it out of this cell block, if they got past the soldiers on guard duty, if they could get beyond the garrison walls, if they could make it out of the village without getting shot . . .

If they succeeded, they'd be penniless fugitives in an unstable, impoverished country whose new leader wanted them dead. If they failed, they'd be shot trying to escape, or else turned over to the Seguridores in the morning.

How had Caroline described the fate of Escalante's victims? Arrested, beaten, tortured and—if they were not executed—locked up in some dank, rat-infested cell and forgotten about.

She wished Caroline hadn't felt compelled to tell her about it. Now she couldn't stop imagining it. Who would have thought that she would become one of Escalante's victims? But, for once, even being a Barrington couldn't protect her. Escalante could indeed get away with it. No one would ever know the truth.

Her dinner churned in her stomach. She shifted restlessly, fighting her terror.

"What's wrong?" Ransom murmured. He was sitting on the floor, his back resting against the cot, his head leaning back. She shifted again, so that his hair brushed her arm. He turned his head slightly to look at her. Night had fallen, and they could scarcely see each other now; there was no light or lantern in their cell.

"Just thinking about something my sister said," she answered, recalling Caroline's warnings again.

He evidently sensed it upset her. "Tell me."

To her amazement, she didn't tell him what Caroline had said about Veracruz and Escalante. Instead, she heard herself saying, "She said . . . Both of my sisters said they're tired of me being . . . so perfect."

After making such a huge admission, she was surprised to hear him say casually, "Oh. And here I thought I was the only one who got tired of it."

"What do you mean?"

"Well, sometimes you really piss me off," he said mildly.

"Spoken by a man with the personality of steel wool," she shot back.

"Are you calling me abrasive?" He sounded amused.

"Attila the Hun was probably an easier companion." She sighed reminiscently, remembering her first impressions of him. It seemed so long ago. "You know, you were a perfect stranger."

"And you," he said, "have never been perfect, no matter how hard you try."

The vehemence in his tone made her say defensively, "I've never . . . I don't try . . ."

"Don't you?" he challenged.

"I'm just trying to do my best. Be my best."

"Sometimes," he conceded. "It took me a while to come round to admitting that. But you also like to hide behind that shield of perfection, using it to intimidate people, to make them keep a respectful distance from you."

It hurt. She was stunned at how much it hurt. More than Caroline's criticism, more than Stephanie's hostility, Ransom's matter-of-fact appraisal of her character hurt.

As if aware of this, he reached for her hand and drew it to his cheek. He kissed it softly, taking the sting out of his words. "You don't need to be perfect, you know. Or is the thought of being just another flawed human being who makes mistakes too terrible to contemplate?"

"I don't like making mistakes."

"No one does, but we survive it."

"Not necessarily," she remarked.

"Oh, come on, do you really think it's your fault that we're here?"

"Yes."

"Let me tell you something, Maddie. Shit happens. You can write that down, if you want. You can't control everything. This time, we're just stuck playing the cards we were dealt."

"You're a fine one to say that. Blaming yourself for Miguel, blaming yourself for Escalante's revenge, blam—"

"I never said anything about—"

"You don't have to. I know you. You're stewing about how I'm going to die at Seguridore headquarters because Escalante hates you." His silence was admission enough. Smiling faintly, she stroked his hair, wishing she could see his expression. "We're more alike than you admit, Ransom." He relaxed after a moment and tilted his head to invite another caress. She obliged, but added wryly, "And certainly more alike than I would like to admit."

"I've got better biceps," he said, reacting like a big cat to her caress.

"I have better manners," she pointed out.

"You're just repressed," he shot back.

"Well . . ." She sighed. "I suppose that's another way of putting it. My father taught me to always do my duty. My mother taught me to be a lady. That didn't leave a lot of room for . . . free expression."

"You express yourself pretty freely to me." He added dryly, "Especially when it's something I don't want to hear."

"That's true," she said slowly, surprised. Yes, she said things to Ransom she'd never dream of saying to anyone else. And not only criticisms, either; she admitted and revealed things to him that she shared with no one else.

"Still," he mused, "I suppose it describes you pretty well, on the outside: a perfect lady who dutifully shoulders burdens that would make most men—most people—tremble."

"I tremble," she admitted, her voice barely a whisper. "But no one sees."

He took her hand and held it against his chest, so that her arm draped across him. "I see," he assured her. "I saw it the first time I looked at you. I see it every time you're willing to let me see it. Even sometimes when you're not."

She took a shaky breath. Her hand quivered in his.

"That scares you, doesn't it?" he probed.

After a pause, she admitted, "Everything about you scares me."

"You're afraid of me? Why? Jesus, Maddie, what have I ever done to make you afraid of me?" He tightened his grip on her as he drew a sharp breath. "Are you afraid I'll talk about that night?"

She knew which night he meant. "Would you?"

"No! Of course not."

"But you said—"

"I know what I said," he snapped. "I was mad enough to bite someone that day. I only said it because . . . Shit."

"Why?" she prodded, listening alertly.

"Because . . . I knew it would scare you." He lowered his

head. "I was fighting dirty. And I'm . . ." He drew in a steadying breath. "I'm sorry."

She took her time before saying, "Apology accepted."

"Are you smiling?" he asked suspiciously.

"Maybe."

"Well . . . Some men talk, but not me."

"Oh, really? You told me about that woman," she challenged.

"What woman?"

"The one you slept with the night before we left New York."

"Oh, Gwen."

"That's her name? Gwen?" she pounced.

"Yeah, that's her name. And I didn't tell you about her. All I said was—"

"But what if I'd said I did want you to tell me about her?"

"You wouldn't have."

"But if I did?"

"I wouldn't have told you," he said impatiently. "What goes on between a man and woman is their own business and nobody else's. I don't kiss and tell. Got it?"

She relaxed. "Got it."

"But there you were, making damn sure I knew that what's-his-face had slept in your bed that night—"

"Graham. And it was his idea to make you come up to the apartment. I didn't want you to know about my private life."

"I can't believe . . . I mean, how can . . ."

"Yes?"

He blurted, "Are you really gonna marry that guy?"

"No."

"No?" he repeated. "No?"

"No."

"No?" Her answer seemed to incense him. "What do you mean, no?"

"You sound like you had your heart set on giving me away at the wedding."

"No, but I was trying to get used to the idea that you belonged to some other guy, and now you're telling me—"

"Belonged?" she repeated in an awful voice. "Marrying someone and becoming someone's personal property are two different things, Ransom, and the latter has been illegal in the U.S. for over—"

"You know what I mean!"

"I don't like the way you phrase it!"

"Why aren't you going to marry that twit?"

"Because I don't love him!" she hurled at him.

"Oh." He mulled that over, then repeated, sounding rather pleased, "Oh."

"Satisfied? Is that a good enough reason for you?"

"Well, don't you think you should tell the poor sonofabitch? He seems to think you're going to marry him."

"I really hate it when you use that tone," she said through clenched teeth. "And, yes, I'm going to tell him when I get back to New York." She paused. "Oh, God. If I get back to New York."

"You'll get back. I have no intention of dying in Montedora." He kissed her hand again, trying to reassure her.

"And you?" she asked hesitantly. "Is there someone waiting for you back home?"

"A woman, you mean? No."

"What about—"

"That's over," he said briefly.

"Over?"

"Uh-huh."

"You slept with her just three nights ago, and now—"

"We said good-bye that night."

"Oh." She thought it over. She had to ask. Nothing could have prevented her from asking. "Was she someone special? Did you . . . Were you in love with her?"

She felt him shake his head. She tightened her grip on his hand, feeling the coolness of his ring against her flesh.

"It was just . . . Oh, Christ, Maddie, how much sleazier do I have to get in your eyes?"

"What?"

"It was just sex, okay? I mean, I liked her, but basically, we got together for sex. We were both single, busy, lonely . . ."

"And randy." Surprised at her own comment, she laughed.

"That, too," he admitted dryly.

"Just sex," she murmured. "I couldn't do that."

"It's not the best," he conceded, "but it was enough until . . ."

"What?"

"Until I met you," he said in a rush. "I could always . . . keep sex separated from everything else. It was easy. Things were simple, my head was clear. But you . . . you confuse everything."

"I do?" Her heart started beating harder.

"Oh, yeah." His response was heartfelt.

"I don't mean to."

"I know. Doesn't make a difference."

"I knew I confused Graham, because I was so unfair to him."

"My heart just bleeds for him."

"But not you. You never seem confused."

"Then you're just not paying attention."

"Oh, I pay attention," she assured him. "How could I not?"

"To me?"

"All of the time," she whispered, frightened by her own honesty. Why did she always give him more ground?

"Maddie, did you . . ." He hesitated, and she felt his tension before he finally said, "Did you ever think about me after the night we spent together?"

Madeleine could hear her blood thundering in her ears as he waited for her answer. "All of the time," she whispered at last. "Did you?"

She knew what would happen now. They shouldn't do this. He should rest his battered body, she should go over their plan again in her mind, they should focus on their escape. But all of that faded into insignificance as she felt him turn towards her. She shifted her position to accommodate him.

"Yes," he whispered. "All of the time."

And he reached for her.

CHAPTER THIRTEEN

This is crazy, she thought, welcoming his weight with open arms and an open heart. Someone could come through that door at any minute. The guards had no reason to bother them again tonight, but that didn't mean they wouldn't. And the bed was narrow and sagging, and they were both filthy, and the hot cell stank with ancient odors she preferred not to think about. She knew he was more injured than he was willing to admit to her, and they were going to risk their lives in a few short hours.

Yes, it was crazy, but she didn't even hesitate as he found her in the dark and kissed her deeply.

I may die tonight.

The realization was sharp and stirring, and this was her last meal. If something went wrong, then she wanted to die with the taste of this man on her mouth, the scent of his skin on her skin, and the feel of his thrusts still aching sweetly inside her body.

He held her face in his hands. The darkness hid their expressions from each other.

"I wish I could see you," he whispered, arching his hips into hers.

She felt his erection stir between her legs, and she ground herself against it, so relieved to feel him in her arms at last. How had she waited so long for this? How had she borne all those nights without him?

Hungry for him, starving for him, she kissed him until she thought her lungs would burst, then pressed her face against his bare chest, inhaling him with fevered pleasure. His kisses were demanding, almost frantic. She struggled to get closer, to have more of him. They nipped and bit, aggressive and clumsy in their passion. He started pushing her slip-on blouse up over her arms and head, and she arched her back to help him, longing to be naked with him. Then he sighed and got distracted. His mouth was hot on her breast and his hands fumbled with her bra, while her arms tangled overhead in the gauzy sleeves of her blouse. Her face was smothered in its folds.

"Ransom," she squawked in a muffled voice, choking on the fine material.

"Hmmmm? God, you taste good."

She moaned when his mouth closed over her nipple, trembled and sighed as he sucked, squirmed under the rough stroking of his tongue. His hand slid between her legs. She thought she might suffocate. She made a strangled sound of pleasure.

"Oh! Sorry." He pulled the blouse over her head. "My mistake."

"You used to be smoother," she chided, catching her breath and going after his zipper.

"I'm under stress tonight," he reminded her, unfastening her trousers and pulling them down.

"Not on the floor!" she cautioned, grabbing at her pants before he could toss them aside. "God only knows what's been on that floor."

"All right, all right." He shoved all her clothes into the corner behind her head.

She sighed with pleasure and relief when he kicked away his mud-caked pants and she felt the length of his naked body relax against hers. The scattered rough hair on his legs teased her skin. The hair on his chest abraded her breasts, and the contrast delighted her. The smooth warmth of his back, shoulders, and buttocks drugged her senses as she stroked and caressed and reveled in him. His arms were like steel bands around her, possessive and impassioned and excitingly male. His mouth was greedy and wet and restless as he kissed and nibbled and devoured her. Every touch, every whisper, every desperate sigh took her further and further away from herself as she journeyed deeper and deeper into him.

"Now," she murmured. "Now, now, now."

She used her hands and hips to show him exactly what she wanted. It was so easy. She felt so free and uninhibited, so outside of herself and all the wearisome strictures of being Madeleine Barrington. With the merest touch, he had helped her shed all of that, and nothing was left but the essential woman, unburdened and unashamed.

He murmured something unintelligible when she found him with grasping fingers. Breathing raggedly and kissing her over and over, he let her lead him where she would, entrusting himself to her less-than-gentle handling. He took the long, deep ride she invited him on, finding his way with no hesitation or awkwardness, filling her with perfect, stunning intimacy. It was more than she could bear in silence. But Ransom put a hand over her mouth to stifle her soft cry.

"I don't want them to hear you," he whispered, trembling with restraint.

Eyes squeezed shut with that combination of agonizing pleasure and exquisite torment that he himself had taught her, she rolled her head back and forth, swallowing her moans as he held himself taut and still above her.

"Quietly," he murmured against her hair.

Desperate and impatient, she shifted her hips against

him, moving with a mindless rhythm she couldn't control. He ruthlessly pressed her down and held her still.

"Quietly," he repeated, nipping her ear. "All right?"

Helpless beneath his weight and his strength, she squirmed restlessly in the dark, her eyes misting as emotion and sensation tore her apart. She was imploding, heat coursing through her, rushing toward the pulsing core of her body. Her muscles contracted in secret, sacred places, massaging him, milking him.

"Oh, Jesus," he choked. "Jesus, Maddie." His whole body shook and lost its rigidity in a sudden, convulsive movement. His hand slid away from her mouth and into her hair.

"Ransom," she moaned, unable to stop herself. "Ran—"

His hand covered her mouth again, roughly this time, squeezing her jaw and pressing her head into the mattress. She wrapped her arms and legs around him, clinging to him, rising off the bed and then crashing back down into its sagging frame as he thrust into her, his self-control shattered and forgotten.

They struggled together in darkness, her cries silenced by the hand clamped over her mouth, his own groans choked back by sheer effort of will. Tears crept past her tightly shut lids. Everything she thought she knew about herself gave way to everything she really was, as she heaved and strained and fought for satisfaction, locked together with this man in the most primitive embrace of her life.

She climaxed with stunning force, her limbs melting, her spine arching, her whole body going blindingly hot in a long, violent orgasm. She felt him shuddering in her arms, his hips pumping compulsively as he came, his teeth sinking into her as he tried to stay silent. His palm pressed even harder over her mouth, smothering her moans until they finally subsided into soft, breathless sighs. And by then, he was too weak to have silenced her anyhow.

She lay quiescent beneath his limp body, slick with sweat, gulping for air as frantically as he did, still holding him so closely she couldn't tell their thunderous heartbeats apart.

She turned her head slightly. He shifted in the dark, and pressed his forehead against hers.

After a long moment, he breathed, "I wish I could see you."

She had never known Ransom to be silent for so long when he wasn't actually asleep. And she knew by the rhythm of his breath and the occasional caresses he passed down her body that he was wide awake.

She lay with her back against his chest, his arms around her, the tickling hair and velvety flesh of his loins pressed intimately against her bottom. Occasionally he stroked a hand down her hip and thigh, or moved his head forward to kiss her shoulder. Every so often, he rubbed his palm across one of her breasts, squeezing gently, lightly tracing the areola. He'd kept her in this dreamy state of semi-arousal for what seemed like hours. The slow burn he was creating, however, didn't succeed in eliminating a thousand terrifying thoughts.

"How much longer?" she whispered, needing to say something, to hear him say something.

She felt the slight tensing of the muscular body which lay pressed against her. He shifted a little to study the tiny patch of night sky outside the barred window overhead. The soldiers had stolen his wristwatch after beating him unconscious.

"Another hour," he said, "hour and a half."

Limp with pleasure, she practically purred when he smoothed his palm over her stomach, paused briefly at the triangle of hair between her legs, and then massaged her hip.

I may die tonight. But it was hard to dwell on her fears when he gently massaged her neck and shoulders with expert hands. He did that for a few minutes, soothing her, and then she felt his soft kisses in her hair or on her back. She pressed her bottom against him and closed her eyes.

But he was so quiet, so unusually quiet. Was he as shaken as she was by what had just happened between them? Could he possibly be a little scared, too, for a change?

Everything inside her was trembling. At its best, she had known sex as a pleasurable act—until Ransom. With him, it was something more, and she was someone more.

She thought of herself struggling blindly with him on this ragged cot in this stinking cell, greedy and shameless and eager. Hungry and yearning and torn apart by emotion. Pierced by tenderness when he kissed her, erotically charged when he held her down and smothered her cries, soaring with pleasure and power when he shuddered and trembled in her arms. Even now, she'd be more comfortable pretending that she wasn't that wildly emotional, abandoned woman. But she knew he wouldn't let her pretend, and she couldn't slip away from him anonymously this time.

Even now, she'd be more comfortable pretending it was all him, and nothing to do with her. But she knew from the things he'd said tonight that this heat between them surprised him, too. It wasn't just him or just her; it was them.

Why this man, she wondered? He was so different from what she looked for in a man. He was irreverent and impertinent, frequently ill-mannered, resentful of authority, contemptuous of courtesy, dismissive of elegance, and, yes, cavalier about sex.

And what about the woman with whom it was "over"? Had it really been "just sex" for her? Or had Ransom broken her heart? No point in asking; even if he knew, she doubted he'd ever tell her.

She sighed restlessly, wishing she felt in control of her relationship with Ransom—yet sensing that her inability to control him was precisely what made him so special.

Madeleine's restless sigh cut through Ransom like a knife. She'd been silent for so long. Nothing but a brief question about when they'd leave, and then that sigh.

Did she want to slip away from him again?

The only thing he hated more than that thought was the heartache and panic he felt after thinking it.

Why this woman, damn it?

Yeah, the sex was incredible. He hadn't blown it out of proportion in his mind. Tonight had been even more incredible than his memories. It kind of scared him, because he was honest—and experienced—enough to admit he probably wouldn't get past it. What else would ever be enough to satisfy him after her?

For a moment, he wished he'd never met her.

And then he buried his face in her hair and thanked fate and all his lucky stars that he'd met her, and that he'd found her again after losing her.

But why her? Why this elusive, arrogant, stubborn, and secretly vulnerable woman? Why this woman, who was never impressed by the things that impressed other women, and who unfailingly zeroed in on the things he least wanted her to notice?

He'd like to pretend it was just the great sex they shared that enthralled him, but he was too honest for that. It was the way he felt after sex that really rattled him.

He'd never been the type to just roll over and fall asleep afterwards, and he wasn't a callow jerk who fucked and forgot women. He usually felt some kind of affection, or he wouldn't be in bed with the woman in the first place.

But he'd never felt so tender that his throat hurt, so exposed and vulnerable that the wrong words from his lover could crush him. He'd never before felt like he'd be happy just to lie here and hold her forever. He'd never wanted to ask a woman everything about herself, and just listen to her pillow talk all night long. He'd never felt that he'd gladly give everything, including his life, just to keep her safe—he, who knew quite well what it meant to put his life on the line for someone.

And while he lay here feeling like this, was she lying there wishing she could escape from him again?

God, he wanted a cigarette! But the soldiers had taken those away, too, after beating him senseless.

Thinking of the beating reminded him of his aches and pains. He was hurt worse than he'd admitted to Madeleine. And all of that hugging and heavy breathing they'd done tonight hadn't helped his ribs any, though he didn't regret a moment of it. He inhaled deeply and winced. Yeah, he was hurt, but not enough to interfere with what he had to do tonight.

Madeleine shifted restlessly, distracting him. His arm tightened involuntarily around her waist, as if he were afraid she'd try to disappear on him again.

Like last time.

He had to know. He had to ask.

"Why . . ." He stopped cold, his chest aching. Shit. He still couldn't say the words, couldn't ask. Not right now. So he asked instead, "What are you thinking about?"

"I was wondering . . ." She paused, and he sensed that she changed her mind, too, about what to say. "What's your first name?"

He was surprised into a puff of laughter. "Not telling."

"Come on."

"No way."

"But—"

"Forget it. Sex hasn't made me that softheaded."

"Hmmph." After a moment, she asked, "Have you ever been married?"

"Married?" he repeated, stunned.

"Uh-huh."

"No." He paused. "Of course not."

She shifted a little. "What do you mean, 'of course'?"

"Well, if I'd ever gotten married, then I'd have a wife now and I wouldn't be in bed with you—if we can call this thing a bed."

She relaxed against him again as she said, "You could be divorced."

"No, I couldn't," he said dismissively.

"Why not?"

"Because if I swore to love, honor, and cherish a woman until I died, then that's what I would do."

"People change," she murmured. "I know so many divorced women my age, sometimes it feels like I've merely skipped my first marriage." She turned her head slightly. "No one can see into the future, after all."

"That's true. But I believe in keeping promises. And marriage is a pretty important promise." He stroked her hip. "When did Graham ask you to marry him?"

"About a month ago," she answered, sounding surprised. "Why?"

"And you've been thinking it over ever since then, right?"

"Ransom, I already told you, I've decided not to—"

"What I mean is," he said, smiling at her exasperated tone, "you treated it seriously."

"Well, of course."

"Maybe you took your time because you know marriage isn't like . . ." He searched for an example. "Isn't like your plantation here. It's not something you keep while it's convenient, and then get rid of one day because it's become too much trouble."

"My plantation!" She sat bolt upright, forgetting their discussion. "The German buyers!"

"When are they due?"

"Tomorrow. Late morning, I think."

"Their flight may not even come into Montedora. And if it does, they'll turn around and leave as soon as they realize what's happening here. Unless they're idiots." He leaned his forehead against her arm and added in a low voice, "But I don't think they'll find out what's happened to you, either way."

"My family will be frantic," she said, her voice growing pensive. "Yours, too, I imagine."

"Yes. But we're gonna make it," he whispered, sitting up next to her. "I promise." He pressed a soft kiss on her cheek.

"You promise?" she repeated, her voice wry as his hands roamed freely. "Didn't you also promise never to touch me again?"

"Oh, that was different." He started pulling her back down into the mattress with him.

"Different how?"

"I was lying." He nuzzled her.

She chuckled—then drew in a sharp breath. "You need a shave."

"Sorry." He pulled away. "Did I—"

"Come back here," she commanded, her touch as firm as her tone. He smiled and obeyed.

Madeleine's body was still flushed with pleasure, her heart still trembling with tenderness as she pulled her clothes on in the dark. Strange that his extreme gentleness left her even weaker than his roughness had. Shaky and distracted, she tried to concentrate.

She sat down on the cot for a moment. Lying there, once again wearing his pants and shoes, he found her hand.

"You can do this," he said.

"I can do this." She called upon years of self-discipline.

He squeezed her hand.

"Are you ready?" she asked.

"Yeah." As she rose from the cot, he murmured, "Take your time. Do it when you're ready."

Alvarez didn't like guarding prisoners, and he especially didn't like working the night shift. This was the dullest assignment in Doragua. And his new partner, Rivera, a skinny kid from some obscure mountain village, was about as interesting as overcooked rice. Instead of playing cards or talking about women, Rivera used these dreary hours to try to teach himself to read. He'd gotten some silly-looking book from the local mission last month, and he routinely spent these dull night-duty hours absorbed in it, squinting at its pages in the dim light given off by the overhead lamp. The only relief from the monotony was when the kid drove Alvarez crazy by doing his reading exercises aloud.

Alvarez sighed and picked his teeth, trying to stay awake. He much preferred patrolling the streets, especially in daylight when the pretty girls were out, shopping with their mamas or flirting with single men (upon being transferred far away from his family, Alvarez had prudently removed his wedding ring). However, without enough money or black market goods to pay the necessary bribes, he couldn't get the assignment of his choice. So he was stuck guarding prisoners until his finances improved.

Bored beyond measure, Alvarez got up and paced around the guardroom. This was the hardest part of the shift, these empty hours before dawn. No man was meant to be awake and working at this ungodly time of night.

He could amuse himself with that pretty blonde woman locked up inside Cell Three tonight, he supposed. When he had relieved Blanco from duty, Blanco had said the woman would be easy, if she could be separated from the man.

Alvarez considered it. No, he decided, it might be too risky. He wasn't worried about the American man imprisoned with the woman, despite Blanco's warnings; Blanco was a fool and a coward. Alvarez had already heard that the American had been too badly beaten during his arrest to cause any more trouble. Upon seeing the prisoner before the sun went down, Alvarez realized that it was true. There was a pile of bloody rags on the floor, a deep cut on the man's forehead, and dark, ugly bruises forming on his battered face and his naked torso. No, he wouldn't be hard to handle if Alvarez decided to take the woman away from him.

But the Seguridores . . . Alvarez almost shivered. Though he had once shot someone for calling him a coward, he was honestly afraid of the Seguridores. Any sane man would be. And their orders to him had been very clear:

The prisoners were not to be damaged. General Escalante—Escalante himself!—expected to receive them in prime condition.

Even if you didn't beat them, sometimes it was fun to goad prisoners; it was a way to relieve the boredom. But these were Escalante's prisoners. Special. Off-limits. And so Alvarez had left the heavy steel door closed, not even peeking at them through the little eye-level security flap. A couple of hours ago, he thought he'd heard the bedsprings squeaking faintly on the other side of the cell's heavy door, and he'd wondered if the man was fucking the woman. He had gotten up to look, but Rivera had timidly reminded him they were told not to bother the prisoners.

Alvarez had felt like punching him, but he'd sat back down, afraid the kid might cause trouble. Anyhow, the squeaking was over almost as soon as it began, and the man hadn't made any noise, so maybe they weren't doing anything after all. The man was probably in too much pain to think about screwing.

Still, it seemed a shame to waste such a pretty woman. Someone ought to enjoy her tonight. She'd be dead in a few days, anyhow. Prisoners never came out of Seguridore headquarters alive.

But what if she resisted him? What if he had to knock her around a little? Women could be so difficult sometimes. Would the Seguridores punish him if the woman got a little damaged tonight? And what about Rivera? Would the kid make trouble for him?

Alvarez was scratching himself in indecision when the woman's screams erupted from inside the cell. He jumped like a scalded cat. Rivera dropped his book. They looked at each other in confusion. The woman kept screaming. Loud, hysterical, awful screams.

Alvarez picked up the flashlight on the desk, went to the cell door, and opened the security flap. It was very dark inside the cell. He couldn't see anything. The woman's screams were piercing. He started shouting at her to shut up. She came up to the door, still screaming. She babbled at him in English. He shouted that he didn't understand. She tried to say something in Spanish. Her Spanish was awful. Rivera was hopping around behind him, demanding to know what was wrong. Finally, Alvarez heard a recognizable word come out of the woman's mouth.

Muerto!

Dead!

The American man was dead?

Escalante's special prisoner had died in their care? Alvarez felt his bowels turn to water. Fear made him want to vomit. The Seguridores wouldn't ask questions when they found out. No, they would simply shoot him.

"What'll we do? Mother of God, he's dead! Oh, no, what'll we do?" Rivera shouted.

It's not fair, Alvarez thought desperately. I wasn't the one who beat him!

The woman kept screaming: *Muerto! Muerto! Muerto!*

Alvarez thought his head would explode. "He's not dead!" he snapped. "He can't be!"

"You said he was badly beaten!" Rivera fretted. "He died! He died, and the Seguridores will blame us!"

"He's not dead! She's just a stupid woman! Maybe he fainted or something."

"They'll kill us," Rivera cried. "The Seguridores will kill us!"

"Shut up!" Alvarez shone his flashlight around the cell. He thought the man was lying on the bed, but he couldn't be sure. "I can't see! I can't see! This stupid woman is in the way! Do you speak any English?"

"No!"

"How can we tell this stupid woman to get out of the way?"

Her Spanish was improving. She screamed, "You killed him!"

Alvarez wanted to throw up. He unholstered his Colt .45 and ordered Rivera to unlock the cell door. A moment later, he shoved the woman out of his way, telling Rivera to keep an eye on her. She flung herself at the kid, screaming and weeping. Alvarez flashed his light toward the bed. Yes, the man was lying there—still and pale as death.

Oh, God, oh, God, oh, Mother of God, blessed Virgin, please, please let it not be so, please, don't—

He saw the man move suddenly, but he never saw the blow that knocked him unconscious.

Madeleine had managed to maneuver the second guard so that his back was to Ransom. This was the part of the plan that Ransom hated. No matter how many times he timed it in his mind, it always worked out to eight seconds between the moment he made his first move and the moment he reached the second guard. And Madeleine was vulnerable for those eight seconds. Anything could happen.

But she'd done everything exactly as planned, and things went as smooth as glass. With his back to the dark cell and Madeleine's well-feigned hysteria distracting him, the second guard never realized until the very last second that something had gone wrong. And then Ransom drove the butt of Alvarez's gun into his head.

Madeleine's screams stopped abruptly. Ransom stripped the skinny guard of his shirt, holster, and gun, threw him into the cell with Alvarez, and closed and locked the door.

"That worked like a charm," he said, rather pleased.

"Oh, my God." Madeleine looked like she was going to be sick.

"Not now," he told her, tossing her the cell door keys. "Check the other cells, just in case someone else is locked up in here."

Pale and shaking, she did as ordered while he slipped into the skinny soldier's shirt and buckled on his holster. He secured the Colt .45 to his side, then searched the room for more weapons and ammunition, all the while keeping his eye on the door. The guards had left two Russian AK-47s lying carelessly against the wall. Ransom took the loaded magazine out of one, stuffing it into his pocket, then grabbed the other rifle. The desk yielded up a few useful items: more ammunition, another gun, and cigarettes. Ransom smelled the packet as ardently as a lover, then stuffed it in his pocket.

"You're stealing their cigarettes?" Madeleine said, coming into the center of the room.

"They stole mine," he pointed out. "Cells all empty?"

"Yes."

"Here, take this." He handed her the gun he'd found inside the desk.

"What is it?" She didn't reach out to take it from him.

"A Browning automatic. God only knows who they stole it from. It's in good condition, though."

"I don't want it."

"Take it," he said firmly. "If we're separated, or if something happens to me, I don't want you to be defenseless."

"Oh, God," she muttered, taking the gun with an expression of profound loathing.

He gave her two extra magazines for it, both loaded. He showed her how to load and fire the gun, and how the safety worked. "Don't aim," he instructed. "Just point it like you'd point your finger, and fire. Go for the torso."

"Oh, God."

He told her to stick the gun into her waistband, beneath her loose-fitting blouse. "Don't let anyone see you've got it."

"Uh-huh."

Though the guard he'd taken the shirt from was painfully skinny, his ill-fitting uniform was big enough for Ransom everywhere except the shoulders. Considering the time and risk involved, Ransom had opted against taking the man's pants. Anyhow, his own were so filthy as to be unidentifiable as civilian trousers, especially in the dark. And although Madeleine's expensive shirt and pants were not the usual costume for women in rural Montedora, they were now so filthy and wrinkled that they shouldn't draw undue attention to her. Unfortunately, her fair hair still shone like a beacon. Before alarming the guards, she had pocketed the least bloodstained portion of his shirt which she could salvage. He watched with a grimace as she now pulled it out and tied it over her hair like a scarf. He helped her tuck in stray wisps.

"Well?" she asked.

"Keep your eyes down, they're too blue." He frowned. "You're too fair-skinned, but hopefully no one will notice, if we stay in the shadows."

Ransom covered his own golden brown hair with a soldier's cap. His tan and his five o'clock shadow minimized his foreign appearance, and his green eyes were at least less unusual here than Madeleine's blue ones. If seen, they hoped to be mistaken for a grubby soldier who had sneaked a woman into the compound and was now trying to sneak her back out. It was a weak disguise, but the best they could manage under the circumstances. Ransom reminded her that they should stay completely out of sight, if possible.

She nodded. He could see the tension in her expression and gestures. She was being very brave. He would give anything to spare her this.

"You can do this." He kept his voice hard.

"I can do this." Her voice was threaded with steely determination. "Are you ready?"

"Yeah. Let's go."

He turned out the light, then cracked open the door. They needed to move fast now, to slip away before the imprisoned guards woke up and started shouting down into the courtyard. People all responded differently to physical damage, so Ransom didn't know if they had five minutes or an hour.

There was no one in the dimly lighted hallway.

"Okay," he whispered. "Now."

He took her hand and led her down the corridor. Following the route she had taken while Ransom's unconscious body was dragged behind Madeleine hours ago, they turned into a main artery and continued past a set of windows. They flattened themselves against one wall, hugging the shadows and scarcely breathing, when a soldier on guard duty strolled past them near the stairwell. When he disappeared round a corner, they silently descended the steps.

When they reached the main floor, the alarm went off, screeching wildly all around them.

CHAPTER FOURTEEN

Madeleine's heart stopped. She thought she'd die on the spot.

Ransom dragged her against a wall and froze in the shadows again. Half a dozen soldiers came rushing toward them from different directions.

This is it, my God, this is the end.

The alarm wailed overhead. Men were shouting from every direction. There were heavy footsteps on the stairs above. A half-naked man appeared out of nowhere and ran right past them.

Madeleine's terror was so great that it took her a moment to realize: He ran right past us. But surely he had noticed them? They had been caught in the worst possible place, with nothing to hide behind.

Ransom's grip tightened on her. She shared his confusion as three more soldiers dashed up the stairs without even glancing at them.

The roar of activity increased, and they heard sirens wailing outside the building, too.

"Jesus," Ransom murmured. He stepped away from the wall.

"Stay here."

"No! Where are you—"

She stopped speaking as another soldier nearly knocked Ransom over. He barked an order at Ransom, shoved him, and raced past him.

Ransom turned, grabbed Madeleine's hand, and started

heading down the hall. "It's not us," he said exultantly.

"What is it, then?"

"Who the hell knows? God, we're lucky, Maddie!"

The general confusion was growing by leaps and bounds, and no one could spare them more than a brief glance. They passed several closed doors and turned into the small security area through which they had originally been brought to this building. Chaos reigned. Whatever was wrong, it was clearly something big. Nearly a dozen men roamed around, all shouting orders and explanations. Only a couple of them were fully dressed.

"Doristas!" someone screamed. "Doristas!"

They heard distant gunfire. A few people threw themselves to the floor.

Ransom steered Madeleine away from the crowd and into another corridor. "Doristas are attacking!"

"Attacking the garrison?"

"Probably the district governor's mansion," Ransom guessed. "It's an easy target, and those shots sounded pretty distant. The army will have to go defend it. But once this place is three-quarters empty, the Doristas may attack it, too."

"All the more reason to leave." It was still prudent to avoid people, too, since Ransom now risked being pressed into service with the Montedoran army, if his thin disguise held up in the confusion.

Two soldiers guarded a door near the end of this corridor. They were so agitated they scarcely noticed Ransom and Madeleine approaching. She thought they'd be able to get past these men without trouble if they acted their parts well.

The door which the men were guarding opened. Captain Morena stepped into the hallway—and looked right at Madeleine and Ransom.

Morena lost one crucial second when he stared at them in shock. Madeleine never saw what happened next. She was suddenly kissing the floor, her legs having been kicked out from under her. There was some grunting, and a few nasty smacking and cracking sounds. The AK-47 Ransom had been carrying hit the floor and skittered away. Morena shouted something. Madeleine raised her head off the floor. A limp body flopped down next to hers. She nearly wept with relief to see it wasn't Ransom. She heard more grunting. Sheer instinct made her roll away just moments before four feet shuffled across the spot where she'd been lying. Her gaze fastened on Morena's leg as she heard a bone break in someone's body. A man fell to the ground screaming at the very moment Morena drew the familiar, engraved Bodyguard from its ankle holster.

"No!" she screamed.

Everything came into such sharp focus it made her eyes hurt. Ransom whirled and stepped between Madeleine and Morena. Then he saw the gun and stopped cold.

"Oh, God," Madeleine babbled, "no, please, no, please, don't!"

Morena was panting. Ransom didn't even seem to be breathing. Madeleine was choking with terror.

"I would like to ask how you got out," Morena said.

"Please, I'll go back to my cell," Madeleine begged, "please don't hurt him."

"But I'm too busy right now," Morena concluded with dreadful finality.

Ransom moved. Madeleine screamed. Morena squeezed the trigger.

And nothing happened.

The look of utter astonishment on Morena's face was comical. But Madeleine didn't feel like laughing as Ransom rammed the captain's head into the wall. She stared in numbed silence as Ransom bent over the unconscious body and took his gun back from Morena.

"Come on!" He hauled her to her feet and dragged her down the corridor.

"The gun didn't fire," she croaked. "It didn't fire."

"There's got to be another way out of this place." He shied away from a passing group of soldiers.

"The gun didn't fire." She'd never get over it. He was alive. All because his own gun didn't work.

"Did you see any other entrance when they brought us here?" He took her by the shoulders and shook her. "Come on, Maddie! Think."

"No, no, no . . ." Her teeth snapped together on her tongue. The sting of pain awoke her brain. She tried to pull herself together. He was right. She must think. "There's a . . . a main . . . I don't know . . . reception area, I guess. The front of the building. We went past it when they brought us here. Big pillars."

"Do we go through the courtyard?"

"No! Um, no . . ." She tried to orient herself. "We're on the . . . on the right side of the building now. If we keep going that way, we should parallel the courtyard and come to the front entrance."

"Good." His kiss was brief and hard. "Good girl."

He turned and ran, taking her with him. The few people they passed in this wing of the building were too frantic to notice them. When they reached the vast reception hall she had described, there were more than thirty people milling around. After dropping his stolen AK-47 during the scuffle with Morena's men, Ransom had left it behind. Now someone ran right into him, screamed at him to go get his rifle, and brushed past Madeleine.

They emerged from the building onto a sweeping driveway with a well-tended lawn. Lights blazed all around them. Overloaded military vehicles hurled past them, hurrying toward the front gates, which lay wide open for the men and machines pouring out of the compound.

"Can we make it without getting shot?" Madeleine asked, following Ransom's gaze.

"They're worried about rebels coming in, rather than people going out. Let's just try to get lost in the crowd."

She couldn't believe how easy it was. An hour ago, she had half-expected to die trying to escape from here. They had plotted and planned down to the last possible detail. And now none of it was needed. They simply shuffled into a crowd of frightened, sleepy, poorly prepared soldiers who hardly noticed them, and slipped past the front gates.

Madeleine's heart pounded. Free. They were free! Now they just needed to get away from these soldiers.

A shell went off in the street, sending everyone scattering.

Ransom drew her against the side of a dilapidated building for a moment, and then they were off and running. The additional fear of being killed by rebel fire lent wings to her feet, and she needed no urging to race madly through the uneven, muddy streets.

They didn't stop for breath until they were beyond the town. Then, gasping for air, Madeleine asked, "Where do we go now?"

"The pensión," Ransom decided. "We'll need whatever help they can give us. We haven't got much chance of surviving if we just wander off."

Madeleine doubted the Gutiérrez family would be thrilled to see two fugitives on their doorstep, particularly since the army and the Seguridores were likely to start looking for them there once things quieted down. However, Ransom was right; they needed whatever help they could convince the señor to give them. They quietly approached the inn, keeping an eye out for stray soldiers and Doristas. After Ransom had circled the pensión and satisfied himself that it was temporarily safe, he and Madeleine climbed the steps of the veranda and went inside without ceremony.

The building was dark. Ransom reached for a light switch at the same moment that someone told them in terse Spanish not to move. Madeleine felt the cold barrel of a shotgun pressed against her neck.

"Um . . . Ransom?" she croaked.

"Señor Gutiérrez, it's us," Ransom said calmly. *"Los americanos."*

"Los americanos?"

Someone turned on a flashlight and pointed it at them. Then the señor cried with relief, *"Los americanos!"*

Madeleine found she had underestimated the courage of ordinary people. The señor and his family gave her and Ransom a warm welcome, apparently as happy as they were surprised to see them alive and well. She had also underestimated the honesty of such poor people. They assured her that her and Ransom's belongings were all intact upstairs. And she knew it would have been as safe for the señor to steal from them as it had been for the soldiers.

Ransom told Madeleine to go upstairs and get clean clothes for both of them, his little twelve-band radio, his spare bullets, all the money she could find, and—for some mysterious reason—his necktie. And he told her to do it quickly. They had to be out of here in twenty minutes, he insisted, no more.

"If the army is able to beat back the rebels, then they'll realize by dawn that we're gone, so we need to be far away by then," he said. "And if they can't beat them back, then we could get caught in the middle of a long drawn-out battle here. We've got to get out of the area while everyone's still running around like chickens without their heads."

"Twenty minutes," Madeleine agreed, taking a flashlight and heading upstairs. By the time she came back downstairs, Ransom had collected food and water for their journey, chosen a route, and made an offer on Señor Gutiérrez's ancient motor scooter.

"A motor scooter?" Madeleine said dubiously.

"He won't sell me his truck. I tried. He needs it too much. How much money have we got?"

"Between us . . . About two thousand dollars in traveler's checks, another thousand dollars in cash, and about five hundred dollars' worth of Montedoran pesos."

"I love a woman who comes prepared," Ransom said. Most of the money was hers. "Let's try to conserve the cash. Traveler's checks are a pain in the ass at the best of times in Montedora, and without our passports . . ."

Madeleine nodded and waited impatiently while Ransom tried to convince Señor Gutiérrez to accept traveler's checks instead of cash for the motor scooter. Even the big banks in Montedora City took up to an hour to cash a traveler's check, and there were frequently problems; it was much worse in the provinces. And short of locating and using the black market, which would be pretty risky for foreign fugitives, Madeleine figured there was no way she and Ransom could cash the traveler's checks without identification. Bank services would probably be suspended for a while, anyhow, considering the current situation.

My God, she suddenly thought, will we survive this?

Yesterday, Montedora had been an unstable country

with internal unrest; now it was on the brink of civil war. Things had happened so quickly she couldn't process it. Veracruz had been quietly overthrown by a ruthless killer, and the Doristas were at this very moment launching their most ambitious attack to date.

What will happen to us? How will we get out of here?

She clenched her teeth and tried to repress the voice of fear shrilling inside her skull.

Ransom will know what to do. He always knows.

She twisted her hands together, stomach churning, steeling herself not to flinch at every sound of distant combat while Ransom haggled with the señor. Soldiers could come and occupy the building at any moment. Doristas could swarm into this end of Doragua in just minutes. The gunfire sounded a little closer now.

Come on, come on, come on.

"Eso basta," Ransom said with conviction.

Señor Gutiérrez didn't think the offer was enough, though, and the haggling continued. Madeleine ground her teeth together. She was considering kicking both men by the time they finally agreed on a price and shook hands.

"Well?" she prodded.

"One hundred dollars in cash, and six hundred in traveler's checks," Ransom told her. "Start signing."

"What?" Madeleine's eyes bulged. "I could buy a ticket home for that!"

"Not at this particular moment, you couldn't," Ransom pointed out. "He says, quite rightly, that the traveler's checks are likely to be useless to him."

"But . . . Oh, the hell with it!" She pulled out her checks and started signing.

"Be sure to write your passport information on the

back," Ransom translated for Señor Gutiérrez. "That'll help him when he tries to—"

"I will, I will. Tell him to go get the motor scooter ready, and to make sure it's full of gas. And to give us a jug of extra gas, too." She glanced up and said, "What are you grinning at?"

"You. You're starting to sound more like yourself, milady."

He went into the kitchen to wash up and slip into his clean clothes. When he came back, his shirttails hung outside of his khaki pants. The Colt .45 was stuck through his belt and concealed by the billowing shirt. His necktie was nowhere in sight, she noted with sartorial relief. He suggested she go change while he loaded a few of their possessions onto the scooter and made sure it was ready to go.

Once briskly washed and restored to some semblance of her usual self, Madeleine tied a clean silk scarf over her blonde hair, stuffed most of their money into her underwear, and went outside to find Ransom. She heard a sudden explosion in the distance and resisted the impulse to cower and hide. She forced herself to keep moving. They had to get away. She rounded the corner of the inn and found Ransom warming up the scooter and talking with Señor Gutiérrez.

She stopped and stared. "You just bought that for seven hundred dollars?"

"It's sturdier than it looks," Ransom said. "Come on, get on behind me."

"You paid seven hundred American dollars for that?"

"You rich people slay me." He shook his head. "Does the money matter so much?"

"You've been had, Ransom."

"Need I remind you that we didn't have time to shop around?"

"Next time we buy something, I'll do the bargaining."

"Your Spanish is lousy."

"But it's better than your business sense."

"I will gladly fight about this with you later. But for now, can we please concentrate on escaping?"

He had a point. She climbed on behind him. The seat was hard and narrow, and the little motor scooter scarcely seemed big enough to carry the two of them. Señor Gutiérrez took her hand and wished her a safe journey. She supposed he had no reason to feel guilty; if the traveler's checks turned out to be useless to him, then the cash price they had paid wouldn't even cover the cost of a replacement. He'd taken a gamble tonight—in more ways than one. If the army or the Seguridores came back here, Gutiérrez would claim that Madeleine and Ransom had threatened the family at gunpoint, then stolen the scooter and other supplies. But there was no guarantee that he'd be believed. And even if he was believed, there was still no guarantee that the soldiers wouldn't take out their frustrations on him anyhow.

So Madeleine returned the old man's grip with a firm squeeze and heartfelt thanks. Then she hung on to Ransom as the motor scooter rolled unsteadily into the muddy road.

Ransom turned away from the town and the battle, going back along the road they had originally taken into Doragua. How long ago that now seemed; so much had happened since then. Not the least of which, she mused, was the change in her relationship with Ransom. Well, there was nothing like imminent death to break down social restrictions, inhibitions, and good intentions, she supposed wryly.

And they weren't safe yet, she acknowledged, as they fled into the dark night of the Montedoran jungle.

* * * * *

They'd been on the road for about twenty minutes when they came to a stretch of such vast, muddy holes that even the little motor scooter couldn't safely skirt them. Ransom stopped the sputtering motor, and they got off and walked, pushing the scooter along the very edge of the jungle.

The absence of human habitation and the canopy of trees made it very dark here. Ransom had turned off the scooter's headlight to conserve the battery, and Madeleine stumbled along wearily, unable to see where she was going.

The jungle was full of noises at night, noises she had never before noticed or thought about. Shrieks, screams, grumbles, rumbling, shuffling, scurrying, and snapping. Increasingly uneasy, she edged closer to Ransom.

"You all right?" he asked softly, keeping up a fast pace as he pushed the motor scooter.

"Nerves," she admitted.

"Still got your gun?"

That didn't help her nerves. "Yes." She felt the weight of it in the small of her back, tucked into her belt.

A sudden stomping on their right made them both jump. Then Ransom said, "Just an animal. Running away."

"A very . . . big animal, do you think?"

"Nah. Most of the big animals are extinct, very rare, or too smart to come near people. Nobody in Montedora has ever opened up a nature reserve, you know; they shot most of their wildlife years ago. The rest of it hides deep in the jungles and mountains."

The chattering of a monkey made her jump again. "Are you sure?"

"Monkeys won't bother you," he said calmly.

She suspected he didn't know what he was talking about

and was just trying to reassure her. So she changed the subject. "Where are we going?"

"Well . . ." She heard him sigh and realized he had been thinking hard about this. "We can't reach the western border unless we go back through Doragua, so that's out. Besides, it's probably too far away, and we'd have to cross too much open territory to get there."

"Okay." She considered their other options. "And as long as Escalante is in control of Montedora City, I suppose we can't go back there."

"Right. And since there's no border there, there's nothing for us there anyhow. We can't fly out of the airport without passports. If we go there, all we'll do is attract unwanted attention."

"Can we cross a border without passports, though?"

"I figure we'll have to sneak past the Montedoran border guards, then fling ourselves on the mercy of either the Brazilians—"

"To the north."

"Or the Argentines."

"To the south."

"Uh-huh."

"Meaning we have to go through the mountains, one direction or another." It wouldn't be easy.

"Las Lunas or Las Verdes. I favor going south."

"Las Verdes," she said. "Bandits."

"I know." She could hear that he was still wrestling with this problem, looking for another alternative. "But the Doristas are based in the Luna Mountains. Even before tonight, those mountains were thick with army patrols searching for Dorista groups. After tonight, it'll be a war zone."

"What about the Verde Mountains?"

"Banditry is a concern, but it's an old story in those hills. The army may even divert some of their forces from there to fight the Doristas, and since we want to avoid the army . . ."

"I see." She thought about his prediction. More troops sent to fight the Doristas? "You think this attack tonight is the start of a civil war?"

"Yes, Maddie," he admitted reluctantly. "That's what I think."

"Oh." She stepped in some mud. He caught her arm before she could fall. Abandoning her pride, she slumped against him, her arms around his neck, her belly pressed against him despite the discomfort of his gun poking into her abdomen.

"I hope I'm wrong," he murmured against her hair, holding her tightly with one arm.

"But you don't think so."

"No," he agreed. "And it'll only get worse when the country finds out Escalante has staged a coup. The Seguridores will have even more power than ever, the army will split up into factions with divided loyalties, and the rebels will see a chance that may never come again."

"But didn't Escalante guess this would happen?"

Ransom shook his head. "He must have underestimated the Doristas' strength. No one knows for sure how many of them there are, how much support they have, or how well-armed they are. Until tonight, I'd have said they weren't ready to attack a town with an army garrison."

"Civil war," she repeated, frightened. Their fate was even more uncertain than it had been a few hours ago. If the country was plunged into chaos, there wouldn't be anyone for her father, or Marino, or even the State Department to contact about their disappearance. She ground her teeth and sought some measure of courage. "All right," she said at last, drawing away from Ransom. "All right. We go south. Through Las Verdes. To the Argentine border."

She felt him reach up to touch her cheek. Then he turned and started pushing the scooter forward again. "We should stay off the main roads, so we'll be less likely to encounter military checkpoints."

"Right."

"A few more miles down this road, we'll come to a crossroads. According to Gutiérrez, we can head south from there."

"Do you think . . ."

"What?" he prodded.

"I was wondering if we might have any luck after sunup. Finding a telephone, I mean."

"To call the States?"

"Yes."

"It's worth a try. I don't think anyone can help us much while we're here, but maybe they could make things easier for us when we reach the border."

"What about trying the U.S. Embassy here?" she asked.

"We'd have to go back to Montedora City to get to the embassy," he pointed out. "Or call them and then find someplace to hide while we waited for them to pick us up and try to sneak us back to the embassy for asylum—or out of the country somehow—if they don't evacuate as soon as they realize what's happening. Under the circumstances, the embassy staff may not be much safer than we are by this time tomorrow."

It didn't sound any more promising than heading for the border on their own, so she let it drop.

He added after a moment, "There must be Catholic missions out here, Red Cross workers, flocks of foreign journalists, UN observers . . . if only we could find out where."

"I take it Gutiérrez had no idea?"

"No. He only knew of one Catholic mission, right in Doragua."

"Oh."

She tried to keep the fear out of her voice. She wanted him to respect her. He didn't need a hysterical companion on his hands. And his honesty about their situation meant a lot to her, because she knew he didn't like telling her all this any more than she liked hearing it.

Walking through the dark together, the two of them seemed very alone in the world.

CHAPTER FIFTEEN

Ransom looked terrible in the daylight. He needed a shave, one eye was blackened, his jaw was bruised and a little swollen, and the cut on his forehead stood out angrily. Since Madeleine's own cut feet and scraped knees were now feeling the unpleasant sting of infection, thanks to filth and to the prolific bacteria of this humid climate, she decided that they must buy some antiseptic today. That cut on Ransom's forehead looked bad enough without becoming infected, too.

His eyes were red-rimmed and bloodshot. His hair was more unkempt than usual, and she could tell by the way he held himself that his ribs hurt. How this man had made passionate love to her—twice—after the beating he'd taken baffled her.

She added painkillers to the mental grocery list she was compiling. Considering how much cash they were carrying, purchasing power shouldn't be a problem when they finally reached a town. Whether the supplies she wanted would be available was another matter.

Bottled water was high on her list of requirements. They were drinking sparingly, but they'd need more than what they'd taken with them upon fleeing Doragua. They obviously mustn't drink from rivers and ponds, and she was also reluctant to risk amoebic dysentery by drinking untreated water from pumps and wells. But plenty of drinking water was essential. Dehydration could set in fast, and it would weaken them more than anything they had so far endured.

The scooter labored slowly as it carried them up into the Verde Mountains. Listening to it squeal and grind, Madeleine wondered how long the sorry-looking thing would last—and would they walk the rest of the way to Argentina after it died on them?

When they reached a ridge overlooking a village, Ransom drew the scooter to a halt and stared down at the place.

"We need to buy some things," Madeleine said, getting straight down to business. "Water, some kind of antiseptic, aspirin or something for you—"

"I don't need—"

"Yes, you do," she insisted. "More gasoline, a flashlight, jackets or ponchos or something, since it'll get colder at night now that we're higher up—"

"Jesus, you'd think they had a Wal-Mart down in that village. Anything else on your shopping list, milady?"

"Food. I'm hungry."

"So am I," he admitted.

"So what are we waiting for? Let's go."

He didn't start the motor again, just kept staring down at the village. Something was worrying him.

"What is it?" she asked at last.

"I don't know." He shrugged. "Maybe it just seems too quiet, after everything else we've seen. Stay close to me, keep your gun handy, don't talk to strangers, keep your eyes open, and don't leave the scooter alone."

"Anything else?"

He didn't answer her. Instead, he pulled the stolen Colt .45 out of his belt and checked it. Then he bent over and checked the engraved .38 which was concealed beneath his pant leg, strapped to his ankle—she saw with amused surprise—by his wine-colored necktie.

"Why are you even bothering with that gun?" she asked impatiently. "It's pretty, but it's broken, Ransom."

"No, it's not."

"But it didn't fire when Morena tried to shoot you!"

"It's my backup gun," he said, tightening the makeshift ankle holster. "For when things go wrong. I'm not going to carry a backup gun that can be used on me."

"I don't understand."

He gripped the barrel of the gun in his right hand. "The ring," he said cryptically. She glanced at the simple ring she had noticed before, remembering that he had first worn it after arming himself at the Montedoran airport.

"The ring?" she repeated blankly.

"I had a Magna-Trigger safety installed on this revolver. It only fires when the user is wearing a special magnetic ring."

She stared at him. "You're putting me on."

He grinned at her expression. "No. It's something built into the grip. Customized."

"It sounds like some toy at the bottom of a cereal box."

"It saved my life last night," he pointed out.

She sobered as she realized how true that was. "Yes. Yes, it did." She stared at the ornate little gun with new respect. "My God, Ransom, I thought I'd die on the spot when he pulled that trigger."

"I thought you thought I'd die on the spot."

"Well . . . despite our personal differences, I'm rather glad you didn't," she said.

"Aw, now don't go all mushy on me, Maddie."

Their gazes locked, and she was glad to see him look briefly amused and energized. She felt a sudden impulse to kiss him, to lavish a little affection on him. It was an unfamiliar urge, outside of her normal range of expression.

She was a reserved woman—or had been, until she met him. And she felt . . . shy, too. They'd been sexually intimate, but their strange relationship had yet to include the usual physical contact of lovers—hand-holding, snuggling, casual affection. She discovered she felt almost as shy about touching him right now as she would about taking off her clothes right then and there.

Realizing the silence between them was thickening, she said, "You're not planning to shoot anyone this morning, are you?"

"It wouldn't be my first choice, no." His smile had disappeared and his expression was unreadable now. "Remember what I said and stay out of trouble."

"Of course."

Strangers in a small isolated village like this couldn't avoid attracting attention. The way the men ogled Madeleine bothered Ransom even more than the fact that they'd definitely remember the two of them if any Seguridores came by to ask about the missing *americanos.* Even in the sensible shirt and slacks she was wearing, with a scarf covering her moon-spun hair, Madeleine looked as out of place here as an orchid among weeds. Nothing could hide the sculpted elegance of her face, the fairness of her skin, or her unconsciously aristocratic manner.

It was the same manner which had automatically clicked into place the moment he had thought about kissing her while they were sitting on the scooter and overlooking this village an hour ago. Damn her, she didn't need to disappear in order to slip away from him. She was doing it right now.

He knew she needed him too much to go back to their former, hostile relationship. Anyhow, they knew each other too well now. Even when he didn't like her, he still liked her (for all the sense that made), and he had a feeling she rather liked him, too. But her ladyship was apparently regretting that she had succumbed to her anguished last-meal mentality before facing death last night and had had sex with him again. Really shameless, animalistic, mind-blowing sex. At first; later, it had been so tender and gentle he had trembled like a virgin discovering passion for the first time.

Shit. He knew he shouldn't have done it. He knew it even while he was doing it. He'd recognized her mental state. She wasn't trained to face situations like last night, and he was. She had lost all judgment by the time they reached for each other. His judgment had been perfectly intact, and he'd never once suggested she might want to look before she leapt.

His father had always warned him that sooner or later you paid for everything, and the old man was right, as usual. Because now Ransom was going to pay all over again for sleeping with that damned woman. And he wasn't gentlemanly enough to endure this torture with good grace, either. Why the hell couldn't Madeleine just drive some other man crazy when she had these emotional crises, and leave him alone?

Of course, like the dog in the manger, he'd kill any other man who tried to touch her when she was feeling weak and irrational—or even strong and rational. Yeah, he'd still like to get his hands on her fiancé, he admitted to himself. Ex-fiancé. Never-was-fiancé. Christ, Ransom thought with redoubled irritation, that poor schmuck was probably as messed up by Madeleine as he was. Maybe he should just let these horny Montedoran villagers have her.

Recognizing that he was being a trifle bad-tempered, Ransom pulled out the money Madeleine had given him, paid for the supplies he had been able to gather in this pitifully poor town, and carried them back to where Madeleine waited in the road with the scooter. He was feeling the full effects of yesterday's beating now, and the ache which began in his toes and continued straight up through his body until it reached the tips of his hair didn't improve his rapidly deteriorating mood. Nor did the frustrations of the Montedoran telephone system. He hadn't been able to get a phone call through to Montedora City, let alone the States. It didn't surprise him, since rumors were already spreading through this isolated village that there was fighting in the capital today. No one seemed to know any more than that, though.

He was scared. Gut-churning scared. Right now, there was no one in the whole world but him to protect Madeleine. If anything happened to him, she'd be alone and undefended here. At the rate they were going, he couldn't get her across the border for two more days. God, if anything happened to her . . . He couldn't even let himself think about that, any more than he could afford to let himself wonder what was going on in her mind right now when she thought about last night. And he knew she thought about it. He could see her thinking about it.

Tired and in pain, hungry and thirsty, frightened and afraid of his fear, and feeling rejected by the one woman who could really make it hurt, he was spoiling for a fight by the time he reached the scooter and met Madeleine's appraising gaze. Gritting his teeth with growing fury, he silently dared this impossible woman to make just one comment about the supplies he'd scrounged up, and he'd—

"Whiskey?" she said. "Is this your idea of an antiseptic? And what about bottled water? And where's—"

"No one in this town would waste half a day's pay on a bottle of water when they can get it from a pump," Ransom snapped, pointing to a public pump thirty feet away. "Even if some trucking company was stupid enough to haul bottled water out to such a godforsaken spot. And I couldn't find any antiseptic either, milady, but whiskey will do. If you're going to keep nagging, I'll want a stiff drink every so often, anyhow."

"Water from a pump?" she said doubtfully.

"It's that, or do without."

With reluctance written all over her face, she handed him their two water bottles and said, "Well, then, go ahead and fill them."

"What am I, a butler?" He found her unguarded reaction to this salvo very satisfying. "You fill it. I've got to get gas for the scooter."

"Very well." Madeleine made sure her tone froze the air around them as she took the bottles back from Ransom. "Go on. I'll meet you at the gas pumps."

He looked over his shoulder. The pumps were at the other end of the village. Doubt crept in as he considered it; he had tried to keep her in sight the whole time they'd been here.

"Go on," she prodded. "Exercise your vile temper on someone else for a change."

Ransom hesitated for another moment, then said, "Don't be long."

She didn't even acknowledge that she'd heard him.

Madeleine resisted the urge to kick Ransom, turned her back on his scowling face, and stalked off in a temper. God, that man could be aggravating when he wanted to be!

Half the village, it seemed, turned out to watch her use their pump. She apparently made a fascinating spectacle as she filled her bottles. Not so fascinating that they let her do it for free, however. After getting her water, she was informed that there would be a five-dollar charge, since she was not a local taxpayer. Recognizing this strategy from many meetings with corporate sharks, Madeleine bargained the self-appointed local "water official" down to about thirty cents' worth of Montedoran pesos.

Having concluded her business, she started walking toward the gas pumps at the other end of the village. Two young men got in her way. She held her head high and tried to walk past them. They blocked her path again. Using her best glare, she frostily told them to get out of her way. They grinned, one of them revealing surprisingly good teeth; the other was missing two teeth. The women and children who'd been dogging her heels drew back. The men who'd been ogling her now watched with tense interest. She suddenly sensed what had been bothering Ransom when they rode into this village, what was apparently bothering him still. People here were not like people in Doragua. Oh, there were some curious, good-natured women and children, but there was a strong, seething hostility among the men. And for eons beyond counting, men had expressed hostility toward women with sexual violence.

Madeleine was suddenly afraid.

Could Ransom hear her if she screamed? Would screaming be the wrong thing to do? Would it escalate a situation which could somehow be diffused? Suppressing her fear, she once again told the two men to let her pass.

They laughed, which made her belly clench. Then, to her relief, she saw Ransom coming toward them, riding the scooter along the muddy road. She took a deep breath and waited, refusing to let herself back away when one of the men moved in on her. Backing away from a bully just encouraged him to come closer, she told herself, hoping she was right. He was awfully close by now.

The scooter stopped. Ransom got off and came up to Madeleine, his posture relaxed, his attitude casual.

"Problems?" he asked.

"I was just coming to find you," she said, hating the breathless quality she could hear in her voice.

"Shall we go then?"

"Yes." She cradled the bottles against her chest.

When he took her free hand, she felt all the tension that he was hiding from everyone else. He stared down her two would-be assailants and courteously asked if there was something they wished to discuss with him.

There was.

Changing tactics, they now said they wanted his scooter.

Keeping his tone and manner pleasant, Ransom told them that it wasn't for sale. In English, he told Madeleine to get on the scooter and be ready to go. Feeling like she might be sick at any moment, she followed his instructions.

The confrontation became more insistent. Madeleine had trouble following the particulars, but she caught the gist of it. The young men claimed the scooter was clearly the property of a local, just as Ransom was clearly foreign. He must have stolen it, they said. They would take it back to its rightful owner.

Madeleine listened with growing dread. As pitiful as the scooter was, she and Ransom would be lost without it. Besides, it was obvious that the scooter wasn't the real issue. These men were simply probing for a sign of weakness in Ransom; if they found one, they—and the gathering crowd—would descend like ravening wolves. She and Ransom had no hope of escaping an angry mob alive—unless they shot some of them, which she couldn't imagine doing.

For one awful moment, the more aggressive of the two

men seemed ready to fight. He stood nose-to-nose with Ransom and goaded him with all the insolence at his command. Madeleine felt her own fists clenching with the urge to wipe that malicious grin off the man's face. But Ransom refused to rise to the bait. And finally, to Madeleine's relief, the two bullies backed down. Something, in the end, convinced them they were about to bite off more trouble than they could chew. Ransom had managed to diffuse the situation.

Keeping a careful eye on the retreating bullies, he got onto the scooter behind her and quietly told her to drive like hell.

Not wanting to leave an easily detected trail, they avoided people and towns for the rest of the day, either bypassing or speeding through any populated areas they encountered. Exhausted from their active night and increasingly uncomfortable due to the hard, narrow seat of the scooter, as well as the rough roads they traveled, they finally pulled off the road before sundown when they came upon a small abandoned group of brick buildings set well back from the road.

"It was probably a school," Ransom said. "A lot of them have had to close in the past decade. Wait here."

Madeleine stayed with the scooter while Ransom investigated the sad, forgotten little schoolrooms. Since they were partly overgrown by jungle, he checked them for snakes, burrowing animals, rotting wood, crumbling roofs, and other hazards.

The equatorial sun, so merciless by day, was now sitting low on the horizon, getting ready to dip behind the mountains. It cast a warm golden sheen across the sky, gilding the fat rain clouds in fiery colors; it looked like there'd be another storm tonight. The surrounding mountains were lush, green, and wild, and the air here was crisper, cooler, and more enervating than the thick, heavy air down in Montedora City or the Calentura Valley. At moments like this, Montedora seemed to be a country again full of green promises and fresh possibilities, as it had once been.

A rustling in the nearby trees startled Madeleine. She looked up and saw a bird spread its glorious wings of scarlet, indigo, orange, yellow, and blue as it flew across the clearing. It perched on a sun-kissed tree limb and seemed to preen especially for her. Madeleine laughed.

Ransom returned and said, "You look happy about something."

"Look," she said. "Isn't it beautiful?"

He followed her gaze. "Scarlet macaw."

"You know birds?"

"I know all sorts of things, Miss Barrington."

"But birds? I didn't know you had it in you, Ransom." It felt good to banter with him after the tense day they had spent riding through the hills.

He shrugged. "Well, I've been in South America on more than a dozen different assignments, for Joe Marino and for the Secret Service. I got interested in the things I saw. All over the world, actually." He glanced at her, a gleam of amusement warning her before he said, "Would you like to hear about some of the adult entertainment in Japan?"

"Not just now," she said in her most queenly manner. It drew a grin from him.

"It's very educational," he said.

"Save it for a moment when I'm desperately bored."

As if piqued at being ignored now, the scarlet macaw flew directly over their heads, letting the sun's rays shine on its multicolored wings with breathtaking effect. After this impressive display, it perched on the roof of one of the school buildings.

"Find anything?" she asked.

"People were living here not too long ago."

That made her uneasy. "Do you think they'll be back tonight?"

He frowned absently, looking around. "No. I'd say the place hasn't been used for a few weeks, maybe longer. And there wasn't anything left behind to indicate they were coming back."

"Bandits?" she asked, the possibility ever-present in her mind.

"Probably." He added, "But I don't think we should risk going to an inn, and I don't think we should sleep in the open; it looks like it's going to rain tonight." He studied the surrounding area for a moment before concluding, "This place is probably our best bet. But we should keep a watch tonight."

"I'll go first," she said. "You'll drop if you don't get some rest soon, Ransom."

"I will not drop." He looked offended. "I'm fine."

She ignored this patently untrue assertion and said, "Come on, let me have a look at you." She pushed him toward the scooter.

"Oh, please, don't make me sit on that thing again."

"Just for a few minutes, while I check you out."

"You're not a nurse," he grumbled. "You said yourself you don't know anything about—"

"I can certainly pour whiskey on a few cuts and look at your bruises," she pointed out. "Take off your shirt."

"Right now?"

She eyed him. "As you once said, I've already seen everything there is to see."

He rolled his eyes and started unbuttoning his plain cambric shirt, then laid aside the .45. He couldn't suppress a slight grimace when he shrugged out of his shirt. Nor could Madeleine suppress a gasp when she saw the huge bruises which had fully blossomed on his torso.

"Oh, my God! Does it hurt?"

He scowled at her. "Of course it hurts."

"Do you think we should . . . I don't know . . . bind your ribs or something?"

"I'd much rather you didn't touch my ribs at all. Now are you satisfied? Can I get dressed again?"

"When did you become so modest?"

He put his hands on her waist, stilling her when she would have turned away. "On the other hand . . . Wanna show me your bruises?"

She shook her head. "Mine aren't as bad as yours."

"Then do you maybe just want to take your shirt off for me?"

Her breath caught. Her gaze locked with his, and what she saw there made her blood thrum in her veins. She put her hands on his shoulders, feeling hard muscle beneath smooth skin. "I don't think you're in any shape to, uh . . ."

"Fool around?" He tilted his head. "Well, maybe not," he admitted reluctantly. Then he surprised her by asking, "Are you relieved?"

"What?"

"You heard me."

"I heard you, but I don't underst—"

"Don't you?"

"No." Wondering what he was getting at, she said with quiet honesty, "I was willing last night. I was willing every time we've . . . slept together. You know that."

"Willing?" he repeated flatly.

"All right, more than willing. I was . . ." She felt her cheeks flush under his searching scrutiny. She had never been comfortable talking about sex. "You know how I was."

"And how are you now?"

Uneasy about this conversation, she tried to squirm away. His grip on her waist tightened.

"Don't try to get away from me," he growled. "Not again."

His words fell on her like a bucket of cold water. Ashamed, she looked away. "Look, I've told you I was sorry. Do you want me to tell you again?"

She felt the growing tension in him. She heard the control he forced into his voice when he said, "I want you to tell me why you did it."

Her breath quickened. "Why I . . ."

"Why you walked out on me that morning."

"I . . ." What could she say? How could she tell him? God, how could she put it into words? "I . . ."

"You what?" he ground out, pulling her closer.

"You're angry," she breathed in surprise. She hadn't expected it, not after last night.

"Jesus Christ, Maddie, of course I'm angry! And also . . ." He stopped himself and tried again. "What was it about me, or that night, that sent you running away like that? Were you that afraid I'd talk? Did you think I'd blackmail you? What was it?"

This time she did pull away, and he didn't try to stop her. She turned and fumbled for the whiskey, feeling his gaze burning into her back.

She took the whiskey and some toilet paper he'd purchased and turned to face him. "I don't really want to talk about it."

"Tough shit. I do."

She wrapped some toilet paper around her hand and made an efficient pad with it. Then she recklessly poured whiskey all over it. "What does it matter now?"

"Ow!" He winced when she slapped the whiskey-soaked pad against his forehead and started cleaning his cut. "Give me a slug of that, would you?"

"Here."

He took a short swallow from the bottle, then said, "It matters because I can't forget about it, and because I'm sleeping with you now." When she didn't respond, he grabbed the hand tormenting his brow and said, "Or am I?"

She didn't know what to say. She stared at him mutely, wishing he'd let it go.

"Was last night our last night, Maddie?" he prodded.

"Are you leaving it all up to me?"

"You can be as chilly you want, but I'm not going to drop it." He took the soaked pad away from her, stood up, pushed her into his place on the seat of the scooter, and examined the scrapes on her elbows. "Are we lovers now, or are you through with me? Or maybe you just want me to be available for sex whenever you're having a personal crisis?"

She glared at him and tried to pull her arm away. He didn't let her. Then, with more relish than she thought appropriate, he slapped the soaked pad on her inflamed abrasions. She winced. "Ow!"

"I know you were a little drunk and depressed and lonely the night we met," he said, cleaning her elbow. "Your guard was down."

"I—"

"And last night . . ." He picked up her other arm, examined the elbow, and started cleaning a scrape there. "Last night might not have happened if the circumstances hadn't been, uh, extraordinary, to say the least."

"And I haven't made any excuses for it, have I?" she challenged. "I haven't tried to pretend it didn't happen or claim I wasn't—"

"Why the hell would you want to make excuses for it?" Finishing with her elbow, he squatted down to push up her loose-legged trousers and look at her knees. "I'll bet these hurt."

"They do."

He got the roll of toilet paper and made another pad. He soaked it with whiskey, then handed her the bottle. "Here. Have a slug of this." She did. Then he warned, "This'll sting."

"And you'll enjoy it."

"To be honest, yeah, I will."

"Ouch!"

"Told you so." Concentrating on his task, he continued, "So what do you want to do? Keep me handy for your occasional dark nights of the soul—"

"That's not fair!"

"—or consider the possibility that since we have such great sex together, maybe we should do it more often. Even when we're not both unhappy or afraid of dying."

Annoyed, she lashed out, "Is sex all you can think about?"

"No," he shot back, "but it comes to mind a lot when I'm with you. And you think about it just as often as I do. Don't pretend, Madeleine. I can tell."

Since he was right, she prudently changed the subject. "What are you doing?"

"Relax," he said, untying her shoes. "I'm checking the cuts on your feet."

"Oh."

"Don't change the subject." His gaze was piercing. "Well?"

She felt her lower lip tremble. His eyes narrowed, but he didn't back down. Knowing he'd never relent after all he'd said, she gave in. "All right." Her voice was low. "All right. I guess we have to do this, don't we?"

"Yes. We do." He waited. When she didn't speak, he prodded, "Go on."

She cleared her throat. "This is hard for me to talk about, Ransom."

"I can tell." He took off her shoes and socks, and he examined her feet, letting her take her time now that she had finally agreed to talk about that night.

Looking at his windblown, golden brown hair made her long to touch it. Suddenly she thought, Why not? They were lovers, weren't they? Shyly, she reached out and stroked his hair. He stilled for a moment, then continued dabbing at her cut feet with the liquor-soaked tissue.

"I'd never done anything like that before," she began.

"Sex with a stranger, you mean?"

She smoothed his hair. "Yes. I was shocked at myself, but I wanted it. Wanted you. Later, I blamed my decision, and the way I felt that night, and . . . and . . ."

"And?"

She said in a rush, "And the way I behaved in your bed."

"Maddie, you behaved great in my bed."

She closed her eyes, remembering. "I blamed it on the alcohol. Three drinks—four?—on an empty stomach. I pretended to myself that was what made me go with you. Just the alcohol."

After a moment, he said, "Did you leave me like that because you were so embarrassed about a one-night stand with a stranger?" He started putting her socks back on her feet. "Because you wanted to blame it on the booze?"

"Yes." She hesitated a moment, then acknowledged that

she had to say more. To tell him everything. He'd made it clear that he wanted honesty between them; she realized that, now that he'd pushed her this far, she wanted it, too, even if she felt anxious and awkward about discussing this. "I mean, yes, I was embarrassed about that, but also . . ."

"What else?"

"I was . . ." She folded her hands tightly together and looked at them. "Well, I was just . . ."

"Come on." His tone urged her to trust him. "Tell me."

"I was never like that before," she said at last, aware of his tension. "The way I behaved. The way I felt with you. I had never . . . And with a total stranger! I just couldn't . . . Well, I've always been pretty reserved. Even in bed."

She watched in awkward silence while he put her shoes back on her feet and tied them. Her sensible shoes, now smeared with mud and dust and god-only-knew what else.

Still crouching before her, he looked up and met her gaze. Now those changeable green eyes were soft and serious and—she realized with astonishment—vulnerable.

"I've never been reserved," he admitted, "but that night was special for me, too, Maddie. Being with you was special." He rose to his feet and then perched next to her on the hard scooter seat. He was gentle now, approachable. "And I wanted to wake up with you. That morning and . . . other mornings, too."

"I couldn't," she blurted.

He took her hand in his. "Why?"

"I was too embarrassed. I—I didn't know myself. I didn't know the woman who had been so . . . so . . . who had been like that with you. With a stranger. With anyone. It wasn't me."

"Yes, it was," he insisted. "It was one of the very best parts of you. But," he added with a soft smile, "to be honest, I'm pretty pleased if I'm the only one who knows that part of you."

"You are. You must have figured that out by now."

"Yeah, I guess I did."

Now she wanted to tell him. She wanted to share this with him, to start over. "I woke up at dawn. I could see you, see the way we'd wrecked the room, see myself in the mirror . . ." She shook her head. "I didn't know you. Good God, I didn't even know your name, and we'd . . . we'd . . ."

"Oh, I remember what we did. Believe me."

"Well, in the cold light of dawn, with the alcohol worn off—because I was a little drunk, even if that wasn't the real reason things happened between us—and with you asleep and looking like a total stranger in the daylight . . . I was ashamed and embarrassed . . . and afraid."

"Afraid? Of me?"

"I was afraid you'd wake up," she admitted. She remembered dawn creeping across the shabby room, the stranger in bed beside her, unfamiliar street sounds coming through the window. And her shock. "God, I was horrified. Waking up like that . . . the night we'd spent together seemed sordid and shameful instead of . . . of wonderful. Instead of . . ."

"Yes?"

She told him what he deserved to know: "The best night of my life."

"Mine, too." He squeezed her hand. "I wish I had woken up. I wish we had talked then."

Madeleine shook her head. "I don't think I would have talked, Ransom, even if you'd woken up. I was confused and ashamed and, well, pretty emotional that morning. I mean, you'd spent all night stripping away years of defenses, and—"

"So did you," he said. "I guess that's why it hit me so

hard that you left. Hours of mind-blowing sex left my mind . . . pretty blown."

"Mine, too." She shook her head, wishing she hadn't been so self-absorbed. "But it never once occurred to me that you might feel the same way. We were strangers. We'd spent all night wrapped around each other—"

"Getting naked in every way."

"That's what made me panic. I'd never been so naked in my life. But we were strangers. So I never thought about how you'd feel, waking up alone. I just thought about . . ."

"How naked you felt."

She nodded. "And all I wanted was to run away."

He brushed his knuckles along her cheek. "I'd never been that naked either, and all I wanted was to know why you'd gotten me that way and then . . . skipped out."

"I kept thinking it was just your pride that was hurt."

"Oh, Maddie, everything was hurt. My pride was just the one that I was willing to admit to."

"The truth is . . ." Her heart ached with regret as she admitted, "I never did intend to tell you my name. From the start. When I went to your room, I had already decided that if you insisted, I'd just make up a name, and we'd never see each other again. I never wanted anyone, not even you, to know that I had slept with a stranger." She held his gaze. "I'm sorry, Ransom. I'm so sorry now. I wish—"

"Shh." He brushed her hair off her face. "That night, I thought we had a great beginning. But maybe it was the worst beginning we could have had."

"Maybe. I don't know. Maybe it would have just happened the next time we met, because I . . . Whenever I'm with you, I want . . ."

"So do I," he whispered.

He didn't move at all, and she knew he was trying to let

her decide, without pressure, what she wanted their relationship to be. And she didn't need to think about it anymore.

"My name," she said slowly, "is Madeleine Elizabeth Barrington. I'm thirty-one years old. I live at 74 East—"

His kiss stopped the rest of her words.

CHAPTER SIXTEEN

They lay together inside one of the little brick buildings, listening to the rain outside. It was coming down in sheets, and the roof leaked. They had scrambled around wildly when the storm began, seeking an island of dryness within the schoolhouse, laughing as cold water hit their naked bodies every time they settled in a new corner. Now, sprawled out in the last remaining dry area, they held each other and talked in lazy whispers. They had found a few candles someone had left there, and they'd lit one so they could see each other. Ransom had bought two ponchos when stocking up on supplies that morning; they had spread one across the hard wooden floor and were using the other as a blanket. But it was cool at night this high up, especially with the rain, and only shared body heat kept them warm enough now.

"You know," he murmured, "you're so rich and I make decent money, and yet we've only ever made love in hovels."

She smiled and burrowed closer to him. "I wouldn't call the Hotel Tigre a hovel."

"Oh, wouldn't you, milady?"

"All right, it's a hovel." She was too content to argue.

After a moment, he said, "I'm sorry about this morning."

"Which part of this morning?"

"The part where I left you alone in a village I knew was dangerous."

"Oh, that," she said, eyes closed.

He jostled her. "Yes, that. You could have been hurt."

"You stopped anything from happening."

"There are some fights that it's smarter to avoid. But the point is—"

"You were angry about something or other—"

"I was thinking about sex," he admitted wryly.

"And so you—"

"Made a stupid mistake. And risked your safety." He was silent for a long moment before adding, as if to himself, "I've got to keep my head clear."

She propped herself up on an elbow and looked down into his face. "And will it stay clear . . ." She kissed him lightly. ". . . now that you know . . ." She kissed him again. ". . . that you can have me . . ." And again. ". . . whenever you want me?"

His answer was silent, but very satisfying.

She winced when he was done. "You really need a shave."

He ran a hand over his jaw, and his eyes widened. "I sure do. Sorry."

She stretched languidly, then lay with her cheek against his shoulder. His fingers gently kneaded the back of her neck. She practically purred with pleasure.

"Do you have a family somewhere?" she asked after a while. "A mother who worries about you?"

"I did have a mother," he replied. "She died a long time ago."

She slid her arm around his waist, careful of his tender ribs. "When?"

"When I was a kid."

"Do you remember her well?"

"Kind of." He sighed and added, "My dad loved her to

death, I remember that. He's never remarried."

"There's just you and your dad?"

"And my brother. He's a sportswriter. Wife, kids, house."

"And this?" she asked, fingering an old scar she had noticed the first time they'd ever slept together. A patch of silvery skin on his belly. "What's this from?"

"Oh, that. I was shot there."

"Shot!" She sat bolt upright and stared, appalled.

He grinned at her. "It's all right. I lived."

"Who shot you? How did it happen? My God, you were shot?"

"My very first day on active duty with the Service," he said ruefully. "I set a new record."

"What happened?" She resisted the hands which tried to pull her back down. "Tell me."

"I joined a field office out West. The guys picked me up at the airport. But instead of taking me straight back to the office, they took me on a call to investigate some counterfeiters. Things went wrong, and I didn't duck fast enough."

"Ransom."

"That's about all there is to the story."

"Oh, really?"

There was more to the story than that, of course, and she forced it out of him. Funnily enough, he liked telling her. He liked talking to her. And listening to her. And lying quietly with her in his arms. And looking at her. And just knowing she was near.

As the rain pattered around them, he told her things he hadn't talked about in years, and even a few things he'd never told anybody before. He told her what he could remember of his mother, as well as stories about his wild teenage years—including a minor arrest that the Secret Service never found out about. He told her about the chain of maturing experiences that led to his decision to apply to the Service as a young man.

"It was a mission I believed in. Not just protecting the President, which was pretty important in itself, but also protecting his opponents. I helped keep dissenters alive, and that's what the American political system is all about—challenges and choices at every free election. Candidates all had a right to be heard, and I was part of the team that made sure they lived long enough to have their say."

And, of course, she asked why he had finally quit after nine years.

"It was all the accumulated years of a lifestyle that left no room for a life. Changing my sleep cycle every few weeks, combining that with jet lag from hopping across time zones all around the world on a weekly, or even daily, basis. Years of waking up every day and wondering, 'What time is it? Morning or night? What day is it? And where the hell am I?'

"I missed every important event in my family for years. I was home so seldom that my phone was disconnected one time and I didn't know about it for two months. And women . . ." He shook his head. "I once dated a woman for ten months but only actually saw her six times.

"I could have asked for a desk job or a field office assignment," he admitted, "but I was a speed freak in those days. I wanted to guard the President and his family. I wanted to 'get that gun' before it took him out."

He shrugged, stroking her smooth back. "And so I burned out. Resigned. Went home to my father's house and just fished for two months. Nothing else. Just slept all night and sat by the lake with my rod all day."

He told her about finally answering Joe Marino's phone calls after two months of ignoring them, feeling ready to return to the world after his long, peaceful rest. He'd been successful at Marino Security and loved his job. "I feel like hell about this business with that rock star I hit, though."

"Maybe Marino's lawyers can work it out."

"I sure hope so."

And, because he wanted to know everything about her, he asked about her past, her work, her memories and plans and life. And he no longer wondered about her loneliness on the night they'd met.

"You know," he pointed out, when she told him about her family, "you could disappoint them—all of them—and they'd go on living, Maddie."

"Ah, but would I?" she asked ruefully. "How would I get along if they all found out I wasn't . . ."

"Perfect?"

"Well . . . yes."

"I know you're not perfect, and I let you have your wicked way with me anyhow."

"That's big of you."

He rolled her over onto her back and met her gaze in the candlelight, serious now. "You don't need to be perfect," he told her. "Don't you know what an amazing woman you are?" She gazed back at him uncertainly. "I don't know any woman who could handle all the things I've seen you handle, Maddie, and that includes handling me at my worst. You've got guts and brains and heart. If I was ever in trouble, I'd always want you on my side. And I know damn well that you make mistakes and do things you're ashamed of and lose your temper and get scared. And it doesn't make you any less amazing to me."

Her answer was better than words.

* * * * *

The mid-morning air was fresh and crisp, heavily scented with rain and greenery. Ransom awoke slowly, stretching with contentment, wincing slightly at his many aches and pains. Then he reached for Madeleine without even thinking about it, as if he always woke up next to her.

The space at his side was empty.

His eyes snapped open. Yes, she was definitely gone. He sat bolt upright, experiencing a horrible flood of déjà vu.

"Maddie?" he called hoarsely.

"Out here!" she called back.

He sagged with relief, heart still pounding. Madeleine appeared in the doorway a moment later, fully dressed. She was smiling.

"I decided to let you sleep. You were dead to the world," she said.

He looked around groggily. "Shit."

"Has anyone ever told you how charming you are first thing in the morning?"

He ignored her wholly unjustified sarcasm. "We were supposed to keep watch last night."

"Oh." She shrugged. "Well, as you can see, we're still alive."

He shoved aside the poncho covering him, stood up, and walked naked to the door.

"Where are you going?" she asked as he passed her.

"To take a leak."

"Don't you want your clothes?"

"Why?" he shot back. "Are we expecting company?"

"I wish we had some coffee," she muttered as he walked away.

He had a cigarette when he returned to the schoolhouse, and that made him feel better. He got dressed, then went outside and washed his face and hands in a puddle of rainwater. When he made some mildly civil remark to Madeleine, she offered him the rest of the bread he'd bought yesterday, as well as an orange.

While he ate, she scattered the remains of her own bread across the schoolyard as an offering for the scarlet macaw. It watched her with interest, then swooped down and examined her leavings.

Ransom drank some water, then unpacked the twelve-band radio. They listened to an English language news broadcast while Madeleine continued watching the bird.

Word of the rebellion had reached the outside world. The Doristas had taken the town of Doragua after a full day of heavy fighting, the BBC informed the world.

"I hope the Gutiérrezes are all right," Madeleine said.

"They're not army, government, Seguridores, drug dealers, or the upper crust, so the Doristas will probably leave them alone—except for possibly taking some provisions from them," Ransom replied, tossing some bread toward the macaw.

Escalante had seized power in a silent coup, the news broadcaster said. The Presidential Guard, having been formally dismissed, had mounted a counteroffensive on the Presidential Palace last night, in an attempt to free Veracruz. Fighting continued today. Casualties were heavy, and no one knew the fate of Veracruz and his family.

"Jesus," Ransom said.

"It's so hard to believe," Madeleine said pensively. "People we saw a couple of days ago might be dead now."

He took her hand. She scooted closer to him.

It was believed that the Doristas, upon learning of the chaos in the capital, would use this opportunity to launch the nationwide rebellion which pundits had been speculating about for months now. As for the LPM, Montedora's secondary, hard-left rebel faction, no one knew their plans, their strength, or their deployment at this time, though it was a safe bet that their response to Escalante's coup would be violent opposition.

"What a mess," Ransom said, turning off the radio.

"I wonder what's happened to Martinez," Madeleine murmured.

Ransom recalled their conversation with the nervous minister. "He'll be halfway to Wyoming by now, if he's smart. Come on, let's hit the road. I want to cover as much ground as possible today, and the roads will be bad."

"The roads will be bad," Madeleine repeated. "What a surprise."

He smiled and helped her to her feet. "Got your gun?"

She nodded and patted the automatic, which was concealed beneath the billowing poncho she had donned in the cool morning air. "I'm almost getting used to it."

"Good." He draped his own poncho over the scooter seat. "Too bad we can't take the bird with us. I think he has a crush on you."

The macaw preened nearby, occasionally eyeing Madeleine as if to make sure he still had her attention.

Ransom started loading up the scooter. He noticed Madeleine walking off toward the bushes. "Where are you going?"

She looked over her shoulder. "To take a leak."

It made him laugh to hear her clipped, aristocratic voice utter those words. "Here. Don't forget this." He tossed the toilet paper to her, reminding her to bury it when she was done, rather than leave litter in the jungle. She nodded and disappeared.

He'd had no coffee this morning, he longed for a decent

meal, his body ached, and they were still a long way from home, but Ransom felt great today, all the same. It was funny what a woman could do for a man's outlook.

But he wanted to get to that border. He wanted to be there now. If Escalante was under attack in the capital and Doragua was now in the hands of the Doristas, he and Madeleine probably didn't have to worry about the army and the Seguridores anymore; they'd be too busy fighting a civil war to pursue two escaped Americans. But Ransom knew how fast law and order broke down in a situation like this. Madeleine wouldn't be safe until he could get her to the Argentine authorities. And the knowledge of her vulnerability here was like a spur in his gut, urging him to haste.

However, he still saw no alternative but to ride to the border on this coughing motor scooter and these muddy roads. And the sooner they got on the road, the—

He heard Madeleine scream.

He didn't remember racing across the schoolyard or plunging into the jungle directly behind the little buildings. He didn't remember anything before the moment he saw Madeleine struggling with a hairy young Montedoran.

He pulled out the Colt .45 and shouted, "Let her go! Now!"

Something crashed into his skull. He cursed himself for an idiot, for a lovesick fool. He knew better than to simply plunge ahead without checking for . . . He hit the ground as everything went black.

Ransom fumbled his way into consciousness to find Madeleine holding his head in her lap and stroking his face as she murmured to him, "I'm right here. Shhh. No, don't try to move yet."

He looked up into her face and groaned, "My head."

Someone poked him with a rifle. Madeleine impetuously pushed the rifle barrel away and snapped, "Leave him alone."

"Maddie . . ."

"No, just lie still for a minute," she insisted. "Shhh."

He wondered how long he'd been unconscious, and guessed by the ragged concern in Madeleine's expression that it was more than a minute or two.

"Am I bleeding?" he wondered groggily.

"No." She kissed his throbbing head. "How do you feel?"

"Help me sit up." He realized he was lying on the hard ground of the schoolyard. Someone must have dragged him here. Once he was propped upright, he looked at the two men guarding them. They were dressed in an eclectic array of rags and they carried—what else?—AK-47s. "Oh, Christ," Ransom muttered, wanting to lie back down.

"We seem to be waiting for someone," Madeleine murmured.

"Who?"

"El Martillo," she replied.

The name drew a reaction from their captors. Ransom ignored them. "The Hammer? That doesn't sound encouraging."

"No, it doesn't."

He looked searchingly at her. "Are you all right? Did they hurt you?"

"No. Scared me, mostly. I never even saw the first one until he grabbed me." She frowned. "Do you think they're kidnappers? Or bandits?"

At the mention of a word he recognized even in English, the older of their two captors expostulated angrily in Spanish. His thick, guttural accent was hard to understand, but the gist of it was clear: They weren't no stinking bandits.

"Not bandits?" Ransom repeated, eyeing the rifle pointed at him. "That leads to an obvious conclusion."

"Doristas?" Madeleine ventured.

This produced an even angrier response from their guards. Clearly, the notion that they could be stinking Doristas was an insult nearly worthy of murder.

"My mistake," Ransom said as a rifle poked him in the shoulder. "Hey, don't point that thing at her! I mean it."

The younger guard blinked at Ransom's tone.

Madeleine said nervously, "Please don't antagonize him."

"Jesus, look at him. He's probably sixteen years old. What a mess."

"They're LPM, aren't they?"

"Looks that way." He asked them. The young one confirmed this before the other man told him to shut up.

"What do you think this means for us?" Madeleine asked with studied neutrality.

"Well, LPM is hard-left, but its only known leader never expressed any anti-American sentiments before the Seguridores killed him," Ransom mused. "Of course, maybe the guy just never had time to express such sentiments before he was butchered. Anyhow, let's hope we can talk our way out of this when El Martillo gets here." His head ached, but he was starting to pull his thoughts together. "It's beginning to make some sense to me."

"What is?"

"Remember that village yesterday? Extreme hostility to city people, foreigners, and anyone with money."

"Yes. So . . ."

"Well," he said slowly, "with the Doristas already so influential in the north, it makes sense that this area would be prime recruiting ground for the LPM. And they're Marxists. Sort of. So those villagers probably—"

The older rebel told them to stop talking. The younger one noticed the macaw perched in a nearby tree, and he raised his rifle to shoot at it.

"No!" Madeleine cried, leaping up. "No, don't!"

"Maddie!" Ransom grabbed her at the same moment that both rifle barrels swung around to point at her.

The rebels shouted at Madeleine. The bird left its branch and flew overhead. Madeleine pointed to it and begged them not to shoot it, saying it was her fault that the bird was there, she'd been feeding it. Apparently realizing what she meant, the boy who had been about to shoot the bird now smiled condescendingly and agreed not to kill it. The tension dissolved, and Madeleine let Ransom drag her back down to her seat in the mud.

"Do that again," he growled, amazed his heart hadn't stopped beating when they'd zeroed their rifles on her, "and I'll shoot you myself."

"You could," she said quietly, keeping her eyes on their guards.

The moment she said it, he felt the weight of the .38 strapped to his ankle, so familiar that, in his groggy state, he hadn't even noticed it until now. "They didn't search me," he whispered incredulously.

"No. Or me," she added.

He blinked, "You've still got—"

"Yes."

He couldn't believe their luck! No wonder the LPM rebels weren't anywhere near as effective as the Doristas. "All right. Here's what we're gonna do. You—"

He was interrupted by a vocal signal from the jungle.

The rebels perked up excitedly, and one of them answered it. A moment later, three more scruffy-looking armed men came out of the jungle. The rebels greeted the newcomers enthusiastically, as if they hadn't seen each other for a long time. Ransom guessed they hadn't. The elusiveness of LPM probably meant its members lived a scattered life, constantly on the move. He certainly hadn't counted them among the dangers he and Madeleine were likely to encounter; he hadn't even known they were based in Las Verdes.

"They seem to have forgotten us," Madeleine murmured, watching the reunion. "Maybe they'll let us go?"

Smiling and greeting each other, these men didn't seem as threatening now, but . . .

"Oh, shit," Ransom blurted. "We're in trouble."

"What?" Madeleine felt the blossom of hope wither inside her. "Why? What's wrong?"

"Don't you recognize them?"

"Recognize . . ." Suddenly, she did. "Those are the three men who ate at the Pensión Doragua the night we arrived there," she whispered.

"Uh-huh."

Their young captor gestured to them a moment later, explaining how he had discovered Madeleine in the bushes. The moment the leader of the group—El Martillo—looked at them, Madeleine knew he recognized them. His expression hardened with hatred.

"What were they doing in Doragua?" Madeleine wondered.

"Probably coming back from the capital after looking for another way to hit the President," Ransom muttered.

"This is bad," Madeleine said with dread.

"I can't believe the week I'm having," Ransom said wearily.

El Martillo and his two companions came forward and studied Madeleine and Ransom. The Hammer's Spanish was as clear as Madeleine remembered it, enabling her to understand what he said; it occurred to her with some surprise that he must be an educated man. His comments, however, were discouraging. He said that he had met these two oligarchic pigs before, and he congratulated his men on capturing them.

"Now wait a minute," Ransom began in Spanish.

"You think I do not remember?" El Martillo sneered. "You had an arrogant lackey with you then, a silly young braggart who openly boasted of his association with that murdering swine Veracruz and the whore he calls his wife."

He prodded Ransom with his rifle. Ransom didn't react. El Martillo loomed over him and snarled, "He also boasted of your association with Veracruz."

The two men who had captured them looked stunned, then appalled, then positively venomous. Madeleine became very, very scared. The two men started speaking simultaneously, excited and bloodthirsty now. With cold bitterness, El Martillo repeated for them everything Miguel had said about Ransom in his good-natured effort to charm the provincial Gutiérrez family. And upon realizing that they had captured a man who was not only a friend of Veracruz, but one who had actually made him harder to kill, the rebels demanded the honor of killing their captive.

"Oh, my God," Madeleine moaned, terrified beyond rational thought.

One of the men who had been at the pensión grinned and said something to his companions that made them all look at Madeleine and laugh. Then he reached out and traced the neckline of her poncho with the barrel of his rifle. Cold terror immobilized her as he leered at her while fondling her with his weapon.

Ransom said something so insulting and vulgar to the man that all laughter ceased immediately. The man forgot about Madeleine and hit Ransom. Ransom barely blinked. He said something else to them all that made El Martillo furious, though Madeleine didn't understand the vernacular. The youngest rebel, flushing with insulted manhood, kicked Ransom. Madeleine screamed and flung herself across his prone body even as he struggled to sit up again.

"Please," she begged them, "please don't do this!" Her meager Spanish deserted her, so she begged Ransom, "Don't make them hurt you!"

He ignored her, pushing her aside as he sat up and delivered a blistering commentary in flawed Spanish about how pathetic he found their obscure, cowardly, ineffectual, so-called rebel army, and how all real men in this country became Doristas. Madeleine thought El Martillo would kill him on the spot.

But then The Hammer remembered his debt to the two men who had captured Ransom and said to them, "I have no time for this. Kill him now."

"No!" Madeleine screamed, clinging to Ransom once again. It took two men to pull her off him. They hauled her to her feet and dragged her several yards away.

The boy raised his rifle and pointed it at Ransom. Madeleine went still with horror.

"Oh, come on," Ransom said, clearly enough for Madeleine to understand, "not in front of the woman. Do you really think she'll let you fuck her with my brains splattered all over her poncho?"

And as terrified as she was, she caught the significant

glance Ransom sent her and realized that, appearances notwithstanding, he was orchestrating this entire scene. Only he hadn't had time to tell her her role! What did he want her to do? Oh, Christ, what should she do?

He was still sitting on the ground. His hand was close to his ankle, where the .38 was concealed. She reasoned it out in a split second and realized what he needed from her. There were five men. He couldn't take them all at once. So, with a screech of sheer hysteria, she started struggling wildly with the two men who held her, taking all of their attention. She kicked out, and one of them dropped his rifle.

Ransom made his move. Madeleine heard the shots. Deafening. Earthshaking. Terrifying beyond belief. Two fast shots, then a whole round of confusing explosions from different weapons. She was down on the ground now, smothered beneath the body of one of El Martillo's companions. When she felt him try to rise, so that he could shift his rifle and join the fight, she clung to him. He fought her off. She heard him curse and then felt his hand scrabbling at her stomach. He had felt the gun concealed there and was trying to get at it through layers of rough poncho material.

There was a lot of shouting. Madeleine choked on muddy water, rolling over and over in various puddles as she fought for survival against this brutal stranger. She saw his fist coming straight at her, heard the dull smack of flesh against flesh, and saw blood splatter. Her blood. She felt no pain, only blind fury. Her knee found his groin with satisfying force, and while he was helpless with pain, she rolled away and climbed to her feet.

"The jungle, Maddie! Run! Run!"

Blinded by sweat and dirt and blood, she obeyed Ransom, turning around and running straight into the bush. She tripped and fell, then hauled herself to her feet and plunged ahead. After a moment, she realized he wasn't right behind her. She stopped and scrubbed at her tearing eyes. There was no way she was leaving without him. Where the hell was he?

She went back the way she had come, able to see a little more clearly now as she crouched behind a leafy bush. Two bodies lay inert in the schoolyard. Ransom fought El Martillo; both of them were unarmed. The man she had left lying in agony was now fumbling one-handed for his rifle, which lay several feet away from him; his other hand still clutched his crotch. Sick with fear, Madeleine pulled the Browning from her belt, undid the safety, and fired at the man. She missed, but she got his full attention—and she nearly dropped the gun. It felt like a wild thing trying to escape from her hands, as if it had suddenly come to life.

Recoil, she realized with distant surprise, never having fired a gun before. So that's recoil.

And the noise. It made her ears ring and her legs shake.

She held the gun more tightly, afraid it would jump out of her grip, and fired again, keeping the man pinned where he was.

She only counted four men, she realized, firing again from her leafy shelter at the edge of the jungle, keeping her enemy separated from his rifle. Where was the fifth man? She wiped at the blood still dripping from her nose as she looked for him.

Finding his advantage, Ransom did something horrible to El Martillo's knee. The Hammer screamed and wallowed helplessly on the ground.

"Ransom, come on! Over here!" Madeleine shouted.

Ransom rolled to his feet and ran. Someone peaked out of the nearest school building and fired his rifle. The fifth man! He had a clear shot at Ransom, who was running toward Madeleine, unarmed. She fired rapidly, again and again. A cloud of acrid smoke rose around her as she emptied the magazine.

The man on the ground heard the pause when she ran out of ammunition. So did the fifth man. He stepped out, raising his rifle just as the man on the ground finally reached his and seized it. Madeleine fumbled for the spare magazine in her pocket. Her hands were clumsy with fear and inexperience.

She finished loading the Browning just as both rifles sent a barrage of bullets into the bush.

"Go! Go!" Ransom shouted, just steps away from her. "Run!"

She ran. The sound of gunfire followed her. Through its deafening roar, she heard Ransom's heavy, harsh grunt.

She turned around just as his body crashed to the ground.

CHAPTER SEVENTEEN

Madeleine's hands operated independently of her mind. She raised the gun as two of the rebels tromped into the jungle just ten yards behind her. Both men fell back when she fired, ducking out of sight. She risked a glance at Ransom.

He was hauling himself to his feet. His face was contorted in pain, and there seemed to be an enormous amount of blood in his lap all of a sudden, but he was alive. Relief made her stupid, and she stared at him as men shouted just a few yards away.

"Where's the other magazine?" Ransom demanded, taking the gun from her. He turned and fired twice more, silencing the raised voices coming from just beyond the trees.

She pulled the last spare magazine out of her pocket and handed it to him as he fired again. Then he shoved her and said, "Let's go. And don't turn around again. Just keep going."

Breathless as she shoved her way through the thick bush, she tried to protest. "But—"

"I've got the gun now, okay? You just keep going."

She wouldn't, but this wasn't a good moment for an argument, so she just kept plunging ahead, frantically wondering about his fresh wound, heedless of the branches and bugs hitting her in the face, careless of the thorns scratching her arms and tearing at her clothes. She risked a glance over her shoulder and saw that he was limping so heavily he almost seemed to be running on one leg, propelling himself forward by pushing against trees and thick plant stalks.

It was her painful breathing, rather than her other senses, which finally made her realize they were running uphill. She stopped for a moment when Ransom did, hearing what he'd heard: people crashing through the jungle behind them. Shoving her ahead, he crouched low and fired until the magazine was empty. The crashing stopped. He reloaded the gun, then turned and followed Madeleine again, gesturing that they should be as quiet as possible now.

When they reached the summit of the hill, he steered her to the left and slightly downhill, into the thickest jungle growth in sight. She heard more shouting behind her, but it was farther away than before.

"We're losing them," she whispered, afraid to hope.

"Keep going." He steered her in a new direction.

"But your leg," she began, horrified by how much blood there was.

"Keep going," he gritted out.

After ten minutes, they came to a narrow river. "You shouldn't get into this water with an open wound," she protested as he plunged unsteadily into the moving water. He pulled her in with him. "Ransom!"

"I'm leaving a trail of blood, Maddie," he panted. "If they pick up on it, they'll find us. But they can't track it through this." He gestured to the murky water which was carrying away his blood.

"Oh, God," she groaned, thinking of parasites, amoebas, infectious diseases, and predators as she followed him through the waist-high water. It seemed a good quarter-mile before he hauled himself up on the opposite bank and led her into the bush again. He was pale with blood loss, drenched, shivering from the cold water, and sweating. Madeleine decided it was time to put her foot down. "We're stopping now," she said in a voice that had made CEOs and corporate lawyers do her bidding in the past.

"No, let's—"

"You'll die if we don't stop the bleeding," she snapped, pushing him down against a fallen log, so worried about him that she forgot to check it for snakes and other hazards. The fact that he was so weak she could push him down scared her.

The river water had cleared away enough blood that she could now see where the wound was. A bullet had pierced his inner thigh from behind.

"At least the exit wound isn't bad," he said, looking down at the front of his thigh.

"It's not?" It looked horrible to her.

He shook his head. "Probably a 7.62mm bullet. Missed the femur and the artery—and, thank you, God, my balls."

"And what a loss to womankind those would have been," she said, striving for a dry tone. She failed, but he smiled weakly even so. She met his eyes. "I don't know anything about this. You'll have to tell me what to do."

He looked down at the wound again, which was still bleeding profusely. "Put pressure on it to stop the bleeding. Then we'll need to make some kind of pressure bandage." His eyelids were drooping with exhaustion. "Here, we'll have to use my shirt."

"Let's use my shirt. I've got this poncho."

"No, I don't want you wandering around shirtless when we meet more people," he said wearily, stripping off his shirt. "Damn, this is my favorite shirt, too."

That's why she had chosen it for him the night they had fled Doragua. "Ransom . . ."

"God, I wish I'd been able to bring those cigarettes with me. Here." He handed her his shirt. "Since this'll hurt me a lot worse than it hurts you, just think of all those times you wanted to hit me and didn't."

Realizing that he was right, that she'd have to hurt him, she clenched her teeth and muttered, "I can do this."

"Jesus, I hate getting shot," he ground out as she applied pressure. "I really, really hate it."

"We'll have to stay here for a while," she said, trying not to look at his agonized face. "You'll just bleed more if we start walking again."

He ignored her words, staring hard at her. "What happened to your face?"

"What?" She glanced down and saw the dried blood on her blouse. "Oh. That man hit me. It doesn't hurt."

"But you—"

"It doesn't hurt," she repeated, scrubbing at her face. "How many . . . how many of them are left?"

He didn't have to ask who she meant. "El Martillo won't be walking anytime soon. One of the men I shot is probably dead. The other may be," he shook his head, "but I'm not sure. But he won't be running through the jungle today, that's for sure."

"That leaves two."

"Uh-huh."

She swallowed. "Have you ever . . . ever killed anyone before?"

"No." He didn't look away. He let her see what was there: the mingled revulsion and acceptance. "No," he repeated, "but I've spent years being prepared to do it, Maddie."

"Are you—"

"I'm all right," he said. "Or I will be. That's the first thing you learn about a gun, you know. How easy it is to kill someone. You learn to respect that."

"Oh, God, Ransom." She started shaking again. She tried to concentrate on the problem at hand, tried to force the schoolyard scene out of her mind. "I—I think the bleeding is slowing down. Tell me what to do now."

Following his instructions, she balled up the shirt against the wound as best she could and tied the sleeves tightly around his leg. The pathetic, blood-soaked bandage would do him very little good, she realized, fighting tears.

He stayed still until she was done with her task. Then he handed her the gun. "Take it."

"No, you keep—"

"Take it."

She did so with great reluctance, tucking it through the back of her waistband, beneath her shirt. "Where's your .38?"

"I dropped it back in the schoolyard. It's empty anyhow." He grabbed her hand with surprising strength. "Listen, Maddie. If you hear them coming, you've got to leave without me."

"No. I won't."

He buried his hand in her hair and gripped the back of her neck. She met his eyes without wincing or blinking. "You have to," he said fiercely. "They'll just kill us both."

"I won't leave you," she repeated stonily. "And you can't make me."

"There's no point in both of us—"

"Or even one of us—"

"I can't run anymore."

"I can see that."

"Damn you, just do what I tell you!"

"No."

"You can't let them get you," he said desperately, weakening even as they argued.

Realizing how this was taxing his strength, she sat next to him, eased him into her arms, and said, "Just rest now, all right?"

"Maddie . . ."

"Shhh."

She kissed his sweat-soaked hair and tried to soothe him. When he went still, she wasn't sure if he had fallen asleep or passed out.

He slept for over an hour. When he awoke, he insisted they move on. She protested, knowing he would start bleeding again, but he was adamant.

"They've probably given up looking for us by now," he admitted, "but we've got serious problems. We're lost, and we've got no supplies. We need drinking water, and I need help. If we sit around here so that I don't bleed to death, then I'll certainly succumb to infection. But by the time that happens, you'll be too dehydrated to get out of here on your own. We've got to find a farm or village as soon as possible."

Realizing he was right, she relented, only delaying their departure long enough to look for a big, sturdy stick he could use as a cane. When he rose to his feet and put weight on the wounded leg, she saw sweat bead his forehead. He told her he'd be all right and irritably insisted they get going. She guessed that his leg hurt far more than he was willing to tell her; she vaguely remembered some long-ago classroom where she had learned about the bundles of nerves running down the inside of the thigh.

Not knowing this region, they decided to try to head toward where they thought the road ought to be, hoping that the LPM rebels wouldn't be traveling that same road. Although the thick jungle disoriented his sense of direction, Ransom estimated the road should be due west of where they were now; they adjusted their course as the sun started lowering in the afternoon sky.

Their progress was laborious. Ransom's wound and growing weakness kept his pace slow, and they were both hampered by the thick bush. Madeleine discovered why heroes in jungle movies were always hacking their way through everything with a machete; she couldn't see three feet in front of herself half the time, and they were both covered in scratches and welts from all the thorns and branches and sharp-edged leaves that lashed out at them as they passed. Madeleine forced Ransom to don her poncho, seeing the abuse that his bare torso was taking—on top of the bruises left by the beating he had endured. He resisted at first, and only the argument that she couldn't afford to let him get any weaker managed to sway him. She didn't like him going bare-chested in this climate, anyhow. It was cooler this high up, and very damp. He'd soon take a chill, the way he was sweating.

She studied him during their increasingly frequent rest stops. He looked terrible, worse than she could have imagined. Beneath his three-day growth of beard, his face was drawn, sweaty, and haggard. He was so pale that his cuts and bruises stood out sharply. His eyes were glassy with pain and—she feared—the start of a fever. He was breathing hard all of the time now, even when he rested. Wading through the river this morning had washed a considerable amount of the blood out of his pants and left them a murky, muddy color, but she could still see the red stain slowly spreading around the shirt she had tied over his wound.

She wanted to fling herself at him and weep. But a show of weakness from her would only require more strength from him, so she confined herself to seeing to his comfort whenever possible.

Unwilling to risk drinking from the streams they occasionally encountered, Madeleine realized they could keep their bodily fluid levels up by consuming fruit. She collected whatever fruits she could find as they tramped along—mostly mangos—and forced a grumbling Ransom to eat one every time they stopped to rest.

"I hate these things," he said. "They're so sweet and messy and—"

"And full of sugar and vitamins and fluid," she said. "Eat it."

"I want a cigarette."

"Eat your mango."

Afterwards, they'd be sticky from mango juice, and flies and other insects would buzz around them until they found a puddle or stream in which to wash.

By sunset, they still hadn't come to the road, and Madeleine wondered if it really was where they thought it was. It was so hard to get her bearings when she was surrounded by bush everywhere she looked, even overhead! And the thought of spending the night in this damp, misty, chattering jungle terrified her. But, with her own vision failing as darkness descended, and with Ransom badly in need of rest, she knew that they had no choice. Summoning her resolve, she announced that they were stopping for the night.

"I can keep going," he lied.

"I can't," she lied. "And who knows what we'd walk straight into in the dark?"

He relented, too exhausted to argue anyhow, and started helping her search for a likely shelter. They found a little dome of bushes growing together, with soft earth beneath it. After ensuring that nothing else lived there, Madeleine lined the ground with enormous flat leaves, then urged Ransom to come inside and lie down.

"And eat this," she added, handing him a mango.

"Oh, Christ." He tried to shove it away.

"Eat it," she ordered inflexibly.

"I'm going to turn into a mango soon," he complained.

"It could be a distinct improvement," she told him.

The macaw swooped overhead, its scarlet and indigo wings blurring in his vision as it flapped and fluttered. The woman at his side admired it, but he was busy admiring her. She was so lovely, even with blood on her face.

Blood?

Why was there blood?

He tried to ask her, but he couldn't get enough breath to speak. His chest burned as he ran, and he couldn't get enough air.

They were running? Running. Running. Trying to escape.

The macaw followed them, circling and plunging. It turned into a vulture and swooped down on the woman. He ran faster, trying to reach her, but he couldn't breathe and his leg wouldn't work. Paralyzed, he watched in horror as the vulture turned into a leering Montedoran, carrying a gun and dressed in rags. The man attacked the woman. She fought back wildly, but without sufficient strength or skill.

Desperate to save her, Ransom shouted with terror as he tried to force his unresponsive limbs to move.

"No," he moaned, trying to reach her.

"Ransom."

"No!"

"Shhh. It's all right."

It's not all right, damn it!

"Wake up."

"No, no . . ."

"Ransom!"

He awoke gasping for air. A whimper caught in his throat, humiliating him. His heart pounded so hard it hurt.

"Oh, God, oh, God," he murmured brokenly, burying his face against her.

They were lying somewhere dark and damp, smelling of earth and greenery. Her arms were around him, and she was stroking his back. As he lay panting and shivering with reaction, she slipped one hand between them to unbutton her blouse and unfasten her lacy bra. He gratefully pressed his face between her bare breasts a moment later. She didn't smell as sweet and clean as usual, but she smelled like her, and that was what he needed right now.

"Tell me what you dreamed," she whispered.

"I was trying to . . . trying to get to you . . . and I couldn't move . . . I couldn't help you . . ."

"Just a dream," she murmured, shifting to hold him more comfortably. "You help me every time I need you."

"I couldn't get to you, I c—"

"But you always do," she whispered. "You always will."

He recognized she was humoring him, soothing him; he let her.

He needed it. And he realized she was seeing him as no one in his adult life ever had—helpless, scared, weak. And he let her. He tightened his arms around her fiercely and rubbed his face against her soft skin, heedless of his scratchy beard.

After a few minutes of her stroking and murmuring, he calmed down enough to ask a rational question. "When did I fall asleep?"

"The minute you lay down."

"Oh. Has it been long?"

She shrugged. "A few hours. I doubt if it's midnight yet."

"Are you all right?" he asked. "You were bleeding."

"Just my nose. It's fine."

He shivered. "Aren't you cold?"

"Are you?" she asked.

"I'm freezing."

"Your skin is hot," she said. "I think you have a fever."

"Great."

She chuckled at the disgust in his tone. "But you're starting to sound more like yourself."

"You could try to make that sound like a compliment."

"No, I couldn't."

"Hmph."

They lay silently for a while. Then she said, "You know, there's something I keep wondering."

"What?"

"What's your name?"

"You know my name."

"Your first name."

"I'm not gonna tell you. You're just malicious enough to put it on my tombstone." He felt her stiffen and realized what a bad joke that was, under the circumstances. He burrowed closer, seeking her warmth. "We'll find the road in the morning."

"Uh-huh." He had a feeling she didn't believe him. After a long moment, she sighed. "I'm sorry. I'm really sorry."

He frowned. "About what?"

"Everything. About leaving you alone at the Hotel Tigre. About bringing you back to Montedora with me. About—"

"Maddie, it's—"

"About your getting shot."

"That's hardly your fault," he pointed out.

"But I . . . Oh, God . . ." He was surprised to hear tears in her voice. "I was so mad at you when we left New York, I told Graham I hoped you'd get shot by rebels," she blurted guiltily.

"You did?"

"Yes."

Yeah, she was definitely near tears. And if he was kind and understanding, it would probably just make her feel guiltier. So he said, "Jesus, I can't believe you said that!"

"Well, you were being so awful to me." She sounded a bit less guilty.

"A little, maybe, but, I mean, what kind of a person are you?"

"The kind who doesn't like to be goaded and bullied," she said, defensive now.

"Goaded and bullied? Oh, come on."

"You were the one who threatened to tell people about us. You were the one who said you could prove you'd seen me naked because you knew about the birthmark on my bottom. You were th—"

"It's a really sexy birthmark." He heard her sharp intake of breath when he fondled her bottom.

A moment later, she laughed shakily. "Why don't you just let me wallow in my guilt?"

"Not in the mood."

"Well, I'm sorry anyhow."

"They didn't shoot me just because you once upon a time wished for it, Maddie." He kissed her breast.

"No, but . . ." She stroked his back. "Does it hurt?"

"Of all the stupid questions," he grumbled sleepily. "Of course it hurts. I can tell you've never been shot."

"Well, no, actually."

"It hurts." He left it at that. Why mention that his leg throbbed like it wanted to fall off, or that a red-hot poker seemed to be piercing his thigh again and again and again?

"A farm or a village won't be enough," she whispered. "We need a real doctor and real medical facilities."

"One thing at a time," he murmured, drifting away. He was so tired, so incredibly tired. Just talking wore him out. Snuggling into her as he gingerly kept his thigh from touching anything, he slipped over the edge again.

She made him take off his pants at dawn so she could get a good look at the wound. She didn't know anything about such things, but it looked awful to her: angry, oozing, and swelling. Considering the wound and the hot flush covering his skin, she had no doubt that infection had already set in.

He was slower today, and obviously in even more pain. Putting his pants back on was an ordeal. Within a half-hour of their setting off, he was drenched in sweat and breathing like he'd just run a marathon. Madeleine helplessly watched him struggle to master his weakness and conceal his pain from her. The terrible, insidious fear that he wouldn't make it started settling into her bones, chilling her with cold dread.

Realizing that, at this rate, dehydration was a more serious concern than additional infection, she insisted he drink from the next stream they found. The water was moving sluggishly, but it was cold and clear, and she harbored some faint hope that it bore no parasites or disease. Feeling light-headed, she decided she'd better drink, too.

A couple of hours later, he seemed to have reached the end of his rope. He sat down, refused the mango she tried to force on him, and regarded her with serious, glassy eyes.

"When you find the road," he said between long, exhausted breaths, "don't get into a vehicle with more than one man in it, unless there are women, too. Or women and children." He closed his eyes for a moment as a wave of pain washed over him. "You know. A family."

"When we find the road," she corrected, her stomach churning. She knew what he was about to say, and she didn't want to listen.

"I might not be there."

"Then neither will I."

He sighed and finally said it: "I can't go on, Maddie."

She could see what it cost him to admit that. She could see that the wound was bleeding again. She could see him close to collapse.

"Then neither can I," she said, meaning it.

He seemed too tired to discuss it for a moment. Finally, he said, "Look, if I wait here, and you leave a trail that you can follow back to me after you've found help—"

"No."

"Maddie, you—"

"No! I'm not going on without you. I'm not leaving you here. I'm not discussing it." Her voice shook, but not her resolve.

"You have to," he said, too weary to get mad at her. "I'm sorry," he added.

"I'm not going."

"I'm not giving you a choice," he explained. "You're going on without me."

"What are you going to do? Pick me up and hurl me through the bush?"

"I'm in charge," he reminded her. "When it comes to your safety, you agreed to do what I tell you."

"I don't remember ever agreeing to that, regardless of what your contract with my father says. Besides, wouldn't you say these are rather extraordinary circumstances?"

"Maddie, you have to do it," he said gently.

"Why?" she demanded. "Why do I 'have to' to go off and leave you to die?"

He held out his hand. She scooted closer and took it.

"Don't let me fail," he whispered.

"What?" She didn't understand the non sequitur.

His face paled, and she knew he was in the grip of another wave of pain. Then he said, "I came here to protect you. The moment . . . I knew who you were and that you were coming back here . . . I would never have trusted anyone else to take care of you."

Her throat felt tight. "Ransom . . ."

"Only reason I came," he murmured. "To keep you safe. Please . . ." He held her hand against his burning cheek and closed his eyes. "Please stay safe."

"We'll both stay safe," she said firmly. "We must be close to the road by now."

"Maddie, I can't help you anymore." His voice was thin, wispy, unfamiliar. "I can't protect you."

"Then I'll protect you," she said fiercely.

"Christ, do you think that's what I want?" His snap lacked its usual crackle.

"No, but you'll just have to let go of some of your pride." Her snap was as sharp as ever. She was pleased to see him glare at her. Fighting all the softness she longed to give him, she forced steel into her tone as she added, "Now shall we just sit here and wait to die? Or are you going to make a little effort, get off your butt, and keep going?"

"God, you are so fucking stubborn!" But he was pushing against the ground, trying to get back on his feet.

"I prefer to think of it as resolute." She helped him get up, relieved that this crisis was past, terrified about what the next one might bring.

"You can think whatever you want, but you have the disposition of a mule. A mean one."

She smiled. Right now, a flare of temper from him was even more welcome than tender words.

The blood loss and infection continued to weaken him, however. He soon couldn't walk alone, and they made slow progress with his arm draped over her shoulder and his weight dragging her down. A lifetime of self-discipline kept her going, but she knew her body would soon quit under the strain, especially without sufficient food and water.

When he finally collapsed, they both fell down. She lay there winded and dazed, too exhausted even to examine him for the first few moments. When she rolled over to look at him, he was unconscious. She knew, with a certainty she railed against having to accept, that he wouldn't go any farther.

"Ransom," she breathed, devastated, lost.

He no longer looked like the smooth seducer from the Hotel Tigre, or the quietly alert bodyguard who had saved so many lives from a terrorist attack, or even the deadly combatant who had engineered her escape from El Martillo. Her chest hurt as she looked at him and saw how much it had taken to bring this man down. She brushed his hair off his forehead and simply stared, too stricken to know what to do now.

And perhaps because she, like he, was now pared down to nothing but the essential, basic qualities of her character, striving for nothing more glorious than survival, she realized what her preconceived notions and stubbornly narrow self-image had made her so slow to acknowledge: She loved this man with all her heart.

Now that she recognized it, she couldn't imagine why she hadn't known it sooner. In the short time she'd known Ransom, she'd shared more with him than with anyone else in her life.

Amidst her fear and sorrow, she was aware of something strange and surprising, something she hadn't thought about until now. That sense of aloneness, the hollow burden she had carried all her life, was missing. Gone. Vanished. For better or worse, Ransom knew her. He understood and accepted her as she really was. And no matter how uncomfortable and potentially painful that was, it was also the most extraordinary feeling she'd ever known.

"Ransom," she whispered, touching his pale, bruised face.

There was no one else like him. Not for her. He was the one. How brutally unfair that she should only realize it as he lay dying in a patch of mud, hungry, thirsty, feverish, and in terrible pain, thousands of miles from home.

She was so exhausted, she couldn't even weep as her heart was breaking. She could only stare dumbly at him, wishing she could give her life for his. She would do anything for him. Anything. But she couldn't think of a single damned thing that was within her power now.

"Ransom," she whispered again in stark misery. She slipped her hand into his unresponsive one. She gripped hard, needing him, needing his strength and resolve and courage. Lips trembling, she whispered, "Please, don't let me fail you. Please."

He never moved, never stirred.

But a moment later, she heard the faint rumble of a car engine.

CHAPTER EIGHTEEN

Madeleine blinked, not believing her ears.

An engine? A car!

"The road," she choked, stumbling to her feet. "The road!"

She didn't even realize she was running until she tripped over a tree root and fell flat on her face. She jumped up and kept heading straight for that sound.

"Help! she screamed, not sure how far away the sound was, terrified that the car she heard might pass by before she reached the road. "Help!"

As it happened, she nearly got hit by the vehicle—an ancient pickup truck with less-than-reliable brakes. It rounded a bend just as Madeleine stumbled into the road, which was so narrow that she didn't see it until she had plunged right into the middle of it. She jumped just in time to avoid being hit, then turned and ran after the truck as it skidded to a shuddering halt on the slick, unpaved road.

"Help! Help! Please, you must help us!" Madeleine cried, running to the driver's window.

The driver, a grizzled old man, looked at her with obvious alarm. The young man next to him got out of the truck and rounded the hood. They both looked wary and shocked. Realizing she had to get control of the situation, Madeleine tried to coax some Spanish out of her agitated mind.

"Ayúdame! Por favor, ayúdame!" Please, help me!

The young man got a good look at her head-to-toe appearance and seemed appalled. He said something to the old man, who nodded and tried to ask her who she was and what had happened to her.

"Americana," she said, gesturing to herself. She nodded when he asked if bandits had done this to her. Why bring politics into it?

The two men exchanged some more comments. Madeleine realized they were father and son. The warning that there were bandits around here frightened them, and they urged Madeleine to get into the truck so they could depart immediately.

"No, no, mi esposo," she insisted. My husband. The lie would simplify matters.

She pointed into the jungle. The two men looked at her doubtfully. Afraid they'd refuse to help her, she plunged a grimy hand into her pocket and pulled out about fifty dollars' worth of Montedoran pesos. She held it out enticingly, seeing their faces light up with interest, and repeated that she wanted her husband. After a brief discussion, the son decided to go into the jungle with her while the father pulled out his shotgun and said he would cover them.

Madeleine tried to guess how much ground she had covered in her frantic dash for the road. One hundred yards? More? She suddenly realized that she hadn't paid any attention to where she'd left Ransom. Terrified that she might not be able to find him again, she tore through the jungle with reckless haste, leaving behind her companion as she ran forward shouting Ransom's name. All the trees and plants looked indistinguishable now. Which way should she go?

Mercifully, Ransom groaned in unconscious pain. Madeleine scrambled toward the sound, tears of relief streaking down her face when she dropped to her knees by his side. She took his hand, kissed it, and looked up at the young Montedoran.

"This is my husband," she said. "He's very sick." She pointed to the wound in his thigh. *"Necesita un médico."* He needs a doctor.

"Sí, señora."

She had trouble understanding his accent, but she realized he was promising to help her. She nodded gratefully, accepting his reassurance. Then she helped him lift Ransom and drape his inert body across his shoulders. All the way back to the truck, she chanted silent prayers of thanks and of hope. Please, please, let him live, please, let him live.

The young man shouted something to his father when they reached the road, and his father opened the truck's tailgate and helped them lay Ransom down in the flatbed. It smelled like live chickens, but Madeleine supposed it smelled better than she did by now. She climbed in with Ransom and held his head in her lap as the truck set off.

They were on the road for nearly two hours before Madeleine saw the refugees and began to understand the scope of what was happening in Montedora. When the little road they were on met up with another road coming from the east, their progress was slowed to a crawl. The road was packed with thousands of refugees heading west with whatever worldly goods they could carry.

Donkeys, mules, horses, and occasionally men hauled carts loaded with family possessions. Some people traveled in battered cars or on motorbikes, but most were on foot. Babies and toddlers were carried by their mothers and older sisters, but small children had to walk. Everyone Madeleine saw looked stoic and tired. No one paid any attention to her, and she realized that as filthy and ragged as she was, and traveling in this old truck, she undoubtedly looked like one of them. Even the color of her hair was dulled by dirt.

The young man who had helped her stuck his head out of the truck window to chat with her every so often. His name was Pedro, and he and his father—Tito—lived in San Remo. They had been selling their chickens in Montedora City when the fighting broke out. They had waited too long to head home, and now they were barely ahead of the fast-spreading violence. He thanked her for the money she had given them, adding gallantly that they would have helped her even so.

Madeleine nodded and smiled. The thousand U.S. dollars that she had stuffed inside her underwear clung damply to her skin. It was a veritable fortune in Montedora, she knew. As long as she didn't let anyone steal it from her, she ought to be able to get whatever help she needed.

When Pedro asked her about herself, she relied on her poor Spanish as an excuse to keep her answer vague. She'd been accompanying her husband on a business trip, she said. Now she just wanted to get help for him, and to go home. Pedro nodded sympathetically.

"Where are these people coming from?" she asked, gesturing to the sea of refugees around them. She had heard him occasionally exchanging news with people walking alongside the truck, but she hadn't understood anything.

The army was splitting into factions, Pedro told her, some loyal to Veracruz, others to Escalante. They were fighting east of here now, and, of course, didn't care whose villages they destroyed, whose homes they burned, or who they shot in their effort to conquer each other.

"Ransom was right about the army, then," Madeleine murmured, tightening her hold on him. Still unconscious, his skin was burning hot. *"Necesita un médico,"* she told Pedro.

He nodded and said something. She had to ask him to repeat it. Then she said, "A mission? In San Remo?" When he nodded again, she asked how soon they would be there.

He gestured to the muddy road and the throng of people congesting it, and he shrugged. Madeleine gritted her teeth, knowing that nothing she could say would make a difference in their speed.

They finally reached San Remo at sunset. It was a small, unremarkable town set in a lush valley, but it had apparently undergone some changes since Pedro and Tito had left it; they seemed shocked by what they found here. Refugees had been streaming into the area for two days, and rumors said their numbers would increase tenfold as fighting continued east of here. Within days, they would outnumber the inhabitants of San Remo.

The Catholic mission was the destination of most people pouring into San Remo. As Tito drove her there, Madeleine could see hundreds of people camped around the mission's walls. Some erected simple shelters to mark their space and protect themselves from rain, but most hadn't yet had time to do this. The noise and confusion were overwhelming, but nothing compared to what was actually going on inside the mission. Tito drove the truck right up to the gates. Madeleine watched Pedro get out of the truck and speak to a couple of teenage boys guarding the entrance to the mission. Beyond the gates, she could see a dense crowd of milling people. Many others were lying down, right there in the middle of the courtyard. And children—there seemed to be more children here than in all of Montedora!

The two teenage boys came back to the truck with

Pedro. Madeleine tensed, recalling the LPM rebels and feeling afraid, but their manner was serious and gentle. They took one look at Ransom, conferred together, and then studied Madeleine. Then one of them spoke to her.

"You are American?"

"Yes," she said with relief. "You speak English!"

The boy smiled modestly. "A little. Your husband is . . . shooted by bandits?"

"Yes. Yesterday. He needs medical attention or he will die."

The other boy shook his head and said something she didn't understand. The two of them started arguing. Pedro interrupted them and delivered an impassioned speech. Seeing that nothing was being solved, Madeleine said, "I can pay for medical help."

"Payment is not—" The boy was interrupted by his companion, who seemed to be saying something negative again. Something about too many people. The boy cut him off and told Madeleine, "You will need to speak to Sister Margaret."

"Where is she? Can I speak to her now?"

"I will bring you to her."

She hesitated, afraid to leave Ransom. Seeing this, Pedro reassured her; he would watch over her husband until she returned.

Jorge, the boy who spoke English, led her into the mission's main courtyard. His gloomy friend stayed behind to guard the busy gate. Once inside the walls, Madeleine started to realize the extent of the problem. There must be a hundred sick people lying around the courtyard. The mission clearly wasn't prepared to handle a disaster of this size. Some of the injuries Madeleine saw as she passed through the crowded courtyard looked superficial, but there were several people who looked as bad as Ransom. Fear tightened her belly as she realized that he probably couldn't get priority treatment here.

She followed Jorge through a confusing series of courtyards and small buildings. He asked for Sister Margaret everywhere they went, and they always seemed to have just missed her. Sister Margaret, Madeleine reflected irritably, must be one hell of a sprinter; Madeleine was getting breathless just looking for the woman.

There seemed to be an inordinate number of children here; they were everywhere she looked. Jorge told her that the mission was an orphanage. The mission had been overcrowded even before the refugees started arriving, he told her, and they still didn't know where to put all these people. The children were willing to vacate their dormitories for the wounded, but Sister Margaret hadn't yet figured out where they would sleep instead. And with so many strangers descending upon the town, she wasn't willing to let the children run wild.

"How big is your hospital?" Madeleine asked, following him into yet another courtyard. The mission was old and simple, but big and well-tended.

"Twenty beds."

"Oh. I see."

"And the specialty here is the maternity."

"Maternity?" she repeated after he finished asking yet another person if they knew where Sister Margaret was.

"Yes. The hospital is really for mothers, to help them have a safe pregnancy and to have a baby safe." He showed her into a schoolroom. "Otherwise, the work here is to care for orphans and teach them school." His face brightened and he cried, "Sister Margaret!"

"Yes, yes. Just a minute, Jorge," said a tiny, ancient

woman with a strong Irish brogue.

Madeleine approached the woman and stared at her with something approaching awe. She couldn't be five feet tall, and her tiny figure was so adorably chubby that she looked like a cartoon character or a doll. Her curly, pure white hair was cut short, and most of it was modestly covered with a utilitarian blue veil. Her calf-length dress was made of similar material, now filthy and wrinkled. As Madeleine watched, this tiny woman gave instructions to a young man three times her size. He was lying on the floor, covered in sweat, and clearly in terrible pain. He nodded and grunted something at her. Then Sister Margaret placed a dainty, sensibly shod foot against his ribs, grabbed an arm which lay at an odd angle, and yanked with all her might. The man screamed horribly—and then stopped, blinking with surprise.

A dislocated shoulder, Madeleine realized.

By the time the man's face cleared and he said his shoulder had stopped hurting, Sister Margaret was already turning away to sign some papers that one person handed her while simultaneously giving orders to a young nun waiting nearby. She dealt with four more people in that efficient manner, then started heading out the door. Jorge ran after her, as did Madeleine.

"Sister, Sister!" Jorge cried.

"Yes?" she said over her shoulder, not even pausing.

"This lady needs your help. She is a lost American, and her husband dies."

That was apparently surprising enough to get her full attention. Sister Margaret turned around and looked at Madeleine. After a quick assessment, she said, "Where is your husband?"

"Outside the gates," Madeleine said. "He's been shot.

He's very ill. We were lost in the jungle for over a day, and he'll die without medical attention."

Sister Margaret nodded briskly, instructed Jorge to get help and bring Ransom into the mission, and told Madeleine to come with her. While dealing with a dozen other people and problems, the Sister extracted the salient details of Madeleine's story from her.

"The Argentine border?" the Sister said while calming a hysterical child. "You'll never make it now."

"I know. Can we contact the American embassy?"

"Not until communications to the capital have been restored. Nor can you contact the United States until then. Not from here, anyhow."

"No one here has a cell phone?"

"No one that I know of."

"Is there someone here who can help my husband?"

"I can." Madeleine didn't doubt it, but her heart sank when the nun added, "But I'm afraid that we've already run out of almost all our supplies. And what's left must go on a first-come, first-serve basis to those in need." Her features softened for a moment as she added, "I'm afraid there's a long list ahead of you."

"I can pay you," Madeleine said desperately.

Sister Margaret shook her head. "I can't allow you to buy your way past other people who also need medicine and bandages, Madeleine."

Abandoning all pride, Madeleine seized the old woman's arm and begged, "Please, help me! Please. I love him."

Sister Margaret stopped moving and focused all her attention on Madeleine for a moment. Her pale gray eyes looked sad. "Yes, I can see that you do." She sighed. "But look around you. Life is cheap here. Before your husband dies, many other women will lose their men. And worse—

their children." Her voice roughened as she added, "I've made it my life's work to change that. And I can't."

"But—"

"We must pray," Sister Margaret said, managing to make this sound like a practical suggestion. "And not for a miracle, either. Just that fresh supplies can get through to us."

"Does anyone even know you need supplies?" Madeleine demanded.

"No." The nun's voice was flat, but Madeleine recognized how scared she was. "Communications were cut before I could tell anyone."

Ransom was allotted a space in the corner of a small, airy classroom. Madeleine realized wryly that it was the nicest place they'd been in since leaving Montedora City. The walls were covered with cheerful pictures painted by the children, and big windows let in air and light, while heavy awnings shielded the room from direct sunlight. She pulled the poncho off Ransom and tried her best to make it into a little bed for him.

Although she was on a waiting list for antibiotics she'd probably never receive and painkillers which had already run out, Madeleine did at least have access to water. And although bandages were at a premium, someone found a few rags she could use. A child who should have been too young for such responsibilities offered to stay with Ransom while Madeleine went outside to boil her rags in a communal pot. She returned a half-hour later with clean rags, boiled water, and drinking water.

She hung two of her rags up to dry, planning to use them as bandages in the morning. Then she wrestled Ransom's pants off his body, relieved that he wasn't awake for this process, as it clearly caused him pain even in his unconscious state. The wound looked even worse tonight, and his thigh had swollen more. It was a good thing she'd never been squeamish, she thought, and started cleaning the wound.

When she was done, she gave him a sponge bath. While she was bending over him, she heard Sister Margaret's voice from behind her.

"What's that beneath your shirt? That lump?"

Madeleine felt the weight of the Browning in the small of her back. She reached under her shirt and touched it self-consciously, then looked over her shoulder at the nun. "A gun."

"I thought so." Sister Margaret held out her hand. "You'd better give it to me."

Madeleine glanced at Ransom. "He wouldn't like that."

The Sister glanced at him, too. "He won't be needing it for a while, and I will not have a gun around all these children."

"I wouldn't let any of them—"

"What if one of them takes it away while you're sleeping? What if he gets delirious and tries to take it from you?"

It was harder to give up the gun than Madeleine would have expected. She was still afraid, having been subjected to so much violence recently. But, realizing that Sister Margaret was right, she handed it over.

Sister Margaret unloaded it with practiced ease, as if she took guns away from people every day, then bent over to have a look at Ransom. She touched the skin around the wound. A dark, strong-boned hand suddenly grabbed her wrist, startling both her and Madeleine.

"Ransom!" Madeleine cried. His eyes were open!

"What the fuck is going on?" he demanded blearily. Then he noticed the nun's habit. Madeleine had seldom seen him look so stunned. "I mean, um . . ." He looked back at Madeleine.

"This is Sister Margaret," Madeleine said helpfully.

"How do you do?" the nun said, examining the wound again.

"Hi, I . . ." Ransom looked down and drew in a sharp breath. "Christ, I'm practically naked, Maddie! And who are all these people?"

She'd left his briefs on for decency's sake, but he clearly didn't feel that was enough to be wearing in front of a nun and all the other adults and children currently residing in the schoolroom.

Sister Margaret, however, had no time for this uncharacteristic display of modesty. She pulled a small bundle of dried leaves out of her pocket, handed them to Madeleine, and briskly explained, "Boil these for about ten minutes, then wrap them in a cloth and apply it to the wound."

"A poultice?" Madeleine guessed.

Sister Margaret nodded. "It will help draw out the infection. I'm sorry. It's the best I can offer you right now. But it can be quite effective." She gave Madeleine additional instructions about keeping the wound clean and warned that delirium might set in if they couldn't bring the fever down.

The rest had apparently done Ransom some good. After Sister Margaret strode off to investigate some other problem, with the Browning tucked firmly into the pocket of her habit, Ransom asked Madeleine where they were. She recounted finding the road, the journey to San Remo, and the problems they now faced.

"At least no one will shoot us here," she concluded.

"Unless the army extends their battle to this area. They won't attack the mission, but they won't take pains to avoid it, either," he muttered. "God, I'm thirsty!"

She opened a bottle of water she had gotten earlier. "I'm told that this has been treated," she said, helping him drink. "Are you hungry?"

"No. Does anyone around here have a cigarette?"

"I'll ask," she promised dryly.

Just the effort of talking and drinking quickly exhausted him. He fell back into a restless slumber within a few minutes. Madeleine asked another child to watch him, and then she went into San Remo in search of food. They were rationing food at the mission and would run out if they didn't get more soon. Madeleine decided not to help deplete their supplies, since she had enough money to buy her own.

A sleepy town like San Remo would normally be closed down by this time of night, but nothing was normal now, and the streets and stores were as busy as if it were Saturday morning. Supplies were dwindling fast, and Madeleine was glad she hadn't waited until morning to go shopping. Since Ransom was in no shape for solid food, Madeleine bought canned broth, bouillon cubes, tea, honey, and the last bottle of fruit juice she could find. She investigated the local pharmacy for anything that might help Ransom. Not much was left, but she came away with some aspirin and a bottle of Listerine, which was a good all-purpose disinfectant. Her own cuts and scrapes stung, and she knew she shouldn't neglect them.

Suddenly feeling hungry enough to eat a boiled shoe, she bought some solid food for herself and sat in the dirt at the side of the road to eat it. She doubted that anyone at home would recognize her if they could see her now.

The thought brought a sudden wave of homesickness upon her. She thought of her family, her apartment, her office, her favorite restaurants, Central Park, Chateau

Camille. She thought of Caroline and Stephanie, and she didn't want that silly argument she'd had with them before leaving New York to be the last thing they remembered about her. She had so much to tell them. She wanted them to know how much she loved them, how hard she had tried to be the best sister she could, and how she had failed them without even realizing it. From now on, she wanted to be someone they could talk to rather than look up to.

She knew her father would be stricken with guilt right now, desperate for news about her. And that her mother would freely inflict more guilt on him, frantically running from her own fear for Madeleine, finding it too painful to endure.

If she got home, Madeleine decided, there were things she would start doing differently. She had seen and experienced too much in Montedora to simply fall back into old habits.

And as for Ransom, whom she fiercely chose to believe would return to New York with her and make a full recovery back to his usual irascible self . . . Her previous fear that he might tell people about their one-night stand was laughable compared to the vulnerability she felt now that he held her heart in his hands. He could break it so easily, but she wouldn't take it back from him, even if she could. She wouldn't run away from legitimate pain anymore, or keep people she cared about at a convenient distance.

She returned to the mission as soon as she was done eating, conscious that Ransom needed her. Sister's Margaret's help would, of necessity, be limited to advice and occasional visits. Other than that, Ransom was completely dependent upon Madeleine's care. She felt inadequate and wished she knew more about medicine.

Despite being cut off from the outside world, Madeleine

harbored a hope that someone would send supplies soon, before Ransom got any worse. With all the refugees streaming into this area, surely someone—the Red Cross, the UN, someone—would learn what was happening in San Remo before long.

But how would the supplies get here? She understood logistics and operations far better than physiology, and she pondered the question as she returned to Ransom's side. He was resting fitfully, his skin flushed and hotter than ever. She decided it was time to make that poultice and went back outside.

A young girl saw her looking for a small pot in the kitchen yard and offered to help her. Madeleine accepted gratefully and watched in silence as the girl went about preparing the poultice with apparently experienced hands.

It would be hard to bring supplies overland, Madeleine reflected, yet the enormous quantity of food and medicine and other supplies needed here, as well as the lack of a local airstrip, would probably make overland delivery necessary. If they came across the nearest border—Argentina—they'd still take a full day to get here after entering the country. Maybe longer, considering the condition of the roads, the cumbersome weight of the trucks, and the unpredictable outbreaks of violence throughout Montedora now. Add on the time it would take to mount such an operation, as well as the time it would take various organizations even to realize the scope of the assistance needed in San Remo . . . Madeleine felt panic stirring in her stomach again, threatening to bring up the food she had recently consumed. Could Ransom hold on that long?

Sternly suppressing her fear, she accepted the young girl's offer to apply the poultice for her, led her back to Ransom, and watched everything she did, trying to learn.

Ransom woke up long enough to tell her what a terrible idea he thought this was.

"Would you like me to pour some Listerine on your wound instead?" she suggested.

He glared at her. With his growing beard, cuts and bruises, and glittering eyes, he looked menacing. The girl glanced doubtfully at Madeleine.

"You're scaring her," Madeleine chided.

His gaze slid to the girl. He said something in Spanish that made her giggle. When Madeleine suspiciously asked what he had said, he told her, "I said you're a shrew and a witch."

"Here, drink this," she ordered, ignoring the girl's giggles.

"What is it?"

"Juice."

"I don't want—"

"Your body needs help. Drink it."

He was too weak to lift his head without help. She forced half a pint of juice down his throat, bit by bit, before he quit.

When the little girl left them, Ransom groped for Madeleine's hand, then said, "I'm sorry, Maddie. Hell of a thing for you to wind up waiting hand and foot on me, cleaning up all my blood and—"

"I don't mind," she interrupted, seeing how his weakness shamed and frustrated him. "I just want you to get better."

"I'll be fine, now that we're not on the run."

He was lying, and they both knew it, but she didn't contradict him.

He was much worse by morning. He was sweating heavily, but the fever wouldn't break. Madeleine sponged him down again and again, to no avail. He started shaking with chills, and by mid-morning, delirium had set in. Shivering and twitching and sometimes struggling violently, he moaned and muttered unintelligibly, restless and tormented. Sometimes he shouted. Madeleine understood a word here and there, but none of it seemed connected or made any sense.

The fighting was closer today. She could hear shelling in the distance. Some of the refugees packed up and moved on, even as new ones streamed into San Remo in a constant flow.

"Maddie . . ." Ransom moaned.

"I'm here," she said, as she said every time he called her name. "I'm right here."

His eyes were open this time. He seemed to be looking at her. "You've got . . . get away . . ."

"Shhh . . ." She bathed his hot forehead with a cool cloth.

"Please . . . safe . . ."

"We're safe," she lied, hoping he didn't hear the shelling through his delirium. "We're safe."

When he fell asleep again, she finally gave in to tears.

CHAPTER NINETEEN

Like everyone else that evening, Madeleine heard the helicopter as it approached San Remo. For a moment, she was afraid they were going to be bombed. But then she realized it was only one helicopter, and she let herself hope.

Ransom was so ill by now, she was afraid to leave his side for more than a few minutes, so she waited for the children to bring her news. After a half-hour, one of the boys came running into the schoolroom.

Journalists, the child cried. Foreign journalists! They had flown in from across the border. There was a camera, the boy told her, and he had waved at it. He might be on television!

"Trust journalists to be on the scene like vultures," Madeleine muttered, having no particular fondness for the media. However, she felt a glimmer of hope. Now that someone was reporting the chaos at San Remo . . .

She gasped as the realization struck her. Of course! She didn't have to wait for help to reach Ransom; she could get him to where the help was.

"Where are the journalists now?" she asked the child.

"Somewhere outside with Sister Margaret."

"Stay with the señor. Watch him, okay?"

"Sí, señora."

"I'll be back. Don't leave his side."

"No, señora."

She went running off to find Sister Margaret and the journalists.

* * * * *

The journalists wouldn't help her. The helicopter was already carrying the heaviest load safety permitted, they told her, and couldn't take on two extra passengers, or even one. However, with so much at stake, Madeleine wasn't about to give up. She used the influence of the Barrington name and millions and her own considerable powers of persuasion to convince them. Although they were interested to find a Barrington in this obscure spot, they couldn't be convinced.

But Madeleine studied the quietest of the journalists, a young newcomer named Lyle Higgins, and recognized the eager light of ambition in his eyes. He was hesitant, and he wanted to be daring. He was shocked by the scene at San Remo, and he wanted to be shrewd and world-weary. Most of all, he was obscure, and he wanted to be notorious. A civil war in this forgotten backwater to which he had been assigned was his big chance to make a name for himself in his brutally competitive profession, and she could see he was wondering how to do it. So Madeleine offered him a perspective he hadn't considered. He could break away from the pack and get noticed; all he had to do was save a hero.

"Ransom is the man who saved dozens of people from a terrorist bombing at a café in the capital just a few days ago," Madeleine explained, getting Higgins away from his colleagues so she could talk to him.

"The bombing that LPM claimed credit for?"

"LPM?" she repeated. "Really? We never knew—"

"He's the guy? Everyone was wondering—"

"He saved Martinez's life, and Veracruz personally commended him the next day. He's also a personal enemy of Escalante, and was arrested without charge within hours of Escalante's seizing power."

Higgins whistled, furiously scribbling notes. "But how—"

"He's a former Secret Service agent: an American hero, ready to give up his life for the President." She moved in for the kill. "And what a story it would make, Higgins, if you saved his life."

He blinked. "What?"

"Change places with him."

"What?"

"He'll die if he doesn't get treatment. He's very ill, and supplies can't reach us in time."

"A lot of people in Montedora are dying," he pointed out, trying to sound tough.

"I know. I've seen them," she said stonily. "This is the one I can save."

"I don't think—"

"You'll put him on the helicopter in your place, and your colleagues will take him back across the border with them. You save his life, and you stay here for a firsthand account of the misery and deprivation that pervades San Remo until the arrival of the relief trucks."

"There may not be any relief trucks if the fighting keeps getting closer," he pointed out as another shell went off in the distance.

"Well, if you're afraid—"

"I'm not afraid!" he said, stung. "But I'm supposed to be back at the bureau by tonight to file my report. If I'm not—"

"What, you'll get in trouble?"

"Well . . ." He shifted and shrugged. "I've only been on the job for three months. I don't have any authority to make a decision like this."

"Come on, Higgins! Do you think award-winning journalists just sit around on their butts waiting for other people to make important decisions for them in the field?" Seeing his expression, she pressed her advantage home. "This story could make you a media darling. You'd be brave, daring, resourceful, making a spur-of-the-moment decision to risk your own life to save a dying hero. Or," she added, scuffing the ground with her ruined shoe, "you could just forget about it and leave now."

He regarded her suspiciously. "And you'd tell the whole world about this as soon as you got back home, wouldn't you?"

"Well . . ." She smiled sweetly at him.

He sighed. "I think I hate you, Miss Barrington."

"I sometimes have that effect on people."

A bird swooped overhead. Its scarlet and indigo wings burst into flame as an explosion made his head ache. Oh, how his head ached! And his leg, his leg, his leg. . . . Throb, throb, throb . . . KABOOM! in the distance, and ka-boom, ka-boom, ka-boom in his body. Children running around, chattering, the chattering of birds, twitter, twitter, the sound of a roller coaster, he was falling now, falling . . . The roar of the New York subway. A dragon breathing fire in the dark tunnels. Someone pulled a gun and shot him in the belly! The pain, oh, God, the pain . . . The pain in those eyes. He watched the eyes of the crowd. Eyes, eyes, those sociopath eyes, those strange eyes looking right at the President. He was worried about those hostile eyes boring into the target. Don't shoot, man, he thought, don't shoot, don't pull a gun, don't move too fast, don't do anything, I'll have to fucking kill you. Don't make me do it, man.

"I'll fucking kill you," he muttered.

"What did he say?" A stranger's voice.

Then her voice. "He's delirious. Pay no attention. Come

on. Lift him." Her voice. His only lifeline.

Then those hard eyes, staring, threatening. "Fucking kill you!" he warned.

"Uh, how delirious is he?"

"He doesn't know we're here. He's dreaming something. Come on, lift him."

She touched him. He knew her touch, the cool, gentle strength of her hands. She touched him, and now he remembered. He knew what he had to tell her before he died. He'd tried before, but it was so hard, so hard to speak with the vultures swooping down with blood-red wings, with explosions and chattering and all the guns and strange eyes, and the pain, the pain, the pain . . . But he had to try, he had to tell her, because he'd never have another chance. He knew that by now.

"I l . . ." His throat was so dry. Desert and jungle mingled in his mind. Running. Running. Must save her. Must tell her, so she'd always know.

Water trickled down his throat. He choked on it.

"Jesus," someone murmured, "how did he get like this?"

"Infection. Germs breed quickly here," she said.

"L . . . Love . . ." He tried again. "Llll . . ."

"What's he saying?"

"I don't know." She sounded so weary.

"Sounds like 'love.' "

He felt her hand on his forehead.

I love you.

He opened his eyes. The room spun wildly. Her hair flowed and swirled. Her eyes glowed.

Then he saw the men looming over him. Over her.

Two men! Sensing he was too weak to protect her, he lashed out at them even so. One of them screamed. He heard it with satisfaction.

"Ransom! No!" she cried, forcing him to lie back again.

He struggled, desperate to save her. The effort was too much. Darkness enfolded him, leaving him alone with his nightmares.

It took some talking to convince Higgins's associates to take Ransom with them after that brief and terrifying attack he had attempted in his delirium. He'd hurt one of them, though not seriously. However, once he was mercifully unconscious again, they carried him out to the helicopter and strapped him into one of the seats. Madeleine gave one of the journalists information about how to contact her father to tell him she was all right.

"My father will be able to give you Marino's phone number, and Marino will have all of Ransom's passport and medical information. Oh, and one more thing." She stared hard at the journalists, who were clearly eager to get back to Argentina to file their reports before San Remo became old news. "I have never before abused the privileges of my family's power. But if Mr. Ransom doesn't get help in time to save him, then I will personally see to it that none of you ever works again. And believe me, gentlemen, a Barrington can do it."

She didn't care what they thought of her. Only he mattered now. She never really got to say good-bye to him. His head lolled forward in unconsciousness, and he was too far from the door of the helicopter for her to even touch his hand. She took a long last look at him, then allowed Higgins to draw her away from the helicopter so it could take off. Tears streaked her face as she watched it fly away.

"He'll make it," Higgins said reassuringly. "He looked like one tough sonofabitch to me."

She gave a watery smile. "He'd be flattered by the description."

Considering the enormous amount of work that needed to be done at the mission, Madeleine volunteered her services to Sister Margaret as soon as Ransom left. She also turned over all of her money—American cash, Montedoran cash, and remaining traveler's checks—to the Sister. Margaret reflected wryly that this money would be a godsend if there was anything left in San Remo to buy, but the town was cleaned out. Using a little ingenuity, Madeleine asked Margaret for a list of the most urgently needed supplies and then began scouring the town and the ever-growing refugee camps for a black market. She was partially successful, although it was clear that the disaster was too new and had happened too fast for much to be available here, even illegally or at exorbitant prices.

The fighting moved southeast, and reports on the radio in Sister Margaret's office said that the Argentines had closed their border with Montedora for the time being. It was the BBC which reported that a former American Secret Service agent, now acting as a private security consultant, had been brought out of San Remo by journalists; though wounded and seriously ill, the man was now recovering in a New York hospital. Madeleine wept with relief.

LPM rebels passed through San Remo, fleeing the fighting. Madeleine would have preferred to stay out of sight until they were gone, but she had to stay close to Sister Margaret and keep the old woman from getting herself killed. Margaret furiously opposed these armed rebels as they raided the mission for food and medicine. One of them hit Margaret hard enough to draw blood. Madeleine bitterly regretted that she'd let Margaret take her gun away from her; she could have shot these brutes without regret.

"Cowards, bullies, and murdering fanatics," Margaret said after they left. "They aren't like the Doristas."

"You know the Doristas?" Madeleine asked, washing away the blood on the Sister's face.

The old woman nodded. "I have defied the Church and given them aid many times. Half the men in San Remo have gone off to join the Doristas in the past year. They are just ordinary people who want a decent life." She accepted a drink of water, then continued, "They are tired of the poverty and misery brought upon them by the excesses of this country's self-appointed leaders; and they are tired of seeing anyone who questions the government being hauled off by the Seguridores, to disappear forever."

"Do you think the Doristas can win?" Madeleine asked.

"I only know that they will never stop trying."

They saw more journalists at San Remo before they saw supplies. However, everyone who arrived, including a Red Cross representative, assured them that help was on the way. The delay was now only due to the fighting south of here. Trucks were waiting just across the border, and they would enter Montedora as soon as they believed they had a reasonable chance of reaching San Remo. Meanwhile, a few daring helicopters flew across the combat zone to bring the most urgently needed medical supplies to the beleaguered town.

"You know," Sister Margaret said to Madeleine one evening as they watched another helicopter depart, "you could have left in it."

Madeleine kept her eyes on the departing helicopter. "I'll stay until the relief workers arrive."

"What about your husband?"

She glanced at the old woman. "I think you know we're not married."

"You worry about him constantly. It's in your face."

"He's safe and recovering. I just worry because it's my nature."

"He will worry, too. Terribly, I imagine."

"I told that journalist to call New York and tell my family I'm all right. They'll tell Ransom."

"But y—"

"Are you suggesting I'm no longer needed here?" Madeleine asked.

"You know how much you're needed," Margaret said as they turned to go back to her office. "I will not feed your vanity by saying more."

Madeleine smiled. "I've never been one to shirk my duty, Sister. I will leave when the relief trucks arrive."

Escalante's army supporters fell back, heading east again, while the Veracruz faction went west to regroup. During the lull, the supply trucks crossed Montedora's southern border and headed for San Remo. They arrived a week after Ransom's departure. Things had gotten very grim in San Remo by then, but Sister Margaret managed to prevent a food riot through the sheer force of her personality. So many people had already died, and so many more would. But now there was help and hope.

While assisting the Sister in organizing the many newcomers, Madeleine absorbed whatever news she could gather.

The LPM, whose numbers had been depleted by an ill-considered assault on Escalante's army forces during the recent fighting, was now requesting an alliance with the Doristas, who were ignoring them. The Doristas, meanwhile, were gaining territory in the north, taking advantage of the way Escalante's and Veracruz's factions were destroying each other.

The Presidential Guards had suffered heavy casualties while rescuing Veracruz, who had survived and fled the country with his family. Martinez was in Brazil, reportedly petitioning the United States for political asylum. Escalante secured the capital, and communications were finally restored.

It took Madeleine three hours to get a phone call through to her family, but she finally managed it. Her mother was tearful, but it was the relief in her father's voice which brought tears to Madeleine's eyes. Her first question was about Ransom's health.

"He's getting better," her father said. "Released from the hospital two days ago. Still weak, according to Joe Marino, but able to walk."

"Really?" More tears streamed down her cheeks and she laughed with relief.

"He blames himself for what happened down there, Madeleine."

"That's ridiculous!"

"I saw him at the hospital when he was first allowed visitors. He said that he shouldn't have gotten wounded, shouldn't have let you stay with him, and shouldn't have let you send him away."

"He was unconscious at the time. It's not as if he had any choice in the matter."

"All the same . . . He's been very anxious about you. Asked me to call him whenever I received additional news about you. I'll phone his office today, of course."

"He's back at work?" she asked, annoyed with Ransom. He should be resting!

"Since being released from the hospital, and against doctor's orders."

"Naturally," she muttered.

"For your mother's sake, by the way, I thank you for the messages you've had journalists pass along to me while you've been in San Remo."

"Of course, Dad." She knew full well he wasn't really just thanking her for her mother's sake, but she let him maintain his stoic image.

"And there's money waiting for you in Argentina, to help you get whatever you need for your journey home." He gave her the necessary information. "When will you leave?"

"Probably the day after tomorrow."

"Can't you leave any sooner?"

She explained about the chaos reigning at the mission, with so many eager relief workers, fresh supplies, vehicles, and refugees still pouring into the devastated area. "Sister Margaret still needs my help, Dad," she concluded. "I can't leave her right now."

"Well, yes, I can see your point. You've always done your . . ." She heard him clear his throat roughly. "Excuse me."

She smiled. "Besides, I'll still keep my promise and be home in time for your birthday party."

"Oh . . . Actually, we had decided to cancel it, considering—"

"Oh, no, Dad, you mustn't. We'll have a double celebration now. Your birthday and my homecoming."

"Of course, Madeleine. If that's what you want."

"Be sure to invite Ransom when you talk to him again." She wanted him to meet her family, and a party seemed like less direct pressure on Ransom's fragile social skills than an intimate family dinner.

"I will," her father said.

"And tell him I . . ." She paused uncertainly. There were a hundred things she wanted to say to Ransom, but her father wasn't an appropriate conduit for any of them.

"Yes?" Thackeray prodded.

"Tell him I said hello," she finished lamely.

"Of course."

"I'll call you from Argentina," she promised, knowing he would continue to worry.

"Yes. Don't forget, honey."

She smiled as she replaced the receiver. He hadn't called her that in years.

Madeleine's departure, so long anticipated, was now breaking her heart. It was painful to say good-bye to the brave people she'd met here, hard to walk away from those who still needed her, and difficult to turn her back on the complex tapestry of Montedora.

"I meant to say good-bye to Higgins," Madeleine said as Sister Margaret escorted her to a waiting helicopter.

"He's far too busy," the Sister replied dryly. "I'll tell him for you."

Madeleine smiled. Higgins had put these past ten days to good use, making a prominent name for himself. San Remo had wound up becoming a huge international human-interest story, and Higgins was the source on what had been happening here since the start of the crisis. He knew many locals, refugees, orphans, and nuns on a first-name basis, and Madeleine knew from listening to the radio in recent days, where broadcasters mentioned him often, that he was quickly becoming famous.

As they paused before the helicopter, Sister Margaret pressed a rosary into Madeleine's hand. "I have little enough to give," she said, "and I know you aren't Catholic, but I owe you more than I can say. This was my grandmother's, and I brought it with me from Ireland over fifty years ago."

"Margaret . . ."

"Vaya con Dios."

Madeleine hugged the tiny old woman, grunting at the strength of Margaret's arms around her ribs. She took one last look at San Remo, then began the first leg of her journey home.

Ransom replaced the receiver on the telephone in his office and lit up a cigarette, in defiance of the whole building's ban on smoking. Barrington had called to tell him that, after more unexpected delays, Madeleine was on her way home at last. She would arrive shortly before a big party being given at the Barrington family home out on Long Island. Barrington had reiterated his invitation to Ransom, and Ransom had again hedged, saying he would come if his leg wasn't bothering him too much.

He flexed the leg now. It was tender, stiff, and a little weak, but getting better every day. No, it wasn't his leg that would keep him away from Madeleine tonight. Not by a long shot.

His stomach churned when he thought about going to that party. For the first time in longer than he could remember, he felt indecisive and nervous. It wasn't like him, and it annoyed him.

He ground out his cigarette after just a few puffs, then restlessly lit another one a couple of minutes later.

He had to see her, to talk to her. He wanted to be with her more than he wanted to go on breathing. He'd nearly left for Argentina two days ago, but Joe had stopped him.

And now that she was so near . . . Now he was scared. There was so much at stake. How could he talk to her at a big party, surrounded by people? What if she'd been rethinking everything? He'd hardly turned out to be a hero, after all, he thought with heavy self-disgust.

The phone rang again. He picked it up. "Ransom."

"A call from New Orleans," said his secretary. "Someone who claims that it's his fault that you were wounded in Montedora."

He frowned, knowing it was his own damn fault. "Who is it?"

"He says his name is Miguel Arroyo."

"Jesus, he's alive!" Ransom sagged into his chair. "Let me talk to him."

CHAPTER TWENTY

Madeleine studied herself in the full-length mirror in her old bedroom at Chateau Camille. She was wearing an evening gown; Caroline had stopped by her apartment this morning to pick it up for her, while she was napping at 30,000 feet somewhere over Brazil. The gown was one of her favorites, a form-fitting, cream-colored, satin confection which left her arms and shoulders bare. It usually suited her. But although daily application of Listerine had helped heal the cuts and abrasions she'd collected in the jungle, many of them still showed faintly pink against her white skin. There was one on her left arm and another above her breasts that looked particularly unattractive.

"It never even occurred to me," Caroline said, looking at Madeleine. "Sorry. I should have brought you a few dresses and let you choose."

Madeleine turned her back to the mirror and looked over her shoulder. "Oh, well. Nothing to be done now. It'll have to do."

She saw both of her sisters blink with surprise at her casual tone. Caroline and Stephanie had hardly left her side since she landed at JFK that afternoon; her parents were now downstairs, welcoming the first few guests of the evening. The Barringtons were not a demonstrative family, but Madeleine's homecoming had been warm and emotional, thawing the chilliness that had existed between her and her sisters only a couple of weeks ago.

"We could put some concealer on those scratches," Stephanie suggested.

Madeleine studied her reflection doubtfully. "I think that might just make them look worse. Anyhow, it's no big deal."

Caroline laughed. "I don't believe it! I've seen you get rid of shoes that were one shade lighter than your dress, and I've never known you to leave this room without every hair in place, but now that you look like you've been beaten with a rosebush, you don't even—"

"I can't sweat the small stuff anymore," Madeleine said distractedly. "As long as I look good enough for . . . I mean, as long as he'll think I'm . . . Well, he just gets annoyed when I look perfect, anyhow."

"Who?"

"Ransom."

Caroline glanced at Stephanie, then asked, "Is he coming?"

Madeleine fumbled with a string of pearls. Stephanie offered to fasten them for her. Madeleine met Caroline's eyes and admitted, "I don't know. He didn't give Dad a firm answer."

"So call the guy," Caroline said.

"I tried," Madeleine replied. "He wasn't in his office, and they wouldn't give me his home phone number. Or his cell phone number. Company policy." She and Ransom had given each other oral sex, but not their phone numbers. She felt her cheeks flush as the thought crossed her mind. What a strange courtship they'd been having.

"It means a lot to you, that this guy should come tonight," Caroline observed.

"Yes."

"Madeleine, are you and he, uh . . ." Stephanie glanced

at Caroline and tried again. "I mean, is there—"

"Yes." Madeleine slumped into a chair. "I'm in love with him."

"Madeleine!" Stephanie embraced her. "That's wonderful!"

"Hah! You don't know him. He can be so . . . difficult when he wants to be." She gripped Stephanie's hand as it slipped into hers. "When I was down in Montedora, I thought I knew how things would go when I got home. What I'd do and say, what he'd do. But now that I'm here . . ." She shivered. "I'm so nervous I feel like I'm going to be sick."

Exposing her vulnerability to her younger sisters was something she hadn't done in well over twenty years. And they lost no time in showing her that they valued her trust. They asked her about Ransom, about how she had fallen in love with him, and assured her that he undoubtedly returned her feelings.

"Unless he's a jerk," Caroline added, making Madeleine smile.

Feeling sheepish, Madeleine told the story of how she'd met Ransom, including the fact that she'd slept with him without knowing his name and disappeared on him without saying good-bye. Both her sisters were openly astonished by this story, trying to rearrange their mental image of Madeleine to suit this new information. Stephanie found the story delightfully sordid; Caroline kept laughing with delight over Madeleine's bad behavior.

Madeleine endured their teasing, finally accepting that she hadn't done the most terrible thing in the world by sleeping with a stranger, even if it was unwise—and even if she'd made a foolish mistake by walking out on Ransom. Imagine if she'd never met him again! The very idea was unbearable. Anyhow, although she had indeed made mistakes, Ransom was right—people made mistakes all the time, and she was only human, like everyone else.

"And to think that I always thought you . . ." Caroline's voice trailed off. She sat bolt upright. "Ohmigod!"

"What?"

"Graham! What are you going to do about Graham?"

"Graham," Madeleine repeated. "Oh, no! I completely forgot about him." She hadn't thought of him in . . . she didn't know how long.

"He's been calling Dad every day for news about you. He wanted to come to the airport with us, but Dad convinced him to let the family have a private reunion before tonight's bash."

"Is he coming here?"

"Yes. Do you want me to keep him away from—"

"No," Madeleine said. "He deserves better treatment than he's ever had from me, and I want to let him off the hook as soon as possible. I'll talk to him tonight."

Their mother knocked on the door and stuck her head into the room. After a bout of mild hysteria over Madeleine's scratches, she whirled on Caroline, who was still wearing her jeans. "Why aren't you dressed yet? People are already arriving!"

Caroline sighed. "I'll go change. Excuse me."

Eleanor followed her out the door, urging her to do something with her hair, too. "And you have such lovely hair, dear, I don't know why you never—"

"Go tend your guests, Mother," Caroline snapped.

Stephanie and Madeleine smiled ironically at each other as the door closed behind their mother. Stephanie picked up a brush and looked in the mirror as she touched up her own hair.

"Mother's still furious at Caroline for her campaign against Randall Cosmetics."

"Is that continuing?" Madeleine asked, putting on some eye makeup.

"Oh, yes. With a vengeance."

"Does it bother you?" Madeleine asked.

"I haven't really had time to pay attention to it." Stephanie paused before admitting, "I've been sick while you were away, Madeleine."

Madeleine paused. "Oh?"

Stephanie bit her lip, keeping her eyes fixed on the mirror. "I've been diagnosed with some problems resulting from . . . from bulimia."

"Stephanie!"

"So I haven't really discussed Richard's business problems with him, and I—"

"Stephanie. Bulimia? But how . . . I mean, what—"

"Trying to get thin. Trying to stay thin. Trying to . . . Oh, God, you know how I . . ." Her hand shook.

"But we've all seen that you scarcely even eat anymore."

"Right. That's what you've seen. Because I binge in secret. Just like I purge in secret."

"Oh, my God," Madeleine said sadly. "Steph . . ."

"You were right, Madeleine, when you said I—"

"No, I wasn't right about anything."

"You were. I've really messed up my body and my health."

Madeleine embraced her. "Oh, Stephanie, I'm so sorry."

"I'm scared," Stephanie whispered, trembling. "I'm afraid I won't be able to stop."

"Yes, you will," Madeleine said firmly. "I know you can do this."

"I've only told Caroline and Richard," Stephanie whispered. "I don't want anyone else to know."

"No, of course not," Madeleine murmured, hugging her, hoping Richard Randall would be supportive of his wife. "Thank you for telling me."

Stephanie fought back her tears. "I felt . . . Tonight I felt like I could tell you."

Madeleine hugged her harder. "I'm so glad. I want to be someone you can tell anything to, Stephanie. Anything."

Madeleine pressed her sister for details about the treatment she was seeking, listening and offering her support. They talked until their mother came back and insisted they join the party. And Madeleine realized that a rewarding part of being so imperfect was that the people she loved were willing to share their own imperfections with her.

Ransom arrived at Chateau Camille around nine o'clock. The party was in full swing, with a band playing oldies from the forties, food and champagne flowing freely, and overdressed guests filling the mansion to capacity. Ransom entered a vast reception room and looked around for Madeleine. A pretty blonde woman caught his eye and approached him. She was accompanied by another woman who would have been just as pretty, if she weren't so painfully skinny. Something about them looked familiar, and by the time they reached his side, he realized he'd seen their picture in Barrington's office.

"You're her sisters," he said without preamble.

"I'm Caroline. This is Stephanie. And you," said the blonde one, "must be Ransom." She glanced down at his thigh. "How's the leg?"

"Okay." Aching a bit. He ignored it.

"Madeleine didn't think you'd be wearing a tie," Caroline observed. Stephanie tried to hide a smile.

"Uh, your father told me it was a formal affair." He plucked self-consciously at the bow tie that was strangling him. "Where's Maddie?"

Stephanie blinked. "She lets you call her Maddie?"

"To her face?" Caroline asked.

He grinned. "Where is she?"

"With Graham," Stephanie said.

Ransom frowned. "With Graham?"

"Uh-huh." Caroline studied him, amusement dancing in her eyes. "Surely he doesn't worry you?"

He scowled at her. "No. But your sister does."

She grinned at him. "My money's on you, Ransom."

Stephanie pointed to a set of double doors. "They're in the adjoining room. Just through there."

Madeleine's private talk with Graham had lasted about twenty minutes. She had apologized profusely for her behavior, assured him that she found neither his character nor his virility lacking, and explained that he deserved a woman who could love him with all her heart. He was, of course, determined to be a gentleman about the whole thing, and the entire scene had been far easier than she felt she deserved. She was relieved when it was over. Now, in the civilized spirit of "no hard feelings," she was having a glass of champagne with Graham and her father when Ransom walked through the door.

The sight of him, so eagerly awaited and nervously anticipated, unraveled her wits. She choked on her champagne, dropped her glass, and created a small scene as Graham patted her on the back, people watched with concern, and a caterer came rushing over to clean up the mess.

She felt Ransom's presence at her side even before her watering eyes cleared. "You came!" she blurted.

"Ransom!" Her father shook his hand warmly. "I'm so glad you decided to join us!"

"Thank you, sir," Ransom said. "I hope I look as good as you on my sixtieth birthday."

"You're wearing a tux," Madeleine said in disbelief.

He shifted self-consciously. "It's rented."

"It looks it," she told him.

"Don't be such a snob."

Graham's eyes bulged at their rudeness. Her father smiled. Looking from his daughter to the man whom he had hired to protect her, he said, "I'd like to talk to you sometime about some security ideas for Barrington Enterprises."

"Uh-huh," Ransom said, not taking his eyes off Madeleine. Those glittering green eyes burned straight through her. She couldn't have looked away if a bomb went off nearby. He didn't look tender, though; he looked ready to fight.

"But, of course, this is a party," Thackeray said.

"Yes," Madeleine murmured. Ransom's bronzed skin and gold-streaked hair showed the effects of the Montedoran sun. His bruises had faded and vanished, but the cut on his forehead was turning into yet another scar. She was relieved to see him looking so healthy and strong. Of course, he was a little thin at the moment; they'd both lost some weight during their adventures in Montedora. But he looked wonderful to her, rented tux and all.

"Why don't we get together to discuss some ideas next week?" her father suggested.

"Sure," Ransom said, still staring at Madeleine.

"Meanwhile," Thackeray said, his voice a little amused, "I'm sure you and my daughter have a lot of catching up to do."

"Yes," Madeleine said through a tight throat.

"Come, Graham," Thackeray said. "There's someone I'd like you to meet."

As her father led him away, Madeleine heard Graham object: "You're not going to leave her alone with him, sir? Didn't you see the surly look in his eyes? I really don't think—"

"She can handle him," Thackeray insisted, dragging Graham away.

"Didn't you give that guy his walking papers?" Ransom demanded in a low voice.

Madeleine nodded. "Tonight. That doesn't mean he doesn't still care what—"

"As long as he knows to keep his distance."

"He knows," she said coolly. "Some men are gentlemen."

"And some men are wimps. But in his case, it's just as well."

Madeleine frowned. "Can't you j—"

"Do you have something to tell me?" he interrupted.

Startled, she said, "Well . . . yes."

"Where can we talk?"

She licked her lips. "Um . . . There's a small sitting room at the end of—"

He took her arm. "Let's go."

"Does your leg still hurt?" she asked, hesitating.

"Only when people keep asking about it." He propelled her through the double doors.

"But you're limping!"

"I was shot ten days ago," he reminded her tersely.

Madeleine realized he was determined to be as disagreeable as only he knew how to be. She ignored her sisters' knowing gazes as she led Ransom out of the main reception room. Wondering what had put him in this abrasive mood, she was increasingly nervous as they pushed their way through the crowded corridor. She risked asking, "What happened with that Sex On The Beach singer? Steve—Steve—"

"Steve Keller."

"Yes. Is he going to sue?"

"No, he decided it would make him look bad in the press if the full story came out, which Marino's lawyers assured him it would if he didn't drop the whole thing."

"Look bad? You mean the part about him being abusive to his girlfriend?"

"No," Ransom replied. "The part where it took one punch to make him squeal like a schoolgirl."

Madeleine sneered aristocratically. "Men."

"Sometimes I actually share that sentiment, Miss Barrington."

"Really?" Her nerves were releasing her tension as anger now. "And what about you, Ransom? Blaming yourself for getting wounded in Montedora. Of all the ridiculous—"

"Is this the room?"

"No, the next door down."

"It is my fault." He propelled her past more guests. "I knew better than to try to run clear across that schoolyard, unarmed. El Martillo's rifle was lying not three feet away from me. I should have picked it up and taken out those last two men."

"You don't know that that's how it would have happened if you'd gone for the gun!" She let him shove her through the door of the sitting room, then whirled on him as he locked it behind them. "Anything could have happened!"

"I made myself a target when I—"

"Then blame me! I was the one who shouted at you to run to where I was waiting."

"That's why I did it," he said, his voice heavy with self-condemnation. "I heard your voice, and I forgot everything I knew. I could only think of getting to you. Maddie . . ." He shook his head. "I lost my head, and you could have been killed as a result."

She stared at him. "My God, is this what you've been stewing about while we've been apart?"

"No," he snapped. "I've been 'stewing' about what I'd say to you when you finally got home—if you got home. What were you thinking of, to put me on a helicopter bound for Argentina, and then stay there, right in the middle of—"

"You were dying! It took the supply trucks another week to reach us! You couldn't have lasted—"

"Clients," he interrupted, "get protected and preserved by their bodyguards, not the other way around."

"I can't believe you're saying this to me! I can't believe that you, even you, have the utter unmitigated gall to—"

"I know." He looked a little guilty. "I'm being ungrateful. It's not that I don't—"

"Grateful?" she repeated in an awful tone. "Do you think I want your gratitude, you sonofabitch?"

He blinked. "Now, Maddie—"

"I'd have done anything for you—anything!—and all you can do is lecture me about what's appropriate for your goddamn clients and talk about gratitude! Sometimes you make me so mad, I don't need to wonder why two people in this world have already felt compelled to shoot you!"

"You're . . ." He cleared his throat. "You seem a little emotional," he ventured.

"A little?" She wanted to hit him.

"I've heard about hormonal changes happening early on, but I never—"

"What hormonal changes?"

"You, uh, said you had something to tell me."

"So?" she challenged, hardly interested in telling him now, while he was being so difficult.

He frowned at her tone. "Look, I'm willing to be as understanding as I have to be, Maddie, but don't push it, okay?"

"Understanding? About what?"

"The next nine months," he said gently.

That stopped her cold. She stared at him in stunned silence. Then she looked down at her stomach. "What on earth makes you think I'm pregnant?"

He started to look a little uncertain. "You said you had something to tell me."

"Yes, but not that. Ransom, I—"

"We didn't have any condoms with us. It doesn't take a genius to figure out—"

"I'm not pregnant. I can guarantee it."

He looked sharply at her. "You've had your period since the last time I saw you?"

She was as startled as ever by his frankness. "Yes. Last week."

"Oh." Their eyes locked. "Then what did you want to tell me?"

"This isn't exactly how I pictured it."

"Too bad."

"Maybe we could—"

"Tell me." He was tense now, his expression dark.

"It's just that . . ." she began.

"Go on." His voice was clipped, impatient.

She clasped her hands. "I, uh . . ." She cleared her

throat and plunged ahead, meeting his hard gaze. "I love you."

He looked as stunned as if she'd flung a bucket of cold water at him. "What?"

Not the reaction she'd been hoping for. Hurt, she repeated, "I love you, damn it."

They stood staring at each other in taut silence. Damn him, Madeleine fumed. He must know how hard this was for her! Why didn't he say something?

"Aw, Maddie," he shook his head, and a slow, tender smile touched his mouth, "you really know how to take all the fight out of me."

"Is that all you have to say?" she snapped.

He grinned. "Not by a long shot."

"Ransom . . ." Her heart pounded painfully as she searched his expression.

He crossed the room to her. "Actions speak louder than words."

She was in his arms before she took her next breath. His kiss was fierce and possessive, telling her everything she needed to know, offering her everything she wanted from him. Then he buried his face in her hair. She clung to him, listening with blossoming joy to the endearments he murmured as his arms tightened around her.

"I'm sorry," he whispered. "I'd have been a lot nicer just now if I'd known that's what you were going to say."

"I certainly hope so." She nuzzled him. "What did you think I was going to say?"

He pressed his forehead against hers. "I was afraid you were going to tell me it was over between us. I thought you were about to rip my heart out."

"How could you think that?" She tried to get even closer. "How could you not know how much I—"

"We never got to talk about . . . about what we'd do when we got home. And waiting around for you . . ." He kissed her, then admitted wryly, "I guess I got a little worked up, waiting for you to come home. I've been so ashamed of leaving you behind—"

"Stop. You weren't even conscious at the time. It wasn't up to you."

"I've been so afraid for you."

"I've missed you so much."

"I couldn't think about anything but you."

"I thought of you day and night."

They kissed again, the warm melding of their mouths trying to satisfy all the longing and hunger of the past two weeks. Their whispers grew breathless and dazed as their hands found familiar ways to delight and entice.

"Wait," he said as she fumbled with the buttons of his rented shirt. "Wait a minute."

"No," she sighed, "now."

He stilled her seeking hands. "Maddie, I know I've never said or done the things that a guy probably should . . ." He took her by the hair and tilted her face up until their gazes met. "But, uh . . ." He swallowed. "Will you marry me?"

She studied his intent, hesitant expression. "You're serious," she whispered.

He frowned. "Of course, I'm serious. Do you think I go around saying this all the time?"

"No, I can tell that you don't."

"It's the first time I've ever proposed to anyone," he said defensively. "It's bound to be a little—"

"It was perfect." She kissed him, her blood thrumming with happiness. "Yes, I'll marry you."

"Oh. Good." He touched her cheek. "This saves me the trouble of carrying you off or something drastic like that."

She smiled and snuggled into his embrace. "But there's something I want to know first."

He ran his hands over her back. "What?"

"Your name."

He went still. "Oh. That."

"Yes. That." She finished unbuttoning his shirt and kissed his chest.

He inhaled deeply and closed his eyes. "Later."

She pressed her hand between his legs and felt him stir eagerly against her palm. "When?"

He undid her zipper. "I'll tell you my name in the morning."

"A likely story," she said as he peeled the bodice of her dress away from her body.

"Hey, it worked for you once." He lowered his head to explore her breasts with his mouth. She buried her fingers in his hair and held his head against her, dizzy with pleasure.

A knock at the door made her gasp and lose her precarious footing. Ransom used the opportunity to back her against the wall.

"Madeleine?" Graham's muffled voice came from outside the door.

Ransom kissed her when she would have answered, then started pulling up the hem of her gown.

"Madeleine, are you all right in there?"

Her breath caught in her throat when she felt Ransom's hand between her legs, pulling away her delicate panties and then boldly exploring her with his fingers.

"Let me get rid of him," she whispered, trembling as he stroked her.

"Ignore him. He'll go away." Ransom unfastened his trousers and pressed himself against her. She shifted her hips—and he winced.

"Your leg!" she said, suddenly remembering his wound. "We should stop."

"Madeleine!" Graham called. "Is that you? Are you all right?"

"I'm fine," Ransom assured her, guiding her hand to his erection and closing his fingers around hers.

"Are you sure?" she asked in concern.

"Yes, I'm sure." He was starting to sound exasperated. "Could we just get on with it?"

"Do you need help?" Graham called.

Ransom laughed. While he nibbled on her neck, Madeleine called, "No, I'm fine, Graham."

"Are you sure? Why is this door locked?" He rattled it.

"Great," Ransom muttered against her neck. "Now he'll never go away. Nice going, Maddie."

"Let me get rid of him," she repeated.

"Not just now," he said tersely and thrust into her with enough force to make her head bang against the wall.

"What was that?" Graham demanded.

"N . . . N . . . N . . ." Eagerly moving to accommodate her lover, Madeleine was breathing so hard she had trouble answering. "Nothing!" She pressed her face into Ransom's shoulder. "Yes, mmmm, yes . . . I've missed you so much . . ."

They kissed, moving together, supported by the wall, forgetting everything but each other—until they heard a woman's voice outside the door. Even Ransom's ardor was dampened by their growing audience.

"Christ, don't these people have anything better to do?" he growled. "What kind of a party is this?"

Laughing helplessly, Madeleine slid her leg around his hip to pull him deeper into her body. She stilled when she heard his sharp intake of breath and felt him stiffen with pain.

"Careful. Here, like this." He gripped her bottom and lifted her higher so that she wasn't putting pressure on his healing wound. Then he cast a glare at the door, where the voices were getting louder.

"It's Caroline," Madeleine whispered against his mouth. "She'll convince him to leave us alone."

"If she doesn't, he'll have the shock of his privileged young life," Ransom muttered, plunging into her.

The voices beyond the doorway rose in volume for a moment, arguing, then faded away and disappeared. Madeleine released her breath on a loud, voluptuous moan.

"That's better," Ransom said, making her do it again.

"Tell me," she panted.

"I love you," he murmured against her throat.

"I meant . . . Mmmm . . ."

"What?"

"Tell me . . . Oh! . . . your name."

She felt his soft puff of laughter against her hair, and then he was driving into her, driving her over the edge, and all she knew was sensation and the breath-stealing joy of his love.

They sat slumped together, leaning against the wall, their clothes in wrinkled disarray, their skin flushed and glowing. Trembling in the aftermath, they nuzzled each other in languid contentment, whispering promises and secrets.

She told him about the daily tragedy she had witnessed at San Remo, the courage of the hungry Montedorans, and the reckless daring and scheming self-interest of the various journalists who had come to the mission. Mostly, though, she told him about Sister Margaret.

"I've never met anyone I admired more," she said. "Someday, I want you to meet her again."

He brushed her hair off her shoulder. "She sounds like you, only celibate."

"She has a true calling. But maybe . . . maybe she never met a man like you before she took the veil." She linked her fingers with his. "I've decided to give her the plantation."

He looked surprised. "Do you even still have control over what happens to the plantation?"

"Not exactly. Even if I could organize a sale now, who would buy it?" The Germans had never reached Montedora, having cancelled their plans upon learning of Escalante's coup. "But Margaret is a friend of the Doristas. If they win the war, they'll let her have the plantation without a quarrel. If Escalante wins, he probably won't interfere with my donation to the mission, especially not with what I can tell the world about his treatment of us in Montedora. And if Veracruz wins—"

"Veracruz is finished," Ransom said with certainty. "How long will his troops stay loyal to him, if he's living comfortably in exile while they're surrounded by Doristas and Escalante's followers?"

She watched him light up a cigarette. "I wish you would quit that."

He raised his eyebrows. "Smoking?" When she nodded, he said, "We've only been engaged thirty minutes, and you're already nagging me about my bad habits?"

"Just this one. It's the one that could kill you, and I want to keep you around for fifty years."

"Only fifty?"

"Well, we'll see how it goes." He smiled, but she said, "So, will you at least think about quitting?"

"Yep, that's nagging, all right," he said with resignation.

Now that she had introduced the idea, she chose a tactical retreat. "We can discuss it later."

He scowled at her. "That would be more nagging."

She smiled. "Much later. Only after lots of sex has softened your resistance."

He considered this. "If that's your strategy for nagging me, I suppose I'll learn to live with it."

She rested her head on his shoulder while he enjoyed his cigarette. After a few minutes, her thoughts turned to one of the things she'd been wanting to ask him. "Do you think Miguel made it out alive?"

He squeezed her hand. "I didn't tell you! He called me."

"He called—"

"From New Orleans. After he left Doragua, he picked up his mother and sisters at the border and drove the car all the way to Rio de Janeiro. Then he sold it and bought four round-trip tickets to New Orleans."

"Round-trip? But he's not going back—"

"No, but it's easier to get through immigration if you've got a round-trip ticket."

"Why New Orleans?"

"He read that it was an easier port of entry than L.A., New York, or Miami."

"He had been planning his escape for a long time," Madeleine surmised.

Ransom blew smoke toward the ceiling. "He was kind of emotional when he called. He knew about the war, of course, so he started trying to get news about us the moment he reached the U.S."

"I hope you weren't too hard on him," she said.

"Well . . . I was a little hard on him," Ransom admitted. "He expected it. And I couldn't just forget everything that happened to you after he took the car."

"You're the one who got shot."

"You're the one I worry about." He kissed her.

"But you're going to help him, aren't you?" she prodded, knowing the answer.

"Yeah."

She snuggled against him, smiling. "You're not half as tough as you pretend to be."

"Maybe not," he agreed mildly, "but let's keep that between us, okay?" He rose to his feet and found an ashtray for his cigarette.

"Okay," she agreed as he helped her off the floor.

She straightened the front of her gown, then turned around to let him zip it up. She tried to tidy her hair, then faced him. "How do I look?"

"Like you've been having sex in the sitting room."

"Maybe we should try to leave without being seen."

"Fine by me." He finished buttoning his shirt, not bothering to tuck it in, then pulled his coat back on. He looked around for a moment, then said, "I think I've lost my tie."

"Male fashion will survive this setback."

"You're the one who took it off. Where'd you put it?"

"Here it is." One of them had kicked it under an end table.

"Oh. Thanks." He stuffed it in his pocket.

"Ready to go?"

"Sure. Your place or mine?"

"Mine. I haven't been home in three weeks." She stretched and added, "I'm so tired, I could spend the next week in bed."

He grinned at her. "Precisely my plan."

She held out her hand. He took it and let her lead him to the door. "I'll just tell Caroline to make my apologies to my parents," she said, unlocking and opening the door, "and then we can . . . Mother!"

Ransom looked doubtfully at the elegant woman who had turned to face them when Madeleine opened the door. Her expression changed from one of polite interest to frosty distaste as she studied them with glacial blue eyes. He realized that their disheveled appearance, added to the locked door, left little doubt about what they'd been doing. Damn it, why did they have to bump into Maddie's mother, of all people? He glanced at Madeleine, waiting for her tact to rescue them.

"Mother, I'm so glad you'll be the first to know. Mr. Ransom has asked me to marry him, and I've accepted," Madeleine said with as much composure as if she'd been planning this moment for weeks.

Ransom grinned. Yeah, she had guts, all right.

Madeleine's mother quickly concealed her true feelings (shock and dismay, Ransom noted) behind a bright, artificial smile. "How delightful, dear! When will the wedding be? Or . . ." She laughed prettily. "Is it too soon to ask?"

Ransom glanced at Madeleine. "Next month?" he ventured, supposing she'd want time to do whatever it was women did for their weddings.

"Six months," she said promptly.

"Six months?" he repeated. "Why can't we do it sooner?"

"Because," Madeleine said reasonably, "we'll need six months to fight about where we're going to live, and what kind of ceremony we'll have, and where we'll—"

"Ceremony? I don't want a ceremony."

"But I do."

He rolled his eyes. "Naturally. But I don't see why we can't just go to a justice of the p . . ." He stopped himself before they had their first argument about it right here. Smiling wryly, he nodded and agreed, "Okay, you're right. Six months." The smile she gave him in return was good enough to make him decide he'd even be willing to put up with her mother now and then.

"Madeleine!" a voice boomed from halfway down the vast corridor. A plump gray-haired man came striding toward them, and Ransom realized they weren't going to escape the party as easily as they had hoped.

"Uncle Winnie!" Madeleine accepted the man's embrace and exchanged a few words with him before her mother interrupted.

"Winnie, dear," Eleanor said, "please allow me to introduce Madeleine's fiancé."

"Fiancé! You're getting married?"

"Mr. Ransom," Eleanor said, "this is my brother-in-law, Senator Winston Barrington."

"How do you do, sir?" Ransom decided he'd better take control of the situation before any more relatives turned up. "It's been a pleasure meeting you both, but we were just about to—"

"You're getting a wonderful girl, er . . ." Uncle Winnie frowned briefly at Ransom. "Sorry, son, didn't catch your first name?"

"Come to think of it, neither did I," said Madeleine's mother.

Her eyes glowing with amusement, Madeleine said, "Don't be shy, darling. Tell them."

"Shy?" boomed the Senator. "Nonsense! We're all family now, eh?"

Ransom looked a little desperately from one

Barrington to the next. Might as well get it over with, he decided.

"My full name is Horace Balthazar Ransom." He glanced at Madeleine and added defensively, "It was my grandfather's name."

"Ah, a fine old family name then!" Uncle Winnie pumped Ransom's hand and cried, "Welcome to the family, Horace!"

Ransom winced. "Actually, sir, I prefer to be called—"

"Sorry, can't stop to chat now. But we'll be seeing lots more of you, I'm sure." The Senator patted him on the back and strode away.

"He's canvassing. As usual," Eleanor said with distaste. She then turned her attention to the happy couple. "I'm sure you want to share this, er, delightful news with your father, dear, but perhaps you should freshen up first. If you'll forgive me for saying so, you look rather—"

"Actually, we were just leaving, Mother. I'll call Dad tomorrow, all right?"

It clearly wasn't all right, but Eleanor Barrington wasn't about to have an argument in front of the virtual stranger who'd been ravishing her willing daughter in the sitting room. She wished them a frosty good night, then returned to her guests. Ransom stared after her until Madeleine tugged on his sleeve.

"Come along, Horace."

"Don't call me Horace," he warned, following her down the corridor.

She paused before a door leading out to the kitchen garden, her eyes dancing with amusement. "Touchy, aren't we?"

"Damn right." He eyed her lazily, thinking she looked pretty good in that gown, thinking maybe he'd pounce on her once they reached his car.

"Horace," she repeated. She shook her head. "No, it just doesn't work, Ransom."

Smiling, he followed her laughter out into the night air.

ABOUT THE AUTHOR

Laura Leone is the award-winning author of fourteen romance novels, including *Fever Dreams* and *Fallen from Grace.* Under her real name, Laura Resnick, she is also the award-winning author of over forty short stories and several fantasy novels, including *The White Dragon, The Destroyer Goddess,* and the upcoming *Arena.* In addition to numerous columns and articles, she has also written *A Blonde in Africa,* a non-fiction account of her eight-month journey across Africa. You can find her on the web at www.sff.net/people/laresnick.